KU-466-497

Kith and Kin

STEVIE DAVIES

PHOENIX

A PHOENIX PAPERBACK

First published in Great Britain in 2004
by Weidenfeld & Nicolson
This paperback edition published in 2004
by Phoenix,
an imprint of Orion Books Ltd,
Orion House, 5 Upper St Martin's Lane,
London WC2H 9EA

Second impression 2004

Copyright © Stevie Davies, 2004

The right of Stevie Davies to be identified as the author of
this work has been asserted by her in accordance with the
Copyright, Designs and Patents Act 1988.

All rights reserved. No part of this publication may be
reproduced, stored in a retrieval system, or transmitted,
in any form or by any means, electronic, mechanical,
photocopying, recording or otherwise, without the prior
permission of the copyright owner.

A CIP catalogue record for this book
is available from the British Library.

ISBN 0 75382 018 8

Printed and bound in Great Britain by
Clays Ltd, St Ives plc

MORAY COUNCIL LIBRARIES & INFO.SERVICES	
20 14 32 09	
Askews	
ʃ	www.orionbooks.co.uk

'Davies's greatest skill is in the depiction of childhood memories . . . Her descriptions gleam with subtle beauty . . . holding at bay the threat of sentimentality as she explores the fine line between the emotions that hold people together and those which drive them apart'
Stephanie Merritt, *Observer*

'Davies brings to life a moment in history when the meaning of family was freighted with ideological contradiction . . . the dislocations that she gives voice to continue to sound a deeply affecting and provocative note'
Alex Clark, *TLS*

'A lovely exploration of the burdens and joys of personal history'
A. L. Kennedy, *Scotsman*

'Stevie Davies evokes an earlier era in delicate, meticulous detail in a story which asks important questions about the boundaries of parental and sexual love. This is a quiet, flavourful novel'
Sunday Times

'The interdependence of Mara and Frankie's relationship is brilliantly captured . . . Peeling back the idealistic notions of universal love and peace, Davies reveals a destructive emptiness'
Kate Riordan, *Time Out*

'Stevie Davies's excellent new novel . . . Her characters have the ring of complex truth. These people can aggravate and endear themselves all at the same time. Just like real life'
Carol Birch, *Independent Review*

'In *Kith and Kin* she toys intriguingly with the conventions of the confessional novel'
Joanna Kavenna, *Daily Telegraph*

Stevie Davies is a Fellow of The Royal Society of Literature and the Welsh Academy, and Director of Creative Writing at Swansea University. Her previous titles include *Four Dreamers and Emily*, *The Web of Belonging*, *Impassioned Clay* and *The Element of Water*, which was longlisted for the Booker and Orange Prizes and won the Arts Council of Wales Award. *The Web of Belonging* has been made into a film for ITV, starring Brenda Blethyn and Kevin Whately.

By Stevie Davies

Boy Blue
Primavera
Arms and the Girl
Closing the Book
Emily Bronte: Heretic
Four Dreamers and Emily
The Web of Belonging
Impassioned Clay
The Element of Water
Kith and Kin

Acknowledgements

I am grateful to the Society of Authors for the Authors' Foundation bursary which helped to support me during the writing of this novel. A version of Chapter Two, which won one of the prizes in the Bridport Short Story Competition, was published in *The Bridport Anthology 2001* as 'Mirrors'.

for Helen
with my love

Rhy dynn a dyrr
  'Too tight breaks'
                        (Welsh proverb)

Echo

He loves the bones of you, I remember declaring, and when there was no longer bone but only ash, I suppose both Aaron and I were still in love with the ash of her.

At Rhossili we poured Francesca away, her ash a sift of fine silver powder. We went out to Worm's Head in a light wind, the two of us, and poured her over the edge, where she was diffused over the rocks and in sea and air, in peaceful handfuls, as I later chose to think, rocking myself in my own arms.

I think now, *That's a typical lie*. Her death was vile, violent. A maelstrom of despair. And we had tussled over her urn. We'd fought over possession of this ash. So many years I'd seen him falsely, as if wearing Frankie's sunglasses, colouring the whole field of perception. For wasn't Aaron just a pretty ordinary guy, when you came down to it? The lustre sticking to him like a child's glitter? Or perhaps it was the hint of incest that created the aura. I didn't know. It was impossible to construe, for I was up too close to his face, her face. We were a tight knot of three cousins born in the same year, the first fruits of our dads' demob from North Africa and Burma.

After her death Aaron and I wrangled, ludicrously, for months. When the coroner had finally released the remains, we even fought over the box the urn came in.

I grabbed at it but he started opening it and then I heard myself yelling, it was mine, get your hands off, and he said, put it down. We finally wrenched it open, revealing a monstrous marble pot, black and heavy.

We stared at this silently.

Her mam, my Auntie Susan, came in, her eyes all swollen, and immediately rushed out again, quavering, *Oh no, take it away.* Jack, her stepdad, came in and said, *A quiet word. You two do the offices would you? You see what a state Susan's in.* He couldn't get rid of Frankie quickly enough. *She was lucky to have friends like you two,* he oozed. *Thought the world of her friends, did our Francesca. Poor Suze,* he lamented to me. *She's a broken woman. Broken, she is.*

Yes, I thought, and I wonder who broke her.

Aaron and I wordlessly resumed our battle for possession. Later, we argued as to who'd won. 'Well, you got her,' I said. 'I let go.'

'No, I let go. I thought, Christ, we're going to drop her. So I let go.'

'You fucking didn't.'

'I did, Mars. You're remembering wrong. I let you win.'

'There was nothing to win. Just rubbish.'

'Don't say that, lovely girl. Don't,' he pleaded. 'We have to let her rest. I think she was just . . . so tired. I think she was tired out.'

And the way he put it was as if you came to a natural end by taking that jump off the ladder in your stepfather's shed. You were weary of being yourself, and it was simply an extreme way of drawing the covers over your head.

As we grappled the lid from the casket, what a surprise, you were in there, Francesca. Quintessentially. Something that had been through fire and was, shall I say, purified? Whatever you were, it was far away from the corrupt pair of us, frantic in our tussle. And even then I was jealous of you, that you should escape beyond being, a scattered handful, a second, a third, as I watched Aaron scoop the silverness of your remains in his beautiful hand with a kind of reverence. I had the strange impression that he was about to lick the dust of you off his palm, a blasphemy of eucharist. He brought it towards his face and stared.

'Of course it isn't really her,' I said.

'What do you mean, not her?' For he must have her, believe himself to be in possession of her, in any form. A kind of pollen.

'How are we supposed to know? I mean, if it's her, or if the last person they cremated got muddled in with her ashes?'

Aaron stood there, a slight wind flicking his long curls. He cupped the ash in his palms to keep it safe. He said, 'Now don't be absurd, Mara,' in just the way his mother talked to his father. The ash stood for Francesca, that was what mattered. He looked at me with a sincere sneer in his eyes. Often he had kissed me with that look; bitten my underlip till I thought the blood must have been drawn. How far from kissing we were then, now that I had won, and got him to myself. But even over Frankie's ashes I was afflicted by that dark jag of envy and took the opportunity to tell myself, *There you are, you see? He never cared a damn for you.*

Yes, well, I think now, with a shrug of my mind, that was a long time ago, when we courted trespass and called it innocence. And we were young and vicious and foolhardy. You think you will not get over things. You do.

But the young desires, the affinities, hang on, don't they? They crowd in where nothing else can grow: where archaic dreams and illusions cling and linger.

There are a few grey strands in my hair, at the temples mainly. It's always a surprise to see them. Frankie of course never aged but she was a heavy smoker and surely she would have aged rapidly: her skin was already lined in her twenties, and sometimes its texture was waxen, bruise-dark under the eyes. Poor lamb.

When Aaron and I stood there on the parapet and threw her, young and perfect as she would ever be, to the winds, some of her dust blew back, lodging secretly in the bud of my eye, and on my lips. The waves curdled far below. My tongue-tip crept to the corner of my mouth and licked the powder's dry, mineral texture. It was a mute and ultimate knowing of her.

Her eyes, I thought, as we turned with the empty urn, a squall billowing my anorak, Francesca's eyes were jewel-blue. And when Aaron had taken that powder in his palm, the thought that it might contain the residue of those eyes, that hair, astounded me. That we should come down to this. Aaron had cradled your arid residue but I had made him throw you away, and he had

3

complied, saying, *We need to let go of her, don't we, Marsie?* After which she had stealthily come back into me and become me.

1

In the valley between Oystermouth Castle and the fortress of flats, smoke from the allotments loses itself in an ashen haze; the earth is the colour of charcoal. I've been prey to eerie dreams and I seem to lie all twisted in my sleep, crushing an arm, which for half an hour will be fizzing with pins and needles. Well, what do you expect, coming home after twelve years?

Auntie Hen has told the family the news that Mara is back but 'not to go bothering you all the time, I've said you're an Important Person, Mara dear, with Work to do, isn't it?' And indeed no one has bothered me. I seem to be able to do that for myself. Plus, Aaron is not here. I calm myself with his absence. After all, this position at the Institute was far too exciting to turn down. Sick of academic life – well, where was I getting? – and with Menna having flown the nest, I could hardly turn down a job at once so high-powered and worthwhile, setting up a unit like this. In point of fact no other such unit exists. This is my baby.

Daily before my eyes pass persons lacking some part of themselves. Breastless, legless, footless or handless – but healed – they smile grimly or clench their faces and tell you of inexpressible pain that nobody will credit. I step round their pain at a quiet distance: hands-on loving care has never been my thing. I'm here to manage and administer, not to treat. But I wonder if it is beginning to get to me? Meeting my own face in one of the mirrors we're experimenting with, I was struck by the tension in my features. Of course the necessary refusal of sympathetic distress is, in itself, draining. As is having to fight prejudice and ignorance in high places, every step of the way.

That quietly spoken consultant surgeon in the restaurant, Mr Pritchard, with his sceptical smile and disarming tone, questioning the existence of the pathology we are underfunded to study.

There is not sufficient research, according to this elegant lopper-off of legs and sawyer of arms, to indicate that the syndrome has any physiological reality. And, with all due respect, he has always put it down to neuroma on the stump or psychological trauma. Plus, if schemes like this were to gain credibility, might we in fact be creating the very condition we claimed to be examining? He genuinely hoped he was wrong.

Elin leant forwards and told him in her lilting way about the Gulf soldier who not only feels his toes burning in his boot but also, as he walks on his prosthesis, feels blood running down into the boot, where it pools, so that when he walks it squelches. She gave no sign of anger but I saw that her cheeks and delicate neck were flushed. I put my hand lightly on her shoulder and asked without undue mildness what Mr Pritchard's purpose was in casting doubt on our work?

Not his intention at all, apparently. Just thinking aloud. He sat daintily, stirring his coffee. It was, after all, a sexy topic. The blur between physiology and psychology seduces us all. That very word 'phantom'. Poetic rather than scientific.

'You know,' he said, 'I have amputated innumerable limbs and truly I have yet to see one definite example of the syndrome.'

'There is a great deal of denial about. This pain is real. We believe it pertains to the somatosensory cortex. But if it were caused by a magnet in the moon, it would still be real.'

My manner despatched him. It frequently does. They used to lobotomise for phantom pain. 'Physician, lobotomise thyself,' I murmured. Elin giggled.

We finished our tea and returned to the unit, where the new mirror system was in place. I allowed myself to imagine how it would be to reach for a cup with a hand that was not there, a hand thrilling with pain so pure as to be off any known map of pain. I watched a diabetic patient, whose left arm had been progressively amputated, collude in tricking his brain by viewing his right arm performing the actions his absent left arm was failing to perform. His focused gaze gave the impression of a man in a dream. I think it was then that I felt the headache setting in.

Elin drove me home: 'You overdo it,' she said. 'You are so dynamic, Mara. Put on your cold cap when you get in.'

The cap is cold therapy. Elin more or less invented it for me. We've run tests on cold therapy for the amputees. It works for me but not for them. My cap lives in the fridge and smells of pre-cooked meals. You fit it over your head, blacking out your vision, and just sit with your head in a cold sheath.

The clamour of pain drew off and the throbbing in my right temple at once began to shrink until it became, not pain, but the memory of pain. Exhausted by the headache's aftermath I dozed, lulled by the murmur of the television in the background. As the smoky sleep began to wreathe me, I thought of Uncle Pierce, Francesca's and my Uncle Pierce, so like a man I sat behind on the bus this morning that he might even have been Uncle Pierce. No. He'd have to be in his late eighties or early nineties. And men like that are too dear to live long. Take our fathers, Francesca's real dad, my Uncle David, Menelaus the Bread — small-boned, the soul of kindness and, like kindness, mortal. My dear dad, Evans the Post, doing the bee-bop in the kitchen. It had seemed at one time that fathers had taken to dying in the way they haunted their locals, gratefully taking refuge from their responsibilities. The dead surround us like smoke, I thought, fuddled.

When I come to, I have the sense that she is with me, here in this room. She's singing softly and intimately. A tedious delirium of dreams has dogged me since I arrived back at Oystermouth, so at first I pay no heed to the voice. Stale from sleep, I open my eyes and there she is.

Francesca's lovely, long-ago face.

I slide to my knees, holding my breath. It seems to be some kind of home movie but which of us could have afforded a cine-camera back then? And how dated Francesca appears in the old-fashioned colour film, her gingerish waist-length hair a childish confection of beaded plaits, with horse daisies and a homemade butterfly. Oh yes, that butterfly Jade constructed with her small ingenious fingers from bits and bobs picked up along the tideline.

As Frankie sings, her kohl-blackened eyes hold the camera with that air of pouty provocation she had, the *I'll take you on and who do you think you are anyway?* expression, and she's singing, whatever's she singing? She finishes. Childishly pokes her face up close to the lens and sticks out her tongue.

I fumble for the video-button. Catch her, before she runs between your fingers, all that heart-rending beauty poured away again. She has on a piece of cloth George and Jade claimed to have brought back from Nepal, though I don't think they were ever in Nepal. I don't think he ever went east of Norfolk or west of Milford Haven. It was an orange and white wisp of fabric you could see through. No one's clothes belonged to any one person then. I wore it too. Aaron wore it like a sarong. But here Frankie wears it with one shoulder bare. (*Disgraceful, acting like trollops, ungodly hooligans, showing us up terrible*, said the family. *Seen them wearing a tablecloth, aye, a tablecloth, what would their daddies have said?*)

I have time, in these few seconds, here on my knees inches from the screen, to note her fingers on the blond guitar with the inlay she created herself in Red Indian patterns. It's here, the guitar, amongst Menna's old toys, with the same gut from which Francesca plucked her melancholy magic.

Young she looks, young. Stranded there in the past, the raspy, bluesy singing in her throat. In suspension. As if she'd been detained while the rest of us were allowed to pour out at the school bell. In detention. As she often was, and I'd wait outside in the lane, kicking a can around, eating blackberries off the briar. Sometimes, bored, I'd trail off home, crimson-mouthed, dragging my scuffed satchel, leaving her to it. Her mam Susan never cared. Or only cared lightly. She'd look up from a magazine and greet

Francesca as she might have welcomed an acquaintance, *Oh, it's you. How about a brew?*

Who took this film? Why's it being shown? Its novelty suggests she has never gone away; that Aaron and I were wrong in supposing that hers were the ashes we scattered, for, look, here she is. But even as I think this, I recognise that the image on the screen is blurred, a surface only.

Now it seems the camera has got bored with Frankie and drifts off to dwell on a group of fuzzy, junky figures round the remains of a fire, prone and (presumably) spaced out, or doing their own thing. One hairy, balding and bearded man seems to be attempting to dowse, though without getting up from where he's draped. Feebly his hands reach out the hazel twigs, which twitch from time to time.

It flashes through me to hope that I am not going to figure in this film. Anticipation of Auntie Hen's horror, Elin's startlement, the management team's prurient distaste at the TV revelation of Ms Mara Evans' bare bum turns me hot with embarrassment. For things are livening up. A cluster of female figures sways towards the edge of the cliff, a circle, wearing, it is revealed, nothing at all. Oh Jesus, am I there? I never went for the earth-mother, we-are-the-goddess-Selene thing; I was the tough-talking politico all set to change the world, single-handed, but you never knew what you might find yourself up to when the acid took you. The camera, however, is uninterested in faces. It shows a ruck of anonymous bodies. I couldn't have been one of them, could I? Am I about to rush pell-mell, face to face with my young self? But no, the camera returns to the lone girl with the guitar, seated on what looks like a rubbish tip, but to her the bottle tops shine like emerald stars, the cans and bottles glow like bronze and copper, vibrations of the universe speaking to Francesca, in Francesca, singing her way back to where the stars attend to her song.

It's over and the credits are going up. A voice is telling us in Welsh that important documentary material has been dug up.

Dug up? How can she have been? No. Only Aaron and I can fully know the completeness of her annihilation.

The whole thing has taken no longer than three or four minutes and I have only a fraction of that on the video. But now she is hurting in me.

Up till now, forty-three ineffective treatments were in common use for the pain we are working on. Forty-three, I think. All as bloody useless as one another. We know they are useless but we fall back on them. Cold and heat and electromyography, sympathectomy and biofeedback and murmuring mantras and cutting the nerve and anti-depressants. A hall of mirrors our greatest hope. Trick the brain. Remap the cortex. Which is what I have done over a period of two decades, saying to myself day in, day out: *no part of you is missing. You are whole.*

It has taken a film of a few minutes' duration to undermine all this painstaking work. *Been dug up* are the only words I caught of the commentary. They recall the knowledge of the noose that ended her. Twenty-three years old and her dream stillborn in her throat. I'm double her age now and Menna is a year older.

Better not have dug her up. The questions we never answered are awakening, I can feel them stir.

It must have been the despair and the drugs that killed her, for she feared pain and made a wild fuss about the most trivial injury. Frankie could never consciously have looped that rope around her own neck, leapt out into that horror, the garage Jack destroyed afterwards.

I walked down the lane a few months later and found it gone. Where she had thrown away her life, there was emptiness. I remember stopping to stare into that void. I examined it. From then on, every time I went past, I was shocked afresh by this nothingness. Later Jack had a garden chair placed there, under a sort of awning. Just where she had jumped, I thought, staring over the wrought iron gate to where he and Susan – *those paramours*, said Frankie, *those concubines, that old lecher and his moll, that pair of dimwits* – where he and Susan used to sit on a warm Sabbath, in earshot of the bells of St Michael's and All Angels across the village.

Once I stood behind the gate observing them. His brown, brawny arm lay draped around the back of the garden chair, nicotined fingers on her bare arm, and they were – as Francesca used to observe – *canoodling*. At the centre of that emptiness, there they were, a happy Sunday couple, canoodling, while the roast seethed in the pan indoors and the bells rang from the church where Francesca's real dad lay buried. The babble of their chat dismayed me and I ran.

The coroner had designated it a clear case of suicide under the influence of hallucinogenic substances.

Even so there had been the irrational terror that I would be unmasked. For I was part of the transgression. And Aaron. Had he been worth it? The family split apart into a feud of epic proportions after her death. Well, of course, that was the nature of the beast. Too close, always unhealthily close. The Evanses, Menelauses and Thomases were linked by intermarriage and sundered by grudges of fabulous longevity and labyrinthine complication. They had been in convulsive throes of mutual hostility for so long that it seemed like a *raison d'être*. Who knew where this feud had originated, when archaic betrayals were compounded by a dispute over the descent of some paltry property, garnered by thrifty women from the pay packets of boozing but chiefly amiable menfolk? We had crept from the underbelly of Port Talbot to Newton and Oystermouth. Aaron's parents had scaled the hill to Sketty. That in itself was cause enough for rancour.

But when Jack came along, after Frankie's dad's death, he bonded the tribe in an orgy of reproach. The wagging tongues. The gossips' reverberating phone lines. They had always known, they agreed, that Susan was no good. A lost cause, Susan, if anyone ever was, not content with decent widowhood or a suitable widower to marry after the elapse of a proper time, but falling with spaniel eyes for crude, base Jack, given to the bottle and blue jokes. Sex. Tattoos all across his shoulders, man. And him hammering her, no doubt. But then making up. Sex. And them coming round on the scrounge, saying they hadn't enough to feed the girlie.

And spending it down the White Rose.

No shame.

Fear of shame was social glue. It kept the feuding Evanses, Thomases and Menelauses together.

And then our antics. Shaming the respectability of the family names, so that the Evanses, Thomases and Menelauses were a laughing stock. We, the spendthrift wreckers of everything they had so carefully built up. Recycled soap. Milk bottle tops in saucers. One lump of coal on the fire rather than two. They had scrimped. We had squandered.

And then the girlie goes and hangs herself.

It was as if she had cut the web at its secret, weakest point. As if all stood accused and, being human, must rush the imputed blame to the next in line, running for cover. You never get over it completely. That emptiness where the garage once stood still gapes at me as I pass even though I've lived away for twelve years. Because if there is no garage there, that means part of me is still missing.

This is my logic. It is pitiful. I am not one of these foolish, frilly women who cannot accept, say, her widowhood. Not that I stand in any danger of the loss of a husband I am never going to have. Even when Jo left me, I let her go. I rededicated myself to my work. I can't remembering crying. Jo was furious that I didn't give her the satisfaction of my tears. Cold, she said I was. Congenitally cold.

'Ah, Susan is not well,' said Auntie Hen, my Nana's sister. 'In the poor head, you know, and that Jack such a womaniser, he went off with a proper floozy but now he's down and out.'

I've never been to visit Auntie Susan. But she's there for the visiting. My father's sister, whom I can't bear to look in the eyes. From my flat, Susan is no more than three hundred metres distance as the crow flies. And, it's weird, I think now: whenever I pass that ex-garage, that corroded relic of Jack's garden chair, something long numb in me tingles unpleasantly, and I hurry on. As if Susan and the interior of that house exist across an unbridgeable divide, where time is different. She doesn't go out, apparently, which makes it easier to sustain this sense of her elsewhereness.

I rewind the video. How much of the film did I miss? I was asleep when Frankie woke me. She was in the room while I dozed, my feet tucked up, arms folded over my belly, in the solitude of the flat; a forty-seven-year-old woman becoming with every day more at ease with her banality and isolation. What woke me? How did I know she was there? For the sound was low. I turn on the picture at the point where I began to record and turn up the sound.

Her voice, smoky and contralto, fills the space I am in. She sings with harsh, intemperate asperity to the mothers and fathers throughout the land, counselling them not to despise what they can't understand. In her touching female impersonation of the Dylan raunch, into which sweetness would keep breaking through, the girl in the orange and white toga was bragging that she was immortal. Whereas the older generation were faded has-beens, the young would go on forever.

I switch her off, with a sense of desolation. The intimacy and invasiveness of voices.

I remember how I reassured her that time about Aaron, when she was in the maternity ward, 'He loves the bones of you.' I went on to tell her that the whole tribe, the Beloved Community, all of us at Breuddwyd, we all adored her, and how could she allege we hated her?

She hesitated; I saw her lip quiver, her eyelids. Perhaps, she was thinking, all her hectic fears were fantasies, projections of her own insecurity. Dope. Paranoia. The baby whimpered and she laid her hand on his head. I loved the hand. I had in some sense betrayed it, but I did love it. Although, given that all the rules were gone, all the codes broken, how could I have betrayed her by loving? Aaron suddenly seemed of low account, beside the bond

13

with Frankie. Not only of small account but a shoot thrown off the mother branch. Not intrinsic or vital. Not really. He joined Frankie and me at the root, just as we all at Breuddwyd shared one mind.

That was it, then, was it? Francesca and Mara shared Aaron in order to share one another? Yet when I see him now in my mind's eye, I'm suddenly ready to faint with longing. He was the first and last man I gave myself to, and what do I make of that?

It's our first case of phantom pleasure. Elin and I are astounded at this woman's revelations. Thirty-six-year-old victim of a car crash. 'When I make love,' she says, her face burning crimson, 'I get this, well, what can I say? orgasmic feeling in my feet? Well, it's some sort of compensation, isn't it?'

She beams, somewhere between embarrassment and triumph, and Elin laughs out loud with delight. We pass the phantom pleasure round with a joy that registers our relief after the totality of pain we view here daily. We've heard so many cases of a searing ache or an 'electrocuted sensation' that is referred to the genitals from a missing foot that we want to cheer for the one who got something, however bizarre, out of the equation.

2

Menna will get hold of a copy of the whole tape for me: apparently they're doing a clear-out of an archive of local footage at BBC Wales, unearthing Sixties and Seventies stuff; interesting stuff, the guy she's spoken to reckons, though not all as spectacular as the material they showed yesterday. Stirring up a lot of memories round here, the guy says. Real honey pot, and more to come.

'Were you into drugs, mam?' she asked on the phone, cautiously inquisitive. 'They all looked well out of it.'

'I was more into, you know, political things. Moon goddesses and druids not my cup of tea.'

'No, I don't suppose they were. I can't imagine it. Don't you think ... it's, well, time you spoke to the family again? Blood is blood, after all. They honestly couldn't have been nicer to me. Everyone asks after you.'

'Well, I will: no, really, love, I will. Haven't had much time, Menna, what with setting up the unit here.'

'I spoke to Uncle Aaron, by the way.'

'Ah. Did you?'

'Yesterday. He's in Japan. But as soon as he gets back, he's coming to see me.' A trace of little-girl appeasement, apprehension, shades the excitement in her voice: 'You OK with that?'

'Of course. Why shouldn't I be? Whatever is best.' There's a lump in my throat like a rock. 'For you.'

Menna winces. She has linked up with every single relative in the area and traced one or two to the US. I've only really kept in touch with dear, gentle Hen, who, in her wisdom, keeps to safe topics like the weather and my Work, which she reveres. But Menna's deft fingers have been knitting together our family's shattered bonds. What have they been telling her? She's timid of passing on to me the extent of her knowledge. But that was all so long ago. Why rake it up? Of course the young crave secrets. She has the right to seek out mine. Yet Menna is gentle with me, wiser than I ever was, more careful.

My hand on the receiver trembles when she speaks his name. And sometimes I read Aaron's face in her, and sometimes Francesca's, and sometimes my own. There are occasions when, to complicate things, I see someone else submerged in my own eyes, a younger self who looks back from the mirror scandalised. As if, in growing middle-aged, I had been guilty of some impiety in relation to this younger person.

'We should talk more,' I suggest softly. 'We will. If you like. When you come over from Cardiff, let's do that.'

'Please.' Her voice brightens.

'By the way,' I add, 'I thought I saw Uncle Pierce on the bus. But it couldn't have been Pierce, could it? Pierce could not still be alive . . .'

'Oh yes,' she says. 'He is. Apparently. I haven't seen him yet. Face to face.'

Twenty-four years ago there came to me that heart-shaped face with a clear vision of her absolute priority in my life. In that first year Menna's face lay so close against my shoulder and breast that the rest of the world was blocked off. Wholly for the better.

When we put the receivers down, I keep Menna's darling voice in my inner ear to balance me against the buffeting of the imagined voices of the tribe, awakened to its long-ago shame by this film. But not Pierce: he would have understood. What was it he said? That was it, needy: Francesca was a needy, manipulative waif, said Uncle Pierce after her death. Aye, but she was a vulnerable lass, he added, and could be so lovable. It was Society, said Pierce, that had insulted her, dealing the blows that put her so beyond help. He was a kind man and spread his compassion in a wide abstract arc. By Society, I suppose Pierce chiefly meant Auntie Susan and Uncle Jack.

All along the gossip-web, the tribe is doubtless back in touch, receivers nuzzling warm against elderly ears, lines buzzing with salacious or piteous shock.

—Did you see?

—See what?

—The girlie, our poor girlie. On TV.

—Not Francesca? But she's . . . so long gone.

And for a moment her wraith would stand in the air like a wisp of smoke.

—A film with her on it. Singing.

—What was the programme then?

—About drugs.

—No! Drugs!

—Flower-power on the Gower, remember all that? Nearly died of shame.

—Well. There you are.

—Naked girls there were. Dancing!

—No one we knew, I hope. Well, they were quite a depraved bunch at one point, came down from the north of course.

—Tribe, they called themselves.

—Communards! I'll give you communards, I said. Never had to work for a living. Always had it easy, that's the thing. Not like in our time. Penny a day I got and Mama had it off me as soon as I was in the door. But these young ones, they thought money grew on trees.

—Remember the beardy one like a goat?

—Well, at least you can't smell them on a film.

—That's something.

—And look at Mara Evans now: big fish in the NHS, who'd have thought it, keeps herself to herself, mind. Better say reclusive rather than rude.

—Temper on her when a child, mind.

—Remember our girlie's eyes? Ah, God love her.

The recurrently warring Evanses, Menelauses and Thomases,

inveterately fratricidal, occasionally litigious, hanker after one another terribly when they've stopped speaking and internal gossip sources dry up. They think of one another incessantly. Love each other warmly. Forget their differences. Lapse into a good-natured lull of uncertain longevity, passing round reminiscences like stale bara brith. Oh and what a relief it is to get back in touch, or even cross the threshold to where the teapot sits beneath its cosy.

In the street I bumped into a second cousin this morning: embarrassing that I could not remember her name, Becca, until she'd gone into the fishmonger's. But of course: Becca the Mouth. Where had I been? she wondered, without stopping to hear the answer. I remembered my mother casting up her eyes lamenting, *Oh what a talker! Does she ever stop? And gossip!* Becca said Uncle Tony had seen Jack. She tutted. Sitting outside the White Rose dressed as a Russian, with a fur cap and those flaps down over his ears. Looking skew-whiff, half-seas-over.

'So that's the pair of them gaga. And who can be surprised after the life they led. Well, Jack must have had a few put away, not to feel the cold, I wouldn't wonder, Tony said. What an exhibition.'

'Not with his current woman friend then?' I asked.

'Apparently he hasn't got one.'

Never. Pigs are flying. I see him now, randy Jack the cossack hobbling around minus stallion.

'Reprehensible creature,' said my cousin. '*Rep-re-hens-ible.* Did you see the film?'

'No.'

'Well, there was a film of the whole hippie crew of you misbehaving at Penmaen.'

'I never misbehaved at Penmaen.'

She took no notice, surging on. I could see her relish. Something to keep the tongues wagging, a chance for a blaming session. 'And that was Susan's doing, mark my words. She it was who let him in and she it is who's paying for it. There's a justice in things, always say so. But also,' she added, staring into my eyes through the thick panes of her glasses, then swerving her gaze away, 'the poor girlie got into thoroughly bad company. *Lewd* company. And what was she doing then . . . on the film . . . there at Penmaen? Not one of us could work out what on earth she was doing sitting in the middle of a pile of rubbish!'

I could imagine their voices, shocked and shamed, sad and intrigued, because what Frankie and Mara and Aaron had got up to in the previous generation with those addicts and tramps and gypsies and thieves was only a symptom of their own disease, like the rash that proclaims an infection.

'Lovely little girl, she was,' said my cousin. 'Once. Poor dab. Come and see us, Mara. I'll be off now, I've to pick up some mackerel, lovely mackerel he does here, you should try it, come round and have a fish supper, there's no pollution any more, it did get polluted, we couldn't touch the whelks and why call it Oystermouth, I used to say, when the oysters have gone? Well I'll say no more but you know you're welcome any time. We shan't last for ever, you know.'

I drift to the window, brimming with the sense of Francesca's childhood. She comes tiptoeing, breathes on the back of my neck.

Sometimes there was a harmony and a peace between Frankie and me, such as I've never known since, and I'm old enough to realise will never come again. We were little girls sitting at the edge of the sea. We sorted pebbles, wetting them to find the most beautiful – opal, agate, some like pear drops, lemon drops – you could scarcely refrain from putting them in your mouth, so perfect was the illusion, but they'd jar against the enamel of your teeth. And all manner of pearly shells, with the sea fizzing in where we crouched, emptied of their fleshy innards.

When we were small, and this must have been very small, I'd kneel on her bed in my nightie, hugging her teddy, and watch Auntie Susan brush her hair. Her real dad might pop his head round the door. The brushing was like a blessing. The presence of my quiet uncle, the baker, in his socked feet, a blessing too. He was a plain man. He knew the decencies, did Uncle David, and did not so much insist on them as assume them. An ordinary and an orderly grace, which you do not recognise until it has been displaced.

When Frankie's real dad was in the world, her home was more pleasantly cosy than mine, more easygoing. It was not exactly messy, because Susan liked to have the best she could afford, and adored her furniture and her ornaments with fervid passion. But their house was unregimented. Ours never seemed to have recovered from my mother's wartime stint as a nurse in the Wrens. And Susan was rounded, bosomy, unlike my mam, though she could be warm too: be fair, she could. Susan, as our uncles murmured, had an hourglass figure. And our aunties, pretending not to hear, were saddened and offended by this phrase. I laid my head on Susan's bosom once and learned its spongy give.

I lay in my cousin's place and lazily hankered. Mam's brushing of my hair was military – I got a quota of strokes. Frankie's was brushed in an intimate humming trance.

In came the dad with a plate of cheese straws. Cheese straws! We shot up. Warm from the oven! Eating in a bedroom! That would not have been permitted in my home. But here if Uncle David brought warm goodies, you all tucked in. And Susan was a creature of appetite. She shouldn't, she proclaimed, considering her figure, but she'd just have a nibble. Or two. We all four sat on the beds and munched. Drugged with the scent of baking, I filled my belly on good things. We slept in the one single bed, Frankie and I.

Whereas our relatives were joined by bonds of blood, we young ones were united by pure, elated, rebellious choice. *Inseparable they are, those lovelies*, our families said of us two girls when we were very small. We shared our dinner mathematically, to the last pea. Francesca and I would eat a banana starting at either end and working inwards. We were blonde and played up to the notion of being angels, false smiles rewarded by barley sugar or ice cream. Our egalitarian distribution of booty was admired by all and praised by Uncle Pierce as a fine example of Socialism, by Uncle Tony as implying elect status, by our mothers as a sign of superior upbringing. We had our own private language before we acquired English or Welsh, which spooked some and charmed others.

I've no crumb of that language left on my tongue. The bananas I do remember and the ice creams: I licked, she licked; I licked, she licked. One bleated if the other suffered a bruised knee. But our touching sisterliness was policed by both parties, vigilantly mirroring eyes ensuring equality of distribution. Aaron we petted and occasionally slapped. He was one of three ductile Thomas boy-cousins, whose descent from the heights of Sketty brought our families out in their Sunday best. Annie was all gracious condescension, her boys the apple of her eye, especially Aaron, the gentle eldest. He bunched his mam's skirts in one fist, sucked the thumb of the other hand, and was not rebuked.

Eyebrows were raised in the gossiping wake of their reascent to Sketty. For whereas the Evans and Menelaus families had achieved a certain respectability, our means were modest. The Thomases owned a large house with four bedrooms, two bathrooms and what Aaron's mother was pleased to call 'land'. Annie was a queenly woman, who had married old money and extended invitations to 'Come over, dears, and eat a simple picnic in the grounds'. But what could you eat when you got there, the family puzzled, since it was all foreign food with spices that detonated coughing fits.

'Such a mummy's boy.'

'Give him a chance, bach, he's only five.'

'Six. Same age as the girlies almost, and you don't see *them* dribbling all over their mams' cardies. Do you?'

'Too much money, too little sense.'

'Course, the money's not *earned* . . .'

Yack yack yack on the relentless topic of property. Who would Nana leave Breuddwyd to? Who should have inherited Pierce's crazed great-uncle's house? A crime it was to leave it to a cattery. Flea-bitten mogs eating off gold plates.

Vague notions tickled us of cats lapping milk from golden dishes. This memory must derive from a time very near to Frankie's dad's illness because its quarrelsome serenity is tinged with black, like a view seen through dark-framed glasses. We sipped Coca-Cola through green and white striped straws, staring at the amount remaining in one another's ice-cold bottles. We were pledged to drink slowly, hoarding the precious liquid. I privately deplored the game, since the bubbles went flat, and bubbles were the gorgeousness of Coca-Cola.

'Can we have a cat, Mam?' asked Francesca.

'No, we don't want a cat.'

'I like cats.'

'Well, we're not having one.'

'Why not?'

'Because of your dad's chest and you know that quite well.' It was certainly Before Jack then, when Francesca was unacquainted with death and the replacement of all she held dear.

'I don't.'

'You do, pet. It's the cat hairs, see.'

'How can they get into his chest?' I asked.

'Allergy. He's got a weak chest, and cat hairs make it worse.'

'A dog then?'

'Don't go on, there's a love.'

'A rabbit? A gerbil?'

'No.'

'But why, Mam?'

'*Because.* I don't want no more to be looking after.'

'Now now. The kiddie,' intervened her dad, in a tempering voice.

'Not even a lizard? A newt? A stick-insect even? Or an ant?' Frankie persisted. I had finished my Coke and was blowing a dolorous note across the bottle's mouth. 'You've finished yours, Mars,' she observed. 'Now you ent got none left.'

'But I've had all my bubbles.'

'Mara's got a puppy.'

'Well, maybe one day,' said her dad, and he laid one hand on her pale curls.

This is what haunts me: the stilling power of that hand on Francesca's head. I can see the hand now, as if it were extended from some merciful place high up, its fingers spread to cup the silky crown of her head. Calming. Our dads were second cousins who had been close from childhood and through the war. It was in our dads' laps that we sought sympathy and security, the mams positioned apart, and apart from one another, hers all fluffy and with a pretty face whose artistry fascinated me. It was a blank space on which Susan daily painted a crimson pout, a startlement of the eyes, a rouge blush. 'Muck', my mam called it, busy with practical tasks. But I lived in awe of Auntie Susan's glamour – her hourglass figure, her matching handbag and shoes. I liked to walk down the road beside her pretending she was mine. It was difficult to credit that she was my dad's sister.

'Maybe one day,' said Frankie's dad, and the hoarse voice sticks in my inner ear, implanting its wistful lie.

'It's all right, da. I'm not bothered,' said Francesca.

'Ah, the angel,' came the auntie-chorus.

'Good girl,' said her dad. 'Lovely poppets, aren't you?'

And then suddenly we weren't good girls any more. We were hooligans, and whatever would become of us, unless we mended our ways? Come on, what?

Francesca plunged from grace and I followed. Turning tomboy, we taunted and walloped our Thomas cousins. I thrust Aaron and his younger brother Seth down a steep dune, cutting Aaron's calf on a buried, rusted can, for which he had to be rushed to casualty for a tetanus injection. Francesca and I rolled down in one another's arms, tumbling over and over like one creature, screeching with orgiastic laughter, sand in our hair and mouths.

The Thomas boys gazed yearningly at our rough and tumble. Their hair was parted low on one side. Joe, Seth and Aaron had almond-shaped eyes, quite pale, and were gentle with one another.

'Why do you do it, cariad?' asked my mam.

'Oh it's a phase, most like,' said dad. 'And look at poor David. He's fading fast.'

What was that about fading? I disliked the idea of fading but it did not sound violent: more like the chrysanthemums my mother kept on the sill beyond their time.

'Aye, but we don't want it damaging our Mara,' Mam went on, and there was a feeling as if the chrysanthemum fade might prove contagious. 'She's impressionable.'

'Oh well,' said my dad.

Later in the maelstrom, when I snatched at Aaron, although I knew quite well what I was doing, I had little comprehension of my own voracious cruelty. But now I see Francesca as a creature deserted by its pack, that's got detached somehow, and swims in bleak waters.

I am no longer the same person. I walk down to the shops for milk, past the house in which Susan is said to be immured in a state of premature senility, and remind myself that I was young then: I am not the same person. Or if I am, I have taken steps to render myself harmless. The flight from Wales when I lived incommunicado, on the run not so much from my kin as from the shafts of memory they awakened, has left me cautious and almost pathologically sensible.

A plane flying across the sun makes the day give a cynical wink. For the first time, it occurs to me to knock on that door and find out what my aunt's mind – full of holes as it is – remembers. Next time, maybe, next time I go past, I will knock.

I remember Frankie's father in the last winter of his life. Uncle David was out of puff, moved heavily, and stayed on a bench overlooking the bay at Caswell.

He waved, her dad, as we chased one another with bladder-wrack. We waved. Then we climbed on the rocks, prising off limpets. We waved again. Higher and higher we climbed. Beyond the pools with their magical crabs and minutiae of shrimp. Above the barnacled limestone, till we had neared the cliff path, and, turning, looked down over the beach. There sat Francesca's dad, peaceful-looking, arms spread out to either side on the bench, wearing his old tweedy jacket. He looked straight out to sea, his corduroy cap on the bench beside him. His face seemed ashy-pale. As I look back, I realise how wasted he must have been. I did not consciously see it then. I saw one of our dads, Francesca's and mine, eternal and dear. Ordinary.

We could not hear the labouring of his breath, the curdled lungs thick with tarry mucus. All our menfolk had coughs, many had emphysema. Their teeth were nicotined, their fingers stained. All smoked as they talked, smoked as they drank, smoked as they washed the car. David didn't smell simply or predominantly of tobacco. He smelt of baking bread, of pastry and griddles, his baker's trade, though by then he must have given it up. And of smoke.

Francesca stood silent. Her thin arms dangled. The strap of one sandal had broken.

'My da,' she murmured.

In the grey sweep of the bay, he was a recessive figure. A grey man dissolving in a grey scene.

'My da's lungs is popped.'

'What?'

'My da's lungs. Popped.'

'Lungs can't pop.'

'My da's have.'

'If they'd of popped, he couldn't breathe.'

'He hardly can't.'

'He can so.'

'It's not the whole lungs. It's the baby pods in them. Your lungs are full of pods. Like seaweed. When you got what my da's got, your pods pop.'

He sat with his hands on his knees, looking concernedly over and up at us, shouting something, but the sound didn't carry. Francesca crouched on the peak of a rock-slab fiddling with her buckle. I considered popped pods. A chill went through me and I laid my palm over my own chest. Uncle David was beckoning now, in a rather frantic and uncoordinated way.

'He's calling us.'

'I'm not going back. It's not time.'

'We better . . .'

'It's *not* time.' She turned her back and began to climb again.

'But we haven't got a watch,' I protested. David was on his feet and looking helplessly across the bay. I stood still, between retreating daughter and panicked father. That beach must have looked immense to him, the rocks a fortress he couldn't even think of scaling.

'Uncle wants us.'

'Cowardy custard,' she threw over her shoulder. A stammer of rock fragments ricocheted from her climbing feet.

She dared me. Beyond that, she dared him. *Come and get me.* Beyond that, she was defying his death, his power to die, the steady haul of the line drawing him in. Frankie began to sing, a tuneless screeching that got into my fillings like paper on a comb. She refused to countenance the supremacy of the popped pods.

I obeyed their imperative. Shinned down and jumped the rock pools from bone to bone of the great limestone dinosaur whose innards held the tiny worlds of rockpool and caves. I ran to Uncle David.

'Good girl.' Though his voice was reedy and hoarse, he looked all right. Perhaps she had made it up about the pods. Frankie was full of lies and stories. 'Won't she come?'

I shook my head. But I knew she would come, now that I was with him, sitting here discussing ice creams beside the closed and rickety café. She would be angry that I stole her dad. Had him all to myself while she punished herself clambering about on boring rocks. I nestled in to him. Examined the buttons of his woolly waistcoat at close range. Heard tides surge in his chest.

Francesca came sauntering back over the sands, her skirt tucked up in her knickers, as if she didn't care. There was a clump of tar on her sandal. She shot me a vindictive look.

'You gave your old da a fright there,' he wheezed. 'Come when I call, my beauty girl. Next time.'

She whipped out a piece of bladderwrack, pinched a pod between her fingers and snapped one after another viciously in his face.

That is how I remember him, her lovely dad, who was also a little bit mine, and how it was not within the bounds of my limited comprehension that he'd gone, or where he'd gone. I sit at the window and try to focus her in the wake of his death. I know she looked for him, stopping dead and swivelling her neck, as if hearing his voice or catching his familiar smell. Tense and quivering she stood, her naturally pale face drained of blood. It was somehow violent, a shock to me, as if I'd heard the report of a gun but she'd been struck by the bullet.

An aura of violence surrounded Francesca. Auntie Susan with stiletto heels, was dressed to kill, my mam said, and trailed a gallimaufry (said the uncles) of scrofulous no-good boyfriends. Call a spade a spade, the woman's a tart, said Tony. Well, I mean, look at her legs, my mam hissed, showing them up to the thigh, at her age . . . What was one to think of the spectacle of such legs? Brazen though, wasn't it? Well, I've nothing against Susan's legs, my dad said. Oh haven't you? Is that right? said my mam, that's men all over, budge up, I need to hoover by here, lift your feet, man, this is a decent house. No, I didn't mean that, my dad said, but it's these unsuitable types she brings home to little Francesca that troubles me.

They must have Francesca round more often, my mam switched off and agreed. And she would have a word with Susan.

Well, be careful, we don't want her taking the hump.

I knelt at the kitchen table and helped Mam rub in crumble ingredients. I never felt as anchored, and at the same time more endangered. The kitchen exhaled good smells, of stewing apples, of dog, of wellington boots and coal. I half-listened as they commented on Frankie's starved look, her big eyes.

'You be a good friend to her, Mara,' Mam instructed me,

unknowingly weakening my bond to Francesca by construing it as a duty. 'But don't be influenced. Llew, look at her neck, it's a sheer disgrace! You do let us down, don't you?'

Dad agreed he'd seen cleaner. I was vigorously lathered and scrubbed.

'Little Francesca should have someone to do this for her,' Mam wheezed. 'Now you keep clean and set an example. I won't tell you again.'

'Good.' I muttered.

'What was that?'

'Nothen.'

'Now don't cheek your mam. She does her best for you.'

'And,' said my mother, 'speak proper English.'

I writhed away from her clutch, my neck and hands raw, terminally bored by their everlasting carping.

'Look at your mam *nicely*,' said my dad.

I aimed at her an evil skull-grimace.

Suddenly she giggled, as if a carefree memory floated up of an epoch when her own neck was none the cleanest and she came home with a skirt full of burrs, slimed with cockoo-spit. She caught me up in her arms and kissed me mercifully.

So I had a mam, the real thing, but Francesca had Susan. I think of Susan as she was in that year when she married Jack, when Frankie informed me with perfect gravity, *she is not my mother*. We'd been up at Oystermouth Castle with a perfume bottle of brandy nicked from Jack's 'dispensary' as he called it. He had a whole cupboard stacked with booze, brought home mainly as duty free when he travelled with his firm. You could filch freely. I'd never seen so many bottles, cans, liquid refreshments of every sort.

I told Mam about it. We had just been rubbing noses like Eskimos and the admission burst out. She went quiet.

'I seen that in the war,' she said. 'People with whole rooms full of black-market cans of food. But never the hooch. Oh dear.'

Susan stalked on precipitous heels, for like Francesca she was tall, and one must limit one's height with any man under six foot. Jack was six plus. He towered and leered. He had unified the whole family, which knotted together in a scandalised bunch to denounce him, regret her, and devise ways to see him off. Men and woman who had not spoken for years, even if they met in the street, wiped their feet on one another's doormats as they met to deplore Jack.

Susan's ecstasy was unquenchable. 'He's so tall,' she exclaimed. 'Isn't he tall, Mara? You don't get men this tall in Wales generally. Welshmen are, well, squat and weasly on the whole, isn't it? Well, of course, Francesca's dada was a good man, without having the height, see, but my Jack, he's got height as well. And manners, well! And he thinks the world of the girlie.'

I had never seen a rapture as stupid, an instinct so suicidal, displayed as nakedly. Even a child could see she was blind.

She's not my mam. I was switched at birth or something. Look at her sitting there on the bar stool noon and night going 'Oh aren't you dishy,' sucking the cherry on her Babycham while he gets more and more pickled. Make me puke.

I stared at Susan thinking, you are not her mam.

'Oh Mara,' said Susan, 'wouldn't you love to marry a really tall, lean husband like a film star when you grow up?'

'Seven foot?'

'Oh well, not that tall, dear.' Susan sat at her dressing table, her blotted lipstick the colour of strawberry ice cream. 'That would be – well – out of proportion. What I adore about my Intended is, he's like an American, without actually being an American. Or an Australian.'

'Oh.'

'Can I have a ten bob note?' Francesca demanded. 'For fish and chips.'

'Money doesn't grow on trees.'

'That's because you and Creepy drink it all.'

'Now, come on, don't be nasty about Jack. He never says a word against *you*. He could do, mind, but he keeps it all back.'

Frankie had gone livid around the mouth. Bile rose in my own throat, as if I were experiencing her pain, her revulsion. With dismay I caught the whiff of her grief, the eternity of her loss.

Our two sets of eyes met Susan's in the mirror. My hand stole into Frankie's and we stood arm to arm, thigh to thigh, staring at the woman who was leaving her dad's adored memory behind. Frankie was singing again, that strange and eerie guttural song. I don't think she knew she was doing it.

You are not alone, my fingers linked in hers assured her. *Whoever else is against you, I am for you.*

'If you want to marry something tall, marry a lamppost,' said Francesca.

'Silly girl, we have to marry men, not lampposts.' Susan fussed with her pots and jars, the scenty array of cheap unguents and perfumes with which she beautified herself. Her face in the mirror was blank. 'Skip off now, dears. Auntie says you can have tea with Mara. And say thank you very much, won't you?' She swivelled round. 'You don't mind too much about Jack, do you, cariad?' Her scared eyes pleaded upwards to the tribunal. 'He's a good chap, I promise you. You don't want me to spend all my life on my owny-oh? I know you don't.' She pouted, seeming somehow disturbingly younger than us. With so much to learn in life. How come she lacked this vital and elementary information about whom to trust, whom not to? 'After all,' Susan went on, 'you'll be grown up soon. And I'm not getting any younger. You have to take what's on offer, while you have the chance. Otherwise you might get left on the shelf.'

'*What – about – my – Daddy?*'

Once Francesca's tears broke out, she was unstoppable. Her breath pumped in great surging sobs. She trembled as if having a fit.

'Oh *dear*,' said Susan. 'Don't take on. Look, Dada would have wanted me to marry again, he did want me to, he said so. See here, everything will be all right. It will. Tell you what, we'll all go, all three and Mara as well, to sail the pedal boats at Singleton Park at the weekend. Shall we? Like a proper family. You used to love that, didn't you?'

'Nah. Just give me the ten bob.'

As we walked from Francesca's to mine, I kept an arm stiffly round her waist. We knotted a school tie round our ankles, to form one three-legged creature, and sucked ice lollies with our free hands. I loved her but, glancing sideways at her swollen and still watery eyes, I was afraid of Frankie suddenly and would not have been her for anything.

3

Anna, who is twenty-nine, explained how she'd got disastrously drunk: 'I was legless,' she said. 'It's all right, you can laugh, you're supposed to laugh at this bit. Paralytic, I was. Drink begins with the letter "V". Spirits. I slid out of bed for a pee and crashed on to my stump. Fucking pain was like nothing on this earth.'

'Oh God, that's awful,' said Elin. 'Awful. Can you describe it to us? Do you mind?' We fill in the questionnaires with the volunteers, because sometimes talking about it releases extra information.

She didn't mind, she was up for it, but to be honest, she didn't know any words for that quality of pain.

'No,' I said. 'Pain is really hard to describe.'

'Like childbirth, isn't that what they say? Doddle is childbirth, compared. You got children?'

'A daughter.'

'Then you'll know.'

'Not really.'

Anna gave me a funny look.

'So,' said Elin, busy ticking boxes, 'shall we just say "Indescribable", Anna?'

'No. Wait. I can say something. The next time I did it, because of course you keep doing it, there was blood from my stump soaking the bandages and pain like shit, like all the shit in hell, and all I could think of was the V-word.'

'Vodka?' I asked.

'Just don't say it! Don't say that *word*! I could taste it on my

32

tongue. Couldn't spit it out. Whenever I so much as see a bottle of that stuff, I gag.'

'What you are describing is a body memory path,' I told her. 'That isn't imaginary. There's a path in your brain that links this ... drink ... with the most extreme fear and pain.'

'Is that right?' Anna lightly touched her temples with her fingertips. Her blonde hair was cropped short and she had the sleek build of a swimmer. 'Better be careful then, hadn't I, with the dope?'

'How do you mean? No, it's OK, you can say. This is in confidence.'

'Marijuana's the only thing that really helps my phantom. Like, it rests it. There are times when my leg – the one that isn't there – is in spasm so bad it's coiled round my fucking neck, honest to God. You take dope, the pain goes all quiet and hazy. Don't want to fuck that up by jumping on the stump, do I?'

I nodded and, retreating towards the computer consoles, heard her whisper to Elin, 'What's she? The doctor?'

'No. She runs the unit.'

'Up her own arse, isn't it?'

'Shush.' What's Elin going to say? I hold my breath. Something like *She's my boss* or *Don't, she'll hear you.*

'Oh no, she's great. She looks after us all.'

'Rather you than me.'

'Anyway we've finished Section 4. Now we'll go on to Activities. Do you exercise? If so, what?'

'Let me see, I'm a mountaineer. I do the high jump. I excel at potholing . . .'

'She's a swimmer,' I called over.

Nice to see them both gape. Later, I looked over at Elin, her fingers poised over the keys, deep in thought. Ah but, Elin, do you like me a tithe as much as I like you? Her wide oval face, the fine hair drawn back in two swathes that linked in a slide; her delicate wrist wore a tiny silver watch from her fiancé. If only she knew there was a time they used to call me Mara Marijuana.

'Are you looking at the pimple on my chin, Mara?' she asked without turning her head or moving her hands.

'No, I'm not looking at you at all.'

'You are.'

'How do you know?'

'I can feel you looking.'

'OK, I've stopped. I was just admiring, if you want to know, the bloom on your cheeks.'

'Oh please.' She takes her flushed face in both hands. 'How embarrassing. My skin is awful. It's pitiful. All pock-marked and disgusting.'

Frankie in the video will never break the pattern. She is condemned to perform that same set of actions and no other. How many times have I watched the sequence through, pausing her, letting her go, rewinding? I'm painfully aware of the bloom on her cheeks that all young people have and, if they could only see it themselves, even the plainest and most gauche would walk taller, freer. You only register it when it's lost.

I pause her now as she is singing. Her skin looks thin, nakedly open to every impression. I wonder how long that poetry in Francesca could have lasted. She hadn't proper boundaries, it dawns on me. None of us had. In our flower-power kit. Our ethnic dresses. Our denims. For all the beauty of her up-tilted head, we can see she's smashed. Out of it. She would have aged speedily. I can imagine Frankie dying fucked-out and friendless, lying in a pool of her own vomit in some squat. She escaped both that and the conventionality that lay in wait for the rest of us after the Sixties had turned.

How would she feel if she could see Menna as she is now, bonny and honourable and straightforward, bright but composed? Menna immaculate in her wine-coloured trouser-suit, proud of her excellent job at the BBC. Might Frankie have outlived her losses and griefs, I wonder, and submitted to the yoke of the ordinary?

In my mind, Menna tiptoes up behind me as she used to creep

up, years ago. I'd feel sticky little hands pawing round in my pockets, digging for secret sweets which must be there, her logic ran, because she wanted them so badly.

Frankie used to creep up too, long before, and blindfold me with her palms. I am you and you are me.

Menna's arms tightened round my neck. I got up to her nightmares and brought Ribena with ice cubes jingling up the stairs after a tummy upset. Squabbles and tantrums. Running out together to swim at Oxwich that summer when everyone else was pelting inland to their cars because there was a storm coming up ... but Menna needed that swim, oh Mam, oh my Mam, she cried, she needed it so achingly much that I could not deny it, and she rushed along beside me in her water-wings, going 'We're lucky ducks, we're lucky ducks, Mama, aren't we?'

My mother said she never could have imagined I'd turn out to be so maternal.

'She loves that girlie all right,' said Hen in that carrying whisper.

'No, she's a devoted mam, there's no getting round it,' my mother replied, as if she had attempted to do just that. They were eating egg sandwiches in the van as I carried Menna back in my arms from the freezing sea, our teeth chattering, giving each other radiantly cold kisses. I'd towelled her off and got her into warm woollies in the back of the van, then settled her palms round a cup of hot chocolate from the thermos. From the front of the van I heard my mother and aunt discoursing on my unexpected excellence as a mother, never knowing – either of them – that I was in love. I was in love with Menna and there is no virtue in that, only hedonism and irresponsible rapture.

And my bonny girl snuggled up in my arms fell fast asleep, a dribble of chocolate on her chin, while I drew the wings of my grey cardigan round her like a dove's.

My mother had never wasted her praise on me, since I could remember. With forensic eye she had detected my daughterly defects, together with my lack of qualifications for wifedom and

35

motherhood, and frequently warned me that, when the time came, no man would want me. I'd be left on the shelf. Such news was cheering. She could have said nothing better calculated to entrench my bad habits.

I was supposed to be tidying my room but I never did. I informed her that I was too brainy to dust and mop, and anyhow, why didn't my dad have to do it?

After that I was called upon night and day, or so it seemed, to do something about my room. Mam was horrified at the welter of clothes, dirty plates and lolly papers. How could I bear to live in such a tip? When I had a child of my own, how would I feel if she turned out like me? Well? And she'd excavated small change from under my bed. Kept it too, waste not want not: she regarded it as fair pay for her exertions. Did I have no sense of the value of money? She would not clean this infernal refuse heap, no, on no account, and if this unholy mess was not sorted, she vowed to chuck the whole lot out of the window.

Nothing happened. I coexisted amicably with dust and spiders, kicking a path through it all to get to my bed, occasionally dragging out an article of clothing and putting it on. Sniff, she said, go on, sniff, it's offensive. Mam appealed to reason, good feeling, respect for one's elders, good citizenship, the Girl Guides, chapel values, my father's war medals and standards of personal hygiene.

Frankie was at the door after one of these homilies, which had paused to allow me to put my mother's precepts into practice in regard to the hoover.

'Well, she's tidying her room at present, lovey,' I heard her tell Francesca. 'Do you want to go and help her?'

'Yes please, Auntie.'

'What's that nasty bruise on your cheek?'

'Nothing, Auntie.'

'Did someone hit you?'

'No, Auntie.'

Up Francesca skipped, in her second-hand sandals, and actually began to tidy.

'What are you doing?'

'Tidying,' she replied virtuously.

'Why?'

'So that we can go out. Auntie's dead nice, she puts sweets in my dress pocket. Look what I got off her.'

She produced three boiled sweets, threw me one, unwrapped hers and popped it in her mouth, speaking round it.

'What's yours?' she asked, meeting my eyes in the dressing table mirror, her hands lining up combs and brushes in a neat row on the lace cloth. Then the front door went. Francesca startled like a hare, bolt upright, her hands suspended like paws in front of her. Dad had come in and was telling Mam something about Boots being clean out of home-brew kits, it's not on, he had reminded the assistant that he was a reg'lar customer, what was he supposed to do?

Francesca was out of the room and bolting down the stairs.

'Uncle Llew! Uncle Llew!' she called out, as though some exile had found his way home at last. As I slouched out of my room and stood, sullenly sucking my lemon drop at the top of the stairs, I saw that she'd launched herself at Dad, who reeled under the blow of her weight. She was a big girl now. Her arms were round his neck, her feet off the ground, and I had the idea that she would strangle him, like a great blonde spider.

'Hey, girlie, girlie!' he remonstrated, righting his balance with a chuckle. 'Watch out there, you nearly had me over.'

'Uncle Llew!' Francesca crooned rapturously. 'You're back.'

'Only been out to Boots, see.' He patted her back as a comforting signal to disengage, and she slid down to the floor. Stood gazing up into my dad's eyes with what I was sure, without seeing her face, was a gooey look. His hand caressed her hair.

'Well,' he said, 'it's nice to be appreciated. It's normally, Dad, can I have? will you give me?'

Scowling, I sloped downstairs. Frankie worshipped my father with dewy eyes, extracting the third sweet from her pocket and offering it to the beloved on the palm of her hand. 'Would you care for a sweet, Uncle Llew?'

'We gave her that,' I complained to my parents.

'Mara, really. That is a very kind gesture, lovely girl,' said my dad and stooped to his niece to show he valued the gift. 'But you can't go giving away your last sweet. The thought is nice though. Let me see you pop it in your mouth, lovey.'

'It's yours, Uncle. Really it is. I saved it for you.'

Frankie's infatuated persistence was beginning to get on my parents' wick. I saw her welcome wearing thin but she didn't get the message. I smirked to myself. Dad adjusted his attention to my mother, wishing to extend his complaints about the home-brew kit.

'It niggles me, it gets my goat,' he told my mother, 'when people don't do their job.'

'Please, Uncle. I want only you to have it.'

'No thank you, dear. Run along now. After all, I do my job. You don't find me lobbing all the post behind a bush when I don't feel like delivering it, do you, or bunging it back in the postbox?'

Frankie was pale and determined. He must accept the sweet. He must hunker down again and give her the confederate smile that echoed her own vanished dad's. She had no idea that she was at that moment as unimportant in his life as nextdoor's cat, which he'd bend to stroke as it wound round his legs. Francesca never had time to learn that a father is, in any case, more than his fatherhood. She grasped his hand to detain him.

'That's enough now, girlie,' was all he said, without looking down, the mildest of rebuffs. My dad could get furious if sufficiently goaded and I hoped he was about to spring a rage on Frankie. He was nothing like her milky-mild father. She winced momentarily; I winked at her in a way she chose to interpret as friendly.

'I'll eat it for you, Frankie, if you don't want it.'

She handed it over, an inexpressible sadness clouding her face, standing there at the base of the stairs while I jauntily mounted, the pouch of my cheek bulging with my gains. Her melting sadness troubled me so much that I needed to rowdy her out of it; I hoped she wouldn't cry. She would. A wall of tears built and brimmed. Reluctantly, I tramped back down and extruded the sweet from my lips on my tongue. Like a rude gesture. She giggled, put her mouth forward and sucked the sweet into herself. I was relieved by her giggle. Yet at the same time I saw her freckles close-up, like a ginger rash, and thought, I'm glad I've not got freckles. I saw her buck teeth and thought she was lucky her mam didn't harry her down to old Smithers as mine did, to undergo torture by brace and filling. But the next day I would meet those expressive eyes and simply put my hand in Frankie's hand.

Ordinariness prevailed. We would roller-skate along the seafront whooping wildly and, if it was icy, so much the better. *Hellions*, said Uncle Pierce, indulgently *Come on, lovely girls, give Uncle a cuddle*. We sandwiched him with hugs. Frankie's fingers laced with mine and one day our cousin Becca braided our long hair into a Siamese plait so we were joined at the head. Becca's mam, my Auntie Bethan, said it was a lovely thing and a godly thing to see the love between two innocent girlies, which made her think of the Garden of Eden and of Isaiah's memorable vision of the lion lying down with the lamb. Frankie and I took turns to roar and bleat. Mam laughed at our plait, and Dad said we were in one another's pockets all right and it was nice to have close playmates.

Family rows rattled round us like thunder, between long spells of apparent calm. My parents with the uncles and aunts in Aunt Bethan's front room squabbled over my Nana's legacy. And Nana neither dead nor showing signs of ill health. Her pale blue eyes, from which all I considered beautiful derived, looked out with intelligent irony on the strivings of her offspring. The house: who was to have Breuddwyd? Although all had either substantial or adequate means, they tore at her carcass-to-be as if starving. Perhaps, in that begrudging world of tight family bonds, they *were* somehow starving. We young ones were left in Bethan's stuffy, familiar dining room, while the adults collected in an adjacent room. We were told to eat ice cream and play a nice quiet game. The grown-ups were going off to have a discussion.

—You always tried to turn her against me.

—I never. I never did. How dare you say so?

—Because it's true.

—She wants me to have that. She knows you were always a grasper.

—Grasper! I never in my life! Hear what she's calling me, Leah? A grasper.

—Well, you are a grasper. Take, take, take, with you, isn't it? All your life the same. Mama, she sees through you, mark my words, oh aye.

—Don't you speak to me about my Mama. Don't. Don't speak! I forbid you to speak!

Apparently they had no notion that we could hear them loud and clear through the door. That we cousins paused between licks of strawberry and vanilla with widened eyes as insults flew. We monitored the bickering that rose to peaks of rage as passions long pent were unleashed. Some uncles held some aunts back, others egged them on or took the baton when they flagged. My dad poured rancour on Midge, the eldest of his sisters, who had flown in from Texas to claim her legitimate share of Nana's inheritance.

—You filthy rich bitch! I'll legitimate you! he shrieked. What do you want with a penny piece of my mam's stuff? Leg-it-i-mate, is it? Don't make me laugh! You're manipulating her, you are, you're doing me out of what's mine.

—She never cared for you.

—What.

—I was her first-born.

—I was a *boy*.

—Okay, buster, but you were a bad boy. Nothing to be proud of.

—You vulgar Yank.

There was a sort of squawk; then a strange silence. I looked over at Rebecca, who had paused in her execution of 'Chopsticks'

40

on the piano we were not allowed to touch. Then my mother opened the door, and peered through in a quivering way.

'Are you children behaving yourselves nicely in here?'

'Yes, Mam.'

'Well, that's good,' she quavered. 'Don't touch the piano, Becca, there's a good girl.'

'But Mam what's happening?'

'Oh, just a little disagreement. Some sherry got spilt, I'm afraid. All over poor Auntie Midge's nice blouse.' There was a certain mortified relish in her voice. 'We're going home now, Mara. Say ta-ra to your cousins.' I was rushed out of the door in the striding wake of my red-faced father, but managed to snatch a glance at my gaunt aunt with a stain of red over the bosom of her pearl-buttoned silk blouse. Surrounded by sympathisers.

And I understood it was love that had done this; it was my father's burning love for Nana that caused him to attack the sister who claimed Nana favoured her. To love might involve being aggrieved, vicious, raw; it might compel you to cut dead your kith and kin when you met them in the street, because love was rivalrous, was theft and cheating. Love might inhabit a zone of murderous danger and still be love.

Dad was now speaking to no one in his family. If he met them in the street, he crossed the road or whirled the pedals faster. Uneasy as my mother and I were, we knew the sin of hurling best sherry over a silk blouse would be, if not forgiven and never forgotten, buried. But now he was calling my mam 'Woman', and instructing her not to break his rule of non-communication with those who were planning to alienate his Mama from him. She was his, he said. His mother. No one could take that away from him, ever. Plotting they were, he said, plotting his Mama's death. Scavengers.

'Take it easy,' said my mam.

'Don't tell me to take it easy, woman.'

'Keep your hair on. You'll have a heart attack. And they're not worth it.' She resented being called 'woman' in that tone of voice

41

and made sure to give the kind of commonsense reply that would make my dad feel a Charley.

'Just don't, that's all. Don't go colluding. I'll not bear it.'

'I'll do,' replied my mam, with a certain grandeur, 'what I judge right. Without consultation. I always have done so, Llew, and I always will.'

'Oh right, now we know where we stand. Now we know. Where are my cycle clips?'

'Where you put them. Now excuse me, I need to get down the shops.'

'Women,' said my dad. To me. As if I had crossed the gender line for a moment and been co-opted as a fellow male.

'Yeah. Anyway, never mind, dad, Nana loves you.'

He flashed me a complicated look, combining rue with embarrassment.

'Let's go down Oxwich on Sunday, is it?' he proposed. 'Almost swimming weather. I think we could chance it.'

'Yes, and she won't die, daddy.'

'Well,' he said, 'we all do die. One day. Of course.'

In a flash I saw that he too was mortal; he might go the way of Uncle David. He might go out of the door and not come back in again. We too might be left alone in the world, or have a Jack billeted on us.

I therefore persisted. 'Dad,' I said. 'Nana loves you the best. I know she does.'

'Oh well. I don't know about that.' The more he heard me parroting back to him the substance of his fears, the more ashamed of himself he grew. 'It's just I don't want her to feel that people are, well, you know, quarrelling over her home. Don't go telling anyone I said this, mind. Especially outside the family. I mean, family's family.'

I knelt and tied his shoelaces. He had put his hands over his ears when Nana had offered to leave Breuddwyd to him, saying he wouldn't countenance her dying, did she hear? He'd rather die himself. But he would also murder Midge for the legacy.

The boat at Oxwich was on us before we saw it. Its engine was off but it was still in rapid motion. I heard the crack as the prow struck his skull, echoing round the arc of the bay. Dad was a strong swimmer. The strongest I knew. But when I looked up, hearing what had sounded like a shot, my father was not there. He was not there, and the green hull of a powerboat was rushing toward me.

The sailor said he had never seen him at all. Had not reckoned on anyone in their right mind being in the water in spring, and the sky so dark. As if it had been recklessness itself to trust oneself to waves where power-boatsmen might take it into their heads to plough at you and smash your skull open.

Months he was in hospital, and not himself. I was scared of the man in the high bed and kept away. Our house was full of relatives, including the Texan, whom my mother chased out of the door. They had not meant it, said the relatives. They all thought the world of my dad. And how was the girlie, the lovely young one? There were treats and presents of homemade cake left on the doorstep like votive offerings. I ate hungrily, watching from a distance as if detached from myself.

When Frankie came knocking for me in the months after the near-drowning, her face all eyes like Bambi, she'd cower in the porch where it was always dark and fusty. She would not ask my mother for me but just stand on the step gazing from those big eyes, singing that strange keening dirge under her breath. Frankie examined the rack of shoes, boots and slippers by the door, carefully lined up by Mam. For Dada as a postman had needed stout footwear; but in addition valued shoe leather as the sign of a man well shod, released from the underclass of Valleys poor, whose shoes were always down-at-heel. Only the best Clarks lace-ups, fitted to his long, narrow foot, would do for him, he had often explained at tedious length. Francesca noted that his coat and cap were on his peg; his brolly and stick with its knob shiny from the grease of his palm still lodged in the stand.

'Is Uncle going to die?' she whispered, and I hated her for it.

'Oh no, lovey, course not. Uncle Llew just got a nasty crack on the head, that's all.'

They tumbled like dominos, the fathers. They were proving more mortal than our womenfolk. My trouble confirmed the totality of her loss.

In Frankie's eyes, we were coming abreast. Perhaps I too would come to live in the abyss alongside her. Horror and relief fused in her heart. But I displayed minimal concern. I whistled and climbed trees. Dad had never been there first thing in the morning; he'd always materialised later. And after all, he'd seldom been ill, hardly a virus in his life, and always so hale and eager to enjoy the day. It was not the same. Frankie's dad had been ailing, his pods had popped, his voice was an old man's wraith of its original self: he had given every sign of being about to quit. Not my Dada though. Not mine. And my mam was tonic, stoical. She was there behind me, nagging, hugging, a rock and a stronghold. Francesca fought for handholds, ledges. She tugged at me, clung to me and kicked at my bearings as I had seen my father at Bracelet Bay take aim at limpets with the heel of his shoe.

She tagged round my brisk mam, panting for attention like a spaniel pup, Mam said, as if she hadn't enough to do with hospital visiting and worrying. What a child for fantasy! Telling her tall tales and swearing every word was true, cross her heart and hope to die: wouldn't deceive a child. Making life up as she went along. A sweet side to her though, my mam thought. Nicking Mrs James' roses straight out of her front garden to give to her on Mothering Sunday.

Susan had been 'encouraged' by Jack, so she put it, to take over the role of chief wage earner in their household. His back was giving him gyp. He had to rest up. Doctor's orders. Not to worry about the nipper, he would sort her out when she wasn't at school. Francesca did not seem to be benefiting from her stepfather's tanked-up attentions, which chiefly consisted of sprawling in front of the TV with his feet up on the coffee table, filling a saucer with butt-ends, swilling ale, and instructing

Francesca to do her homework or he'd bloody tan her hide. He assured her that her being a girl would make no difference, just watch it, that was all, and do as she was bleeding told or she'd feel his hand on her pert little arse. This hand, you little madam. See this hand? We both saw the hand. White-faced, Frankie tendered no reply. But we both felt that, although he did not turn his greased head from where it reposed on the chair cover, it was a two-way thing, this seeing. We saw the hand. He saw in imagination her bare behind.

Susan had entered David Evans as a sales assistant in Beauty and was recognised at once for her exceptional ability to sell (Mam said) smells and muck to silly females with more money than sense. She was promoted and promoted. She'll be promoted over her own head one day, Jack was heard to brag, braying at his own jest. She's the kind of woman, he explained, that knows how to sell herself, see. I remember how Hen's hand trembled on the gravy boat as she passed it to my Auntie Bethan when he spoke these words, and how the atmosphere at the table became frosted. Jack liked a tuck-in after a pint at the White Rose: *it proper made a Sunday, wasn't it, a good roast dinner, all the trimmings?* You could tell where he had been sitting at Nana's crisply laundered linen tablecloth by the ring of gravy and splatters of custard.

I heard Mam say to a hugger-mugger crowd of family that Jack pimped Susan.

'What's pimped?'

'Not for you to know. Go and do your homework.'

'Not right, to send your wife out to work. Man's place to keep his wife.'

'Well, yes, I grant you. In the normal way. But now, when Llew comes back, he'll not be fit for postal work. I'll *have* to go out then, won't I?'

'Oh aye. If the breadwinner can't ... if he's, er, physically incapacitated ... that's a different thing. But what's wrong with Jack, I ask you, what?'

'Backache! I'll give him backache. How did he get the backache, I'd like to know?'

'Now now. Walls have ears.'

'Well. There are proprieties.'

'If poor David could see it.'

Sighs. Murmurings.

'And drinking your wife's earnings. Pimping a painted trollop!'

'I said, go off and do your homework, Mara Evans, and don't slouch, I've told you that before. Shoulders back. I mean, who's going to want to marry her? You want to do well in your tests now, don't you? Do the family proud?'

'Ah, God love her, she's a brainy original girl and no mistake.' Hen of course, doting, sincere. I flashed her a brilliant smile of gratitude.

'If you want to know me, come to live with me,' my mother said darkly. I pouted. 'See her sulking! Homework you! Vamoose!'

I skulked behind the door.

'Just when I've got my hands full of Llew, Mara starts acting up. Refuses to wear her nice frocks. Cuts off all her hair with pinking shears! Pinking shears! I ask you. Don't tell Annie, mind.'

Pierce: 'Oh, Mara's a dear girl. And her Daddy all laid up. What can we do for you, Leah? Let us take some of the burden now.'

The way he said it, it was as if she were clutching a vast jumble of packages. He stepped forward to relieve her of some. It struck me that he had never married. Was that to do with being a Quaker and a Communist, which my dad snorted at as naive boloney. *You can't beat 'em, you got to join 'em* was his creed. But I thought to myself: I will not marry, I will not wear a frock, I will not be a girl, I'll be like Uncle Pierce.

'We must make open house for David's kiddie,' said my mother. 'The least we can do.'

A flare of jealous rage rushed from my ribcage to the crown of my head.

So Mam pressed my cakes on Susan's daughter, making a great show of putting the stolen Mother's Day roses in water, splitting the ends to make them last. I scowled.

'Mam can't bake,' said Francesca, speaking with her mouth full, so that you saw the yellowish paste inside. 'We get bought,' the child of Menelaus the Bread confessed.

Greedy, I thought. Pig-gob. I darted out my hand and took two.

'One at a time, miss,' snapped my mam.

'She's took two and you never said nothen.'

'Don't speak back. And taken is correct English.'

'My dad done the baking at ours,' mumbled Francesca. 'Here's his pouch, see.'

My mother's face softened as she bent to examine the pouch with respectful fingers. 'Well, what have we got here?'

Uncle David's pouch. With the last shreds of his tobacco.

Mam put her arms round Francesca. I flounced out, slamming the kitchen door; then, when nobody bothered to follow me, slouched back in, dejected. Francesca was kneeling up on a kitchen chair, learning how to rub fat into flour. For an eerie moment I saw myself looking back at me. She was kneeling in my characteristic posture. I stared. Effaced. For I had needs too, with Dad having his head cracked; at night I imagined all his brains spilling out like yolk. Frankie's clever fingers rose and fell, rubbing delicately to keep the flour and butter aerated, so that it did not make nasty clots such as those of which I was allegedly guilty. And she was singing, but beautifully; soft cadences as if blowing a stream of bubbles from her lips. My mother stood to listen, her eyes brimming. That voice had a poetry of its own, chapel-bred but free beyond all imagining. Frankie's hand stilled in our big, cool mixing bowl, her face concentrated and spellbound. The expression in her eyes as she raised them to my mother was silly with worship.

When she'd gone, I hissed, 'She stole those roses from next-door, she did. I saw.'

'Yes. I know.' Mam calmly arranged the stolen property in a vase, and stood it in the centre of the table beside my freesias, eclipsing them.

'So that's all right, is it, if she does it?'

'Well, lovey . . .'

'Right, then, I'll go out and pinch some. I bought you yours. With my own money.'

'And lovely they are. But she's a sad little mite, Mara, she's got no one really.'

I thought of Susan; of tribes of relatives, of Francesca's stepfather and his extensive and chiefly objectionable family. And even though my imagination thronged with these people, I could, against my will, see a sense in which Frankie had 'no one'. And that I was rich in comparison.

'It's not fair,' I said. 'She's allowed to steal and I'm not.'

'I've turned a blind eye. For today only.'

'She's got plenty anyhow. She's got hundreds of clothes, I haven't. She just won't wear them. And a grown-up bike. You won't let me have a proper bike.'

'Less of your lip.' Her temper was beginning to fray. 'At least little Francesca is polite.'

'She is to you. Because she wants something.'

'Exactly.'

You can seek to steal a dad, and then a mam, but you will not succeed. Lovers are different. I remember how he said, Aaron said, my hair was all bouncing and child-soft. That was what he said with his gentle, supple hand on my head. *O Marsie, Marsie, long straight shiningness.* And the way you are an intellectual, Marsie, he burbled, and an idealist, and really mind about the Bomb and things. You will achieve greatness, I know you will.

Which of us was the more infantile? He and I coiled in so close I sometimes liked to imagine we could not tell which was which, like twins in a pram greedily sucking each other's thumbs or toes. Pulling the earth from under Francesca like a mat on a slippery floor. And the pleasure as I took her place was the more violent for that knowledge.

4

Aaron stood on the peak of a dune, scanning the bay. He had shot up tall, overtaking us, and, wearing only a pair of shorts, his body was willowy and pale brown. He shaded his eyes with one hand. His shadow undulated over the dune's whiteness, where thrift, vetch and marram grass cast spikes of shadow. There were blond hairs on his slender arms and his hair was a shock of curls bleached by the summer.

Francesca gazed at Aaron from where she crouched in a rare phase of inaction, the palms of her hands clasping her feet, rocking slightly. We had swum and played beachball, caught crabs, swum again. A dusting of sand coated her legs and there was a green stain over her shorts and a once-white vest of her real dad's that had shrunk drastically in the wash. The studious stillness of her upward gaze impressed me.

I'd come upon them, having toiled up the dune, hauling myself on hanks of grass and sliding back with each step. I seemed to burst up from the scramble into the light that gilded them both. Dismayed, I blundered into their quiet. Looked at Frankie watching Aaron watching the beach. Neither said a word to me. He was staring to where, like a child's toy boat, a ship had run aground and lay stranded.

Most of the caravanners had quit the shore and, lugging windscreens and picnic baskets, and reproving the cantankerous over-tiredness of their young, had yawned their way to primus stoves and hobs for cooking bacon and beans, so that sometimes the salt scent of the dunes was permeated by the smell of frying. Children would be called back to supper with 'Wash your hands

49

before you sit up to table'. Domesticating the beach, so that the marbled formica tables around which we squeezed became an outpost of home.

Frankie and I rebelled, diving out into the head-high bracken which surrounded each caravan. Of course it was the Thomas caravan. Only they had spare cash or the confidence to spend rather than hoard it in a Post Office savings account. The biddable Thomas boys, with confused backward glances, followed. Even the youngest, Seth, had strained away from his parents and he and Joe were trailing me up the dune, moaning. Halfway up Joe hesitated and headed back for home. But Aaron had reached the top and as I burst into the picture, I am certain that something had just been said. Between the two of them. Frankie and Aaron. Something important. About the beached ship, which Aaron was steadfastly observing, his forefingers forming circles with his thumbs around his eyes like imaginary binoculars.

I'd missed the first sizzle of excitement. My struggle with the sand and Seth's grizzling had lost me a place in whatever was being hatched.

'What?' I asked.

There was silence.

Or am I saying, there *is* silence? Am I remembering some photograph now lost, with those two posed and frozen in a gestural language set up by the grown-ups. *Stand there, Aaron, lovely boy. That's it. Look out towards the ship. That's the way. Now, Francesca, you sit there, look up at Aaron. That's the ticket.* Click.

But I don't think it's a photo I'm remembering, though Annie had the latest colour equipment and the memory is in colour. Aaron's easy grace is too vivid. Light edged the curve of his calves, picking out the swell of muscle from flank to slender ankle. But have I imposed a much later time? I recall clasping those ankles in my hands, years later, fingering the joints with the tender wonder of the love-struck.

Seth's head appeared over the peak and Frankie said, without turning her head, 'You're not coming.'

'Where?'

'To the boat, dope.'

'We're not allowed, tho there,' Seth said. He had a lisp and his round specs launched his gaze forward as if he were attacking you with his fears and misgivings. Goofy, we called Seth. Aaron looked out for him protectively, putting himself not only at Seth's mercy but at Annie's, who could control her oldest through her youngest.

'When?' I asked.

'Now, you nitwit.' Frankie scrambled to her feet, wriggling sand out of her shorts.

Aaron hesitated: he slackened his hold on the dream ship, remembering what Annie had confided about the dangers of the coast, the guileful tides, jellyfish that might sting you in the eye, and where was the doctor? You might die before you reached a doctor. Wasn't that right, Pops? Oh yah, said Pops, and we all winced at his English drawl, better safe than sorry. There then, Annie would go on, there are no doctors on the beach you know, and if Seth so much as got wet ... the danger of glue ear, perforated eardrums and deafness were all tolled out. The whole of the beach was out of bounds in the evening. The whole of everything was out of bounds most of the time. Aaron's narrow shoulders hunched and he kicked up a jet of sand.

Seth now claimed to have a fly in his eye, which Aaron must attend to. He knelt and peered.

As Frankie taunted the Thomas boys, her face contradicted the malice of her tongue. The eternal wanting was more than she could contain. She converted it into a radiance that shimmered at you. Now, spying capitulation, she said, 'It's OK, Aaron, take Sebs back. Mara and me will go down to the ship.'

'It's thauthage for tea,' Seth confided to Aaron. 'With beanth.'

'You run back, Sebs, all right? I'll watch you till you get there. No, I will, darling.'

Just like his mummy he sounded, I thought. What kind of cissy would call his brother 'darling'? Yet I liked the tenderness of Aaron suddenly, and the courage of that tenderness.

The ship's allure had grown into a spell. It lay so close to the dunes, straddling the stream called Diles Lake, that it appeared to be breasting the white waves of sand. Its radio mast stood erect but atilt before two funnels. Seth, pouting, retreated to his mother, to whom he would be sure to tell on the nasty girls. It was hard to tolerate such goody-goodies as our Sketty kin had become. But Frankie had the power to ease Aaron from his moorings. Out into her gleaming shallows she floated him.

'I'll come.' My skin was peeling from sun and windburn and I had accumulated wedges of puppy-fat, which gave a barrel-effect to my body, especially when buttoned into the waist-length white cardigan Hen had knitted me. Frankie had skipped the lumpen stage. The tatty old vest she wore veiled budding breasts; her hair, tangled and bleached with sand and salt, was a wild mane. Beside my lumpy solidity she seemed like a gypsy girl, I thought, free.

It cannot have been so long since her dad had died but mine was recovering. Her mam we had left sitting in the caravan, lips coated with a gingery-orange lipstick, a raucous colour and oily. She smoked one Benson after another, so that it seemed her odour reached everywhere, a promiscuous smell which (Annie fussed) got into the curtains of the miniature world of the caravan. Why couldn't Susan smoke outside? Aaron's Pops opened wide every window and the door. Susan didn't take hints.

On and on the orange lips yacked about the charms of Jack. The smoky rings she blew reminded me somehow of her forgetfulness of the buried David. She blew him away. Jack this, puff, Jack that, puff puff. I stared at her mouth till it seemed to occupy her whole face. When she bent to kiss me, I'd bob and duck, dip and weave like a boxer. For the lipstick was not only on her mouth but coated her teeth. She'd give up, with an affected, nervy titter and plump down on the plastic padded bench. With her hair dyed auburn, she reminded me of an over-ripe apricot.

In my memory, Aaron and Frankie pelt across the great pale plain of the bay towards the distant ship, myself lumbering along in their wake. They run wide of one another in arcs, only to close and cross over, so that the pattern of their heel prints makes a looping chain. I lollop along, my detested cardy slung over one shoulder.

The hull bellied over us, corroded with rust, barnacled.

'She's a destroyer,' Aaron told us, as if this were not the kind of thing girls would know. 'From the war.'

'We know *that*. It's the *Cleveland*,' I said. 'The destroyer *Cleveland* is what it is. Everyone knows that. Even Auntie Bethan knows that. Hen knows. Nana knows.'

I went on enumerating who knew, fighting Aaron for possession of the destroyer, even as I experienced the thrill of standing beneath its evening shadow wondering what would happen if it listed sideways and crushed our bones. In that shivery moment I felt as fragile as a bird.

'Even Auntie Susan knows,' I continued. 'You knew, didn't you, Frankie, what it is?'

'No,' said Francesca. And suddenly it was glamorous to be innocent of the *Cleveland*, here in its dark, fish-smelling shadow, examining the barnacles and the rust.

'It was the rope broke,' said Aaron. 'From the tug. Out there.'

Francesca was not listening; she was climbing. Hand over hand up the iffy ladder at the side she went, and I was following her. When we had both hauled ourselves on to the deck and looked down, Aaron seemed puny, standing in his shorts with his arms folded.

'It might not be all that safe,' he called up. 'Actually.'

'Ah actually! *Actually!*' In her shriek of mockery lay the boast that of course it wasn't safe; had it been safety we wanted, we could be sitting outside the caravan shucking new peas into a colander.

'It says about trespassers,' came his plaintive voice. 'Pops said ... we must faithfully promise ... not to ...'

Frankie looked at me, where we stood on the tilting, terrible deck. She was mine again and I was hers. She winked. But, withdrawing her head, she seemed to have pulled him on an invisible rope and, against his own volition, Aaron must already have begun to climb the rickety steps, for he soon appeared on deck with glowing eyes. Now he was firing an imaginary gun from the bow at the ubiquitous Nazis who still inhabited the communal imagination. It stank of corrosion, salt and oil. Frankie and I roamed the deck and climbed into the old hulk's lifeboats, mounted on the captain's upper deck and, from this vantage point, saw tiny figures spill down a faraway dune and hare across the sands. The rate they were going, it would take a quarter of an hour to reach us.

'Nazzies! Nazzies! shoot the Nazzies!' yelled Frankie and we opened fire on the older generation.

We were murdering the fascists.

And the Commies.

We were dam busters, they were Krauts, Huns, Jerries. A small black swarm of enemies on the far beach scuttling towards us. We picked them off one by one, but they kept on coming.

'Kill the old squares!'

Our excitement fed on our alarm. I could feel myself fizzing.

Frankie ran up to the top deck, singing as her feet slammed against the rusted metal ladder. Up there she began to swing and roll her body and pound her feet, chanting she was gonna tell us how it was gonna be. She flung out her arms, jiving with an invisible partner. *We were gonna give our love to her.* Aaron stared, a fascinated but embarrassed smile on his lips. Her voice raged and her mouth pouted as she told him how it was gonna be, in that charged voice that I would have been ashamed to raise. But she was not ashamed. Whereas before Frankie had seemed a skinny tomboy in that tatty vest and stained shorts, now her small breasts bounced and flaunted themselves. She was signalling that she was older, far older – knowing, far more knowing – than her age.

Love that was love would not fade away. Not fade away.

Her voice pulsed downwards, dark and earthy, and dirty, I thought, dirty. I blushed with excitement, began to sway and clap my hands. Her body was sinuous; it knew. Her body knew. She stamped the beat. I stamped the beat where I stood on the salt-shrunk boards of the clapped-out old boat.

She was ready. Ready teddy. I was ready too.

It was at the moment that I raised my voice to join in the Buddy Holly festival that my parents reached the destroyer.

'I'll give you ready, young woman,' cried my father.

'Don't you know,' shrilled my mother when we had been forced to abandon ship and been marched back to the caravan, 'you could have been killed? Killed, you could have been? It's a wreck, don't you know that? Going to be broken up at Llanelli. You stupid, stupid children. And, Aaron, what an example to set to the girls.'

Annie was on her knees, inspecting every inch of her precious son for signs that the rusted metal had pierced his skin, in which case he must be rushed to Swansea for a tetanus injection. Her eyes mutely expressed a grief which he answered with a quiet 'Sorry, Mama,' spoken softly as if blowing a bubble. He placed his hands round her cheeks in a gesture so gentle that it seemed she was a creature he must handle with infinite care. Where had Aaron learned that skill, in his fingers and in his voice, to gentle you? It was a gift, no doubt. And certainly a power.

'Don't worry, Auntie Annie,' said Frankie. 'It was us led him on. It was us done it, wasn't it, Mars Bar?'

'He didn't want to come,' I said, ecstatic. 'He was scared stiff.'

'I was not so scared.'

'Scared of what your mam would say.'

'Ah, bless him,' said Aunt Hen. 'He's a good boy.'

'Pity you weren't more scared, miss,' my mother intervened.

I shrugged and knew that it was only the presence of the elegant Annie that was stopping my mother from hitting the roof. Frankie and I laced hands behind our backs and smiled into one another's eyes. My father exploded. We were not to swim tomorrow. For the rest of the week. For the whole summer. With each extension of the threat, his eyes sought Susan's approval, as she sat in a deck chair, eyes obscured by sunglasses and complexion shielded by a floppy hat tied loosely under her chin with a pink silk scarf. Not to swim! he raged. There'll be no more swimming for you, do you hear?

'You'll make yourself ill, Llew.' My mother laid a hand on his arm. He was still frail. 'Look,' she turned to me, 'you're making your dad ill.'

Susan examined her fingernails.

They could have died or fallen off and broken their legs, my father now informed Susan at the top of his voice. And nobody knowing where they were! Died! No, he told my mam, he wouldn't shush, that wasn't enough.

If these two hooligans didn't mend their ways, he yelled, there would be no swimming – ever – again – in their lives!

Frankie had dropped my hand and her grin. She approached my raving father and searched him with a curious gaze. Her grave, urchin face, with its mat of burnished hair, looked up at him like some lovely ragged boy. She put out her hand, as if to calm him, but palm upwards. The gesture startled him into silence.

'Sorry Uncle,' said Frankie, almost under her breath. 'Sorry, Uncle Llew. Please don't be ill.'

'Well, well. Don't do it again, beauty girl.'

'Do you want to thrash me?'

'*What*?'

'Punish me?'

'Great God alive,' said my dad and he took the open palm in his with anxious tenderness, curling the fingers shut, as shocked as if he had been forced to see some nakedness. A wound she bore. Or was. Was, I think now, the family's open wound. He pulled her awkwardly towards him and, rubbing her head, the nearest thing he knew to demonstrative affection, he asked her mother, 'What is going on, Susan? Susan. I said, Susan, what is going on here?'

She had been smoothing down her skirt and looking at her watch, as if this were a theatrical tableau which bored her and had no direct relevance to her own life. Yet all her actions were marked by a special intensity of affectation. She ignored my father, daintily climbing the little staircase into the caravan to pack the beach-clobber in a bag, humming.

Words were exchanged. What did Jack do to the child? My father insisted on knowing. My mother shushed him and told him to think of his own health but he brushed off her concern and called her 'Woman'. We were told to go and eat lollies together in the bracken and be good children. Seth, Joe, Frankie and I sat cross-legged and licked, listening.

We heard snatches of the row, which was deliberately kept low so as to preserve family secrets and family reputation.

. . . good man.

. . . good man? Him? Smell the booze on his breath the other end of ruddy town.

. . . got to administer correction.

. . . so you admit? He beats her?

Mam was in there too, lambasting her sister-in-law. Look here, the girlie was in rags. In rags, she was. She was dirty. Unkempt. Running wild, she was. Wouldn't do.

. . . Jack has offered to buy her nice clothes . . . good things . . . pretty things . . . she won't have them, Llew, I'm telling you . . . wants to wear that filthy old vest. Not my fault, don't poke your noses in . . . make it worse.

'But look,' I heard my father say in the dim echo chamber of the caravan, 'she just put out her hand to be hit. Is that right? Is it natural? Susan, don't you care?'

'She's out of control,' mumbled Susan. 'It's all very well but you don't know. She doesn't treat Jack with the proper respect, it's no wonder he . . .'

Outside, Annie was brushing Aaron's hair, rhythmically. He had wavy, bushy hair, but terribly soft, yielding to the touch. Seth and Joe went off to bat a beachball relaxedly between them. Frankie and I looked steadily at one another as we listened to the row going on in the caravan. The chemical toilet in its hut exuded a faint stink which somehow mingled with the wrangling.

Francesca hunkered down and wrote in a patch of sand with her forefinger. I watched Aaron watching her, passive to his mother's grooming, his eyes screwed up as if trying to look over a hill. I saw that look so many times later in my life: an

57

attentiveness so concentrated as to confer a kind of blessing, or the promise of it. A promise that might or might not be redeemed.

'I'd bloody take the little waif in myself rather than see her thrown to that wolf,' my father snarled.

'Llew,' warned my mother's voice. 'And be careful with that table.'

He had pounded the none-too-sturdy formica table that opened out from the wall with his fist.

'I will, I'm telling you, I will – take – her – in – myself – if that's what it takes.'

Frankie's head had swivelled. She rushed to the caravan, colliding with my dad on his way out, red and sweaty, his shirtsleeves rolled up.

'Oh *please*, Uncle, will you, Uncle?'

A threat to my space. Darkening of clouds over the low sun as my world faltered. There would be two of me. She'd edge me aside. She was hungry: she'd consume what was mine and mine alone. His ireful enthusiasm had already faltered, however, for my father was physically too weak to sustain such intense emotion. My mother's eye had informed him that one dippy coot of a girl was enough and, if it was not enough, why had they stuck at an only child in the first place? His eye had argued, But look at the state of our niece. David's child. Her eye had counselled prudence: there would be mayhem in our household and in any case, didn't she have a say in it?

'Oh, Uncle,' breathed Francesca in ecstasy.

'No, you poor dab, I can't do that,' said my father, abashed now at how far he'd gone, overreaching his concern into a form of hospitality his means could not afford. 'But I'm keeping my eye out, Susan, he'll have me to answer to. Oh yes. You got to dress her up nice, see, so she doesn't play the tomboy. And, Francesca, be a good girlie, and have a nice life.'

At Dad's refusal, my feeling turned round upon itself. I went whining up to him and begged him to change his mind. Let Frankie come and stay with us. She and I together would balance out the two of them. Midnight feasts and moonlight walks on the beach. Stealing lipstick and putting each other's hair up. Lovely gossips under the fuggy quilt at day's end. Someone to be close to and share my secrets with.

Squirming, Dad said he was sorry to disappoint us but there was the legality to be thought about, see? Annie asked, who was for cocoa? She bustled. Francesca's shoulders hung limp; despair seemed to have stunned her for she made no further complaint. The birds were all swarming home in black flocks.

Where was Jack that day while a nice life was being wished on his stepdaughter? Turning a liquid lunch into a boozy fraternal afternoon crawling from pub to pub along the seafront? Reeling home late in the evening maudlin or violent? Behind Susan's casual front there lurked a sulky self-preoccupation that suggested to my parents, driving home from Llangennith, that the two lovebirds had fallen out. Perhaps, they speculated, Susan would get quit of him for good, find some respectable bloke. After all, she was a good-looker, my dad observed. Kept herself in good shape. Well, didn't mean shape. No, not shapely in *that* sense, Leah, though he supposed she would count as a bit of a fine woman, she was a looker no doubt about it, always had been glamorous, his sister, not that he personally went for that style of woman, the Monroe type.

'Oh indeed, and what *style of woman* might you go for?' I couldn't see Mam's face but I knew the tightness around the mouth.

'Well . . . you, of course. Obviously.'

'And anyway, there's no question of divorce. The *shame*. No, she must lie in the bed she's made for herself. Just a pity the little girl has to suffer for her mother's folly.'

I thought about the destroyer *Cleveland* and how we had climbed aboard, just Frankie and me, and then cissy Aaron. Her raw, raucous singing on the bridge. I sucked the memory like sherbet through aniseed all the way home and knew that, because of Jack, because he was vile and violent, and mean and weak, and had caused Dad a digressive swerve, we would swim again tomorrow.

If they all returned, the Thomases, the Menelauses and the Evanses, and burrowed like moles from underground or collected themselves together from where their ashes lie scattered, they would find little essentially altered today. Beyond the addition of a few Chinese takeaways and student lodgings, I think, as I walk down the lane to the village, round blind curves where the castle wall is swathed at all seasons in ivy.

I pass Old Mr Davies' rickety shed with its motto forged in childish joined-up lettering: Castle Light Engineering. The iron shutters are speckled with a rash of rust and lichens stain the walls. Inside beneath naked bulbs, works of light engineering are still in progress. A power lathe, Sixties music throbbing. Young Mr Davies is in charge now, Old Mr Davies being long gone. But I feel as I walk past that, if I were to go in, Old Mr Davies would look up from his work with some characteristic quip.

The houses along the lane are all seen from their nether quarters, long strips of garden leading to tumbledown sheds and the odd derelict Ford from another era. But today there is a sudden, elderly face. Pouchy and forlorn, it peers out between gate bars. I generally look away and hurry past the place where the garage used to be.

But there's the face. Or rather an expression. Without particular hope or expectation, but betraying an absent-minded yen to escape her prison, confounded by forgetfulness of what lies out here. Susan pushes her face up against the cold black wrought-iron bars and I'm glad she's past feeling mortified by the absence of make-up behind whose mask she once proudly hid.

'I thought you were gone,' she calls to me.

'I did live away for ages – years,' I explain. 'With my work, you know. I've got a job back here now.'

'I thought you were dead. You've been dead for . . . ages of time, haven't you?'

Glancing down, I take in her drab, old-fashioned skirt and the drooping belly of old age. On her feet, baggy blue slippers saturated from the damp grass.

'No ... oh no. I've just been away.'

'Oh.' Baffled and unconvinced, she is reluctant to contradict. 'Are you sure?'

'I think I would be, don't you?'

'If you say so.'

'Auntie Susan, your feet are soaked. Don't you think you should go in and ... is there someone with you?'

'Well ...' She places her little finger in the corner of her mouth and sucks. My heart squeezes at the helpless gesture. The child in her. I wish I had not seen her. Not chosen to see her. The last thing I want is ties and I think at my age, I've a right to cut them.

'You were always very difficult,' she says distinctly. 'Always. It wasn't my fault. Mind that.'

'Of course not. No.'

'None of it.'

'No, Auntie. No one said it was.'

'Where's Jack? And why are you calling me Auntie? Where's he got to? Have you seen him? Is he down the pub? Do you drink too? You used to take everything, heroin they said, LSD, oh the shame of it, I never got over it. They put me on drugs, you know. I've never held with drugs, not that I made a fuss, mind, when you used to ... never mind ... I'm not one for judging, I leave *that* to others. High and mighty, hoity-toity (Midge, dear, I'm talking about Midge. She's dead too.) Swimming in their birthday suits at midnight, don't think I've forgotten – down by Ron's Rendezvous at Rotherslade: in the *News of the World* it was, I mean, the shame! In the Gower! He was a rotter, was that Ron. On the make. Is he dead too? I did think you were dead, see, especially with there being an inquest, but then they tell me such lies, you don't know what to think.'

'Will you go indoors, Auntie?' I quail. I do, however, remember Ron's, and the *News of the World* article, and, for all the sadness of the sight of Francesca's mother, a smile trembles on my lips. 'I don't take drugs, I hardly drink.'

Her face brightens. 'Oh, but sherry now, that is nice. I love a sherry. Or fizzy wine, you can get that. Up your nose they go, the bubbles, so nice is that. Can't get sherry nowadays of course. They say it will interfere with my drugs, but give me sherry any old day. I used to like sitting in the snug, down the Oystercatcher . . .' On and on. A fine drizzle nets us both, the Swansea mist that seems to come up from the very ground around you.

I panic. I've allowed myself to be tempted back into the net. 'Well,' I said. 'Well, I should . . .'

'It's no good saying that,' she says. 'Jack would have tanned your hide.'

'Auntie.'

'For less. I saw you the other day. Up to your old tricks. You never learn, do you. I saw you. Showing me up. The Eye sees everything.'

The Eye? Saw what? Behind her comes a small, chivvying figure in green overalls, calling, 'Naughty girl, Susan, come back in this minute!'

'Saw you on TV. Brazen! See what I mean? The Eye?' she blurts. 'You're never free. Since Jack went off, it's never been the same, not at all. And it was you sent him away, don't deny it . . . No,' she expostulates, turning to her minder, 'I won't come in. I'm talking to my . . . this one,' she says, turning back to face me suddenly, truculently. 'Exhibiting yourself to Tom, Dick and Harry. Is it any wonder I'm alone and no one comes?'

The carer asks if I am a visitor.

'A relative.'

The old woman has sagged; the hope quits her like a limp sail, and with that comes a numb reconciliation to things as they are.

'My daughter,' she explains to the carer. 'On telly she was. Misbehaving.'

'Auntie Susan, can I come in? It's not Francesca. I think you're confusing us. We were so alike, weren't we? It's Mara.'

'Is it? Is it Mara?' And her face lights up, before fading. 'Where's your dad? Who is Mara though? I used to know you, did I? Once?'

'She's due her medication,' the carer says as if in explanation. 'Then a nice little nap with her hot-water bottle. But come in if you want. You'll have to go round the front, there's no key to this gate, well, there probably is but I don't have it. She doesn't get many visitors. People don't care these days, do they? Not like the old times.'

I don't want to follow. But I am curious, and stricken with momentary ruth which seems to march me round to the main road. I pause in front of Susan's front door. Perhaps I won't ring.

5

'Where's Jack? Have you brought him home? Did you see him down the White Rose? Jack.'

His name caws at me again from the once proudly lipsticked mouth, which now is bare and slack. This could never happen to *me*. *I* won't get senile like this, unappealing and confused. I smile falsely, to cover my vain distaste.

'No, Auntie, I've not seen him, I'm afraid.'

'Seen who?'

'Well . . . Jack.'

'Oh aye, Jack. Don't talk to me about Jack, it isn't very pleasant. No.' Susan turns and cranes her neck toward the net curtains, as if to pick a passage out of this decaying mind marooned in a decaying body. 'Jack made blood puddings. He did, you know. He made me eat them.'

'Oh, Auntie Susan, you're all right now.' Unexpected tears spark behind my eyes. 'He's gone,' I try to comfort her. Disastrously.

'Oh! don't say that. Do you mean . . . I'll never see him again? What'll I do then? How will I cope without him?'

She wrings her hands and her eyes are blue and baffled. These are my family eyes: I can neither duck nor evade their claim. I find myself reluctantly kneeling beside the wreckage of Francesca's mother, trying to stem the moment-by-moment panic of her. She smells faintly of urine and talc. Her classy perfumes in their chubby bottles with rubber sprayers are years in the bin. To live in this pastless, futureless moment must be to awaken perpetually

64

into nightmare. There can be no relief, no reasoning yourself into a state of quiescence, for you are at the mercy of the here-and-now, like a baby.

'What'll I do? What'll I be?'

'You'll be fine, Auntie,' I lie. 'Let me give you a big hug. There, you see, you're better already.'

'But which one are you?'

'Mara ... I'm Mara Evans. I'm her cousin.'

'Well, don't you start crying too, I thought you were supposed to be comforting me, for goodness' sake!' In her exasperation is mingled just enough of a hint of amusement, a ghost of normality, to bring a smile to my lips.

'There you are now,' she says. 'And don't come up so close, stand back a bit, sit over there, that's right. Crybabies I can't stand. Now what about a cup of tea – with ginger biscuits, or some nice bara brith, cut it thin, mind, with lashings of butter, after all we don't have to think of our waistlines now do we, it's not Lent, er ... what's your name? Sorry, it's gone. Don't think me rude, now, all the young people look the same to me.'

'Mara,' I remind her gently. 'Mara Evans. And it's a few years since I heard myself called young. Very nice too. Say it again if you like.'

'You want me to say it again? What again?'

'Just a joke, Auntie.'

'Oh. A joke. Well then.'

The carer brings tea and says she'll be in the next room watching TV if we need her. After setting the tray between us, she bends to my ear and whispers, rather carryingly, 'Don't mention the J-Word. Sets her off.'

'She means Jack,' Susan says, accepting the cup of tea with pleasure. 'J for Jack. *He* doesn't bother me. Set me off? Not one itsy bit. Plenty more fish in the sea, I can tell you. Anyhow,' she dunks a ginger biscuit and pauses to suck, then daintily wipes the corners of her mouth with a tissue from her sleeve, 'there were all sorts of men after me, swooning they were, in the aisles. I was a film starlet. Did you know? Or an usherette. At the Elysium. You were always a naughty girl, you brought great heartache,' she adds stagily. 'You did – but you've calmed down now. Apparently.'

She observes me doubtfully and I can tell that she is hiding one confusion behind another. Who I am. Whether I am a dowdy middle-aged niece, or whether that is just a surface from beneath which Susan's dead will explode like grenades. She follows my eyes roaming the many framed photos on dresser and mantel-piece. I try to hide my greed and to negotiate a polite means of examining them more fully.

'*I* know who you're after,' she comments.

'Who?'

'Ah-hah.' She taps the side of her nose with her forefinger.

Brainwave: 'I'd like to see pictures of you, Auntie, in your lovely frocks.'

Her face lights up. 'I did have some smashing togs, didn't I though? They're all upstairs, you know, in the wardrobe. I put Llew's Leah in the shade, such a drab woman, poor thing.'

'I thought you were absolutely It, Auntie Susan. You still are of course. I used to admire you in your finery ever so much. Show me the pictures you like best.'

'He absolutely worshipped me, that boy. Never looked at another woman. He was a butcher, you know. By trade. And inclination, he said. Pass me that picture there . . . on the side . . . that's right.'

But it isn't of Susan. It is Frankie. I pick it up and take it to the window. My heart clenches to see the bloom on her skin as she looks out of the window at Breuddwyd, a youthful and dreamy urchin-mother minus her child, wearing a cream turtleneck sweater. It may be winter, for the light on her face has that blanching effect that radiates the glare of snow. Before her, Nana's garden in Newton; behind her, shadow. She looks calm. Too calm.

'But this is . . . not you,' I point out to Susan. I'm timid of saying Jack's name, Frankie's name. To speak those violent names in her presence seems gratuitous cruelty, and besides I need her to talk. I'm tickling trout.

'No, not me. Jack chopped that one up. That girl. He chopped her to pieces with an axe. Yes, I don't mean that one. The one next to it.'

My head is ringing with the word *axe*. Of course he didn't, couldn't have, but maybe he . . . attacked her with an axe, once? What is Susan trying to tell me? She says the word so placidly – *axe*. It is normal in her skewed mind, to think that thought.

'Look then. You're not looking.'

Here hangs Susan, fashionably resplendent on Jack's arm, with her hair in a priceless arrangement of sausages. One sausage is pinned up above her forehead; the others are rolled up at the bottom of her hair, the whole coiffure bagged in a fancy hairnet. Jack looms, outrageously debonair, dark-suited. The picture was taken in the garden at Breuddwyd, I recognise the pampas. But all the time I'm admiring this with Susan, I'm clutching the likeness of Frankie behind my back in the other hand.

I do remember this picture of Frankie, and intend to keep it. Her hair was shorn. The calm eyes of a Madonna, resigned to grief. I remember showing this picture to Aaron, who said, off-guard, 'Temazepam', but then coloured up and went on to deny that it had got into the milk and affected the baby, for she'd contracted mastitis and had to give up. Didn't I remember? So it couldn't have affected the child, could it? Obviously.

In the picture, Frankie looks breastless, or breast-free. It could not be said that she had persevered in her role of earthmother. At the first sign of a problem, and to the health visitor's chagrin, Frankie left off nursing, saying, 'Yeah well, they're my tits, I suppose? Or do they belong to the State now, has there been an Act of Parliament? I need to breastfeed that geezer's kid like I need a hole in the head.' She had treated the health visitor to a spaced-out appraisal, while, in the chaotic living room at Breuddwyd, rock music jangled, spices and joss sticks sauced the air and young men in floral skirts wandered from room to room.

I almost thought she might offer the health visitor a joint and urge her to hang loose.

Yet when the intruder had gone, she crushed the child to her as if she would squeeze him to death and kissed his fat cheeks with desperate greed.

I'm going to spring the baby on Susan. I'm going to ask the forbidden question about her grandchild. For she does recall things; she is not half as amnesiac as she first appears. A strange cunning characterises her fits of forgetfulness as if one part of her brain leans across to camouflage the gaps, bringing with it illuminations of its own.

'About Zack,' I begin.

'Jack. Have you seen him then? You have! You've seen him! Where?' She leaps to her feet, so nimbly that I am taken aback and stumble into a coffee table covered with china rabbits, half-inch miniatures that spill over the floor. I bend down to retrieve them, as if gathering together particles of our childhood. I replace them on the table, while Susan cranes from the window into the garden, towards the garage that was dismantled, towards the rusted garden swing she shared with Jack on those sensual Sabbaths when the church bells pealed over Uncle David's ashes and beer poured freely into the happy couple's glasses. I reach round her agitated shoulders to calm Susan. How she has shrunk.

'Is that him out there? Jack!' she calls. 'Yoo hoo! Is he coming back home soon? I'll take him back, of course I will. It's a wife's duty after all to turn the other cheek. He made some jokes about that. Cheeks. Men can't help it. But joking aside now, loyalty is . . . what is loyalty though?'

She shakes like a leaf in my hands. Down the garden lies the oblong concrete slab that represents the space into which her daughter leapt. And Susan stuck to Jack, so that in the end, Frankie could find no security, but took the extreme gamble of that leap.

'I'm Mara, it's all right.'

'That's you in the picture. Over there. You and the others by the ship that was wrecked at Llangennith. You were spanked good and proper after that, when I told Jack. Oh yes. I did tell him, what else could I do? Wives keep no secrets from their husbands. Jack gave you the thrashing you'd asked for. But you deserved it, see.'

You bitch, I think. You had no need to tell him that. It was a thrashing you could have saved her. The memory scorches me of Frankie standing with her hand out for punishment, that pathetic semaphore, warning my dad, telling him of her great hurt, and how it shocked him. Ranted about how he would take her in. But didn't. Susan bleating and querulous. Goes straight home and tells Jack.

'Did you watch?' I ask coldly.

'Watch what?'

'When "I" was spanked? Did you watch other things? What did he do to me?'

'Now you're being nasty to me,' she sulks. 'Unkind. Nobody comes to see me, my own family, nobody loves me.'

Well go and eat worms then, my mind snaps. This is the same Susan, oh yes. Same as she always was.

But gently. Keep tickling. 'No, truly, I wasn't meaning to be nasty.' In the picture, which I now have in my hand, Aaron is looking through binoculars made of his fingers towards the ship; Frankie, with an expression of unappeasable yearning, gazes up at Aaron gazing away. And I am crouched like a frog about to spring, on the dune, looking gormlessly at Frankie. Let me try once more.

'Auntie, I didn't say Jack. I asked about Zack.'

'Mama never allowed Welsh spoken in the house. Infra dig it was, the Welsh.'

'Zack isn't a Welsh word, Auntie. It was the name of . . .'

'*Wash your mouth out with soap*, Mama said. I'm not having that gibberish in the house. Language of baboons, she called it. Jack doesn't know Welsh. I don't. You see, the best people don't. And there's a pride in that, though I say it myself.'

A pride in not knowing, I think. Yes, but you knew one hell of a lot, Susan, and you can't contain the infection of that knowledge any more than I can.

'I'll go now, Auntie. I think I've tired you. I'll come again. Is there anything you'd like me to bring?'

'Love Hearts, my favourite. And I've got something here for you. Here, here . . .' She is fumbling off a locket from her neck, a cheap silver locket with a thin chain.

'No, Auntie Susan, I can't take your special things . . .'

'Please. It's yours, darlen. Open it up. Go on, you'll see. You can't put it back on your head now of course. The colour's changed, that's odd, because look at you, you're going to be grey as a badger one of these fine days (pardon me – how rude), and look at this here, it's gone all red, mind, you were ginger at one time, your hair was my despair. But they say beautiful hair and so on skips a generation so if you'd *married* and had children, they would have taken more after me, but there you are. No, no, don't pick at it, dear, put it away. I can't abide fuss.'

It comes to me warm from her bosom, her intimate skin. My thumbnails prise at the tiny silver hinge.

'It doesn't want to open,' I say.

'No, well. Look later, is it? I snipped it off you when you . . . passed over. Go on, and have the album as well.' She shoves a photograph album in my hands and then looks round for something else to give me.

'I'll have it on loan. I can't keep it.'

'Course you can, Frannie. I've got my memories, haven't I?'

As I walk home along the winding path behind the terrace, I pause at Susan's back gate, with its massive lock. Look into the vortex.

It must have been a sensation untenably pure, like being a body without a shadow, a mass in freefall, that moment when Frankie jumped. You wouldn't feel despair then. There might have been an anaesthetic rapture in such a moment, or perhaps a climactic astonishment as you saw that you had actually done it. Flown free. What you had frequently threatened, perhaps without meaning much by it, you had achieved. But now, at this peak of decision, you found yourself not free at all. Noosed to the consequence of a wanton action, which maybe you saw too late for what it was, in all its shallowness and show. But they say that hanging is not quick. You may have struggled on the end of the line, hooked in through the gills.

And then afterwards, when they found you, instead of hysterics Susan produces – from a pocket? from the sewing basket? – a pair of scissors, hares out and snips a curl from your bright head.

Here is Dad arm-in-arm with Annie. In my mind, I can hear his voice, exclaiming that Annie's boys gave him the pip, they were pansies fit only to be put in a vase. *E-fem-in-ates!* he cried. *E-masc-ul-ated!*

Here is Dad having a jolly joke with his dear youngest sister Susan. *Common trollop! Her and her fancy man!*

Here he stands with his arm around me wearing a CND badge. And ranting on afterwards, what did I know about war? Had I been in the Western desert eating corned beef, sharing the Hardships and fighting for Freedom? He didn't think so.

Here's Dad with Midge, dressed in furs. *More bloody money than sense, living in that pseudo-bloody-Texan-palace.*

Susan is here too, her skin peachy in the early photos, her face suggesting in the midst of our Evans plainness and poor skin an extraordinary sweetness. And perhaps she had it too, I think, as the door bell goes. It's probably for the old lady downstairs. I've been hunkering down for several days, nursing the memory of Susan and convincing myself I'm starting a virus, with the face-to-face knowledge of this broken human on whom I've turned my back subdividing and multiplying in me by the hour.

The album's leaves of tissue sigh as I turn them, as if to lament all the smiling lies. I shiver with my flu or whatever it is, as the buzzer carries on ringing. Go away, leave me be, I'm sick.

I hid the locket away. In the drawer, which I now open and take a covert peek. Jack with an axe, Susan with a pair of scissors. I'm not opening that and I don't want to touch it. Or even keep it. Or have anything to do with it, but how could you throw something with that . . . provenance . . . away? It is in the shape of a tarnished heart.

Of course Susan can't have meant it literally, that she cut hair off the corpse. It's no doubt invention. She doesn't talk sense and it's just neurotic of me to take it like this. Most likely there's nothing at all in the locket.

Even so I play it over in my mind's eye, in a variety of scenes. Jack cuts my hanged cousin down with the blade of a handy axe. The look on his face? His face is blank. Enter Susan with a pair of scissors. What kind of scissors? Kitchen scissors, sewing scissors from her beaded work basket? Oh I must have a souvenir. Just hang on there a moment while I snip a curl. There she kneels in all her warpaint, a froth of slip showing from beneath her pencil skirt. Her idol standing there behind her with the axe.

I should really prise the locket open with my thumbnail; it would take a second. But my fingers shake; the palms of my hands and the soles of my feet tingle unpleasantly, because I have got flu, real flu, I ought to be in bed. My stomach is queasy and something here is desperately awry. We are a family that keeps a record and then locks it away. And I am no different. For instance, look what I am doing with this locket. I reopen the drawer. And there are tapes of Frankie singing, those big plastic spools in the trunk. We don't chuck stuff out but we don't examine it either.

Someone has been let in. A clamour up the stairs. Menna's unmistakable rap on my door. I huddle the album away as if I were the child and she the mother, and I'd been caught out yet again (and hasn't it always been like that, really?)

'I wasn't expecting you.'

'But you're pleased to see me, aren't you? Course you are!'

She stands there, radiant, in a dazzle of deep blue. Menna is not, in any conventional sense, beautiful, but there can be a magnetic vitality in her dark looks when she is excited. I have the feeling that I am about to be found out. A qualm goes through my heart; Menna's love and trust are my sanctuary. A video in her hand and a man in early middle age hovering behind her. It's

Aaron: surely it is? All last night I was dreaming of some man very like Aaron and woke shuddering with remembrance.

'Hi, Mara. It's been years. I heard you were back. We didn't like to intrude, but Menna said . . .'

It isn't Aaron but Seth and his gauche fifteen-year-old son Tristan. My social manner is momentarily lost, but Seth seems to intuit my confusion and chats away to cover it. Memories come pouring out thick and fast.

I hear myself ask, 'Do you remember that ship that was beached at Llangennith, Seth? I was thinking about it just the other day.'

'Do I remember it? The *Cleveland*. The destroyer *Cleveland*. One of the high points of my childhood,' says Seth. 'Black for me, please, Menna love. Tristan, there was this clapped-out ship ran aground at Llangennith. You'd have loved it,' he pleads to the turned back of the terminally bored boy. 'We climbed up on to it and there was hell to pay when Grandpops found us.'

'*We* climbed on it!'

'Oh – well, not you girls, of course, but your Uncle Aaron and me, we were up there like a shot, Tris. Parents none too thrilled, if memory serves. Shouldn't really be making these revelations about our misspent youth, should I?'

Appraising Seth, I think back to a tot with his thumb permanently in his mouth, Annie's skirts bunched in his fat fist, whining to be picked up. His sole ambition in life was a kangaroo-pouch, where he could stay for all time, peering down from this position of coddled privilege. Tristan at the window probably knows his father's innately mushy nature as well as I do. The set of his shoulders speaks the immemorial disdain of the adolescent for parental humbug.

'Seth,' I say gently but implacably. 'Are you sure you were in that ship?'

'Of course. I can see it now. In glorious technicolour. There was hell to pay. I don't mean we were walloped or anything. My parents didn't believe in smacking. They just explained the dangers and so on.'

'You can't have been more than four.'

'Oh gosh, where Aaron went, I went. Law of nature.'

'Are you sure it wasn't Francesca and me on the ship?'

'As I recall,' he says, 'you were keeping watch. Singing. *N'est-ce pas*?'

'Yes, we were singing Buddy Holly. But *on* the ship, Seth. Not off it.' I turn on my professional voice to reinforce the authority of my memory.

Tristan, turning from the window, looks me in the eye. Cynicism flows two ways. Yet all the while, I am thinking that Seth seems a decent enough man, courteous and thoughtful, doing his best for everyone, as did his mother, carefully checking that we all had plenty on our paper plates and begging us to eat, eat, be happy. Even her unruly niece.

'On the destroyer. We were dancing. Aaron was there with us. You were with your mother. Seth, you were quite a baby.'

He colours up but so do I. Constantly in my mind last night's melting dreams of the man who must have been Aaron drip like candle wax scalding the fingers. I am aware of Menna studying me, confronting perhaps for the first time the past from which she came. I sit very still and prim, maintaining the authoritative and neutral surface which has served, with her careful collusion, to keep intimate questions at a distance.

'So . . . how about you, what do you do, Tristan?' I enquire, and when will the visit end, I wonder? In our parents' time, families would 'pop in' and stay put for seven hours, gassing. I hope they aren't expecting to be fed.

'Drore. I do drore. Hash. Weed, you would have called it in your day.'

Seth swallows and affects to ignore this but he jitters. They have all seen the full video presumably: Francesca of legendary memory, smashed out of her mind. Heard her sensuous, smoky contralto song of how the times they are a-changing, of how everybody must get stoned. Menna has seen it. How much more than the snatch I have seen is on the full film? Menna lays it down on the TV without a word.

'So how are you liking being back?' Seth asks me.

'I like it fine. Of course I'm kept busy at Singleton. It's a demanding position.'

'Important though,' he says. 'Important work. You must feel it's tremendously worthwhile.'

'Oh, well, I . . .'

'Pain relief, we're all going to need that at some stage in our lives.'

'Oh goodness, Seth, I don't relieve any of the pain myself. I'm just a facilitator. And I trust that your leg isn't going to fall off, or mine for that matter. It's phantom pain my unit's been set up to study. Real, of course, but the limbs aren't there.'

'Fascinating,' he says, as everyone does.

'I saw Susan, by the way.'

'Terribly sad.'

'How long has she been in that state?'

'Hard to say, Mara. A gradual decline, sort of thing.'

'But nobody visits?'

'Oh, they do.'

'Really?' I press him and he doesn't like that at all.

'Certainly. We do so religiously.' Thomas sanctimoniousness creeps into his voice. 'But often she doesn't want us, or doesn't seem to know who we are, or, I don't know, doesn't like to admit it. And, if I'm honest with you, Mara, it isn't easy. To see her in that state. Of course she's well taken care of.'

The memory of Susan's soaked slippers intrudes before I can politely agree.

'She got away yesterday. From her carer. She was at the back gate.'

'But she can't get any further. It's padlocked.'

'Never seen such a massive padlock,' I say. 'In all my born days. Wormwood Scrubs isn't in it.'

'Well but, Mara,' Seth says correctively. 'Think what would happen if she did stray out. The cars come down that lane like nobody's business. It's for her own safety. And we do visit. Not the kids, of course; I don't think that's fair, do you? She says such

75

way-out things. She accuses Jack of . . . well, it depends which day you visit, what she accuses him of. It sort of makes sense in my view: I mean, the guy has behaved disgracefully. I don't have any time for Jack, never have had. He's a sot, Pops used to say, I wonder his liver can stand it.'

'Yet but, Seth, what actually *does* she say?'

'Accuses him of murdering girls and cutting them up with a fretsaw and burying their bodies in concrete in the cellar. Only problem is, they don't have a cellar. She's quite unhinged. On other days she denies it all: says Jack was a saint and where's he gone? Poor soul. She had a bad deal out of life in some ways. I always remember her amazing high-heeled shoes. Real stiletto affairs, do you remember that? She wore them once at the caravan. Shouldn't laugh, I know, but honestly, the sight of her picking her way along the grass, sinking in at every step, well. Look, we'd better go. You are a busy lady.'

'Woman. Or busy person.'

'You mean you're not a lady?'

'Exactly that.'

'Oh pay no attention, Seth,' Menna intervenes, having come through to the study. 'Mam is second-wave feminist. Incorrigibly. Women's Lib. It's hopeless.'

'Blimey,' says Seth. 'I'm out of my depth here.'

'Enjoy,' Menna says, patting the video.

'Have you seen it?'

'Yes. It's wild, honestly Mam, what you all got up to.'

'Shock you, did it?'

'No way. You were all . . . kind of innocent, really, like big hairy babies. Actually I couldn't see you there at all. At one point there is a pile of bodies, like pink grubs on top of one another. Was that a love-in?' She directs a piercing look at me, as if to suss out my part in this ruck of flesh. For all she knows, she could have been witnessing her own begetting. I wonder what she has made of Francesca but I flinch from asking; perhaps she will bring it up.

'Well, we must talk, love. When are you coming again?'

'Soon. Not next week. Aaron's coming then.' She has me in surveillance, watching every flicker of my eyelid, every shadow of expression. 'I expect,' she says, 'Uncle Aaron will fill me in. On things I don't know.'

'Uh huh.' *Don't bank on it*, I think, refusing the bait. I detain her, my hand light on her velvet sleeve. Then it dawns: George will be on the rest of that film. Yes, George, I remember you, I think, and a throb of fear and violence comes punching up through my pelvis into my ribcage. Menna must be able to smell my fear.

'What is it, Mam? You're all hot and bothered.'

'Oh – nothing. Touch of flu.' I laugh artificially, to cover the fear. There is electricity in her hair, which she has just washed and fills the hall with scent. Electricity too, I feel, in her veins and nerves, exciting her to an intensity I've seldom seen in my steady youngster, a hunger in her face that makes her seem younger, thinner-skinned. She allows my hand to linger on the nap of her sleeve. That expensive jacket of electric-blue, which awakens the colour in her eyes and makes me long to catch her to me and not let go; to hide her eyes in my shoulder so that she will be blind to anything that will hurt her.

'Hey you, don't be getting yourself all knotted up and anxious,' she says, seeing my eyes brim. 'All's well.'

I hang on to her hand, a moment too long, because I want to beg her, whatever she finds out, to go on loving me. But you can't ask of your children the understanding you owe to them.

I'll not look at that video: why should I? It's all dead and buried. Why not go into the unit instead and do some preparation for the inspection we're due next week from the Funding Committee? I scoop up the video and shut it in a drawer.

6

Lying together on Oxwich Beach in the lee of a boat, we were seventeen years old. Up for anything, rebellious as hell. The cool of the shadow was sensuous out of the pulsing heat of the day; a fishy smell, the sand clammy and cold.

'Got a present for you Mars Bar.'

'What?'

'Just make sure no one's coming.'

We dipped out our heads; Aaron and Seth were idling down the beach towards the sea. The dunes lay hushed and empty. A crisp bag lodged in the reedy grass. Thrift and vetch put out tiny flowers.

'I've got some stuff,' she said.

'What stuff?'

'Magic blissing mushroom.'

Into the shadow-zone Frankie drew me to her and kissed the corner of my mouth, where sometimes apprehensions of cold sore tingle. She kissed me with such thrilling delicacy that a moth's wing seemed to have brushed me. Later on the beach she wrote a piece of music without a tune and played it over and over, trapping me in the mystery of her harp-like guitar.

We kissed. Then we took the stuff. Perhaps I also tasted, incestuously, Aaron there. I lay the length of her and, oh it was blue. Blue was my colour. Blueness pulsed in the spacy shadow under the boat and aquamarine tides broke between lens and lid.

'Oh cool,' said Frankie. 'The vibrations in your skin. Your skin, my skin, which is which?'

Francesca Menelaus and Mara Evans were inseparably one.

When you peel away you still have the imprint, so I've read: that's how it is when you first take stuff. Forever that special bond between the two of you, because you dissolved minds, or thought you did.

'We need a world of our own,' said Frankie. 'Me and Mara is one brain.'

'Well,' said Jack, 'let's hope it's Mara's and not yours.'

Upright in her chair, Nana levelled her blue gaze at Jack, who was the only person apart from Francesca not to notice that she was anatomising him: that her eyes had pierced through to the corrupt heart, the toxic liver.

'You let the child be,' she said.

Rows with Mam. Rows with Dad. Rows with the family as a corporate unit, the lackeys and lickspittles of capitalism. Warmongers of the blackest ilk. Colonialists intent on oppressing the southern hemisphere. Vegetarian rants over the Sunday roast. Sabbath rows with Uncle Tony and Auntie Bethan about God. How, actually, if there was a God, he must be an evil maniac. Gasps, followed by promises to pray for the backsliding daughter. *Of course she doesn't know what she's saying, she's only a schoolgirl.*

Private rows about my knicker-revealing skirts; my homemade paper panties. About my hipster jeans, which seemed to come lower even in the moral scale than the depraved skirts, for they had a zip down the front like a fly. Why did I need a fly? my father demanded, since I did not possess the Wherewithal?

'What wherewithal?'

'You know perfectly well what I'm talking about. Flies are masculine. And slacks are masculine, come to that. It's a matter of utility and a matter of logic and a matter of modesty. Try to look like your mother and you can't go far wrong. Yes, and turn that filthy racket down.'

'It's not a filthy racket, it's a tape of Frankie singing at the Cross Keys. Listen, don't condemn what you can't understand, Dad,' I parroted.

'Show some respect for your elders.'

'Just because you're older doesn't mean . . .'

'Don't speak like that to your father, Mara. It's rude and it's raucous and it's ignorant. And put your shoes on. Your feet will splay out horrible if you go about like that. And what will people think?'

'I don't wear shoes.'

Dad said to Mam: 'You know, Leah, I think I must have wax in my ears. Do you think I ought to have then syringed? I thought I heard your daughter say she doesn't . . . wear . . . shoes?'

'Well, Dad, I don't.'

'Oh yes you do, miss.'

'I think you'll find I don't. None of us do. Why would I need to?'

'Rusty nails? Tetanus? Ever heard of that? Fragments of glass?'

'The trouble with you, Dad, is you've lost the capacity to experience . . . oh, never *mind*.'

'Oh please, don't spare my feelings. To experience what?'

'The grass under your feet. The rain on your face. You're not *alive* if you can't . . .'

'Fetch her shoes, Leah. It's like having a toddler all over again.'

'I've thrown them away.'

'You've . . .'

My blue sandals had been made of soft leather with ties crisscrossing my ankles and I adored them. But it was the day I got my three 'A's at A Level and I felt guilty about that. It was scarcely cool. Frankie had failed her GCEs twice and quit. Busked. Barmaided. Sold ice creams down at Caswell. Took off with a thirty-five-year-old guy from Chicago and turned up four months later with an all-over tan and a motorbike. She wore biker's black leather and her hair seemed to have become several shades lighter. Sang like an angel, like a demon. Met the Carmarthen pagans and shacked up with them for a while; back to Susan; off again, fucked around, stopped eating, started again, sang at every pub within a radius of thirty miles. Walked barefoot singing along the cliff path with an acoustic guitar.

This was cool, such as none of us could pretend to. I sat in the classroom throttled by my school tie and considered the Origins of the First World War and the Origins of the Second World War and the pending Third World War, which made all this sitting at desks making marks on paper seem rather pointless. If there was to be no future, why not race round on a clapped-out motorbike with a skull and crossbones on your back?

My authoritarian yet innocent parents were unable to believe in the possibility of a mushroom cloud spreading across South Wales. I looked over at Port Talbot where the steelworks belched filth in a great bank of dark cloud that loured over the bay. This was how it would end, a discharge of death on us all from an apocalyptic cloud, one very ordinary day like today. I could see it so easily. Why couldn't they? Why did they say the Bomb was a peacekeeper? *A Hard Rain's Gonna Fall,* Frankie sang at the Cross Keys, and afterwards there was silence. She modelled herself on Dylan, I thought, but the boys did not realise this because she was a girl. They thought she was a one-off job, midway between freak and genius. The smoke and jarring, off-key voice, the nicotined nails slashing metal strings. Laconic. Got up like a homeless person. I pondered with chagrin the extent of my uncool.

And now the greatest and most paroxysmic shame of all: my three Grade 'A's. Some sacrifice was demanded.

On the bridge I bent to untie the straps of one blue sandal. Appreciated it for the last time and sniffed the supple leather. It smelt of the creature from which it had been stripped on my behalf, and for whose loss I felt remorse. It smelt of me and told of my comings and goings over the earth and the tarmac, the beach and the grass. Exact to my foot with its high arches; still warm from my wearing. A lovely thing that had been transiently mine. I would cast it away and send it down to the sea. I untied the other, placing the pair on the stone parapet.

Hurled them high, one after another and, resting my elbows on the warmed stone of the parapet, watched them tumble downstream, the ties streaming back like ribbons. The effect was marred by one of the sandals becoming lodged in a mass of rubbish, sticking there like any other junk.

'. . . thrown them away. I don't need them. By the way I got my results.'

A fierce, fearful look came over both my parents' faces. They were thinking I must have failed. For all I did was mooch, sulk, declare against the bourgeoisie and refuse to make the toast. And now I was snarling that I had tossed my favourite shoes away and got some results I hadn't bothered to declare.

'Yeah. Got 3 "A"s.'

'You mean – three A Levels? What grades though, girlie?'

'A.'

'You mean Grade "A"?'

'Yeah.'

'Three.'

'Llew! She can go to university! Are you sure, *bach*?'

'Course I'm sure.'

'Well . . . why aren't you looking pleased? Why didn't you say?'

They wanted to see the certificate, to make sure I was telling the truth. There it was in black and white. They read it over and over, passing it between them, and tears welled in my mother's eyes. Ecstasy. Even I was affected. I was the best. I was an intellectual. I'd be a student and have my own bedsit, if the Russians didn't drop their bomb till next year. I'd get up at midday and sit in, march, work for Peace, drink. I'd denounce the South Africans, I'd live my life barefoot, in my own way. Meanwhile I was the toast of the Evanses.

After the first rapture, it occurred to them to wonder what Aaron's results were.

'Not as bright up-top as our Mara of course.'

'You ring, Llew, and find out. Tell them what Mara got. Go on. You couldn't get better than that, in any case.'

Dad rang everyone in the family except for Annie, knowing that the news of my success would wing its way to her via fourteen phone calls. Then our phone began to ring.

'One C and two Ds!'

My parents flung their arms around one another in pure *Schadenfreude*. They jumped up and down, and my mother said she'd never been so happy, in all her born days, and it all went to show. One C and two Ds was of course very sound. But it didn't have quite the ring.

'Oh well,' Mam said with happy hypocrisy, 'he's done very well, considering. They've perhaps not got the brains on that side, not really. And I don't suppose he did much swatting, did he, Mara, what with chasing around after Francesca. She'll be feeling very out of it, poor dab, with all of you going on to college and higher things.'

'*Out of it*'s the word,' I smirked. 'Higher plane.' I thought of Frankie inhabiting the astral regions in someone's slummy bedsit or wandering the heathlands toward Neath, hearing the bells of ling chime, or seeing constellations and stars or shoals of fish stream across the moors. Yet a part of me knew that Frankie took stuff and freaked and strutted in defiant high boots with rough lads and played riffs on her guitar so harsh your teeth grated, not just because it was the end of the world and a hard rain was going to fall, but because, with her unbearably thin skin, she had been left behind. We were all on our way: for, although the Bomb was definitely coming, it also was somehow not going to fall. The futureless generation was going to take over the world. We had that power or would have. Our music pledged it, drummed the message home to our hearts while we danced.

I consoled myself that Francesca had her art. If she lived in a cruddy parochial bohemia, that was because she had everything she needed, she was an artist, she didn't look back. Or something. So, while my heart winced momentarily for Frankie, I thought: well, if you're a genius, you had to be like that – an outsider, a stranger on the earth.

'Have a sherry, we'll all celebrate with a sherry!' said Dad. 'The first one in our family to go to university. Well! You are the very first.' He stared at me for a moment, as if it was hard to credit that this filthy-footed, long-haired savage could be the same as the person with three 'A's under her belt. 'Here's to Mara! And her brilliant future!'

As they lifted their glasses, a pang went through me. It meant so unimaginably much to them. For a moment I saw their struggle in a long perspective: saw them leave school at fourteen, the canning factory, the War, the austerities of the Fifties. Their life seemed to be one long anxiety. In their blue, incredulous eyes flowed the illusion of release.

I clinked my glass and garnered the grace to say, 'And here's to you both. For all you've done. To make this possible.'

'To us. Now you'll make sure you work hard when you're there, Mara. And, well, consolidate. Don't be led astray.'

'She'll want a haircut before she goes. And we can afford some good clothes for you, Mara.' My shoulders drooped but she suddenly grinned. After all, I might look like a weirdo, but, unlike my way-out cousin, that was just a front, a kind of carnival costume. Underneath I had proved my worth. I was one of them. One of the tribe who was making good.

'She could be really well off if she finds a worthwhile career, and of course she'll meet Mr Right.'

Their eyes glowed as the sherry worked its warmth into their veins. My father fantasised about my economic prospects and marriage eligibility. The sky was the limit. And after all, I thought, he's entitled to enjoy his own film. Why shouldn't he? Poor man, he'd never been strong since the accident and now walked slowly and lopsidedly with a stick: we had long been reliant on my mother's nursing pay packet. He was given to forgetting what he had just said, and repeating it in identical words. And to realising that he was doing so, the sadder aspect.

'This is the proudest moment of my life. And the next will be when I see you in your cap and gown.'

Heavy, I thought, and managed to escape. So wrapped up were they in the thought that we'd at last arrived, and could hold our heads up, that they did not query my unshod condition as I skipped out into the street. The silky insides of my thighs brushed secretly against one another; the sun fingered my shoulders and arms, intimately caressive. Nothing could hurt me. I was immortal. I shimmied along with self-delight, beaming into surprised local faces which involuntarily caught the smile and flashed it back, like mirrors.

In the crammed, fuggy room with the loud, red walls, I hunkered under a fern with black spores on the underside of complex leaves. The girl beside me was blowing an ocarina. She held it in the bowl of her palm like a china egg and blew across its holes.

This was my first visit to the flat where Frankie often hung out and where the radicals gathered. A high-status place. Having arrived wanting to look serious in denims, I found that only uncool outsiders were dressed for seriousness. They wore long fringed floral skirts and earrings. I shook my hair from its ponytail and hid between its curtains to get my bearings. Sweat, tobacco and joss-sticks mingled overpoweringly.

The men were tongues; the girls were ears. The ears cosied up to the tongues of choice and allowed themselves to receive the benefit of their windbag garrulities with every appearance of worship. It was worse than bloody chapel.

But I had a tongue too. I could speak, couldn't I? Two years into my degree, I had important things to say, which I felt with a passion that throbbed so violently I hardly knew how to contain it. I saw the tender earth, a blue and green globe swathed in cloud, with its precious and intricate cargo of life, hang vulnerable in the vast cosmos. The cosmos didn't care about our planet, so we had to care. We had to love. Urgently. To that degree, love was political. We owed it to the earth to love each other; to oppose with every fibre of our being those who wouldn't, couldn't love. Men with flags. Plutocrats. I kept the image of the fragile globe spinning in my mind's eye, balanced there, like a favourite bauble from the childhood Christmas tree.

So when a pause developed, I rushed into it. The bloodbath in Indonesia, I said, this whole Vietnam thing: we've got to actually get out and act ... and what I propose is ... I mean, every minute, while we sit here and just, you know, theorise, babies are dying. They are dying now ...

Hardly anyone so much as looked at me, except one pale-eyed

man who smirked and winked. Aaron, who was leaning quietly on the end of the sofa, nodded assent and did a thumb's-up sign. But what did the guy's wink say? That I was not a tongue?

I looked over to where Frankie hunched in her leathers. She'd said hi to me and made an odd sign with her fingers from across the jam-packed room. What was that: sign language? A secret code from our childhood, now forgotten by me? But as I struggled towards her, she'd switched off and sat deep in thought, or unthinking, it was hard to decipher which. Now she crouched forwards, elbows on knees, as if suffering from stomach ache. She did not seem to have registered my contribution to the discussion, but perhaps she had, because she arched her back and stretched, then reached back for her guitar, which she laid across her knees and began to tune. Rooting her mouth-organ from a pocket, she attached it to a rack she'd made from a couple of coat hangers, to fit round her neck. Then she began to suck and blow, no tune, no direction, just a dirge-like soughing in and out, a droning two-note accompaniment to the talk in the room. Like a bagpipe, I thought; like lungs. Pods that pop, I thought, and looked away.

We were two groups of people: the old-fashioned Swansea lefties, serious and kempt young men with low side-partings and open-neck shirts, chiefly students, and the long-haired dropouts of no particular denomination or age group; people who came and went without warning, charismatics or lost souls, the unemployed and the artistic. Oddballs. Prophets. What my parents called, on a frightened reflex, gypsies, riffraff, vagrants, scum. They drifted between towns and festivals, dossing and playing for their supper. To me they had a scary glamour, being older than ourselves and privilege-free. They travelled the fabled dark side of the road.

At the group's centre was George Owens, whom I'd mistaken for a postgraduate student or hip lecturer when I had first seen him cruising the shelves in the college Library, hair tied back in a ponytail and hands in the pockets of an Afghan coat. I'd witnessed him pocket a book, having thoughtfully caressed it with his fingers. He'd winked at me and tapped the pocket; then sailed over and offered to show me his seventeenth-century tracts. Any time, man, come and see. He kept them in a tea chest, and where he went, they went. Like, his family were those books. He'd leaned over my chair to see what I was writing, said 'Engels, eh? Well well,' and I'd felt the push of his body at my back, then his beard against my hair. George had freely harvested – that was his phrase – his antiquarian collection from all over Wales. *Bibliophile of the old school, me*, he said. A book cannot morally speaking be owned, your man Engels would agree, it can be sown, it can be reaped, it spreads its seeds through time and space. Later I wondered how George had gained access to all those libraries: presumably by sashaying in, colossal impudence flaunted as his credential.

'Dilly, what about a bite to eat?' the cry went up, along with blandishments: 'Ah Dilly is such a darling!'

The tenant of the flat, Dilly, was an earth mother, she said, or rather, she wasn't at all, she had never wanted to be a mother, not in a world like this, let alone an earth mother, but that was how people needed to see her and she didn't care to disoblige. Besides, she was between spiritual affiliations. She was broadly speaking a pagan, she told me as I followed her out to the kitchen, cutting onions and crushing garlic with the flat of a knife, a fag in the side of her mouth. Yeah, had been a Wiccan. She was ample and handsome in a ruined kind of way, her skin as brown as tobacco and pitted with eczema. Perhaps about forty.

'They always want meat, that lot,' she said, gesturing with her head to the men, whose talk was reaching an angry crescendo. 'But pass the joint round and they'll believe a carrot is a piece of dead cow. They're like walking stomachs on legs with their brains in their bollocks.'

'And tongues,' I said with some bitterness.

'Aye, they could yack for Wales. That blond guy, Merddyn, he's a druid. Makes me laugh, God love him. Claims to be a crowned fucking bard too. Stoned out of his head he was, started to deliver an epic poem in regular cynghanedd – wasn't even in

Welsh. Shove the tomatoes in boiling water, easier to skin that way. There you are, little tip for you in case you ever take to earth-mothering.'

'No thanks.' Her life was no different from my mother's except that no apron was involved. I asked her why she did it. Dilly laughed and said, 'Sucker, that's me, darlen.' In the living room I could hear voices raised in controversy, while Frankie accompanied them with a satiric droning, in-and-out. Aaron sat with his soft hair curling to his shoulders like a spaniel at her feet.

'Didn't think you'd fancy it,' said Dilly. 'You're a free spirit, aren't you?'

Her astringent irony ruffled me. It seemed to suggest that I was young and delusional. That when I reached Dilly's age, I would find out that freedom of spirit had never been available to me.

'Well, I don't know how free we can actually be,' I began. 'But we do need to think about the earth,' I faltered.

'Sure, sure. Anyway, dear Merddyn (not his name of course, he's probably called Sid) he starts this monkey gibberish and goes on and on and insists it's an ancient Welsh poem.'

'So what language was it?'

'Sod all. Speaking in tongues. That's Druids for you these days. Nice guy though. Share his last crust with you. After you've baked it of course. Now, we're going to have oat cakes with this and we'll just let it simmer. God, I could listen to Francesca all day and all night.'

'But she's only playing two notes.'

'You're not listening. Listen with your soul.'

I listened. But there was interference. Not just the raised voices and skirls of derisive laughter but some static of my own. All I could hear was Frankie's dad's lungs above the grey beach at Caswell that winter morning, and his child tugging at the bond between them in her boundless, ireful grief, trying to force him not to die. I could hear the rough tide at its turn, grinding the pebbles one way, the other, one way, the other. Could hear the mourning snarl in her throat; the hectic display of rock'n'roll on the *Cleveland* which said she was ready, ready Teddy, when she was not ready at all.

'We are a tribe!' yelled the shaggy-blond druid with the bare torso sitting deep in a settee covered with a dingy linen throw. Its springs were wrecked and you dropped into a womblike yet lumpy softness, a place where dead sperm, lice, dog hairs and warm bacteria might multiply. There was a sticky mess on the edge of the table on which the pot plant lay and I tried to avoid leaning back on it. 'A subterranean tribe,' said one of the longhairs, 'and that means in principle we love together, we fuck together, we are all sealed in one being, on the literal lateral dimension.'

In the pause that followed this revelation, the harmonica rasped satirically. The guests were either embarrassed or nauseated.

'Don't you think, in the end,' said the earnest and well-spoken young man beside him, swallowing his revulsion and in an accent that told us he came from the Mardy, 'it's not enough to go inward and, well, contemplate our navels. We have to identify with the working-class struggle, and here in Wales we're in the dead centre for protest, there is a living tradition, there is a Marxist-Leninist tradition very deep in the . . .'

A hot battle began about who was working class and who wasn't. Aaron asked what did it matter who your father was, it was you who mattered, the man you were.

I thought: *I'm not even counted as a man. Not really. So where do I fit in?*

'Are they always like this?' I asked the earth mother.

'Yup.'

'Like, when I spoke, they didn't seem to *hear*.'

'Your big mistake was mentioning babies. Babies are chicks' stuff. Anyway they don't listen to us. We aren't people, are we? Fucking useful though, we are. Do you like my mobiles?'

Everywhere was strung with bright aerial decorations. Strings of foil bottle tops. Jingling chimes. Shards of green and blue glass threaded on to revolving cane frames, bowls brimming with gilt buttons, streamers down the windows, so that hardly any space remained. In this immense treasure-house of bits and bobs, everything carried a thick patina of dust, so that for a dizzying reactionary moment I understood why my mother would have demanded to know how all this could possibly be dusted. On Dayglo pink surfaces lay pebbles and bits of driftwood. In its way it was wonderful. But looking at it deranged the eye.

We returned and the political discussion had died, now that a joint was on its way round and another being rolled. The youthful old-style Socialists in their chapel-bred puritanism were pulling down their shirtsleeves and saying they must go; they had a meeting with miners' representatives. *Real men* was the implication. *Not layabouts. Not dope-heads. Noble working people.* We'd talk again. We mustn't be introverted, they warned. It was a mistake. The Revolution could happen.

'It has happened,' said George from Anglesey. 'Happened it already has. It is here.'

'Meaning?'

'We are the Revolution,' said George. 'Don't go looking for it down a coal mine, comrade. Never mind dear old Bevan. Apart from anything else, Bevan sold out, didn't he, over the nuclear? Good man, don't get me wrong, but of his day. If you're going to look into the past, I mean, look into the Good Book. Never mind Marx, go to the Bible. Yea, I say unto you!' he roared in a pulpit voice and the girls around him frothed with giggles. 'Verily verily I say unto you, he who doth it unto one of the least of these my children, he doth it unto me. You dig that?'

Nods. 'Aye. And so does Bevan, man. Where do you think he got his Socialism?'

'Well then. Go to the source. Like, my dad is a minister. Upright minister of the Congregationalist Church. Right? Started with the Independents. In the seventeenth century, do you know what they believed?'

'Yes. I do actually.'

George was only slightly put out at this retort. He was a large-boned man with impressive blue-green eyes and a forceful stare, which he could maintain steadily without blinking. At that time he had not worked on perfecting his eyeballing, for his gaze was a bit mad-looking. He shimmered with sexuality, and with commitment to weird old theology. You felt he could crack these lads between finger and thumb, and that they knew it.

'They believed that the Kingdom was here, man. In the flesh. We are members one of another. Christ had come. But not, like, on a horse wearing a coat of armour, I mean they were not that unsubtle. It is now! It is us! We shall all be changed! Tune in. You heard of the Diggers?'

The young Socialists sighed and bolted; they could be heard clattering down the carpetless stair, slamming the door of their Ford and driving off in relief.

'Well now, have *you* heard of the Diggers?' George rounded on the people sharing his couch.

'Yeah, they dug folk music. Or was that the Beats?'

'No, they dug the *earth*. The common treasury, the earth. They just took it out of the hands of the rich landowners and gave it back to the people. Three hundred years ago.'

'Right.'

'You heard of the Ranters?'

'Nah, but you're going to tell us, right? And here I am only guessing, mind, but: they ranted, yeah?' Another joint was on its way round the circle and a mellow euphoria was descending.

'They fucked.'

'Yeah?'

'Fucked and fucked and fucked.'

'Well good kharma.'

'Fucked whomsoever they loved because God was love, wasn't he, and love was God, and they loved All Flesh. And you know what they called one another. My One Flesh. If a Ranter met a Ranteress going along the road to Brecon, he said Hi, My One Flesh, and they got it together there and then. In a ditch or knoll or in a shady copse or on a grass verge or, whatever. Cos everywhere was holy copulatory ground, see. Three hundred years ago, think of that.'

'I'm thinking. It's a cool thought.'

'God-given sacred orgasms for all. I was writing my thesis on this, you know, at Lampeter, Theology Department, and they said I was making it up. Lewd and obscene, they said. Can't have a thesis full of fornication. Put down your pen Mr Owens they said, and that was the end of my short-lived academic career.' Then suddenly, swivelling his head to me, George changed the subject. 'Wow,' he said. 'I love your feet. I mean, look at the instep of that foot. What's your name again? Mara, what a glorious name. Those are the feet of the Song of Songs, Mara. Did anyone ever tell you you had Biblical feet? No? "How beautiful are thy feet with shoes, O prince's daughter!" Narrow, shapely feet. Do you know what I would like to do to those feet?'

I could imagine him taking one in his hand and giving it a public massage, or licking it: I tucked one beneath the other, feeling a fool. Exposed and braless, with no way to hide the private places of my body. Yet I was roused too, by the attention.

'Fuck off, George,' said Francesca. 'And budge fucking over.'

Francesca muscled in between George and me. She planted herself at the centre of the room and struck the guitar, improvising, cutting from key to key. On and on it went, and round went the joints, the beer, a bottle of wine, gin, and I noticed with slow fascination how George's powerful hand crept up Francesca's calf and how Aaron watched this happening without apparent animus. I watched him play with Frankie's calf and then drift away.

But her cheeks were wet. She was singing through tears. 'Hey, loveliness,' I said, and thumbed away the tears. And she was singing to me, I thought, Frankie was singing Mara's song that she made up after she kissed me that time under the boat, though the lyric was harsher: *Mara bitter as rain on my blinded face.* Up close she did not look well. Her complexion seemed sallow, her teeth and fingers with their long nails coated with nicotine. She looked as if (and here my mother spoke again) she could do with a good long soak in a hot bath with foaming bubbles up to her chin and a month of hot meals and pampering. With a jolt it dawned on me that you could be young and yet expend yourself. Your life-energy might be finite and you might find yourself consumed. This could not be the daughter of Menelaus the Bread.

We hooked into one another's gaze. I thought of our heads on the one pillow whispering in our secret language. Tiny children. Uncle David bringing treats even though we were meant to be asleep.

She looked so hungry.

'I was thinking of cheese straws,' I told her.

'Were you? That's nice. We should find out how to make them.'

'We can ask Dilly,' I said. 'She'd know.'

'I couldn't keep them down.'

'Yeah, you could. Course you could.'

No, she could not eat, she said. Eating was something she just didn't do. It was not normal to her to eat. If other people wanted to shove bits of dead animal in their mouth, she said, what could she do? Anyway, she sat up, all jittery, lighting a fag in fingers that trembled, she was going back to her mam's for a bit.

'Yeah, Jack. Give Jack something to think about, the old lech. The parasite,' she said, fumbling the ciggy and dropping it. 'Bloodsucker,' she said. 'Jesus, I've burnt my frigging hand. If you don't shove over, Mara, you'll be alight.'

I hauled myself up, retrieved the fag and saw Aaron flat out beside her, evidently wasted. Sometimes, she said, she went and parked herself on them just to show the bastard. That seedy sordid mind-fucked anus on legs.

'You don't want to go to Jack. Don't be daft.'

'Yeah but I don't want to go *less* than Jack doesn't want me to come. He would love it if I just buggered off and never came back. I'm not giving him the satisfaction. I remind him, see. I'm a death's-head.'

'Forget him. Move on. We don't need our parents.'

'He's not my parent.'

'Hey, idea,' I said. 'What about moving in with me. No, go on. It would be great. Like old times. Chippie next door but one.'

'I don't eat.'

'No, OK, you don't eat, but how about it? We always wanted to be together. Didn't we?'

'Nice of you, Mars Bar, but I need to get to my bed at home, if you know what I mean.' The child in her was speaking. Her need. I had never been good at coping with that and she knew it.

'Aaron, wake up. Jesus, look at him. He's such a girl of a boy. And you're such a boy of a girl. Adorable though, isn't he?'

I remember her hand laid on his curly head, and brushing the hair back from his forehead. I thought suddenly, as he raised his head and smiled, *Yes, he is.*

Menna on the phone at the crack of dawn. 'I've seen him!' she crows.

'Who, love?'

'Uncle Aaron!'

'Oh, right. That's nice.' My stomach swoops over and over. '*Nice?*'

'Menna, I'm sorry, I've had a lousy night. I'm glad for you. Of course.'

'You don't sound it,' she complains.

'No, I am, really. It's just . . .'

'Just what? You don't have to meet Aaron if you don't want to. And Aaron doesn't have to meet you. That's up to you. He's got six children. Imagine that. Six! Says he'll never be able to afford to retire because they've all got to be put through schools and university. Are you still there? Mam?'

'I'm still here.' Stunned, I'm thinking, *six.* I knew he'd done a lot of procreating but Hen never supplied me with details, nor did I enquire. A tribe of faceless Thomas boys and girls of diverse ages.

'Yes, and he's had three wives. Why do you think Seth didn't tell me all this? And pots of money, he must be loaded. He's an economist with the World Bank. I mean, he must be seriously rich, mustn't he? He was laughing: he said when he was a kid, he used to go round wearing sandals saying all property was theft. Do you think I ought to call him Uncle Aaron, or just Aaron? That seems to be more natural somehow. It's a gorgeous name, isn't it? Anyway, I didn't poke and pry but it seems he hasn't got a wife now.'

'He's between wives? Well, never mind, he's got his six children,' I say dully.

'Yes, and he has custody of the whole lot, what's more.'

'Blimey.'

'Yes, but he must be a good dad, mustn't he? I mean, he must be a super-dad. Says he wouldn't be without his children even though they drive him round the bend. But he takes them yachting, he has a yacht, and he's invited me to go along. I'm so excited.'

'So how many boats has this paragon got? A fleet?'

'Just the one. Mind you, it's big, apparently. Are you still there? This line is weird. Is it you or is it the line?'

'It's demons, Menna. Interference.'

'What's up, Mam? Don't you want to hear?' She doesn't wait for an answer because Menna is eager to tell, to share, but I can feel how the glow is being dissipated, like the bloom off handled fruit.

'Anyhow he wants to sail round the world, that's his great ambition. His friends and some of his children's partners go along and crew. He's so – huggy and warm and hospitable, I can't believe it.'

I sit, numb, with my cup of tea held against my stomach like a miniature hot-water bottle. The six children who are so adorable and richly educated file through my mind, and I dread to ask the names of these six young mariners. Chastened, I slump with my head drumming, and listen to a list of Aaron's other attributes and acquisitions. He has a house, well, really a small chateau, in Provence. But he's so modest that he has informed Menna that chateaux are two a penny in France, and it's really just a glorified barn. However, the alleged barn has several barns in the grounds which he lets out. He has invited Menna to visit the chateau or the barns, bring her friends, any time, come any time. Just ring. What do I think of that?

'Very nice.'

'Well, it is though, isn't it? Don't you think?'

'Oh Menna, you know I don't hold with second homes.'

'God, you're such an old stodge, Mam. You are, you know. You're like, from another age! And anyway, it isn't a second home, he's got four houses or something like that, I couldn't catch it all. He speaks very modestly and swallows his words, and then he goes all shy.'

'Did you meet any of the six sprogs?'

No, Menna didn't, because they are all massively active, doing expensive or lucrative things in all sorts of places. If I asked their names, I might hear among them the name Zack. And if he came up from burial in my memory, I would have to go and see him. There could be no rest until I had seen his face. None.

7

I close the door on these echoes; the door with my nameplate which tells me who I am, satisfyingly, each time I enter and, by reducing everything to order in the unit, I compose myself. The office is in a state of gossipy anticlimax after the bigwigs' visit and Elin is going on about her synaesthesia. She's telling everyone what colour their names are.

'So what about me? What colour's my name?' I ask her.

'Yellow.'

'What? You can't be serious.' Everyone is looking. My voice betrays genuine upset. My PA pauses with her hand on the shredder.

'Well, OK,' says Elin, 'yellow and black.'

'A wasp! You've got me down as a bloody wasp!'

Everyone falls apart, disbelievingly, for if the cap fits I should wear it, Elin (who can get away with anything) has suggested. Only kidding, she adds hastily.

'I can't be yellow,' I stubbornly insist. 'Green or blue, I thought you'd say.'

'It's not a value judgment, Mara.' She puts down a cup of coffee in front of me and I drink. 'The letters literally do have colours. I see them in colour. It seems quite banal to me. It's not a code.'

'Well, what if you called me Marsie?' I ask her, and the office convulses again, since even Elin would never in a month of Sundays venture a nickname with me. But I'm still yellow apparently. Black's OK: I can do black, in fact all of us in this office except Elin wear black – to show we're serious, or, as I said

97

to the Ministry woman, to show we're all in mourning for the imminent death of the Welfare State. It's a disgrace, I told her, we *need* and must have the promised funds. What is more important – tell me straight – than human suffering?

Nothing, she said, but it's not my department.

Not your . . . ? You're going to need us one day and then we'll see if it's your department. Except that you'll go private. All our generation have sold out. Nearly all.

I'm in no position . . .

Doesn't it bother you, being a cipher?

Elin watched me savaging her. She was cheering me with her eyes. Elin can do that; butter wouldn't melt but her eyes are radical. I have hopes of her. Despite her delicate blouses, the blonde streaks in her hair. Even so, she calls me yellow and sticks to it.

'Not as in cowardly,' she rushes to reassure me. 'God, no one could call *you* that.'

I'm not so sure. It's just that I don't show any sign of the panic that sent me on the run from Wales. I don't speak about the steady, tender passion Jo and I shared at the flat in London, when we were such settled partners that Menna would occasionally call Jo 'Mam' too. I don't wear the scars of the breakup or show how lost I felt when she went, because I was 'cold and had stuck emotionally at the bloody potty stage, if you want to be Freudian'. That's why the whole office is staring now, with a smile around the eyes, because I've lost my cool about a whimsy. Mara the controlled and controlling, acting like a helpless brat.

'But I hate yellow!' I squawk.

'I like it,' says Elin.

'I used to be called Mars Bar.'

Whoops from the office. The distance I've held, the body language that commanded respect, has temporarily fled away. Howls of mirth. Everyone, including the lad with the post, is looking on with interest.

'Well, that gives you a hint of . . . red. But it's the M, I'm afraid, Mara, you can't change your name. So you're always going to be yellow. And that, I'm afraid, is that,' says Elin as she straightens the edge of a bundle of papers by slapping it against her desk.

'Goldy yellow or lemon?'

'Mmn. Hard to say.' Seeing room for negotiation here, she flashes me a humouring look. 'Which do you prefer?'

'Neither.'

Another burst of laughter. The atmosphere in the office is so cheerful that the air seems physically warmer.

Daffodils they brought me, after I went for Jack. When I came into my kitchen, the violent yellow hit me, wedged into bottles, vases, strewn on every surface. Amongst their yolky brilliance, a scatter of tulips bled crimson. And in a blue enamel kettle on the stove, Aaron had stuck a message: BIG MARA'S BEAUTIFUL OK. BIG MARA'S WILD.

Frankie had looted Jack's wallet to pay for the daffodils while he was still lying there on the floor, groggy amid the jagged ruins of the glass table. Blood liberally sprayed over Susan's furniture, the pride of her eye. His jacket was hanging on the door. Frankie rummaged for his wallet, casually, as if she had every right to seek compensation, while I stood there in the aftermath of my outburst, shaking uncontrollably. She stripped out a wad of notes, held them up to show me and stuffed them in her jeans pocket.

Wildness was growing upon Big Mara. Here in the drifts of daffodils was its harvest, for in the last months I'd vented spectacular reprisals on Francesca's behalf. So, you see, I tell myself, I did not sit idly by and let her be axed and scissored: I intervened.

Because, look, said Danny the big mouth, at Rhodri's bar, he'd seen my pal Francesca in a field with Hairy George, did I know that? Rutting like beasts, going at it . . . *Shut up, Danny*. Everyone from Llantwit Major to bloody Porthcawl had had her. *I'm warning you*. Oh, says Danny, I'm terrified, man. Off sailed his pint through the air to shatter against the far wall. Rhodri goggled and pointed out that I would have to pay for that and who was going to blinking mop up the mess? Danny gaped. *Now fair do's Mara. The fucking fact is, that every fucking one round this fucking table has fucking fucked Frankie. Not excluding your fucking self, if all I hear is true. Can't be that fussy, can she? Plus, she's up the fucking duff.*

What?

But who's the dad, I'd like to know.

A little beer goes a long way. All cowered: it was precious, the way I told it afterwards, to see these great rugby lads with thick necks and bull heads cower, covering their heads with their arms. Of course, it grew with the telling.

But the daffodils came later. They were a tribute for the exercise of my vicious streak in the greatest cause of all: Jack.

She was pregnant, and very sick. Susan had not twigged but I'm not so sure about Jack. Nothing stayed down. Frankie threw up night and day. He didn't like that, not at all. Hated illness. But also, he was in some unstated way frightened of his stepdaughter, to the degree that he would bestow on her large sums of money accompanied by oily smiles; he reeked of fear when she was around. She sat feebly on the sofa sipping a glass of Ribena, staring expressionlessly at Jack.

Jack watched TV. He did not return her gaze. He'd watch anything while enjoying elevenses of Guinness and a giant bag of crisps which he popped one by one into his small mouth. The sight made Frankie gag but still she kept her eyes on him. He must have felt them roaming his face. He chomped on, darting sidelong glances at his stepdaughter, rubbing the bristles on his chin with his hand's heel. He was still a notably handsome man and imposing, despite an increasing girth and occasional reluctance to shave.

'Going out today, girlie? You taking her out with some of your nice college friends, Mara? Do you good to get a change of scene, you know. You're bored, that's what. Swanning round on that bike has made you sick. And those unwholesome pals – you can do better than that.'

'She's not well enough to go out.'

'Well, what's wrong with her? Ask her what's wrong, go on, ask her.'

'Uncle Jack wants to know what's wrong, Frankie.'

'Does he really?'

'She says, does he really?'

'Well, it's her funeral.'

'He says it's your funeral.'

'Such a gentleman.'

'She says, such a . . .'

'I can effing well hear what she's saying. And as a matter of fact, your mother, who knows a great deal more than you, Francesca, about common courtesy – are you listening? – your Mam's shocked at your bloody insolence to me. Disgrace you are . . . ashamed you ought to be . . .'

All the while he had been losing focus and his attack murmured to a halt. Briefly his eyes met her needy sneer; then swerved to the screen. Following Frankie's cue, I sat mute and studied him. Surprisingly, he was actually following the programme. Jack would watch anything if he couldn't get sport, whether cookery, wildlife films or the news. He lolled now with both arms over the back of the settee, and absorbed himself in the programme.

'I want to be sick,' announced Frankie.

'Stop it, just stop that. You'll be saying next, you've got a polter-bloody-geist.'

'A what?'

'A poltergeist. Hysterical females making clocks jump off the mantelpiece and so on. Look, if you want to be sick, go and do it somewhere else. You've only got yourself to blame. God knows what substances you pump into yourself. And perhaps you'll learn from this . . .' He died away again. It was as if his energy came in small rations, which quickly consumed themselves.

'Don't think I'll bother. Think I'll just sit here and watch you.'

That look on her face was scary. She had used it at school to give kids the willies. Pale eyes staring, the secret being not to blink. The bitter beauty of that face shocked me sometimes, and made me draw back, wary and admiring.

'We are observing a peculiar kind of animal species which feeds on its own young. Gobbles them up whole. It's no wonder I feel bloody sick.'

'What?' His eyes were still glued to the screen. I saw that he was using the television to calm himself. It dawned that perhaps he did not choose these moods: they controlled him, as mine did me. I wanted to signal to Frankie: *enough*.

'It cannibalises its own babies.'

'Quit the back-chat, now darling, and go out for a breath of air. Take her out, would you, Mara? Look, I had a heavy night last night.' He seemed to be pleading with me to help guard her against himself.

'I can't go out. I'm sick. You've made me sick.'

'Well, go to the doctor then. Or tell your mother.'

'Tell my *mother*? You want me to tell my *mother*?'

Jack got up; I froze.

Whistling through his teeth, he reached out to switch off the television. Now there was nothing to calm him.

He seemed to tower. I could imagine him wringing her neck. Easily. She looked away nervously, her face pale and drawn. Having lost courage, she gave me an odd little peep, like a child's. I got up, my heart storming with panic. He bent towards her, and, though it was not a violent movement, it was terrifying. Jack leaned down towards her face and whispered, 'Get rid. Just – get – rid. Or you will wish you'd never been born.'

'I do wish I'd never been born. I wish I'd gone with my dad. I wish I'd never set eyes on you. Animal. I wish I was with him now, under the ground. No, I wish you were. I wish you were dead.'

Panic roared in my skull; I saw it mirrored on Frankie's blanched face. There was a green vase on a doily on the sideboard. It was a peculiarly hateful vase, with a bulbous base, full of bits of rubbish that had been picked up off the carpet: hair grips, Irish coins, paper clips, safety pins. I reached for it with both hands and heard myself scream.

I brought it smashing down on the base of Jack's neck. As it broke and his bulk toppled sideways with a grunt oddly suggestive of appreciation, my own head seemed to explode. I burst into tears. He was silent and, for a moment, it seemed to me I might have killed him. Francesca laughed out loud. Cackled. Whooped. 'You little darling, you little love!' she cried. She took my violent hands and kissed them.

'He's dead, Frankie, oh God.'

'Are you dead, freak?' she asked him and aimed a kick at his groin. He moaned and curled his body into a foetal position. The glass-topped table chose this moment to splinter. I shrieked at the top of my voice and, when the scream died, I was terrified by my own silence.

It was then that Frankie stripped his wallet of notes. While she was doing this, the back door from the kitchen opened and the light snapped on. Susan gave a yelp. All I remember of the turmoil that ensued was Susan's wail of, 'My best vase! They've smashed my favourite vase, oh the hooligans! Are you all right, darling? Oh come on sweetie pie.' Kneeling, she pulled her husband's head on to a cushion. 'How could you?' she demanded of me, then wailed: 'My lovely table, it comes from Norway!'

Daffodils: the most powerful scent comes as they perish and they perish sooner, rather than later. It is a penetrating scent, almost too much and then, suddenly, sickening. The sickly sweetness of other people's sex.

'Frankie, I would die for you,' I proclaimed, taking her back to my rented room at Brynmill. Meaning that I would kill for her, and shocked, now that the adrenalin had died down, at what I was capable of. I shook all over. 'What'll we do, lovely girl? What'll we do?' Taking her distress in the crook of my arm, I stroked her hair from her temples with rhythmic motions. 'What'll you do – about the baby?'

'He wants me to get rid of it. So I fucking won't.' She laid her

103

hand on her still flat belly and the other on my hand that was stroking her hair. We murmured to one another and wept. I tried to decide whose baby she was carrying, enumerating all the possibilities I knew and was shocked to think that she allowed so many men to do God-knew-what to her, as though your own body were a container you could pass round to anyone with a prick. Like a spittoon or a urinal. It was a thought that my parents might have planted and which had persisted, stunted but stubborn, in my mind.

'Oh Frankie, why aren't you kind to yourself? Why don't you take care?'

'Don't keep on,' she grumbled, not unhappy that someone was prepared to nag. 'It's boring. Anyhow, Aaron loves me.' She perked up. 'Aaron will take care of me. Anything I want, Aaron will do for me. I only have to ask. What do you think?'

'Think of what?'

'Of me and Aaron?'

'And me,' I said. 'Don't forget me.'

'Yeah, and you. Of course, Marsie. You've been brilliant today. Wow. Like bloody Tarzan of the Apes. Do you know, I'm starving. I could murder a meal. All because of you. Jesus, you cracked him one. Like an egg. I could fancy eggs actually, Mars Bar. Have you got any?'

It was strange how suddenly the sickness left her. She was calling for bacon and fried bread, and eggs whose yolk she pronged with her fork to bleed the yellow out. She followed this up with a bar of chocolate, washed down with strong, sweet tea, and half an hour later was asking for the whole lot over again. The lace of the egg white bubbled and spat in the pan. As I spooned the butter over the yolks, I wondered when the police would come, or Jack, or some posse of Evanses, Thomases and Menelauses.

'Is it ready?'

'Just a tick.'

'God, I'm starving. I can't wait.' She'd snared my waist from behind and was swaying my body to and fro. I giggled as I swayed, but my mind, always charged with melodramatic fantasies, was envisaging myself in the witness box pleading guilty but justified. I pointed a Nemesis finger at a phantom Jack, only to be led away, still ranting, to serve my time.

Instead of Jack or the police came Aaron and our grandmother.

It seemed to be taken for granted that the child was Aaron's; at least Frankie did not quarrel when he spoke of it as 'ours' and said how thrilled he was, no, really thrilled. He'd leave college, he said, holding Frankie's hand in his, and earn a living for them as a family.

'You will not do that,' said Nana. There was a detachment about her manner. All her children had snarlingly fought for possession of her. She had them on leashes but the leashes were hopelessly tangled and she could control none of them. Us, however, she could take in hand.

'College is a must,' she told Aaron. 'It is in nobody's interest for a young man to lose out on College.' She said the word with reverence, sounding the capital letter. College was the heaven of the underclass. A passport to status. 'I shall sort out the practicalities. All you have to do is study, Aaron, *study* and improve yourself. This family has not striven and saved so that you can tip this chance down the drain. And you too, Mara. No more throwing your weight about. We shall do things in a proper way.'

We were abashed and subdued. Of our whole family, it was only Nana we respected enough to listen and learn from. I was sent out to the shops and, when I returned, she'd gone and Frankie sat flushed and breathless.

'Nana's leaving me Breuddwyd, Marsie. For me and Aaron and the baby. She's moving to a flat – apparently it's all signed and sealed. And we can move in. But you don't think she's ill, do you? I don't want her to die. I don't! She said not to tell you but you gave Jack what he was asking for.'

Uncle Pierce differed, when I described to him, with suitable embroidery, how I'd seen Jack off. It was not his way to lecture, but, a pacifist in two World Wars, he reminded me that violence was not the answer. He had to reach up to me, being a small, wiry man. His hands enclosed my shoulders with the lightest touch and with no hint of a reprimand. He seemed to me even in those days a venerable person, and it soothed me to be taken in hand.

'Apart from anything else,' he said, 'Mara dear, if you lay about you like that, sooner or later either your own fist or someone else's will slam into your own eye. Which I shouldn't like to see. You have such lovely eyes. Oh Mara, get angry by all means. It is only right to feel anger. Rage, even, when we look about us and consider. But get angry about the right things. About Vietnam, for instance.'

'I am angry about Vietnam, Uncle. You know I am. I go to all the demos. I sit in, you know I do care, absolutely.'

'Well, good. But how would it help to go and punch President Johnson on the nose?'

'It would make me feel better. And one for Ladybird too.'

He laughed. 'But would it change anything, dear heart?'

'Well, no. I do believe in Peace. It's just, you've got to stand up for things.'

'And look here, Mara.' Pierce had the tight curly hair and blue eyes of most of our kin, plus unusual strength and fitness: having worked as a steelman. He was no weakling, Pierce. 'Look here, I was a bit of a bruiser in my time. Yes, really. Well, I had it in me, let me say that. We all do, you know. But what I found was that it's better by far to talk it through. Stand, you know, but give the other person a sense that, well, there is someone there.'

I looked at him in panic, my eyes filling up. This was precisely what I did not feel. There were too many of me, inhabiting the one skin. We all jostled in there and sometimes one came to the fore, sometimes another took over. I was nothing but a transparent sac in which vagrant and slippery identities had to coexist in a rhythm of feud and truce.

Whisperings. Disquiet. Shiverings along the whole family system.

Mama given the house away? To Susan's hooligan daughter. Can't be right, can it? Senility. Must be. That's *our* property, by rights. Is there no law in the land?

Did you know that Susan's girl is pregnant? No. *No!* Who's the father then? Well, that side of the family, they've no backbone, never have had, never will, what have I always said? And who's the father? Don't make me laugh, man. The boy's a pansy, I seen him in a skirt. It'll be that beardy ruffian from Anglesey. Words fail me. They really do. I'm telling you, words fail me. Whatever will Annie do?

'Ah, the lovely girl,' said Hen sitting with Nana in the sheltered flat for which she had left Breuddwyd. 'I'll be a great-auntie, there's nice. I'll start knitting, soon as I finish this cardy for young Mara.'

'Silly creature,' Nana said it with testy fondness. She sat erect in her chair and refused to go to bed. She said plenty of people had cancer, and everyone was mortal, it was widely known, so why the fuss?

Uncle Tony spoke of sexual sins in these Latter Days. Strictly speaking, said Auntie Bethan, it's the girl's fault. Virginity in the present day is scorned like sin was in ours. Sex is everywhere. Everywhere you look, on the radio, on TV, on Fairwood Common.

Annie mourned. She had nourished such aspirations for her first-born, plans which had under no circumstances included early marriage with lower and less fortunate kin. A wild girl.

'What do you mean, Aaron?' her voice quivered. 'You're not getting married? How can you not get married? You mean, the child is not yours? Oh the relief, I would have been so ... It is yours? You don't *know* if it's yours? You're going to live with her unmarried?' She could not argue further and turned her face away.

'Tell him,' she begged Pops. 'Please. Just tell him.'

Pops concentrated fire on Aaron's hairstyle, leaving other issues untouched. The lustrous curls that fell past Aaron's shoulders seemed a manifestation of all his son's defects. They were against nature, he counselled, and effeminate.

'I'm sorry you don't like my hair, Pops. I'll have it cut.'

'Oh good. You see, Annie, he's coming round.'

Aaron came back with his hair an inch shorter. He liked to oblige and pointed out that Pops should not worry about effeminacy, since if he were effeminate, he could not have fathered a child. He gravely explained to Pops about free love and how all children belong to the whole community. And he didn't want to upset anyone and he wasn't criticising but when he looked round this beautiful room, with the Wedgwood and the silverware, he felt it was scarcely fair that the Thomases should have so much and the majority so little. Couldn't they give some of their surplus value away? he asked. After all, in *King Lear* . . .

'*King Lear* my backside!' bawled Pops, in a burst of moral indignation. 'I worked my balls off to afford all this, you're the apple of your mother's eye, and you do this to us! Well, watch out, young man, I've two other sons to leave my "surplus value" to.'

Annie confided in my mother, instantly regretting it. She'd had three beautiful boys, she said, like books on a shelf: she'd been gifted with sons, all destined for the professions . . . and now *this*. It was a trick, she said, Aaron was a perfectly charming but not very worldly-wise child, who'd been caught by the oldest trick in the book.

Aaron was gentle under their wrath. The more I saw him with his head against Frankie's belly, listening intently for the baby's heartbeat, caring for her every whim, the stronger grew that ache of tenderness. His stillness and capacity for keeping silent when he had nothing particular to say impressed and endeared. This was a rarity amongst the men I knew. Big talkers, all. Fellowship grew almost unnoticed between us. When Nana died, it was Aaron who told me. He took both my hands in his, up to the wrists, explaining that she had slipped away with no pain. In the night, he said, in her sleep, that was good. We often cried on one another's bare shoulders. I found we could sit together and just be. One evening at Llangennith he lay beside me, our feet fraternally touching, chatting and laughing. As I gazed straight into his long-lashed eyes, he put both hands through my hair and said I ran so deep, it was amazing how deep I ran.

'What you doen, cockles?' asked our friend Aled.

'Discussing Kierkegaard,' I explained. Aaron smiled.

'You got to be blinking bloody bladdered for Kierkegaard,' said Aled. 'The whole frigging universe, see. How's your Francesca then, Aaron? Six months, isn't she? Sorry about your gran, mind. But it gave you a pad, isn't it. Gorgeous voice, your Frankie though, haven't heard her sing lately. All smoky and harsh, dead sexy. Sexy like a snake would sing, if it could sing, if you see what I mean.'

'She could have been an opera singer,' I told him.

'Oh aye, operatic. Plenty of the Madame Patti there.'

He drifted off. We spoke, Aaron and I, of how we would help with the baby when it came, although we didn't know one end of a baby from the other. A Moses basket would be nice. We should all carry the baby next to our hearts, the pulse beat would calm it, Aaron felt, and kind of link it to the life force flowing through us all. For this was all a great experiment in life, like George said. Aaron often quoted George with approval, as if he possessed a rare fund of wisdom.

'Come off it. He's a wanker.'

'You got to see the gentle side of the man, though, Marsie. There's a rough side and a thoughtful one . . .'

'You're welcome to both sides. He's all yours.' I thought of George's hand on Frankie's calf; of what Danny had said about seeing the two of them at it, copulating in a field. Perhaps the child of the universe was none other than the issue of George.

'Frankie cares about him,' Aaron said. 'And I'm prepared to trust her instinct.'

'Oh, right. Yeah. But you know something? I think he's the spit of Jack. No, I do. She seems to need that kind of . . . tough. I don't even think she likes him. I don't like him.'

'Attraction is complicated, isn't it, though? She says he's got charisma. He understands her on the level of . . . well, something deep, musical.'

'Do you want some of this spud,' I said, changing the subject. 'It's hot, mind. Pass that beer, Aaron. Where is George anyway?' I did not add, *And where is Frankie?* They would jaunt off together, Frankie at six months pregnant still straddling the bike, with George's arms loosely clasping her belly as they roared off. Aaron seemed to accept that she must do her own thing; she must be free. Once he asked hesitantly in my hearing where they were off to: according to Frankie they could not know until they arrived. 'The Spirit,' as George explained, 'bloweth where it listeth. Ta-ra.'

'And ta-ra to you,' I thought in contempt.

'Never mind, he'll look after her,' Aaron said concernedly.

Now, eating charred potato out of the foil, washed down with beer, Aaron asked me, 'Do you think I'm weak, Marsie?'

'Nah. Why?'

'Oh, well, you know. People seem to think I'm, sort of, shapeless. Because I can't decide on things. I tell myself it's because I'm growing. I look about me, listen to people. But perhaps I'm just a wishy-washy liberal?'

'Hey, you are lovely. Eat this.'

'Tastes better coming from you. But even so, perhaps I ought to be more decisive.'

'But then you'd not be you, softlad. You'd be someone else and I wouldn't like you.'

If he was weak, it was a genial and appealing weakness, I thought, angling my eye at his softly athletic body. Aaron's capacity to see good in awful people and many sides of a simple question sometimes irked but more often soothed me. It allied me with a quietism not native to me. When I said it was good to be someone like him or Pierce, who didn't whack people over the head with Susan's green vase, my cousin laughed and said he was bloody glad I'd seen Jack off. Then he set his beer bottle down, wedging it in the sand so that it wouldn't fall over, and took my hand, saying he read the tender, loving side of my nature in the curve of the lifeline and, look here, he said, your love line. It

110

occurred to me that he had no character. Or that he was embryonic. Perhaps that was it: he seemed almost entirely latent. I recalled Frankie's saying that he was a girl of a boy and I was a boy of a girl.

In the low sunlight, the lines in my palm were imprinted by shadow, a network of possible destinies. We both stared at the crisscrossing on my palm, and compared it intimately with his: definitely an affinity there.

At Breuddwyd, we'd have a new kind of society, with love and children, and less of the possessiveness and clutter of possessions that had burdened our parents' lives. We deplored their mercenariness but of course, Aaron said, feathering my hair with his fingers and looking into my eyes with tenderness, it wasn't their fault; they'd come up from poverty. Life had been hard for them. Whereas we were in a position to stand on their sacrifices and make a fairer world for everyone. He firmly believed it, he said, which was why he was studying economics, for we'd need that kind of know-how in this new world.

'Can I say something? Something personal?' I asked.

'Of course.'

'I don't . . . know if Frankie wants this baby, Aaron,' I said. 'I don't honestly think she does. She seems to be, sort of, ignoring it. As if it will go away.' The sun had been swallowed by the sea and the air was viscous, the sands tawny. Where the destroyer had been beached at Diles Lake, there were still remnants of the hull, and a funnel poking up out of the sand.

'No, I don't think so either,' he said. 'She pretends . . .'

'. . . it isn't going to happen.'

'But when the baby comes,' Aaron hazarded . . .

'. . . everything will be all right.'

He took my hand and we walked towards the tide, creaming a long way out, assuring one another that it would work out, because there were the two of us standing one on either side of Frankie, to help with the baby and make it easier for her. And we paused to kiss, as friends do.

*

Aaron is coming. He should open the locket with me and hear the tapes, then decide what to do with these things. That's only fair. He and I were co-legatees of all that is mortal of Francesca, and he can't get out of it just because he has seventy children and seven stately homes and any number of barns throughout the known globe. Somewhere in this plutocrat must be the Aaron I knew, who will turn the evidence over with me in his sensitive hands and help me to make sense of Jack the axeman and Susan with her scissors. I shall speak to Aaron strongly, yes, strongly, I think, dumping my groceries on the table. I shall use my professional persona. My iceberg chill. Elin always sends me into action when something nasty needs to be said. Well, even if I don't go smashing vases on people's heads any more, at least my aggression has its uses. Except that the iceberg chill seems to be flaking off and melting. It's odd, mildly embarrassing even, that Aaron keeps invading my dreams and kissing me.

Sensory deprivation, I tell myself, rebuking my anachronistic desires. Plus coming home to where we broke all those taboos, and never really resolved anything. Just ran away. Get yourself a cat like other spinsters.

Three years without being hugged, since Jo, I suppose. My senses have forgotten Menna's passionate, openmouthed kisses on my cheeks or hands or lips, although in dreams her child self comes stealing back, exactly as she was. She's generally about four, a stocky cherub whose strong, enchanted hugs reminded you of your amazing status as the dearest person on this earth, simply the dearest.

I could not bear to lose that, when Menna finds out whatever it is she's looking for. It's not that I have kept things from her: I've played it by the book and endeavoured to enlighten her. Every few years I made a ritual effort, which she always refused.

Whey-faced, Francesca held out the child of the universe for me to take, as if it was my turn, and looked relieved when I accepted him. When Aaron came bounding in to the ward, he found me holding his son, and Frankie outside on the terrace, smoking an illicit fag. Milk crowded her small breasts; colostrum throbbing through to stain her nightie; out there on the terrace overlooking Swansea Bay, she swallowed into her lungs forbidden tar as she felt the trap close. The sad farce of it, the biological mother with her tranny in her hands, rasping out: *Lay lady lay . . . Lay across your big brass bed . . .* Frankie held the smoke deep in her lungs and blew it out slowly, as she leaned on the balustrade, like some scruffy tourist jaded from a night on the town, while Aaron and I struggled with nappies and rubber teats, and the nurse coming on duty wondered ever so politely why I wasn't breastfeeding?

When I called to Frankie, she turned up the volume. 'Come in now, mam,' said the nurse, having located the true and transgressive parent. 'Baby wants you. We don't allow pop music in maternity. Turn it off, there's a good girl.' Francesca allowed herself to be led in by the hand. I half-wondered if she'd taken something. Downers, to dull the pain. She took no notice of Zack. But it was a positive not-taking-notice, as if the child inhabited a zone of terror where her eyes dared not peer. The nurse noted the failure of Mother to bond with Baby. She coaxed Francesca to take notice of the miraculous properties of Zack, his beautiful violet eyes, the searching bud of his mouth. But as soon as the nurse had left the room, Frankie was out again with her Bensons, the tranny at her ear. The child in its perspex crib whimpered and rooted with its mouth. Aaron and I leaned our heads together over Zack. I slipped my little finger between his lips; his gums clamped and he sucked with such power that I could feel blood draining to its tip. Touched, I grinned into Aaron's eyes.

Frankie had stolen up on us, barefoot. 'Ah,' she cooed, her mouth stale with smoke, 'Pretty picture. Aaron and Mara and the Foundling Child. I trust you have been busy knitting it bonnets and boottees. Would you like to keep it, Marsie? Be my guest. What's mine is thine. Apparently.'

Her face was ashen. We tiptoed round her, Aaron and I. We knew nothing whatever of babies. But between us we managed to feed and change the little boy. At the end of what seemed an interminable day cajoling Frankie to bond with Zack, aware to the roots of my hair of Aaron's presence, we were turfed out.

'Enjoy yourselves.' She turned childishly from Aaron's goodbye kiss, his mumbled words of consolation. Then she called him back and held him tight, her arms round his neck, begging him not to leave her, to make everything all right. There was a farcical scene. The nurse came to admonish Mother. Frankie denied being the nurse's mother. The nurse accepted this but insisted that it was time for Father to go. Frankie enquired whether Aaron was the nurse's father, which was hypothetically possible if he had impregnated an Older Woman when he was seven. Aaron said he must go and would she loose her hold. Frankie said it was bloody disgusting the way they locked mothers up in these places and let the fathers go free. The nurse insisted that visiting time was over, it was no joke, and she would have to call Matron. Frankie held on tighter and said she was, oh oh oh, terrified, man. In the end, Aaron, beetroot-red, had to push her away to break the stranglehold. She gave the crib a petulant shove with the ball of her foot and it rolled away a few inches. Then she turned her back and stared at the wall.

As we left the ward, we could hear her calling for George. Half-singing, half-snarling, with that infantile rasp in the back of her throat that threw me back through the years. Where was George? George should come and give her some satisfaction. She couldn't get none.

'Jesus,' said Aaron. 'That was a show.'

'Weird beginning for the poor little chap.' We squeaked down the hospital corridor. 'He's got a dad. Not so sure about the mam.'

'She'll come round, won't she? Marsie?' He blinked nervously. 'It's probably like the nurse said, something postnatal – probably quite normal. After all . . . it's a shock to the system, isn't it, and it must take time to adapt. I think we will all adapt.'

'How's your mam taking it?'

'Popping the Valium. I can feel for her. They want such different things, don't they. Are you coming home with me?'

Aaron unlatched the gate of Breuddwyd and there came the now familiar pang of expectation and loss. Nana should be there, for there she had always been. The coal fires implied her and the grubby twin pouffes at the hearth where Frankie and I had sat to hear her stories recalled her. Only she could have kept us in order.

I gathered him into my arms; we fought our clothes off and against my nakedness he moved in a tender storm. Blinking open my eyes for a moment, I glimpsed Francesca's musical instruments – a dulcimer, her guitar and her childhood cello – amongst dusty piles of books and clothes, and Aaron's tennis racket: someone else's messy heaven. Lamplight slid along the curves of piano lid and guitar. I saw them through my closing eyelashes as he slid into me, like an eel into oil.

Morning: scrambling up from my dreams, I found Aaron perched on the edge of the bed, a blue bath towel round his waist. Leaning his elbows on his knees, he was tousling his hair as if something itched.

'I'm a father,' he said, as if testing out this statement. 'My God. Do you realise, Marsie, do you? I'm a dad. I'm only twenty and I'm a dad!' He got up on to the bed and knelt, his hands on the towel-skirt, damp from the shower. His skin was not quite dry and, when I touched his shoulder with my lips, it felt cool as a mushroom. 'Of a son,' he went on breathlessly. 'I have a son, Mars.'

'I did notice. Especially when the bloody nurse kept calling me "Mam".'

I kissed the insides of his wrists, one after the other, with light, valedictory kisses. Surely he was asking himself what he was doing here with the cousin who was not his child's mother but existed like a third term in a botched equation, fouling up its symmetry. A shadow they both cast. I felt dirty and sick. Creeping into the bathroom, I mooned at my own face in the mirror, its lips fat with greedy kissing, chin rasped raw from Aaron's stubble. Under the shower I lathered him off my body and sluiced his residue away. We can begin again, I thought, and must do so for the child's sake. And anyhow, I privately added, pulling up my wet hair into a high ponytail, this has been no different to the way Frankie behaves: we're even, there's no odds.

8

Mirror Man is here, accompanied by a flock of first-year medical students who hang on his every word. Elin and I have tensely awaited the visit of Mirror Man, who will confer on our work a stamp not only of authenticity but also of being on the cutting edge of science. Even our detractor, Mr Pritchard, has freed himself from his customary irony and his private patients to come along and listen to what this man has to say. Our bid for extra funding will be enhanced by Mr Singh's imprimatur. He is an impressive speaker, at once benign and precise. Tomorrow he leaves the UK for California and we have been lucky to lure him west for a two-hour visit.

Mr Singh emphasises that exact mirror placement is critical: 'A midvertical sagittal mirror,' he says. 'Our patient, Anna here, will place the remaining limb in a mirror-symmetrical location – so. Her mind may eventually be tricked into believing that the movement she sees is actually happening in the absent leg. The pain may shrink. The phantom may shrink. I cannot say it *will*, Anna. It may.'

'I'm up for anything. I'll stand on my head underwater if it will help.'

'Of course you would.'

'Why doesn't anyone laugh at my jokes?'

There is a momentary, queasy silence. A student asks why the mirror can't be used to reinforce the patient's sense of reality, rather than to trick the brain into imagining something false.

'Because this is not imaginary pain we are talking about.'

I steal a look at doubting Mr Pritchard. He is standing

apparently admiring one dapper pin-striped leg in one of our mirrors. But he is taking it in.

'We have nothing to do with the superficies of consciousness. What we face here is deep loss, deep shock, real pain, a destabilising of the very self. We are taking it upon ourselves to remap the cortex. To tamper with the neurosignature. The brain's inherited blueprint of the whole body surface. What constitutes the "I".'

They all scribble on pads 'tamper with neurosignature ... blueprint ... cortical remapping'. Mirror Man is graciously impressed by our work at the unit. If he can aid us in any way ... 'Oh you can,' I assure him, accompanying him and the flock as they flit off across the walkway linking the modern Institute to the hospital.

Mr Pritchard, no less, will see Mr Singh to his taxi. Now we're on the move, I think, mentally punching the air.

I wander up several flights of stairs and find myself in the maternity wing. Whimpers of newborns haunt the corridor and a woman like a walking gourd shuffles toward me in slippers. In one of these sidewards Frankie bore Zack all of twenty-nine years ago. I duck my head into a delivery room and see how much has changed. An auxiliary is scrubbing out a birthing pool, surrounded by soft furnishings, walls of pastel yellow. Which sideward was Frankie's? No idea. They are all the same. Pausing at an open door, I look through to where a French window stands ajar and a film of silvery curtain billows inwards. An empty, anonymous room. On the balcony I stand with my hands on the rail.

Quite a congregation had gathered round Frankie's bedside to worship the boy-child, though conceived in sin and surrounded by tatty pals with whom no one in the Thomas, Evans or Menelaus families wished to be associated. Dilly was there, doing her earth-mothering act; even Merddyn the druid made a brief and silent appearance. He was plainly out of it, and wandered away, unlamented. Zack lay jaundiced in his perspex box, looking like a baby corpse, and nearly as inert. Between him and his mother sat bearded George in camouflage gear, one hand lightly dangling over the baby's head, the other holding Francesca's hand. Annie, at the other side of the bed, was wearing a shirt-waisted shot silk dress which shifted between black and dark green with every gesture, a colour that made her skin look blanched. Her impeccable manners veiled a faintingly intense dismay.

Aaron and I stood outside the window that divided Frankie's private room from the corridor and surveyed the scene within. Danny had visited and on his way out had passed us the tidings: 'Your Frankie's got that rank bloody hippy in with her. And there's a to-do. Brace yourself, man, you're in for a shock.'

'George?' said Aaron uneasily. 'Oh, George is all right.'

'Don't say I didn't warn you. Atmosphere in there, you could cut it with a knife. We said. Rhodri said too. We all said.'

'Said what?'

'Put it like this then, Mara. If Aaron don't mind that stinking gypsy's beard nuzzlen his girl's muff, he's better not be surprised at the consequences.'

The abominable suspicion hit me that George was attempting to perform cunnilingus in full view of our kith and kin.

'Him. In there. Look. Seen them at it – *free* love, is it? In broad daylight down by there on Fairwood. Bloody spectator sport, I'm telling you. Even Rhodri won't have him in the Cross Keys and Rhodri's so easygoing it's criminal.'

'Mars,' said Frankie as we came in. 'Have you brought some booze? This is doing my head in.'

'Nice glass of Guinness does wonders for the milk supply,' Auntie Bethan informed us. Uncle Tony's eyes flicked from George's beard to Francesca's bosom and away to Aaron bending over the crib.

'Cherry brandy's supposed to be just the job,' I said. 'Or whisky neat, I've heard.'

'Why *no*,' Bethan exclaimed, aghast. '*No*. What are you thinking of, Mara Evans, coming in here recommending spirits?

It'll go straight into the milk, see, taint it *horrible*. You won't do that, Francesca, will you? Irresponsible suggestion,' she frowned at me.

'No, really, it's tried and tested. Honestly. Works a treat. Shall I just pop down to the offy, Frankie?'

'Tell her, Granny,' Bethan appealed to Susan who immediately bleated, 'Don't call me Granny!' Several times declaring herself far too young to be a grandmother, she went on to say, darkly, that on her daughter's head be it, for it was none of her doing. The shame! Nevertheless she seemed bewitched by the child in the crib and was beguiled into giving it little smirks.

'Now do tell her, Susan. Guinness is a food whereas brandy—'

'It's a joke, Bethan,' explained Susan, and sighed. She was done up to the nines as usual, but had spotted a catch in her nylons; 'Look at this, fresh on today. Honestly, it's no wonder we're permanently skint. Don't take any notice of anything those two say, they egg each other on. Now she's a mother, Mara, you'll both have to stop it.'

'A joke is it? Well. Why didn't someone say?'

'Anyhow I'm not breastfeeding. I can drink what I like,' said Frankie. 'So.'

'Not . . . Is that a joke too?' Bethan was lost in the minefield of irony. 'Breast is best, you know what they say.'

'I'll drink to that,' interjected George.

Uncle Tony's eyes ranged back to the original source of his perplexity – the unkempt northerner's beard. He folded his arms across his paunch and stared, then sniffed.

Aaron said, 'Hello, Mummy. It will be all right, you know. Don't worry. It will be fine. Better than fine. How are you, Frankie? Did you get any sleep, love?'

'Did I fuck.'

Annie's eyes spoke dolorously to her favourite son, *What did I not give you that you needed? Why did you choose this immorality, this chaos? This inbreeding. Why are you not ashamed?* Her green-black shot silk dress picked up the colour of George's camouflage outfit, creating an unhappy harmony.

'Oh dear. You poor thing. You look all in. Aren't we, er, a bit crowded in here?'

'I think so,' agreed George, and didn't move.

The nurse requested a halving of numbers. She mentioned germs. Mobs of visitors were not good for Baby and not good for Mam, who looked tired.

'I am, I'm bloody knackered. Funny how when your bun's in the oven, everyone makes so much of you and then when it's baked, all of a sudden they're bun-mad and you can go stuff yourself.'

The nurse gave Frankie a humouring look. She observed that mams could feel pretty ropy after Baby was born. We had better decide who was going to leave or she'd just shoo the whole lot of us out. Mam needed to focus on Baby without distraction.

'For fuck's sake,' said Frankie.

'Frankie! Dear! Language! Who taught you to speak like that?' bleated her mother, on her feet and poised for flight.

'Your frigging husband.'

'Oh really. Now that is too bad.' Convulsed with embarrassment, Susan apologised profusely to the nurse.

'By the way,' Frankie clarified. 'I mean Husband No. 2, not my da.'

'Ah, poor girl, she's not herself,' soothed Hen. Chairs were being scraped back and piled by the wall, as family made ready to depart. Pitying looks were angled at Annie, at Aaron, at the fallen angel on the bed.

'She is herself,' said Susan quietly. 'That's how she is. And do you wonder I'm at my wits' end?' She stacked her chair with the rest, taking care that the metal legs should not further snag her stockings. 'That's her all over, don't expect any sense out of that one, or any gratitude come to that, all we've done for her, all thrown back in my face, you can't say I haven't tried . . .'

'Ah, sweetheart,' said Hen, her powdered face bending over her niece, to implant a kiss. 'You take a nap. We've worn you out.'

'Sorry, Henny darling.'

'What you sorry for then, pet? Bless you, I'm not shocked by a

121

bit of effing and blinding. No, no, every girl has a right to swear. I've always said so. My gran, chapel she was to the core, she *amazed* us, the stuff she came out with in her last days. Had to smile, though sad it was, mind. Never knew she had it in her. Mind you, the nice nurse doesn't deserve it. Swear at me if you feel it coming on.'

Frankie giggled and held out her arms for a further hug.

'I don't mind fruity swear words once in a while. Not all the time. Spoils the effect. But your great-gran, she could swear beautiful.'

Three of us remained after the family's departure.

George got up and stretched. Sometimes he did not speak for hours at a time. Then he might become loquacious or break into song or execrable North Welsh. He might strum a guitar and melt you all over with the beauty of his playing. He might pick a quarrel or speak of world peace and the iniquity of the US government. He might go on and on about his aborted theological studies at Lampeter, using tooth-cracking jargon and ending on the word *anti-nom-ian-ism*, which meant that to the pure all things were pure; and that George, as being elect, was whiter than white. Or he might sit and gaze at you, silently. He gave a great yawn and I smelt his breath. I winced back in just the way my mother might have done.

The nurse was back. She counted three persons: reminded us that she had stipulated a maximum of two visitors. Glowered at George, whose uncouthness seemed to get up everyone's nose in equal measure. 'I think this gentleman has been here the longest.'

'Yes, but I'm the dad, see,' said George.

How Frankie crowed, sitting there on the bed with her arms folded as George and Aaron locked horns. She seemed to have set it up and to take a director's pleasure in seeing how her farce worked on stage.

Aaron said George was being ridiculous.

Oh aye? said George.

Aaron wondered if this was a joke.

Never more serious in his life, said George.

Aaron, customarily so tolerant and easygoing, looked down at the sprawled figure of George with what I can only describe as a Thomas look. In that look lay coiled all his respectable family's social prejudice, combined with the uncertainty about his virility that haunted him.

'Tell him ... Frankie,' he pleaded.

'Why?'

'What do you mean, why?'

'Well, like George says, Aaron, *if* you were listening, we are members one of another. I mean, he is me and you are me and ... our brains are one brain. Like, you and Mara are one brain. You are making me a chattel. Trying to—'

'What are you saying? Is my baby George's?'

'Well, he might be, mightn't he?' said Frankie. 'Or he might not.' One prick was as good as another, as far as she was concerned. Jesus Christ, she should know about pricks. 'Why don't you both be dads?' she asked. 'Nice for him to have two fathers. At least, I suppose it would be nice. If you could just cooperate. Or you could draw lots. What do you think, Mars Bar? You've gone all quiet. Don't worry about frigging around with Aaron. You're welcome.'

The nurse was back. Couldn't we keep the noise down? This was a maternity ward, not Cardiff Arms Park. Everybody but the father was to go. For goodness' sake.

'It seems,' said Aaron, white to the gills, 'there's a question of paternity.'

'Hang loose, man, hang loose,' said George. 'What does it matter whose spermatozoon got to which egg first. I mean, what kind of a horse-race is that – George Spermzoon on one side of the egg and Aaron Spermzoon on the other, each fighting to get into that poor fucked-up egg? Brothers we are. Spermal brothers. I mean, a child belongs to the whole race, isn't it? He belongs to the stars and the sea. Anyhow,' the ironic crooning tone was suddenly ditched in favour of a cunningly launched attack on the rival father, 'if you can't tune into the universe, man, why don't we get a test done?'

'What?'

'A blood test. Find out for sure. I mean, if I'm A and you're O, and he's Rhesus negative, or whatever, then . . .' He sat back, arms behind his neck, and grinned. I could scarcely imagine Frankie intimate with this . . . beard. Pubic curls, allowed to run rank, longish brown hair also curly but less so. I realised how much I liked smooth bodies, and thought beautiful men who were as near as possible to girls, their curves gentle and their bearing willowy. George's Army Surplus shirt, tucked into olive green trousers, showed stains of sweat as he flexed his body back in his seat. He made the gesture seem vaguely crude. It was aimed at Aaron, whose mind he could read as well as I could. Aaron's look was saying, incredulously, What are you then, a bricklayer? But then the enlightened Aaron reminded the prejudiced and insecure Thomas part of himself that you judged people not by occupations or background but by who they were. You did not judge at all. You embraced them as friends and brothers. Where they fucked, you fucked, for the world was just one great playground.

The nurse cried, 'Enough!' and clapped her hands but showed a hint of amusement, as if rival fathers furnished a welcome novelty in a routine devoted to the shucking of innumerable human peas. She would have to page a doctor, she stated.

I offered to leave. Then there would only be the regulation two visitors.

'Yes, but how would that solve the problem? You're not the problem, are you?' she confided in me.

But I was a complication of the problem. I was the problem expressed in different terms.

'Anyhow,' said Aaron suddenly, as if awakening from some brooding trance, his fingers on the crib, 'I'm morally the father, whatever. Whatever.' I followed his eyes to where the slatted blinds sliced the late morning light into parallel segments.

Sunlight undulated over Francesca's bare legs. She had shut her eyes.

'Never mind moral rights. Whatever you want, Franks, lovely girl, that's what I want,' George announced. 'In any case, you don't seem to realie she's an artist: she's a free spirit. A pure being. She's not a piece of horseflesh to breed by, come on, I thought you knew that, Aaron, I thought we were brothers.'

And he broke into a rendering of *She's got everything she needs, she's an artist, she don't look back.* Shivers went up my spine from the base; his voice melted me dangerously. He gentled down the Dylan song and made it tender, reverential. Frankie's eyes came open and she joined in, the first time I had heard her sing in months. They repeated that she had everything she needed, she was an artist, she didn't look back. His voice artfully gave place to hers, allowing hers free rein until she stopped singing altogether to allow him to finish that he ended up *on his knees.*

'Why don't you just piss off?' I heard myself shriek at George. 'You fucking goat!'

I grasped him by the hair and hauled him to his feet. George was of a powerful build, tall and muscular, and could have felled me with a single blow. Somehow through practice on Jack and my drunken provocation of pub brawls, I had learned to do on an impulse of rage what I would not have dared do by premeditation. I carried my advantage by heaving him off balance towards the open door, where he stumbled and then turned in his tracks, bewildered. Then he left.

Just like that, he ambled off. It was the weirdest thing I had ever seen. He whistled as he went; turned and waved a cute little wave. Was he actually more high than I'd guessed? Had he been stoned all along? I still felt the surprising softness of George's hair in my grip, like a residue.

'Bloody hell, Mars.' Frankie sounded impressed. She looked wide-awake but fazed, as if my outbreak of violence had broken her line of thought. 'What came over you?'

I stuck my hands in my trouser pockets, where their trembling would not be noticed. 'Do you really like him, Frankie? You don't honestly, do you?'

'Why? What don't you like about him?'

'He's scary. And hairy. And boring, boring, boring.'

'His chest is actually as hairy as his face,' Frankie confided in a hushed tone. 'It goes all the way down to his bellybutton.'

'I know. You can see it at the top of his neck.'

'You two are a right pair of snobs though, aren't you?'

'No,' said Aaron. 'I don't think so.'

'*No*,' she mimed. '*Ay don't think so*. George can sing though, can't he? And he's been to San Francisco. I'm going there. I'm going to hear Janis. I'm going to Texas. *Then* I'm going to India. I'll send you a postcard.'

The tiny bundle in the crib had come alive. It let out plaintive mewings and bleatings which became a regular pumping of needy noise. The noise snared me with a strange pang, dragging at a line attaching to my breastbone. All the alarm bells that should have been rung in Francesca, and weren't, were activated in me. In me and Aaron.

We crouched over the boy. His face was a mottled purple, mouth squared, one curled hand flailing free of the tight sheet. The uproar such a scrap of flesh could produce stunned me. Gently Aaron pulled back the blanket and eased one hand beneath the head, the other beneath the body, lifting the child.

Zack shot up in the air with an expression of pure terror. Aaron was not very expert and huddled the child to his chest, uncertain of how to cocoon him. Zack seemed to be drowning in blanket and jersey.

'Give us a hand, Mars,' he said. He asked me, not her.

'Drop him, why don't you?' said Frankie.

We both froze. She sat cross-legged on the bed, biting at a hangnail. Her face looked vicious.

'*Frankie.*'

'My God, you are both so uptight. I wasn't saying "Drop him", I was helpfully pointing out that that was what you were doing.'

I looked down at her child, fiercely sucking at a teat in Aaron's

arms. Zack's helplessness squeezed me like a powerful fist. Beside
his claim, which ringed Aaron's heart for the next twenty years,
and beside Frankie's as Zack's mother, what was my weight? All
my claims on my cousins were feathers, compared with this
earthing in a child. It was serious, I saw, and cringed into myself,
my abraded body still tender from Aaron's touch. This having of
a child was the most serious thing in life. Nothing else was worth
a straw. It was this absolute imperative that Frankie was rebelling
against, but she would give in too. Her petulant slumping away
from her child and its father, struggling together in the throes of
learning how to give and how to receive this milk, was in itself
prelude to recognising defeat. Aaron said nothing to criticise her.
He just struggled.

I leaned forward and took the curled fingers in my hand; they
were bunched tight as a fern, but they opened me wide. Nothing
as powerful as Zack had ever come near me. The injustice of his
being forced into a world where your mother said, 'Drop him,
why don't you?' appalled me and demanded redress. If Frankie
scared me and dominated Aaron, what would she do to Zack?

Someone had brought her plums. She swivelled round and
reached moodily for the paper bag.

'Want one?' she asked me. I shook my head. Watched her skin
a plum with a penknife, sink her teeth into the plush meat of the
fruit. Aaron burped Zack against his shoulder and a hiccup of
milk poured out.

'Put a nappy on your shoulder,' Frankie advised. 'You'll stink
of posset.'

This was indeed a contribution, which Aaron seized on, as she
spat a plum stone into her palm and discarded it among the litter
of paper hankies and fag packets on her bedside cabinet.

'Baby puke,' she added. 'Get used to it.'

Aaron took this as a further good auspice. 'I think we can live
with baby puke, can't we, little beauty?' he said to the child of the
Northern Lights. 'But how do you know if you've put in more
than comes out?'

Frankie sank her teeth into another plum and flicked through the pages of a magazine. I saw how her shoulders and hands trembled. *She'll cry soon*, I thought. *She'll break down, and then I'd better quit.*

Aaron was going on about posset; about feeding on demand; about how he was getting the hang of this. It didn't half make your arm ache though. And it took forever. By the time he'd finished, it would be time for the next feed. I could feel his antennae alert for signals of Francesca's capitulation.

But his touch was still all over me. Vestiges of his tenderness smeared my skin, at the side of my breast, inside my thigh, glowing and fading. I glowed with thousands of lights, all dying.

By tomorrow there would be no trace. Nothing would be left of him on and in me, except a few tired sperm thrashing their tails as they butted their blind way towards an unavailable egg.

'Does he sleep in the night?' asked Aaron.

'How would I know? They shoved him in at crack of dawn in that bloody trolley and cleared off.'

'You must be shattered,' he said.

'You must be shagged.'

'No,' he said collectedly, rocking Zack to and fro. 'I did want to stay on, you know, last night. It was the nurse that sent us packing. Ah, look, a bubble! He's blowing a bubble! Is he a genius then?'

I marvelled at his far-fetched admiration. But Francesca's gaze slid across to Zack and she smiled. At the moment the smile came, tears overflowed her brimming eyes. My heart contracted, and contracted again, as though trying to force something out.

'Don't cry, sweetheart. All will be well,' said Aaron, his throat hoarse. 'I know I've not always been . . .'

'You have,' she wept. 'You have. It's me . . .'

'No, love. No.'

Somehow or other I was left holding their baby. I received the little creature into my arms, experimentally, surprised at his weight. One eye was glued shut with sticky mucus; the other roved in search of bearings, but as if he didn't care greatly, hadn't invested much hope in the venture, and would find it acceptable to topple asleep, as he did.

You were a parcel we passed from hand to hand, Zack, as we rushed from one to the other in search of resolution. Once you went the whole way round the semicircle of kith and kin, your eyes wide-open and roaming for focus, your nappy smelling high. That was one of Frankie's days of weeping. She cried on and off all day long, the tears oozing out, a tedium of tears which purged nothing and expressed nothing, but fell monotonously as drizzle.

'Baby blues,' said someone. 'Quite normal.' The word 'normal' seemed to comfort the assembled company and glue it together so that the fault lines didn't show.

Another time you had been passed to George, who sat with the bundle of you against his arm, gazing into your eyes with a smile crinkling his own. Your mouth stretched in what seemed an answering smile, so that we all crowed and aahed.

'That's not a real smile. He's done a poop,' said Frankie, 'especially for you, George.'

'Babies can't smile, bless them,' observed a Thomas cousin. 'We just think they do.'

'How do you know?' asked George. His guitar was propped on the wall behind him. 'How do you know what babies think or feel?'

'I believe it's been scientifically proven,' riposted the cousin, bristling.

'Give Zack to Aaron,' Frankie instructed. 'It's his turn.'

George obeyed. He accepted, he said, his place in the universe as being one which might change at any moment under astral influence, for one of his chicks was into astrology, and he would accept the stars' verdict.

The stars, he informed Uncle Pierce, are not hypocrites anyhow.

'There you are then,' Pierce replied mildly.

Aaron received you, Zack, without turning a hair. He was schooling himself to wait, sure that Frankie would come round.

You failed to smile at Aaron. He was willing you to smile, or have windypops, or whatever it was you shared with the bearded pretender, but you did not oblige.

'And when do you return home?' enquired Uncle Tony of George.

'How do you mean, home?' Foot on a chair, George was now strumming his guitar, as if preparing to treat us to a concert.

'Home to ... Anglesey, is it? I presume you've got a family there waiting for you?'

'Oh, my wife, you mean?'

Frankie giggled.

'And seven children.'

'Most amusing,' said Tony, his eyes like those of a startled bird. Nobody in the room was without fear of George, hostility to him on every possible ground, and a sense of affront so gross it could not be mentioned except in gasped confabulations over sherry. Wasn't there anything the law could do to expel such a parasite from the healthy body of a Swansea family? Tony's son, my nerdy cousin Gareth, was an articled clerk. He said you couldn't litigate just because you objected to a chap's beard.

It wasn't about the beard, Tony said, it was what the beard signified. It was what you might call the man's moral smell. A lay preacher had a nose for such things. George was, both without and within, impure. What was Francesca doing allowing her child to be held in such arms? And what was Susan thinking come to that?

'I've never been able to control her,' bleated Susan.

'That's the trouble. You've been too weak with her. She's been out of control for years.'

'Don't you go accusing me.' Susan's habitual whine spiralled into a wail of protest. 'If even her stepfather can't control her, what do you expect me to do about it?'

Pierce took a sip of beer, looking over the glass thoughtfully. 'She never did get over losing her da,' he said. 'Stricken, she was. Like a little ... wounded deer.'

'Yes, well,' Susan rushed in. 'So it can't be my fault, can it? I mean, I didn't choose for him to die, did I? I was as devastated as her. More devastated. *I* was stricken, Pierce, if you want to speak about strickenness.'

'Of course you were, dear. No one's blaming it on you. I was just saying, Francesca never got over it.'

'Well, I never got over it.'

'No one's criticising you, Susan,' said Bethan, in her most censorious tone.

Susan, once launched into the competition for strickenness, was hard to quell. She recited Francesca's acts of adolescent rudeness to her stepfather, complaining that her daughter had never even tried to get along with him. 'Fair do's,' she said: 'if Frankie had even made a tidgy effort, tidgy, Jack would have gone out of his way to be nice to her.'

'But she never took to him. I felt sad for her,' said Pierce.

'Oh, so you don't think I should have married again, is that what you're saying? I only got married for her sake.'

I looked at the hangdog mouth and felt contempt. All those times Frankie had come slinking round my dad, cosying up to him, invading my territory. I had resented it; but I had understood. I possessed the priceless thing she lacked – my dad. Her grab for Dad upped his value to me. Otherwise he would have remained a dull, sweet chap, unlettered, fun to play football with. I knew exactly what Uncle Pierce meant by hunted deer.

'Bambi,' I blurted.

'Pardon?'

'She used to have big eyes like Bambi.'

'Make eyes, I think you mean,' said Susan. 'She does that all right. And where she shouldn't, too. There is such a thing as degeneracy. I will say no more than that. Anyway I'm leaving. I can't be held responsible for Francesca's wayward behaviour. Her dad was always so milk-and-water with her, that's the trouble, let her get away with any naughtiness. He was just too good. Nothing to be done about *that*.' She picked up her crocodile-skin hangbag and hurtled off down Pierce's garden path.

'That's it, you see,' Pierce said. 'Her face seemed all eyes, like Mara says. Hungry eyes.'

'So what does Mara think?' They all turned on me, in case as a representative of my generation I could reveal secret tips on how to winkle George out.

'I threw him out the other day. Actually.'

I said it to impress and all except Pierce were impressed.

'Well,' said Tony, and looked at me with rare approval, 'you've always been a big strong girl. And you stood up to Jack. Perhaps this thug is frightened of anyone who stands up to him.'

'Yes but he came back, didn't he. As if nothing had happened. So I don't think that will work. He may clear off when he gets bored. Just ignore him, I would.'

Pierce said he thought that was right. Tony pointed out that Pierce, as a Commie and a Quaker (two things he could not see had anything in common but let that pass), was always a bit of a sentimentalist. Couldn't the police do something about this George? Was he right in thinking the fellow was a drug addict? Was there no law now in Wales to lock these hippies up?

What did a bonny girl like Frankie see in such a ruffian, they all puzzled. I wondered too. Yet when I was near the two of them, I understood. The scent people were picking up came from a mingling of sex with power, musky and disturbing.

A day came when I arrived early and found Zack in Frankie's arms. Her eyes swivelled guiltily as if ashamed to be caught out in an act as natural as kissing the fluffy dome of her son's head and crooning nonsenses to him. The buttons of her nightgown were undone and the bodice was wet.

'But I thought you weren't breastfeeding, Frankie?'

'Thought I'd give it a go. See what it feels like. Not giving them the satisfaction of knowing, though.'

'So what does it feel like?' I asked inquisitively.

'Be my guest.' She bared her breast, which was large and taut, the web of veins very blue. 'Well, go on, taste and then tell me. What's the point of living, Marsie, if you don't experience everything? Don't be such a fucking prude. My God, Aaron wasn't slow to take advantage of my kind offer. And George had a suck. Come on. It won't poison you.'

She laid Zack in his crib and covered him up. I lay briefly at my cousin's breast, where Aaron and George and Zack had been, my abashed eyes shut, and smelt the warm, mothery smell. Hesitantly I laid my lips to the swollen aureole. Milk, thin and sweet, dropped on to my tongue, then, without the least effort on my part, pooled, and I swallowed. The heavy, uneasy longing that came over me, to suck the breast dry and lose myself in this strange reprise of a long-vanished dependency, did not quite overcome me. I sat up and closed her nightie.

'What's it feel like, Mars? It turned those two motherfuckers on like hell.'

My face must have been distorted with a chaos of tenderness and shame. 'It doesn't turn me on: it takes me back.'

'I wish I could go. Back.'

'I wish we could. Both of us, *cariad*. What'll you do, lovely girl?' I asked and she budged up so that I could sit cross-legged on the bed.

'God knows. It feels as if someone's pulled a fast one on me, Mars Bar. Practical joke. They've made me into a woman.'

'You always were a woman, softgirl.'

'No, I wasn't. I wasn't a woman. I could have been anything. I was a poet. I *am* a poet. I can sing. That's what I was born for – to make music. Now some bugger's been in and pumped up these bloody balloons and hung them round my neck and tied me to this . . . unbelievable boy . . .'

She stared at me with mingled pride and envy. For I was free. My life remained latent, open. Biology had not yet grasped hold of me and determined my destiny. I sat there on the bed while Frankie buttoned her nightgown and I found myself admiring my own waist and hips in tight black jeans. She'd always been the slim one, now her stomach was a slack pouch. It was a novelty to take this fleeting pleasure in my own physique. I'd run along the seafront afterwards and get chips. She couldn't run. She wasn't free to wander off when she felt like it and eat chips on the seafront. She had a ball and chain.

Or an anchor.

For now Frankie reached across and cupped Zack's head with the palm of her hand; and the melt on her face was intense and exclusive. Frankie had come home, while I was still adrift.

'Who is the father, actually?'

'Want to know?'

'If you want to tell.'

'Haven't a clue.'

'Is that true? Honestly?'

She flirted at me with those pale eyes, and I thought suddenly, You're sick. Messing everyone around when there had been no child was one thing, but this dangling of Zack between fathers was another. Wouldn't it have been better to offer him for adoption? Or to decide, however arbitrarily, on a father: Aaron or George, and give him the best possible start. Her flightiness awed me. It acknowledged no boundaries.

'Did you want a baby, Frankie?'

'Did I ... *want* ... a baby?' She stared at me with incredulity, as if I had mooted the possibility of some wild perversion. 'Tell you what,' she suggested. 'You have him. Go on. You fancy Aaron rotten, don't you? Well, here's a chance to rear his offspring. Cost you nothing. Nothing but your life. You'll want for nothing. Aaron will be a devoted father. Ever since he was a kid, he wanted to be a father, according to him. Weird, is that. Still, he'd do the night-feeds and play with it and when all the women come swarming round him – because he attracts, you know, a bit like flypaper, but only the sad cases, the vulnerable ones with thin skin and big boobs, you know the sort' – and she glanced wryly at my chest, and suddenly I felt florid and fat – 'they're everywhere, but wherever Aaron is, you'll find two or three of these jackals gathered together, they have long blonde hair and size 10 mini skirts, generally more petite than present company but he's not fussy – and they'll be all over him with their big eyes and their brittle remarks, because Aaron of course is so sensitive and he'll listen for hours and say Yes and No and Uh huh? and not judge because, being so intuitive he knows not to judge. And besides, he's not all that bright up-top (hadn't you sussed? you must have), but anyway don't worry about all these rivals, Mara, because although he'll be flattered and tempted, he won't do the dirty on you, because you're the mother of his child and he'll do anything for you, and put up with any crap you care to throw at him, except of course competition from your Best Friend. Your Best Friend, who you grew up with, who shared everything with you, your twin, he won't be able to resist. Are you hot, Marsie? You look hot. Funny what a blusher you've always been. Ever since Miss Pugh's in Infants. What did you think of him in bed, then? No, really, did you find him a bit feeble, always asking how you were liking it? I've got a theory he swings both ways. Watch him – no, do. But most of all, watch your Best Friend. By the way, who is your Best Friend, Marsie? Just remind us both.'

'You,' I whispered.

There was a pause. I thought I'd just dash out. My heart knocked but I didn't move. I swallowed. I would ditch Aaron – if Aaron hadn't already ditched me. I hated Frankie for exposing me to this X-ray light. Sorry to her, sorry for her. Because of Zack but more because of our long friendship, its many deceits, but its dearness more so.

'Sorry to bang on like that,' she suddenly said. 'Jesus, I don't know how you put up with me. Must be my hormones or something.'

'You don't seem to trust me,' I accused her in a wounded voice.

'Would you trust you, if you were me?'

'We've been ... like this' – I knitted my fingers – 'since we could walk.'

'So?'

'That must mean something. Do you *honestly* believe Aaron and I would? ... On that night of all nights? If you believe it of

135

me, how on earth can you think it of him? That he'd do that to you? He loves the bones of you.'

I pushed my hair behind my ears, hugging myself in my own arms, almost rocking myself as I struggled to close the circle with Frankie.

Then Frankie said, 'Don't let Jack come. I can stand anything, pretty well, except him. He's scared of you. Whatever happens, promise me you'll keep Jack away.'

How odd, I thought, that she has named her son to rhyme with Jack.

9

A miscellaneous Herefordshire mansion, with a timbered core: the new 'Breuddwyd'. I'm inside Aaron's space for the first time in decades.

'It's so nice that he's called it Breuddwyd, isn't it?' says Menna. 'Don't you think so, Mam? Dream. Like in Newton. Continuity.'

'When we were young,' I tell her, since she is showing unprecedented interest in my reactions, 'we hoped that this kind of thing – excess property, conspicuous consumption and so on – would be done away with. He thought so too. That is how we lived. In a dream.'

'A good dream, Mam. But this is a good dream too, in its way.'

Menna knows everyone, it seems; she has been busy tying up the links we did our best to break. She enters into an incomprehensible burble of conversation with a person called Sasha, who ends by exclaiming, 'Very postmodern!' at which they burst out laughing. Menna tucks her hair behind her ears and her eyes glisten with the joke. What are they laughing at? I wish she'd never persuaded me into coming.

And here is Aaron wearing a mask: the mask of ageing which in his case has not conferred much in the way of wrinkles or significantly greyed hair. His skin is greasier, coarsening his face as if it were enclosed in a transparent sheath, and he seems well-padded in every sense.

'Mara.'

I nod. My face feels crazed as eggshell held together by the membrane. Aaron darts a shy glance into my eyes, then away, for a moment off-balance himself. White hairs in his eyebrows.

Those strong, wolfish teeth. It fazes me to think that we used to cry together for pure joy, joined at the root, throbbing in the dark. Does this quick thought shoot up in Aaron too? *I've been inside that woman once.* Or how would a man say it to himself? *I had her.* Or would he scarcely remember? It might mean very little, at this distance. And of course he is the only man I have ever chosen to sleep with, so isn't it bound to be more of a shock?

We will say something no doubt, in due course, about Zack, about Susan. But now he is greeting Menna. Gentle and easy with her, as if she were his own child.

'Fetch your mum a glass of wine, would you, love? I'll just . . . oh, hi, Stephen, hi . . . I'll be back, Mara. Just make yourself at home.'

It's still the face I used to love but a drowned face, looking with young eyes from the well-fed flesh that at first seems rather to contain than to be him. Someone helps me off with my coat and hangs it up. The greetings we have exchanged (though have I said anything at all out loud? it is not clear to me) are so commonplace that I'm mortified. I think, *he plays golf; he passes the port to the left; he has a fleet of yachts. Annie's boy to a T.* I sink into an armchair in a corner while the rest circulate. My drink comes. Menna says, 'Get a swig of this down you, Mam. Is it all too much for you?'

'Thanks, love. It's fine, go and talk to your cousins, do your own thing, I'm fine.'

She thinks I've gone rather seedy looking: sits down on the arm of the chair and lays her hand on my shoulder.

'If you do that, Menna lovely, I'll cry.'

'I do have some idea, you know,' she says gently. How have I managed to bring up a child with so much kindness and wisdom from the maelstrom of our past?

'Hey, chill. Come and see this. Auntie Hen is holding court in the kitchen: it's so sweet.'

Moving through to the kitchen, I glimpse him. Aaron is here, there and everywhere: laughing with one visitor, taking Uncle Tony by the arm to make him feel at home, cracking a joke with

Menna. He has proliferated into all these children, at the centre of this complex of family. Half a city, I think, with Aaron the founding father, as more and more people arrive. And he has to keep dashing from the opulent room into the kitchen, for he is cooking. Sumptuous, meaty smells waft through. Uncle Tony sits perched on a high-backed, antique chair, looking down on the encompassing taste and wealth.

'And I do like an open hearth,' I hear Hen say. She is old now, but not especially discomposed by the unknown faces and place. 'Oh lovely, that is, Aaron, you got everything a treat. Annie must be so proud. And all these beautiful children, a breath of fresh air to see their faces.' They make much of her, unfeignedly. She accepts a sherry and some nibbles, which she cannot quite bring herself to eat.

'Now, just go through your names again,' says Tony. 'So I get it straight.'

It was what I had asked Menna, my heart in my throat. Expecting, longing, dreading, to hear the name Zack. But it never comes. Instead, there are Henry, Cassie, Florence, Juliet, Petra and Lucian. They line up, giggling, for identification, in chronological order. Then there are the boyfriends and girl-friends; and the friends and kin of friends. Everyone is welcome apparently; there is no sense that Aaron's chaotic kitchen will run out of food or that his hospitality will be crushed under the weight of numbers.

Aaron affects no ostentation. Although he is used to antique luxury, and to knowing whether a cabinet is Queen Anne or Georgian, his pride in possession is exhibited modestly, with a rueful sense that he would love to share it with you. Menna keeps diving over and prompting me to join in, as if she were the mother and I the refractory child. Occasionally I sense Aaron's glance on my face, thinking, no doubt, how changed she is, how dull and faded. The great house, he tells Tony, was originally built in, 'Oh when was it, Cassie? 1565. Full of every kind of rot and fungus you can imagine. We like it though,' he adds, as if most folk would be tempted to turn up their noses at a Tudor mansion. 'Thing is, there's room for our friends to visit, and stay. I wish you would all stay.'

'You'll stay, Auntie Henrietta, won't you?' asks one of Aaron's daughters, leaning down and twining her arms round Hen's neck.

'Well, I don't know about that,' quavers Hen. Juliet or Florence or whoever she is has hit a wrong note here. Hen is already hankering after her own fireside.

'Please,' begs Henry; I think it is Henry. 'It's fabulous to have you here.'

Hen signals across to me with anxious, milky eyes.

'A bit tiring for Auntie Hen,' murmurs Menna. Aaron shows his sensitivity by immediately acceding.

As he leads us through the various rooms, with their prevailing chill, I spot here and there a chair, a desk, from our life together, unapologetically worn and scuffed amongst the display. Each of these remnants jolts my heart. How could he simply subsume these precious things into his collection? The scuffed and worn leather armchair in a corner of the library has a still child on it, curled up reading a book. *But that was ours*, I think, and it's wounding to come upon it so historyless. It is as if I'd come upon someone wearing my old slippers.

Aaron does not want to seem consumer-rich; he needs to be a friend to all, of no rank or caste.

'Bought the house for a song,' he is telling Tony.

'Oh indeed?'

He does not in the least read Tony's expression of distaste.

'Yes, honestly. Amazing bargain.'

'Is that so?' Tony looks me full in the eyes and raises his eyebrows. 'Well well. Annie must be pleased and proud to have a son with such a palace. Mustn't she, Mara?'

The vainglorious palace of Beelzebub, his pursed lips imply.

'Hardly a palace, Uncle. They were more or less giving it away,' Aaron goes on, digging his own grave, embarrassed now, colouring up. 'A picturesque ruin. But I'm making a real home of it. For my six lovely dears, and any grandchildren that come my way.'

They all groan. Tenderly. As if they have been primed to play supporting roles round the paterfamilias.

'No but, imagine a childhood here. I'm going to get the stables opened up and we'll have horses. Remember the ponies in Newton, Auntie Hen and Uncle Tony? I want it to be the new Breuddwyd.'

I remember Zack on the grey pony's back, Aaron and I walking one at either side. A peaceful image. I must speak to Aaron about the child.

I wonder how to broach everything that needs to be said, because, God almighty, he never stops yacking. 'We have super house parties at the weekend,' he tells Uncle Tony. 'Totally informal. Everyone just comes and relaxes or does their own thing. I wonder if you would like to come along sometime?'

'Sabbaths are chapel, see.'

'Oh yes, of course.'

These anglicised Thomases cluster round Hen and Tony, well-nigh their final tie to South Wales, to the pit and the steelworks, to the dearth and dirt from which we climbed. The knot has not been cut as cleanly as Annie could have wished, for there is always this self-deluding *hiraeth*, the hunger to claim kin with the authentic peasantry. To these kids, up to their lips in lucre, the pitprops and the terraces have a filmic quality. They handle Hen and Tony like trophies. Doubtless they'll tell their friends, *Actually we are working class.*

As we eat in the grandiose dining room, our faces lit by candles, I am asked about my work. The subject of pain always excites people. They are bursting to tell you about their toothache, labour pains, arthritis. As the group gets into its stride, my eyes roam the walls and come to rest on two paintings I'd entirely forgotten. I'd painted them for him, painted with so much tenderness, on the floor in our basement, the damp cellar-flat bought for a peppercorn. An Etruscan quoit-thrower and a box held by an Etruscan lady. The thrower is always aiming, the lady always waiting, the quoit never risked. Your hair is chestnut brown and falls to your waist. The next moment, the picture on cheap paper in powder paints inhabits an expensive frame on the wall amongst objects of rarity and value and you are a greying woman, holding your arrogant chin rather high.

I painted those pictures. But whose are they rightfully now?

The mirroring Etruscans were painted in the fullness of love. Answered, equal love. On my knees I painted them for his birthday, mixing my colours on a saucer. Drawing with the brush, so sure did I feel. No prior design, no experimental sketches, just the sure touch, the absorption, chatting as I worked. Then all that was in the past. The Etruscans, as I look at them in their gilt frames, appear coldly archaic, an art which has survived its history.

'The Etruscans look rather good there, don't they, Marsie?' he comments.

I don't reply. I wish he had not plucked out my pet name from the past. We are people with nothing in common.

'Now then, how are Annie and your father keeping?' asks Tony.

'Good, yes, good. They have a flat in the Barbican, and my mother can go to all the plays; she's in her element. And Pops, well, he had a bit of hip trouble but they've equipped him with a new one, and he reckons he's a new man.'

'Aye,' says Tony, to whom this meal has smacked of profanity, in lacking a grace at either end and involving partially cooked roast beef, from which blood runs. 'Annie was always one for the good things in life. Done nicely for herself. We don't see her, you know, or rather, she doesn't deign to see us.'

The unspeakable rift is at last acknowledged. The young ones keep very still and watchful, trying no doubt to fathom the boundless folly that split us a generation back and sent the Thomases and the Evanses as far away as they could get from their nearest and dearest.

The host, troubled, offers Tony brandy, which is refused. 'We must get her down here,' Aaron says, 'and have a proper family reunion. All of us. Every single one.'

To bring so many under one roof, I think, would challenge the dimensions even of this huge house. I have a sense of dispersal. The pod has exploded and shot us all in different directions. He, for instance, married, remarried, married a third time, and presumably will marry again. The once huddled and inbred family became legion and the stock diluted. The hopes and ideals we held so high inverted in our children. From the hippy came the yuppy. Out of the mouth of poverty, capital. But then, with abundance, comes a bereft sense of absent bearings; of turning retrospectively to see where we came from. From the depths of Aaron's careless memory comes my pet name, Marsie.

I wish he had not used that name. Frankie's absence fills my horizon. He called me Marsie, so casually, but, Frankie, you came instead.

'I doubt,' says Tony, with such violent scorn that it silences the table, 'whether Annie would ever deign to attend my vulgar chapel funeral.'

'Don't say that, Uncle Tony.'

'But I have said it, my boy. Said it I have.'

'Aaron,' I ask, in the silence that follows Tony's thunderbolt. 'What happened to Zack? At Breuddwyd. The real Breuddwyd.'

At Breuddwyd pampas grass raised magical plumes beside the monkey puzzle tree. The garden was a haven of wonders, where Aaron and Francesca would lie on rugs with Zack, the summer people lazy and daisy-chaining, listening to the ponies from the stables at Lady Housty clop past in the lane. The scents of the garden rose thick and delicious, an aphrodisiac, I thought, glancing towards Aaron, who rested nearby and feasted his eyes on Francesca and Zack. I was weaning myself from him, from her, from Breuddwyd. Or at least, that is what I told myself.

You could scent the droppings from the ponies in the warm lane. Sweet, good manure, with the innocence of hay in it. Zack lay on his back naked in the sunshine, his little willy erect, and peed in the air. We all admired the arc, and Zack was graciously appreciative both of the rainbow fountain and of our applause.

'Ee widdles something lovely,' said Francesca, in the doting style of Auntie Hen.

'A credit to 'is Mam, is it,' said Aaron.

'Oh that we all could widdle thus. Give us warning next time, boy,' George instructed the crowing Zack, 'give us time to get out of range.' Zack beat his arms and cycled his legs in the air. He had been dopey as a tiny baby, inert: often he could not be awoken to take his feed. He must have passed beyond this phase, for in my memory Zack is quite a big, vigorous, cheerful child.

'That's how they piddled in Eden,' said Aaron. And though it was daft and whimsical to see a man capable of rapture over a child's excretions, we were all touched and thought that, yes, that's how it was in paradise. We were all Zack's mother and all Zack's father, so we told ourselves. Dappled light and shadow chased to and fro across the boy's body and the breeze made the heat of the day gentle on the skin. *That's how it was. Before we got the boot.*

In Eden, Aaron and Francesca, George and Flora, Dilly, Jayne and Mari and Merddyn and I, and whoever else drifted in, could have shared one another at will, without emotional complication. It would be rather like my idea of San Francisco. Frankie said we would all go there, to San Francisco, soon, and to India. But George said that wherever we are, wherever our Beloved Community is, is San Fransisco; we are there already. I sat up and watched the sun silver the leaves of the holly tree and wink on the cider and a bottle of ruby wine nestled on the lawn. Aaron pushed Zack gently on a lopsided swing attached to the bough of a tree. He was crooning some monotonous nursery rhyme which went round and round.

Many mouths kissed Zack's silky forehead; many feet rocked him in the old pear-wood cradle Aaron had rooted out of the attic of Breuddwyd. He'd rubbed it down and painted it daffodil-yellow. In this house, generations had rough-and-tumbled: I felt, in the pauses of the music, the chatter, the presence of a throng of living and dead children.

Dad was a dead child. He had slipped away so gently, one small

144

stroke, then a second; then a cluster of mini-strokes, and one morning he was lying breathless beside my mother.

It had shocked and sobered me. The paradise in the garden lay around my loss, sealing me into solitude. I had intimations of a readiness now to shed my childhood, an itch to quit the security of Breuddwyd and the ragtag tribe that had collected there, in favour of comradeship and purpose. *Oh Mara Evans, the Leftie*, I wanted to hear myself called. *Bit of an intellectual heavyweight.* Was it a desire to step into my father's shoes, taking upon myself seriousness and authority? A quiet transient, I sat reading Trotsky and let their light fingers feather my head in passing, their spaced-out smiles invite me further into their circle. How odd, I thought, that I should be in rebellion against rebellion itself.

Trotsky was tough going and tedious but this was the kind of thing I wanted to master. On the lawn bright figures were lounging or prowling, singing different songs. Perhaps the folk at Breuddwyd were not in rebellion at all? Perhaps they were in retreat?

I kept on my rented room at Brynmill and went home to study and sleep. Frankie, though glad to have me at arm's length, seemed afraid to lose me. When I told her of the closeness with Charley, a post-grad, she looked away and yawned, saying, 'Whatever turns you on.' Aaron pondered me with tender respect as I began to take my leave. I told him just enough about Charley to alert him to the fact that I was on my way. 'I'm happy for you, Marsie,' said his mouth; but his eyes said, 'Stay.'

'Bring Charley here,' he said. 'Do. The more the merrier, and anyone who matters to you, Marsie . . .'

I shook my head. I didn't want Charley sucked into this soft melt of identities. There was more to life. I wanted to forge an identity, not dissolve. It would be easy to let go, curl up and vanish into the Beloved Community. Jade was a mess. She saw monstrous things down the plughole and when she was asked to bring a drink, was alternately frightened of and excited by the patterns of tea leaves in her cup, or might be found rapping the teapot with one of Nana's silver teaspoons, hearing the tinkling of bells. She and Jayne were rarely observed to eat and were gaunt to the point of emaciated. Merddyn was a desperate bore, mystical and humourless.

Even so, Breuddwyd pulled you. It called you to abandon outward concerns, to turn inwards to the spirit. It was a soft mouth sucking at me, a tongue lapping, a kiss out of control.

'I need to see what I can do, Aaron. Things need changing in the *real* world. This isn't the real world, Aaron, is it?'

'Well. I suppose it's part of the world,' he said reasonably. 'And I'm bringing up a child, Marsie. That is a delicate task, and demanding.'

'I know you are.'

'That is the most important thing any human being can do. I really believe that.'

'Yeah, and he's gorgeous.'

Aaron had dropped out of his course and was living on Nana's legacy to Frankie. I admitted to myself that he worked for his living. The others spread litter wherever they trod. It didn't bother them. They illuminated the walls by loading brushes with paint and flinging it randomly when stoned. Aaron picked up, fetched and carried, cleaned and cooked. He worried about the dirt for no one was much into washing: and what about Zack? He might catch all sorts. A little dirt might be homeopathic, brooded George.

What? Germs? Were homeopathic?

All life was sacred, Merddyn chipped in. Even an ant was a precious miracle of mother nature, the goddess Isis and the Welsh Flower Maiden, Blodeuwedd, being of course one and the same.

'What?'

'Well,' said Merddyn, 'you wouldn't kill a ladybird, would you?'

'No,' said Jayne, 'they're so sweet, ladybirds.'

'Ladybirds are just flying beetles,' Merddyn pointed out.

Jayne said no, she hated beetles. 'I had a beetle trip once, do you remember that, Georgie? They were crawling all over me, up my bum, up my nose, you were picking them off for me one by one.'

'Ladybirds are gentle, gentle creatures,' said Mari in her soupy way. 'And oh they are pretty. I love it that they are so red with those sweet black spots and they eat the nasty bugs, don't they?'

'No bugs are nasty,' said Merddyn, 'bugs are emanations of the divine. Earwuggers are maligned.'

'But you have to draw a line,' I said.

'Yes,' Aaron agreed. 'You can respect all life, but you have to protect your human child.'

'Course you do,' said George, and spat. I looked at his spittle (which of course had to be holy spittle because it came from his antinomian mouth) and watched it seep into the soil. George was interested in me. George could remember the novelty of my lambasting him that time in the hospital. He looked at me looking at his spit and asked, 'Does it remind you of anything?'

'No.'

'Oh, thought it might.'

'No.' He meant semen. His semen. His eyes were all over me. He liked to prove over and over again his thesis that he was a charismatic. Was that because he was plug-ugly? I wondered.

Frankie reached for her guitar. She began to sing:

Ladybird, ladybird, fly away home,
Your house is on fire and your children are gone . . .

A melancholy echo travelled between the listening faces. A single expression. They are just lost, I thought. They want their homes. They're sitting round here thumb-sucking.

George said to Aaron, 'Killing is all right. Killing in the spirit of love. That is all right.'

Frankie dropped back to sleep and Aaron bleached the loo.

Why did Aaron put up with it all? I wondered. Because he bent, like a sapling. He bent and didn't break. Beautiful Aaron, I thought, and when he came back, I reached out to take his hand. There were so many different kinds of ideal. His was just gentler than mine. It was quietist. And at least he didn't go around pushing his charisma in my face. He lit up a joint, sitting with his elbows on splayed knees, and I could see the hint of his genitals through the orange cloth sarong. I would not go yet. Why go at all? Ever? He passed me the joint and I took a deep drag. No hurry.

I sang to Francesca, who'd collapsed with her head in my lap, that if she went to San Fransicso, she should be sure to wear some flowers in her hair. She smiled with her eyes closed and her fingers reached up lazily to caress my cheek.

'No, I'm going to Texas,' she murmured, 'to see Janis. Will you come with me to Texas, Marsie? I dreamed of Janis the other night, we were drinking Southern Comfort and necking. Like you and Charley, yeah. What's it like with a girl, Mars?'

'Shush.'

'No, go on. Tell me. Whisper.'

'Shush.'

'Oh go on. It would be out of sight with Janis. Mmn. Then we'll go to India. Shall we, Mars Bar? Shall we? Just the two of us – because we don't need anyone else ever, do we?'

That long afternoon Frankie lay dozing beside me on the tartan rug, her face covered in a swathe of sandy hair. George wearing one of her kaftans and my sun hat was reading in a deckchair, absorbed in one of his antiquarian books. I laid my hand on Frankie's warm head and she purred in her sleep.

George said, 'Hey, Mara, you're an intellectual, this will grab you.'

He handed me his precious book. I took its sun-warmed leather in my hands, interested against my will. It was a book of seventeenth-century prophesies by his supposed ancestor, Jacob Owens, who was bored through the tongue for heresy. In his wilder moments, George proclaimed himself the Messiah as predicted by Ranting Jacob. On the page George had opened for my inspection Jacob foresaw a marriage of the Sun and Moon, fatal to the many but justifying to the Few, and the issue of this marriage was to be a Star. George came over and touched the book with the pads of his fingers, with a certain wondering reverence. He showed me how the pages were freckled with time, the print gingerish.

I asked him where he had got the book.

'I'm a bit of a book-nicker, yep, true,' he admitted with his usual glib ease. 'Or a bibliophile, however you want to put it. I liberated this book from the temple of the profane at Aberystwyth. The living spirit speaks in these pages, man, it's a personal letter from Jacob to George. I would say I'm entitled.'

The book must, I thought, be worth thousands of pounds. And by exposing it to the daylight he was destroying it. Still, for once I could feel a faint quickening of sympathy for George. The desiccated old geezers at college made the past a pile of bones; for us it was alive and we had every right to appropriate it.

'I'm decrypting the prophecies,' he said. 'Keeps you busy, does decrypting. Works up a thirst.'

'Yeah. It would.'

'The Marriage of the Sun and the Moon. The Man that is to come with the Woman that is to come with the Star that is to come . . .'

He droned on but I paid no further attention. There was always a slight discomfort when I had been in conversation with George, as if in some oblique way I had given myself away.

I could not awaken Frankie when we went indoors to eat. She was snoring slightly and her mouth was open, with a little childish dribble at the corner. We decided not to rouse her but to leave her covered in a blanket in the evening air. Mari and Aaron fried steak and boiled cauliflower. The blood ran out into the pan, turned brown and spat. My mouth watered, though as a veggie I could only eat the cauliflower. George stated and Aaron tolerantly agreed that, if you loved the cow, you could eat her meat.

'Not wishing to insult your dearly held principles,' he said to me, 'you veggies are refusing the precious blood of life. Blood is something we are commanded to drink. Eat the cow, eat her! With reverence, man, reverence in your mouth. Like, when I make love, there is reverence to the cunt. With whomsoever, wheresoever.' George rhapsodised as the meat seethed in the pan, and it was impossible to tell whether he was ironising himself or sending me up, or laying bare a claptrap philosophy in which he genuinely believed. 'I'll have that bit, Aaron boy. That looks just right for me.'

It was funny how George always got the biggest, juiciest bits of meat on his plate.

'So we may shed blood,' he concluded as he sawed his pink, soft steak. 'The cow in the field gave his coat for the cover of that old book of mine, Mara, three hundred years ago, and is still alive in that book. You got to think round things.'

'Right on,' I said.

'So do it, man,' said George. 'Never mind the "Right on", Mara baby. Let me see you do it. Look I'll give you the most delicate part of mine. For this meat,' he said, 'for which we are indebted to the gentle cattle of the field, this tender meat offers itself to thee O Mara, to enter into your flesh and be one flesh with thee.'

'Right on, George. But I prefer the sacred cauliflower. For the cauliflower hath a white head, signifying purity, and bunches itself like a fist against the evildoer.'

He had the grace to crack up laughing.

'You'll kill me, Mara.'

'I sincerely hope so,' I replied.

I watched him chew, nodding at Aaron to show that his cooking was sensational. Why did George allow Aaron to monopolise Frankie's bed, I asked myself; why had he acquiesced in Zack's being seen as Aaron's biological son? I'd seen George ogle Frankie's behind as she bent to the child; catching me looking, he winked and said that at present he was into arses. Arses were white as the driven snow, he said. I had seen Frankie watching from a window as George and Jayne, or George and someone, fondled on the lawn. Then she had roared with laughter as nextdoor complained over the fence.

'Grow a hedge, boy,' George advised good-naturedly, 'if you don't like the sight of innocence. My One Flesh, we are.'

'I beg your pardon.'

'We are the chosen of God. My One Flesh. We are all of us under this roof tree members one of another,' he informed Mrs Rees. 'As a chapel lady, you will especially dig this. Come on in, do, come over any time.'

Frankie slept on. Her hair was the last part of her to be abandoned by the retreating sun. The midges were out, inhabiting these last stains of light. Frankie looked, from the kitchen window, like nothing but a heap of clothes. I scrubbed at the bloodied plates and thought of Charley, and how she had asked me what Breuddwyd meant. Coming from Bristol, she knew no Welsh. I had told her. Dream. 'And what's Francesca like? I've heard she's a brilliant folkie.'

'Francesca lives in dreamland. In a house of dreams. With other dreamers. Who never wash. They are killing themselves.'

Charley had said, in her young, stern way, 'That is a waste. Indulgence really.' She was writing a thesis on water and how it was more precious to our world than oil. When people hosed their gardens down, she deplored it and harangued the householder on the thirst and disease of Africa. We'd discussed what we two could do to make the world a better place. But I'd sensed a dangerous quiver of interest at the mention of Frankie's music and the Beloved Community.

'They live in their own film,' I'd said. 'It's hopeless. Just a load of acidheads. And a fake druid. An earth mother in the wrong vocation. A blood-sucking swine from Anglesey. One jelly baby in the form of my cousin Aaron. Concubines. And Frankie.'

As I looked out of the window at the twilit lawn, and in imagination quit Breuddwyd with Charley on our mission to change the world, the more I was aroused by melodies, scents, memories, that would not die away. Frankie stirred in her sleep and raised a floppy hand in what might have been blessing, or valediction.

'Pardon, Mara?' Aaron reaches for the port.

'I wondered about Zack? At Breuddwyd. The real Breuddwyd.'

There is blood all over the tablecloth. Coming from me.

'My God, Mam, whatever is it? You've got a hell of a nosebleed,' says Menna. 'You've gone as white as a sheet.'

When I put my fingers up to my face, there is an alarming slick of blood that shows no sign of letting up. They bring me ice cubes and tissues. Someone mentions blood pressure and having it checked. I inform them that I do not suffer from high blood pressure, I work in a hospital, I never get nosebleeds. Only when I see how ashamed Menna is of me do I let up this belligerent programme of denial and submit to treatment.

'Menna, I think I need to go home now.'

She nods. 'Uncle Aaron, I'm sorry, we should go. I don't think Mam's well and it's quite a drive.'

'Look, we must work something out, yes? A boat trip? And a real family gathering. I will ring you, Mara. Lots to catch up on. Good to ... so good to have met up again.'

Menna drives me home, my nose caked with dried blood.

'I want to ask you something, Mam.'

Every couple of years I've tried to tell her, as they advise you to in the textbooks, but she has not wanted to know. I stare ahead, as if we were driving straight at the wall of the question. Nothing to be done: may as well get it over with. But she is careful to ask not exactly the expected questions. She wants to know if there's any chance that Aaron is her father. She feels towards him in a curious way, she says.

'No, Menna, he is your uncle. And ... please don't take this the wrong way ... Uncle Aaron is attractive but he's not altogether to be trusted.'

She slews the wheel in her hands. 'That's something for me to make up my own mind about. I don't take my opinions secondhand. Any more than you do.'

We plunge, without further speech, from one shadow into another.

10

I had to find myself, I told Aaron. Liberty was everything, I said. Independence. Women had been chattels for too long. Aaron agreed, looking puzzled, for no doubt he had never seen me being a chattel. But sometimes the longing just to, oh well, how could he say it? just to be near me seemed so powerful, he breathlessly confessed, that he would come and stand beneath my window in the moonlight.

But when I wanted you, I thought, *you turned away. And now that you can sense me slipping away, you want me.* It seemed we could know one another solely through our abdications, our vanishings.

I looked out for him at night. But it was Frankie who appeared.

'Let's go away, why don't we, Mars Bar? To see Janis.'

'Who's Janice?'

'Janis Joplin, softgirl.'

'But we don't know Janis Joplin.'

'We do.'

'We don't.'

'Marsie, of course we do. She sings to us, doesn't she?' And Frankie went into a rasping, over-the-top version of 'Ball and Chain', which was excellent, seeing that there was no mike, no backing group, nothing but the raging of Frankie's bluesy tones. She was a mimic, I thought, an incredible mimic. But where was she? She stopped in mid-cry.

'Yeah, OK, she sings to us and to about ten million other people.'

'No, Marsie, she sings to me. In code. I can hear her. No, I do, I've got her in my inner ear.'

'*She* hasn't got *you* in her inner ear, that's for sure.'

'She will though. When she hears me. Don't be so fucking square. How's jolly old Comrade Leon Trotsky these days?'

'Oh Frankie, he's singing in my *inner ear*. I don't care about Trotsky. I care about poverty, I care about the ecosystem. Big things, Frankie, not personal things.'

'Well, personal things are political though, aren't they? I think they are. Tell me a bit more.'

As she listened, my exasperation collapsed. Her hair had been shorn, ragged and elfin, leaving her face exposed and naked and young. She was a tomboy again in tight hipsters and a denim shirt that didn't tuck in properly.

Just one little trip, she wheedled. No, not that sort of trip, Marsie. A jaunt. You and me together. For old times' sake. It might be the last time. Oh go on. Midge wants us to visit. So, come on, why not? We could visit Port Arthur and Austin. And Buddy Holly came from Lubbock, didn't he, so that would bring back amazing memories. Did I remember that time on that destroyer? Just her and me, me and her. Well, and Aaron, but he didn't count, did he.

'You ought to know,' she informed Charley, who was sitting at the breakfast table by the window, pushing toast crumbs round with her finger as she wondered, no doubt, about the irruption of this brilliant, haywire cousin into our quiet space. 'You ought to know, my Uncle Llew, that was Marsie's dad, bless him, and our American Auntie Midge, had the mother of all rows. Years ago, this was.' She laid her palm lightly on my shoulder as she mentioned Dad, and I could feel my tears spark, for she had been silent about that death, and I had not taken my pain to her. 'Anyway, you should also know, dear Charley,' she said, 'now that you are – well – one of us, that our family never forgets a grievance. If there's a grudge or cause for envy or dispute, we have to pick the scab until it festers. But if Auntie Midge has invited us both, Marsie, it may mean a reconciliation. What do you think?'

'I'm supposed to be finishing my thesis.'

'Don't be so bourgeois. Charley won't mind, will you, Charley, if I nick my cousin for a family visit? And when we're back, both of you come over to Breuddwyd. I really wish you would. Stay a while, put your feet up, listen to a bit of music with us, play with my little boy. There are some interesting people there, aren't there Mars? Zack? Oh, Zack doesn't need me. He's got all the Beautiful People, hasn't he, looking out for him. It's in the stars, Mara, you have to come.'

I had never allowed myself to be tugged between Frankie and Charley before. But I didn't want to leave this gossamer web of suggestion that Charley and I were spinning between us. Not for anyone. There was a moment when I looked at Francesca coldly and thought, *Get off my back.* Exerting all her charm on Charley, to the extent that she seemed to be making eyes at her, through her long pale lashes, and, yes, of course Charley took the bait and said, rather radiantly, she would love to come to Breuddwyd. It meant 'Dream', didn't it?

'Yes,' said Frankie. 'A peace dream. Everyone just being tender and open with one another. Simplicity and truth. It sounds . . . oh, a bit daft, doesn't it, if I put it like that. I'm not great with words.'

'It doesn't sound daft at all, not one bit,' said Charley and her severe young heart seemed to go out to Frankie, who said, with a hint of shyness, 'You know, I hope you don't mind my saying – it isn't meant to be condescending or anything—' and she flashed Charley a smile full of indeterminate promises, 'I am really glad Mara has a friend like you.'

We plunged into an airless sauna. Flat plains with straight roads, whole Norfolks mathematically added to one another, in every direction. Oil-wells' nodding heads. Frankie at the wheel of our air-conditioned car, sucking on a straw from the Coke bottle I held, beating her hands on the wheel to Country and Western.

Joining in, sultry and theatrical, self-parodying. What sheer fun it could be, to be with Frankie.

We wore identical twin sun hats and sunglasses; stepped out with newly pierced ears from which hummingbirds dangled and revelled in the sense of being on the road, free of Swansea, free of Wales. A nation whose reputation had not yet reached Texas, apparently, though Texas claimed kin with Scotland and Ireland.

Did we mean Wales, England? they asked politely.

We explained. We mentioned dragons. Taliesin. Lloyd George. Made up Celtic myths off the tops of our heads. Were courteously listened to and wished a good day.

Aaron became a lighthearted topic of doubtful provenance; George dwindled to a joke, Charley to a pal. Frankie and I were kith, were kin. Zack, like a babe in a folktale Moses basket, drifted away relieved of the ballast of our anxiety, and we let him go, trusting he would fetch up in a place of safety. Frankie, released from Breuddwyd, was her childhood self again and so was I. Sitting outside Auntie Midge's house, we contemplated two maroon limousines twinkling in the driveway. Twin flags – the Stars and Stripes on a higher pole and a Welsh Dragon on a shorter – drooped in the stifling humidity.

'Well,' I said. 'Seen that. Let's hit the road, Frankie.'

But out of the house bounced a miniature poodle in a tartan coat, with red ribbons on its collar, on an expanding leash.

'Pearlie!' shrieked our aunt's voice.

Frankie shook with laughter. Opening the window, she clicked her tongue to the dog.

'Come on, Pearlie, come on.'

Pearl, her wits gone, broke into a tempest of yapping.

'Get out of the way, you – bird-brained – fatuous – Welsh – irksome – woman.' Uncle Saul, a burly, well-padded man, came barging out in check bermuda shorts, pursued by Midge's raucous Americanised voice, that summer by summer had pierced the ears of the assembled family group round Nana's hearth, dressed up in Sunday best and on chapel behaviour, as if the mighty dollar itself had come amongst us.

'What is it, Pearlie? Saul, who are those. . . ? Go and order them off.'

Frankie's grinning face poked out of the hire car into the soupy Texan air.

'On your way,' Midge said, without recognition. 'My husband will call the police. Won't you, dear. We've got a gun. My husband will not hesitate to use it. Will you, dear?'

'I surely will.'

'Does that mean you will hesitate, Uncle Saul, or you will use it?' asked Frankie.

'Well, look who it isn't! Midge, look who's here! But where are your shoes, dear? And where's your skirt, Mara? That *is* your skirt! Well, pardon me.'

Hospitality took us over. It begged us to freshen up; crammed us with food; it sat Pearlie panting on our knees turn and turn about; it hungrily enquired after every family member 'back home'. Hospitality exerted heroic self-restraint, casting no further aspersion on our outlandish get-up and only wanted to know who our fiancés were and what were their prospects, for Midge was sure we must have sweethearts? Evidently nothing had filtered through to Midge about the mayhem at Breuddwyd, nor did she appear to know that she had a great-nephew.

Midge exhibited a grand piano on a dais in the middle of the gigantic sitting room. Frankie asked Saul to pass the whisky, downed it in one and said she would play if they liked. Ecstasies: 'You play piano? Saul, young Francesca plays! How about that? Runs in the family. And do you sing too, Mara, dear?'

'Only in the bath.'

Francesca at the keyboard belted out the blues with the pedal down and, when she had done, the body of the piano roared as if a bellowing echo of Frankie's whole rebellious repertoire had got trapped in there. I clapped.

'Nigger music,' Saul said. '*Where* did you pick that up?'

'Dear me,' Midge lamented in the kitchen. The dishwasher whirred and drowned out, so they believed, their conversation. 'Aren't they just savages? Still, what do you expect. I mean, the

157

parents . . . Remember when Llew . . . and *you* didn't stand up for me,' she added, more in sorrow than in anger.

'As I wasn't present, my dear, that could hardly be held against me.'

'Even if you had been, you wouldn't have. Sorry, sorry, I'm overwrought. I'm in shock, Saul. Of course her mother's no better than a tramp. Loath though I am to say it.'

'Cute looker though, Susan. If I remember. Come here, Pearlie. Real generous-looking lady.'

The dishwasher roared.

'Those nigger songs! Obscene! Sexual! Did you ever hear the like? And – come here, dear, I'll whisper . . . no brassieres! Neither one of them. You didn't notice? Well, look next time. No, don't look.'

Frankie got up and cruised, picking up objects and turning them over in her hands. A mammoth picture of Uncle Saul with Senator Barry Goldwater presided over the monumental room. 'Old fascist fart,' snarled Frankie. She took out her penknife.

'Shush. Listen.' I had the feeling we were going to hear something significant.

'Breuddwyd!' wailed his wife theatrically. 'My Breuddwyd! Mama promised me.'

Frankie called into the kitchen, 'Are you a Republican, Uncle Saul?'

'Why, yes, young lady. I am proud to say I stand for Freedom. American Freedom.' Saul was back in the room, holding a soup dish and a cloth with which he was polishing it. 'Freedom from The Hammer and Sickle.'

'Cool. So you're against the Viet Cong.'

'Too right I am. Bomb them into extinction. No other way.'

'And Laos?'

'The same.'

'Cambodia?'

'You got to annihilate them before they kill Democracy. No good whining after the event.'

'Saul! you haven't finished in here,' called Midge.

'So that's Freedom, is it, bombing civilians into extinction? Thanks for explaining that, Uncle Saul. You've made it nice and clear. Marsie and I thought that freedom was *not* bombing people into extinction.'

'Now, honey.' Saul looked at his niece regretfully. 'You have to see things in perspective. You never went through the War. You don't know about the Soviets. Let them get a foothold in Asia, and . . .'

'Saul! I won't call you again.'

'Dominos,' I told Frankie. 'The domino theory. They have to napalm the skin off the children's backs or they'll lose their game of dominos. See?'

'Now that, Mara, is just plain adolescent cynicism and just what I would expect a silly girl to say. I could get cross, but I'm not going to stay and listen to you.'

'And did you know,' called Frankie to his retreating rump, 'that Property is Theft?'

He retreated into the kitchen. I heard the rumble of his voice, denouncing his wife's nieces as Reds.

Frankie selected small valuables, which she stowed in the pockets of her jeans. The rumbling died down. Saul had decided that we were just ignorant females and a problem had occurred with regard to a counter top, which Midge said had been spattered with fat and had all come up in heat bumps, it was ruined. Where was the guarantee? Or had her husband set down a hot saucepan on it? Saul denied having touched a saucepan; it was not the kind of thing he touched.

Frankie slit Goldwater's throat with her penknife. Seized a lipstick. Went wild. I watched, aghast and elated, as she covered the walls with scarlet rage:

BLOOD BLOOD BLOOD BLOOD

BASTARDS

WE'LL BE BACK. FOR YOU! HO! HO! HO CHI MINH!

NAPALM TEXAS, she wrote.

*

159

'Oh my Christ, I need to score, I need a fuck, I need something,' said Frankie, putting her foot down.

We fled beneath billboards and past garages towards the Gulf Coast.

Port Arthur. As we neared Janis's home town, the stink of rotten egg hit us as fumes from the refineries and chemical plants vomited filth into the air. The sulphur seemed to stick to our skins, so we rolled the windows up. In this wasteland we cruised in silence. Some areas were totally black; and a car of redneck youths drove by smashing with wooden boards at black pedestrians. Jesus, said Frankie, Jesus Jesus. I took the wheel so that Frankie could scan for Janis. She won't be just walking round this filthy dump, Frankie. Course she won't. She might. She won't. Love, she just won't. Well, OK, but I want to see. Where she comes from, the badlands. I mean, I gotta know, drawled Frankie, with her new-minted Texan accent. After a while she got sick of it. OK, I know now. This is the kind of hole you leave behind.

We headed for Austin and were comforted by the sight of a few weirdos cruising the streets in long hair and loons. But most of the girls were bubble-heads, their hair lacquered into bouffant helmets. At Threadgill's we heard a folk singer perform earnestly. Is Janis here? Naw, Janis is in Frisco. Fuck, said Frankie, I've come all the way from Wales, England to see Janis.

All the way to Galveston she repeated that she had been so sure. She shook her head and wept and talked to herself. That night in a motel, Frankie cut acid with speed. I awoke to find her thrashing about, clawing at some demon that was apparently coming at her from all sides.

'Bad trip, that's all, you're having a bad trip, Frankie. I'm here. It's OK.'

Television light stained her face bluish as she stared at me; thrust me back as if I were the source of her fear. But perhaps it was the TV that was generating her illusions? We had fallen asleep with it on. Turning on the lamp, so that she would not be plunged into sudden darkness, I padded over to switch off the television. The glow of lamplight softened the cheap, sordid room. I came back; sat quietly on the bed and took Frankie's hands. She shrank from me.

'I can see a hole.'

'Shush.' I didn't want to get sucked into Frankie's trip. The remoteness of home overcame me. There was no one to call for help.

'There it is!' she yelled, theatrically pointing, so that it darted across my mind that she was putting it on. It was all a sham.

'Keep your voice down. You'll wake the people next-door.'

'Next-door?'

'Through the walls.'

'Through the *walls*? Who is it?' Slowly she sat up, cramming her body back against the plastic headboard, hair soaked in sweat and sticking to her forehead. She wasn't shamming. 'Can they get through the walls? Please, please, Janis, don't let them through.'

'Course they're fucking not. Look, have some water, cool down. You're just having a nasty dream.'

'Are you the hole, Janis?'

'I'm not Janis, love, I'm just boring old Marsie.'

'No, I thought you loved me but you *lied*.'

The night wore on and on, Frankie thrashing from one horror to another. *About Jack and Zack, Zack and Jack.* Apparently the incongruous two of them had slipped over the Atlantic and were chasing one another round the room, or the inside of Frankie's skull. She limped into a corner and cowered, asking Zack to spare her from Jack, or was it Jack from Zack? Now one of them was staring at her through a window, how was she going to get away? I could understand how one could be terrified of a baby, yes, for babies are the most threatening beings in this world: changelings from another zone, with infinite claims on their victims.

Charley, I thought. I needed Charley. I could phone. What time would it be in Swansea now? Ten hours behind? A good time, therefore, to catch Charley at work. A vision of the blessed mundanity of the life I meant to lead once I got back flashed over me. I could not carry Frankie. The fizz of her company was not worth the bitter, dreggy taste she left behind. In no way worth it, I thought, reaching for the receiver. Charley and I could whisper. But instead and unaccountably, I rang Aaron.

Sweetheart, he called me. Hang in there with her, he said. He'd dealt with a bombardment of phone calls from Midge and Saul, accusing their nieces of vandalism and theft. Oh love, you poor thing. The rain of endearments. The sense of him and myself sorting things out together. Hang in there, try to talk her into coming back. Where are you? Are you safe? You're sure? If anything happened to you . . . both . . . just take care, said Aaron, and his quiet tone said far more. They believe in Vietnam, I said, that's why she did the deed. They believe in bombing children. So she was right, actually. He said, well, they are not one hundred per cent pleased. They believe in American Freedom, I said. That's a good one, said Aaron, and we laughed.

Aaron had begged Saul and Midge not to call the police out. After all, he had said to Midge, your kin is your kin. You wouldn't want your family in gaol. And he asked me, Marsie, can you try to get her back on an earlier flight?

Then when I was back, Aaron said, and the phone was alight with intimacy, we two must meet up and talk over how things stood – not only with Frankie but between us. He never would forget, he whispered, till the day he died, how my great mane of hair felt in his hands and . . . sometimes, he said . . . but the sound blurred at this moment, and I could not be sure whether he'd really said it or I'd made it up, he thought of Zack, God help him, as somehow my child and not Frankie's at all. Zack looked like me, Aaron seemed to be saying as the sound broke up: he carries an imprint of you, Marsie.

What are you saying? What can you possibly be saying? I yelped, but the phone had gone cold.

In a shack on the Gulf coast, we drank Budweiser. A bar where apparently no one ever came, except perhaps the clientele of Al's Bait Shop, another shack, claiming to sell Live Mud Minnows. There was no door to Al's, the windows lacked glass and Al received no clients throughout our lengthy stop-off. A freezer-tank in his shack advertised Coca-Cola. *Take it ice-cold*, it counselled in red letters.

'That's where the minnows must be,' said Frankie. 'Poor little baits. You OK, Marsie? Have I been a git? Sorry. But they did deserve it. Midge and *Pearlie* and Uncle Saul.'

I began to thaw. It would be all right. Probably. I smoked some grass and life mellowed.

We wondered if Al would appear to preside over his premises. Time slowed and we sat on the verandah of our shack in the wilderness sipping Bud straight from the can, passing the joint, fanned by breezes from the unseen Gulf of Mexico. The round, rackety table had been retrieved from some defunct ship's cadaver, and ropes slung round the salt-eaten pillars of the verandah added to the makeshift marine effect. Behind Frankie, a bank of scrub hid the waterway and a rusted fishing boat seemed to sail up its crest, an amphibious craft on a wave of green.

We drove down over the sands, meeting nobody. The car bumped softly along. When we stopped and opened the window, there was a chemical smell. An emptiness. There were few shells, no pebbles, just sterile sands and a grey and glittering sea. I sat with bare soles on the hot sand, the rest of me in the shadow of the car, dismayed.

'Come on, get your clothes off.'

Frankie was out and haring down across the sands to the mineral-smelling sea. With her cropped hair she resembled some glorious, narcissistic boy. She was into the crashing waves up to her knees. Turned and hollered, 'My God, it's *warm*. Come in with me, Mars Bar.'

I waded in but was immediately surrounded by a shoal of fish, bodies everywhere, jostling round me, thick and squirming. Momentarily Frankie had a fish in her fist, thrashing. It thrust up into the air and flipped back down into waves. A tumult of creatures, everywhere, and Francesca lunging for them, screaming with excitement. Now she stood with a tiny fish spasming in her grasp, drowning in air. I yelled to her to throw it back, throw it fucking back, but she made as if to stuff it in her mouth and chew. *You are sick, Francesca, sick to the soul,* I thought, and watched it die before she tossed it back. The water puckered where it fell.

Sun beat down on my head and I felt nauseous from the chemical smell of the air. How had we got here? Why had I agreed to come? In every direction, land and sea seemed to extend interminably. I thought of Caswell, the cradling circle of the bay, embraced by high cliffs covered in gorse and broom. Uncle David on that bench, his arms wide in an embrace, the grey and dying man. But even this was an image of comfort.

Back in the car, towelling our hair. The radio playing Janis up high, Frankie singing, braying, gargling, crooning along. When the tape came to an end, she still sang, throaty and tuneless, as if working up phlegm from corrupted lungs. She set off on another long lament for Janis: how Janis had not waited for her in the badlands; how Janis had made love to her one thousand times, and then fucked off and left her. And how I, Mara, had no mercy, you have no mercy even though you're my kissing cousin and so is he. She pushed her urchin hair back and moaned: You aren't even listening to me, I hurt, I hurt so bad, I am bleeding, Marsie, because I am an artist and they are turning me into just a mother, and you're not even listening, you're looking out to fucking sea and you think I can't see what you're thinking under your eyelids, you know you've got eyelids like a reptile, did you know that?

She butted her head right up to mine: You know, the way your eyelids suddenly flip shut – and then wide open – is that a nervous tic, Marsie? Or is it guilt? They flip down and then they flip up and your eyes bulge like one of those iguanodons. Stop pretending you're not listening, this is interesting. You know iguanodons? Of course you do. Skin all warty – not that your skin is warty, but your eyes, definitely, those eyes are prehistoric. Cave eyes. Too pale.

The car jostled in a sudden gust of wind and my heart tumbled over. What was she seeing that I could not hide? As if she'd caught a whiff of betrayal. But wasn't she the trespasser? The one off the rails?

'What's that coming?' she asked suddenly. Through the bluish windscreen we could see a car approaching from miles away over the sands. A long locust of a car, a petrol-guzzler, making lazy progress. 'Is it Janis? When Janis gets to me, you will see what blood sisters really are. She's got balls, Janis. You are just a baby doll.'

'I am *not* a baby doll?'

'You are!'

'I'm a serious person, serious, I'm a follower of Trotsky.'

'I'm the fucking man in the moon.'

'Oh shut up. Let's go. I'm sick of this. I want to go home.'

'Ah, baby doll. Janis is orgasmic.'

'Fuck off, Frankie. Just drive.'

'You want me to fuck off?'

'Yes, fuck off. Just fuck off.'

'I will fuck you off, that's for sure, I'll fuck you off.'

During this frenzy, the beat-up car had come alongside. 'Hi,' called a redneck through the window. 'Y'all having a good day?'

Three youths, rangy and drawling, outrageously polite.

'You seen Janis?'

'Don't know no Janis, ma'am.'

'Oh *no*, Frankie, *please*,' I hissed. 'Don't for God's sake start that again.' I put my head in my hands.

'Fancy a fuck?' Frankie asked.

'Pardon me, ma'am . . . ?' The one at the wheel pushed back his cowboy hat and goggled.

'What did she say?'

'I'm a personal friend of Janis Joplin. Yeah? You heard of her? Heard of Shakespeare? John Kennedy? Oh, well done. This lady was just mentioning to me the sad fact that she hasn't been able to get a good fuck since we came Stateside,' Frankie's sunglasses fixed them with an impenetrable brown stare. A sly, appalled look passed from face to face.

'Ma'am.' The blond guy in the passenger seat leaned across his

165

red-faced friend. His look said, *I'm up for it, lady, don't go away.*
'Did you say what I thought you said?'

'What did you think I said?'

'Francesca, cut it out. Not funny. Just drive.'

She ignored me. 'I think I put it quite clearly. A good screw. A
good shag. As long as it's good. As long as you've washed
properly under your foreskins, boys.'

Francesca switched off the air conditioning and opened the car
door. Thick hot air rolled in. Blondie was already out on the
sand. He wore a blue check shirt and jeans, with sneakers; was
well over six foot tall and no more than eighteen at the most. My
stomach turned over in dismay. They had all bundled out and
were standing round and over her. Callow, averagely decent,
averagely stupid young men at that age when the hormones are
amok. And they had not yet enjoyed a taste of the Sixties. I saw
Blondie's erection bulbous in his jeans.

I heard Francesca say, 'Let's try your hat on. See if it fits.'

An explosion of awkward laughter. The ten-gallon hat was on
her head. She bent and slung it through to me.

'Francesca, *please.* Stop it at once.'

'Stop what? Too big, mister. Let's try yours.'

She stood there in a cowboy hat flaunting her pale body in a
light green strappy top. You could see the peaks of her nipples
through the cotton, the tender skin between armpit and breast. It
took me leaping back a decade; her bony little body on the
destroyer at the Llangennith dunes singing that she was *ready
ready Teddy* when she was not ready. Her dead father's vest, tatty
and stained, the armholes looping deep so that you spied the
intimate places of her unripe flesh.

The same child. The same need. And my father nearly taking
her in, so that we would have grown up as sisters, and then
reneging, as I too would always, when it came to it, renege on
Frankie. Compassion stirred in me. I shifted over into the driving
seat; slung the hat out of the window like a quoit and turned on
the engine. 'Get back in the car, my love. Come back in now.'

She smirked. 'No way, Mara Marijuana. You come out and they can lay you. Give them a start in life.'

She waltzed found and fumbled at my door. Rage flared, the stronger for knowing her lethal need. How did I know she wasn't capable of holding me down while they raped me? Offering me around. How did I know what she was capable of? My nose suddenly began to spout blood. In my mind I had been raped already. How could she do this to me simply by thinking and saying it?

'If you don't get in, I'm leaving,' I snuffled, terrified, through the blood.

She knew I wouldn't do it. Drive off into this gaping unknown, leaving her to the mercy of these aroused kids. I reached out and grabbed her arm, which she wrenched away. There was a struggle of eyes. Hers looked mad. She was pumped high, amped up. She dabbed a finger in the blood funnelling from my nose. Dabbed it and licked it.

I put my foot down hard and the car shot forward.

She thought I'd stop. Was right of course. Why right? I'd not stop. I kept going; accelerated. The figure in the driving mirror was running, running, calling. I accelerated again. I could leave her. I could go. The minute I thought this, I slowed down but didn't stop. I crept forward until she had almost caught up; then I took off again.

Her mouth was wide open, I saw in the wing mirror; a wide O, shouting something.

The rednecks and their vehicle had shrunk to toys in the distance. Francesca had stopped running, bending from the hips, breathless in the swelter. As the danger receded, as the power rose in my hands and under the ball of my foot, inveterate anger, chill as the air streaming from the conditioner, rose. But perhaps I also knew more surely that it was a fantasy I was playing out. For that reason, I let the madness rise higher.

The power-steering made it appear that the car was providing active help as I turned. I and it, it and I, became *we*. We circled in a slow, neat arc and bore down on Francesca. She was walking towards us, her body slouched as if weak with relief that the game was over. Blood dripped from my nose and I paused to swab it away with the back of my hand. Something hurt. Something had broken.

I put on speed.

She stopped, waited, hands on hips, panting.

Once again I picked up speed and held it. Frankie gaped; she had been asking for it for so many years, muscling in on my life, everybody's life. Her terrible hunger. The car and I hurtled past her, I banged on the horn and kept my hand pressed down. Another arc on the sands; she watched. Now she was scuttling crabwise. I put my foot down again, hard.

The wheels spun in the sand. The car slewed; the engine raved, then weakened; and my foot came off the pedal. In the wake of anger, fear; in the wake of fear, reason. The car and I uncoupled our wills. It juddered and the engine stalled.

Flushed, tremulous face at the window. Freckles scattered across her nose and cheeks. Nervous lips quivering, the pointy chin. *Elfin*, said my dad. *Mischievous little elf. There's never any guile*, he said, *in these oval faces.* Taking her chin in his fist, with an intimate friendliness that cost him nothing, smiling into the fatherless face.

I leaned over and quietly, coolly, opened the passenger door. She slipped in. Nothing was said. We just sat. I stared straight forward and listened to the hollow booming of the sea, the car rocking slightly in gusts of coastal wind. When we got back to Wales, I would leave her, for my own sake, for her sake. *She is lethal. Look what she's brought out in me.*

Her brains could have been spattered all over the bonnet, crushed beneath the tyres, for all I'd cared. It only takes a moment. In the heat I was cold.

Of course I would not really have hit her on purpose. It would have been a violent accident, as the car went out of control. I am not much of a driver.

Of course I wouldn't.

My hand reached out to the ignition. She watched, hands in

lap. Bit her lip. Waited to see what was coming next. I saw that she had handed over full responsibility for herself to me. Having inspired me to threaten and harm her, she had done all she knew to evoke, provoke the attention she leeched out of you in lieu of love.

'I've got a headache,' I complained.

'Oh dear. And your nose. Have we got any pills? Shall I see if we've got anything? There might be something – in that vanity thing.' Her voice was little and submissive. For a luminous moment, I wondered what she made Aaron do to her in order that she could feel secure.

'There isn't.'

'Oh.'

'Anyway I'm used to having headaches,' I said.

'How are we going to get out?' Francesca asked in a little-girl voice. Then it was as if a switch was thrown. 'Hey,' she said, 'you were marvellous. Unbelievable. I'd never have thought you had it in you. What did you think you were doing, playing cops and robbers?'

The hectic current of her habitual spirits began to stream. She lit up two fags and handed one to me. I shook my head. She stuck them both in her mouth and puffed. Incredulously I pondered the thought that Frankie didn't consciously know how tempted I'd been to run her down. Imagined I just went a bit theatrically haywire. As I had with Jack, and then again with George. I think she had believed I would never turn my violence against her. 'Did you take some stuff, or what?' she asked. 'I wasn't serious back there you know, it was just a laugh.'

I made no reply.

'You don't believe me, do you?'

The Texan boys drove up. They omitted to mention her strange proposition and enquired whether we needed a hand to get the car out of the sand. Suggested we avoid driving too near the apology for a dune. They twiddled things in the carburettor; siphoned off petrol from them into us. I wandered away from the cars, grateful for the show of polite machismo that would deliver us from this hellish beach. My face was wind-scalded. Francesca stood subdued near the amateur mechanics, not responding to their timid innuendos.

'You know something,' she said. She had come up behind me and her eyes were on a level with mine.

'What?'

'I actually don't think I'm going to find Janis. At least not here.'

'No, I am *not* going to San Francisco to look for Janis.'

'I never asked you to, Marsie. Probably I will never get there myself or ever get to see her. It's just a dream, isn't it? Childish really. And George is always saying, *If you want to see Janis, look into yourself. If you want to go to India, drop some acid.* Really I think he's just scared of flying and scared of going beyond Wales and scared of pretty much everything. Definitely scared of you. Anyone would be scared of you,' she said admiringly. 'Still, at least we had an experience, didn't we, Marsie?'

'You handed me round like a plate of meat.'

'Only kidding though, Mars Bar. I wouldn't hurt a hair of your head.'

INTRACOASTAL WATERWAY, said the green notice beside the bridge on the freeway to Houston. A second notice said, HIGH VOLTAGE, KEEP OUT. Her posture in the photo looks uncharacteristically embarrassed, elbows drawn in tight as if trying to shield her breasts. In the picture, her eyes have an odd sheen. I rub at the milky, cataract-like spots with my thumb, as if they were defects of the film or its developer, or impurities that could be wiped from the surface.

11

lways the beach is empty. On the rusted hull of a destroyer listing on a dune, the noise of children. Who's the scrawny girl rubbing herself vigorously against a boy? She's like a leech, she won't be peeled off. In my sleep I try to rouse myself, so that the horror of the dream can't get a grip.

I dreamed of you, Aaron, and look, I've conjured you up. I'm fascinated to have you here in my flat, but listen to you, so otiose and tedious that, if your name weren't Aaron, I'd be asleep by now.

'Will you have a biscuit?'

Aaron shouldn't, apparently, because of his girth, but they are rather more-ish. Get real, man, they are off the Co-op shelf. My God, look at your hands as you yack: how they've coarsened. Your ring finger's indented with an absent wedding band. Of course, you're between marriages, aren't you; between the pledging and the breaking of eternal vows. Is that the price you paid for our bad faith: a slipperiness of attachment?

'Yes, it's a nice view. It suits me here. I like to live simply.'

Oh, so does he, it seems. You always did want to please, Aaron. You'd mouth anything to anybody.

Sipping your coffee, you describe the entire Antipodes, taking in perspectives of New Zealand and Tasmania: cities thereof, surfing, red rocks, roos. History of your six sprogs in relation to wallabies. Are you always like this? You used to be able to keep quiet and we'd listen together to that quiet.

'No, I'm happy to stay put now that I've come home.'

Dwelling on your hands, I'm shaken and blush. Your fingers always knew. They read me minutely, delicately.

'Oh really, do you? And how many cars do you have these days?'

Only three? You don't believe in global warming, it seems. Oh, you ass. When are you leaving? Well at least you haven't lost your hair. Our family doesn't. We're well thatched. But it's cropped close in a schoolboyish side-parting: Annie's boy to a fault. Remember when you had those gorgeous curls all down over your shoulders; when you wore that sarong? How beautiful you were and look at you now.

Being this polite is infernal. Aaron's a mouth and I'm an ear. I punch a hole in his monologue, to tell him about my mother's remarriage and her life in Dundee with Alan. Oh yes, he'd heard about that: jolly good show. I plough on about my work, the years in London as an academic, my long and fruitful partnership with Jo. About the Institute and our new unit, which is high-powered, I emphasise, and on the cutting edge of science, likely to secure a whacking great research grant.

'You always were the brainy one. It's a shame we all lost touch. You know, Mara, it's so good that we can sit here and talk like sensible people. Seth showed me the famous video. Made me realise how long ago it all was. Sad. Another world. Look, sorry I couldn't explain about Zack the other day, or John rather – he uses his second name – not really the time or the place, was it, with dear Menna hovering? What a splendid young woman she is, by the way. I can't tell you all that much actually; John is *very* reserved. A serious, impressive guy though. Spends most of his time at Findhorn. The Findhorn Community. Ecology is his thing. Earnest. Apparently he has a pronounced Scottish accent, can you imagine that?

Aaron flushes to the roots of his hair. A nerve has been hit, an ancient nerve which remains activated after all he has done to deaden it. My resistance to him melts in the moment when he blushes and his hands tremble. It must have cost Aaron so much to free Zack from his claims. Because Zack was the darling of his heart and losing him meant he'd never be the same, however many compensatory children and houses and antique decanters and wives he amassed.

Aaron shifts his weight on the couch, complaining about his back. He'll have to get up and stretch. No reflection on the furniture, nice and homely. 'Age,' says Aaron. 'Not getting any younger are we, Mara. Pierce is your man,' he adds. 'If you want to know about John. Pierce is in touch, he's seen him in the not too distant past. I had to let him go, Marsie, it was better for Zack that way. It turned out well, I mean, he did.'

'Why does he use the other name, do you know?'

'I suppose he wanted to merge with the crowd. All those poor kids called Sunflower and Rainbow and Saffron, it must have been tough growing up with those labels. We didn't give them the most auspicious of beginnings, did we? Does Menna ... know about all that?'

'No. She doesn't ask, Aaron. She skirts the difficult things. Menna is a very prudent person. A bit like Zack, from what you say. Cautious. She draws her boundaries with care and woe betide you if you trespass.'

'You did well with her, Marsie.'

'I'm her mam, that's all.'

'Yes. Yes, of course you are.'

'Actually she brought me up.'

'Kids do that.'

Each of us pauses before we speak. Our conversation glitters with unshed tears. At least we're talking about real things now. But because we're entering difficult terrain, we have to pick our way, tentatively. No, I'll not enquire after George. Glancing down at my hands, I see the freckles as the beginning of age spots. I reach for the locket to tell him what it contains.

'Aaron, I visited Susan.'

'Oh, Marsie.'

'She has all these rings on her hands. I counted eight. Funny, that. And round her neck, she had this locket. Anyway, we had this awful talk. She seemed to think I was Francesca. And then she took off the locket and insisted I have it. I do actually need you to look inside. Please look with me.'

My thumbnails unclasp the locket with a minute click. Francesca's hair. One curl. Reddish. Tied together by Susan with a green embroidery thread.

'She told me she snipped it off Francesca's head when Jack cut her down.'

Suddenly we are having a mad conversation, anything to avoid the conversation that would take us back to that terrible time. We discuss in the most objective way possible the fact that the hair of the dead changes colour. We mention Beethoven, a lock of whose hair was removed, and changed colour from generation to generation. The chemicals that make up the dye change their composition. In that respect, hair no longer remembers the dead. It betrays them, like all mementoes. But really this kind of Victorian obsession is a tad gruesome, Aaron thinks: wouldn't it be better just to get rid of it? he wonders.

'In the swingbin? Down the loo? Where do you suggest?'

Aaron flashes me a look of pure dismay. My arm accidentally brushes up against his bare forearm and the hairs shiver at the contact.

'Or shall we put a match to it, Aaron?'

'That hardly makes a difference now.' He pauses; wrings his hands in an unconscious gesture I remember and which, against my will, moves me. Then he says very gently, 'Bless her, she went a very long time ago didn't she, and yes, it was awful, and no, we'll neither of us ever quite forget. But Mara, this kind of grisly relic . . . it means nothing.'

'In that case, I'll just throw it out of the window, shall I?' I pinch the lustreless curl between finger and thumb; open the window but somehow can't bring myself to let the cold air swirl it away. Aaron's eyes are hooded; his lips thin with tension. I put it to him that there is something weird about Susan going out with a pair of scissors and snipping Frankie's hair the moment Jack lifted down the body. Doesn't he think so? Shouldn't that scene

174

be reconstructed? Does he know she accuses Jack of murdering girls and burying their remains in the cellar?

He shakes his head. Mentions Alzheimer's. Doesn't want to trawl through all this. Is looking at his watch.

I've never really known, I persist, what happened between her leaving Breuddwyd and Jack finding her. Eleven hours, while I was in hospital. We know nothing about those hours, do we? I place a hand on Aaron's bare arm. What do we know about that day? My heart quivers as I sketch out the possibility that Jack in an alcoholic frenzy strung her up and Susan knew, and colluded, as she had colluded for years.

'No,' says Aaron. 'It was the drugs. You and I kept relatively clear of that. The case was cut and dried, Mara. We don't need extra explanations. My thought is . . . and I might be wrong but I don't think I'm wrong . . . Francesca was . . . for want of a better word, maladjusted. Plenty of us were off-kilter in those days. But it's all over. Absolutely. That's why I say *Let it go*. She's at peace. She's been at peace a long time, hasn't she?'

'Peace! Frankie at peace? You have to be joking.' And who wants to be adjusted to the world as it is? You have to be in denial, I think, not to notice the injustice, the waste, the lies. And you, Aaron, are well adjusted to an unhealthy, chronic degree. I begin, out of the blue, to denounce the Gulf War, the iniquity of the world as it is; the vicious lie of the New World Order. Aaron points out that Saddam Hussein is a brutal tyrant who has gassed the Kurds. Oh yes, I say, and who took any notice of that? Saddam was one of America's clients! We armed the bastard. We did! Made in Birmingham, his bloody bombs! Aaron says, now hold your horses, this has been exaggerated, according to what he's read. Oh and where did you read that? In the bloody *Telegraph*, is where.

Suddenly we are wrangling furiously. Name-calling. The row seems to detonate out of nothing and we yell at one another like crazies. Abuse, insults, in the true tradition of our family. In my raucous accusations I hear my father abusing Midge; Annie's slimy respectability in his rejoinders. The terms of the debate are filthy rich womanising prat and Trotskyite out-of-date idealist parrot.

'Have a nice cup of tea,' I suddenly say, and we both laugh. Yes, all right, he will have the tea and hear the tapes. If I insist. They are little decayed, although the recording was never all that clear.

Francesca's in the room with us now. The voice often fails to hit the right note, but she makes a virtue of wrong notes, thrusting them out at you, polishing nothing, pretending nothing. You can hear the faulty breathing, her breath husky with smoke. A singer using her own gut for strings. This is for real. And how can Aaron pretend to himself that the person who sang in this way could ever be at peace? Dead, yes; at peace, no. The qualms I have involve the knowledge, which I'm trying to transfer to Aaron, that we were part of the team of butchers. In the end she's just bellowing and screaming, and the only words I can make out are 'Shootin' *up*, shootin' *up*!'

I turn the volume up high and her intense and brooding sadness is everywhere. I see her more truly than the video showed her, bare feet and dirty hair, the way her whole body sang the notes. Her nerves were so exposed, her skin so transparent, that anything and everything would hurt: the tenor of her songs is that she is alone; she is alone for all time in a world with napalm, bombs, men who fuck children, malnutrition and dead forests. Someone laughs in the background, proving her point. One of the Wraiths or the Weather Balloons. Those bloody so-called Beautiful People who moved in when we got back from America.

Aaron picks up the brittle curl of her hair and tucks it into his palm, thoughtfully. Glances at me, goes over to the window, and gently lets it go.

'Aaron, no!'

I'm down the stairs and foraging among the welter of leaves and last year's cones, a scrolled up bus ticket, thistledown, cigarette ends, beside myself and weeping.

As I scrabble around, birdsong spirals from the remnants of the woods: its brilliance seems manic, many voices thrusting out, clamouring to be heard. So small a throat, for the discharge of such power. And once there was a nest down here on the path. A wren's perhaps, perfectly round and woven of moss, lying tilted where it had fallen. A web of down and thistledown lined it which did give me a queer sensation because at first I took it for grey human hair. No eggs. In the evening when I came back from work, I recognised rags of nest several metres away, torn by people's feet or bicycle tyres.

The bushes shiver in the wind. This is nonsense. It could be anywhere. It was rubbish anyway.

'Hey, hey, Marsie, I'm so sorry.' Aaron, coming up behind me, gathers me into his arms, tight, and sways with me there. I sob as I've never allowed myself to do since Menna's coming and Frankie's passing. Tight, tight, I clamp myself to him and my forehead fits into the space between his chin and his breast, just where it used to.

The Beautiful People had moved in, in extravagant numbers, smelling ripe.

'Who are you?' asked the Beautiful People.

'Oh don't mind me, I just live here,' said Frankie. 'Like, it's my house.'

'Wow! and wow again! Are you Francesca?'

'Yeah.'

'Oh, wild. Hey, guys, she's here! This the musician, Georgie? *The* Francesca? Man, you are a legend in the Valleys!'

She liked that, being referred to as a musician. A cut above the groupie girls who hung around with wide eyes and ever-accommodating cunts. Two bands they were, they said, introducing themselves. But sometimes they cosied up to become one hell of a big band. The Wraiths and the Weather Balloons. They were chiefly males, some pony-tailed, others wearing Hendrix frizzes. Tribal music was what they did, they told us, sheets of sound, like the sea through a thousand mikes, yeah? So in that sense being in tune and in time and all that shit didn't fucking matter.

Improvisation was where it was at. Finding your own way. Extending the limits of . . .

'You mean you can't actually play?' I asked. 'You're using my Nana's house as a squat while you freaking parasites work out how to play G major?'

'Take the bitch out and fuck her!' called one of the Wraiths. A roar of laughter. Braying. Slow handclaps.

I started. Looked towards Frankie. She shrugged but glistened as they swarmed around her and their eyes told her she was the queen bee. Told her she could have so much attention she'd be swallowed in it. Because, of course, she had a pad. Plus she was hip. And off her head wild. And thought she was Janis. And had money in the bank.

Their presence scared me rigid, like invasion by a testosterone-heaving herd of bulls. Looking, apparently, for placid cattle to serve. Later the Wraith informed me he'd meant no offence, it was just that, as I knew, the Revolution was glued on the end of a prick. Like, we were brothers and sisters, yes? Yes, so all the brothers fucked all the sisters, right? Fucked them hard, fucked them good. Then all those fucked sisters were fucked by other brothers. Good kharma to the sisters, mind, as they had the Pill, none of the sexploitation of monogamy. Then – where was he? oh yes – the fucked brothers bonded with the other fucked brothers, and the sisters were sapphic with the sisters. Then when the tribe was fully and orgasmically bonded, that would be such closeness, I mean, he said, that would be intimacy like there never was in Human Society. Power. Then you were a cell. You took your good fucking to the mind-fucked world, and . . . like the Baader-Meinhof, apparently, but, well, more Welsh.

'More feeble. More witless,' I said. 'And more VD. You can't even play, can you?'

'Course we can play! But we're moving with the scene. We've all played folkie-dokie, love thy neighbour, nice vibes. We don't do nice vibes, we do the real genuine authentic acid thing. You want to sing with us, Francesca?'

'I might.'

'We got the strobes, the electrics, everything.'

'Yeah?'

'Well, to be honest,' said Baader-Meinhof, 'it's a bit more of an improvisation. The trippy light show blew. Someone's got to stand there with lamps and wave them about.'

'Aaron, tell me this isn't happening.'

'Don't worry, Mars, it's a shifting population. You've come on a crowded day. Doubt if they'll stay long.'

'They will if you feed the tossers.'

George seemed somehow more looming and rangier. In our absence his sense of humour had eroded further and he seemed to believe his own black fantasies, as if he'd taken some mushroom and the mushroom had told him he was the King of the Jews. He said he was getting aural messages from his seventeenth-century ancestor Jacob Owens. Jacob had been before his time he said, and you're not listening, Mara, I thought you were an intellectual like me, but you've disappointed me sorely. Even so I will forgive, he stated, unto seventy times seven. 'And then, at the four-hundred-and-ninety-first sin, watch me, sister. And watch out for yourself. For that will be the *Dies Irae*. It is coming.'

'Yeah right. You sound the spit of my Uncle Tony. No one saved but you and your pals.'

'Not so, Mara, don't twist my words. Anyone can be saved, they just got to open their ears. Don't say I didn't warn you.'

He and Zack banged the drums together and crashed cymbals and tambourines, and Zack was allowed to accompany the twin bands with maracas. Aaron stood by and smiled. Sometimes, I joined in the vigilant, anxious smiling. Or stared at George with mute loathing. When our family came, summoned by irate neighbours or moved by affection or outrage, there were hot disputes between them and the tribe.

'Now do get that pig out,' Bethan begged us, meaning George. 'And all the other pigs. Who are these people?'

'Did you know that pigs are the cleanest of God's creatures?' remarked George.

'Jesus, Frankie,' I said quietly. 'You don't know where he's been. He is just filth.'

'I'll remember you said that,' George said. 'Yes, I'll remember that.'

'I doubt it. You're out of your head most of the time. You don't know the fucking time of day.'

'What you need is a man,' said George. 'I could help you with that problem.'

'Do us all a favour,' I said, 'and clear off back to Anglesey.'

'George is staying,' said Frankie. 'He belongs with me. He can stay as long as he wants. After all, he's family.'

'Family?' quavered Hen. It was brave of her to come. Timid by nature and tiny in stature, she held her handbag across her breast as if to shield it from assault. 'You've not married him, you've not gone and . . . ?'

'No, Auntie Hennie, of course not. We don't think of family like that. I mean, that's not where it's *at*. We are a tribe. Like, a family.'

'Not . . . where it's at? Wellywell,' said Hen to Bethan, appealing for guidance, 'perhaps she should marry him. Or shouldn't she?'

'Man,' said George, 'that is a deep ethical question. Whether a chick should marry a pig. I'm going to give that serious thought. You see, we're all One Flesh here. Each of us being a member one of another, as the Good Book tells us.'

'How can these be your family, Francesca, lovely, when we are your family?' asked Hen. 'We are your blood, isn't it?'

'Well, Auntie Hen, it's, like, a new concept.'

'Did you pick it up in America? Maybe?' Hen made it sound like an illness, one not native to the gentle Gower. 'I mean I'm your *auntie*.'

'Course you are, Auntie Hen. But this is a new concept, see, because we choose our brothers and sisters.'

'Kin is kin,' Bethan stated. 'And that is that. Flesh and blood. It is the greatest – piety – and – obligation – of our lives. It is the knot that binds society. Your Uncle Tony can tell you that. Now then Francesca, I know that you have not had it all that easy. But that is no excuse. You could make something of yourself. As Mara is.'

'Yeah, I'm going to make it big. In rock. I mean, big.'

Select Wraiths and Weather Balloonists cast respectful glances at the womenfolk on the lawn who had come out of love and concern to make a last-ditch attempt to reclaim their lost sheep.

'Now my dad, as it happens,' said George, 'is a minister of the Congregational communion.'

'Is he now?' There was scepticism on this point. 'Well, he should have brought you up to know right from wrong.'

'In Anglesey. You been to Anglesey? Very spiritual place, is Anglesey. And my dad taught me that the body is the Temple of the Holy Spirit.'

'Well yours, young man, not to mince my words, is the very temple of Sodom.' Auntie Bethan stood over the lounging George. Though little more than five foot two, her stature at this moment impressed me and perhaps George too, who was silent. 'Your temple, mister, is a pit of ordure and iniquity. It is an abomination. A hairy disgrace. And don't think I'm afraid of you, I'm not afraid of a billy goat, no fear. The next time I am here, you, mister, will be gone.'

The aunties chose to wait outside the gate, backs turned to the house of Sodom, for Pierce to pick them up. When he arrived, Bethan got in and murmured to him. He got out.

'One minute, Francesca, my lovely.' She went to him, quietened. I saw her place both her hands in his. Gently. She had mocked her aunts and I could see that already there was appalled contrition. She was no better than her own son. No more ripe. Little wiser. But he was a child of three.

I watched Frankie stand at the gate and allow Pierce to counsel her. I could not hear what she said but she blushed and the mutiny briefly went out of her.

I wondered what to do for Aaron.

Wait for him, said the voice in my mind. *Not long now.* I'd watched them, Aaron and Frankie, since our return from

America. The atmosphere in their house was inflamed, swollen like tainted yeast. The child showed the symptoms of their rancour in a hectic temper and unruly demands.

Frankie in Rhodri's bar wearing a see-through gauzy blouse of midnight blue, knocking back pints, laughing with the lads; Frankie pouring a pint into herself, down in one, standing barefoot on a beer-smeared table, hips swaying, while Rhodri's uncouth clientele discussed her nubile features, her quality of being always up for it. And she was singing 'American pie'. She looked at me as she sang that she had driven *the Chevy to the levvy but the levvy was dry.*

And they were all looking up her skirt. She sang so that glasses rang. Her kohl-blackened eyes glittered. The more the laughter swelled around her and the taunts bit, the stronger she sang, until the audience was gradually overpowered by her and roared greedy applause at the end of the song, hooting, banging tables, demanding more.

I remember the expression on her face as she sucked in the adulation she'd extorted. Knocked back a double brandy. Leapt lightly up to another table and sang again. And a few times when she was stoned and drunk, she peeled off her T-shirt and sang topless. Big hit with the local youth, said Rhodri. Go with the times, he coughed. That's where the money is, with Topless, he said. But not all the girlies will do it. In case their mams and dads pop in for a pint, see.

I watched and registered the fragility of her high: I thought in the midst of her exultation, she'd shiver into a million pieces.

The silence between the Wraiths and Aaron pulsed with a violence that brought me up in goosebumps. Whereas the Weather Balloons were on the whole gentle and off-kilter, the Wraiths were nasty and edgy. Pete was an ex-Hell's Angel, whose manners reflected his pedigree.

Aaron and I pegged out washing while music thudded through the house. I found myself whispering: 'Why do you let him stay?'

'She wants him.'

'But . . . Aaron . . . why do you let her?'

'You don't know, Marsie. You just don't know.'

'Know what? Aaron, what is it?'

I pegged the toes of rainbow toddler socks to the line. In the laundry basket, they intermingled with Aaron's grey socks, Francesca's chunky woollen ones and a selection of George's undergarments, greyish with wear. The Wraiths were not into washing and contributed nothing to the laundry basket. The Weather Balloons would comment on the pong of their brother band, but were not much cleaner themselves. George however made a point of undressing whenever he knew that laundry was about to be done. He'd pad in starkers with a collection of clothes still warm from his body and hand it to Aaron or Jade, or whoever was doing the washing, calling them Good Girls. I tried not to look at his hairy torso or to notice that his arms were hairy, that his prick was half erect and swung as he walked, that he had bulging muscles in his thighs and arms.

'He can fuck his socks,' I upturned the basket over the currant bushes. 'Throw his bloody things away. Sling him out. He can't be good for Zack, Aaron, can he?'

'You don't get it at all, Marsie.'

'Help me understand, lovely boy. Come on, we go back a long way.'

Frankie ambled out, chewing gum. 'What's the tête-à-tête all about then? Can anyone join in or is it secret? I will say this for you, Aaron, you make a smashing little laundress. Praise where it's due. How's your girlie, Mars Bar?'

'Pardon?'

'Your girlfriend. *Charlotte.*'

I hated hearing Charley's name said in that sneering way. I thought of Charley and how she'd drawn away from me, saying she hoped I'd break free one day, she'd always remember the tender times we'd had. Breuddwyd was a cul de sac, she said; she'd looked into the communal dream and seen a narcissistic mirror. A surface with no volume. I saw her thin, oval face in my mind's eye, its delicacy, the tender lobe of her ear. 'I haven't got a girlfriend. Why is that bastard still here?'

'Aaron? Well, he just hangs about, you know. He seems to like it here so I let him stay. His domestic skills come in useful. In fact I would say he was indispensable.'

Aaron did not take the bait. He picked up the laundry basket, dumped it through the kitchen door and came out again.

'Not Aaron. George. Of course. And the rest of the fucking ghouls.'

'Georgie? Georgie's a lamb. He's here to stay. We all get on great. There were three in the bed, and the little one said, Roll over, roll over,' she sang, chillingly. 'There were *thirteen* in the bed ... And they all rolled over and one fell out ...'

'He's an animal.'

'He is, rather. But I'm tolerant, you know.'

'He's a parasite. And what's he doing to Zack?'

'Are we talking about Aaron or George here, Marsie? I'm getting muddled.'

'For Pete's sake.'

'And Pete too?'

'You should be ashamed,' I told her in a frenzied whisper. I sounded like my mother. But underneath I was scared, as if I'd caught Aaron's fear. 'I think you need help.'

Her eyes narrowed. 'Ah, sweet. And you think you've helped me? That was helpful, when you tried to run me down in the little old US of A, Mars. Yeah, the ultimate painkiller. And you stopped me seeing Janis. Yes, you fucking did, Marsie. That was all I really wanted. You knew that. Oh yeah and that was helpful too when you and Aaron were screwing the shit out of each other while I was having Zack. My God, that was helpful.'

'Mara, leave it,' said Aaron with desperate quietness. 'Just leave it.'

If all I could do for him was to leave it, I would comply. He would think, when the time came, Marsie was there, Marsie stood by me. She showed some wisdom, stability. Yet my habitual selfishness was riven with concern. It was as if Aaron had placed himself between Frankie and her own damage to absorb the bruises for her. There was a cigarette burn on the inside of his wrist. I hadn't asked how he came by it. He allowed her to emasculate him in everyone's eyes, and wasn't that courage? Perhaps I loved Aaron more honourably then than ever before or since. For his own sake; for Zack's; for hers.

'I saw Jack off for you, best girl, and I'll get rid of him.'

'You think so, do you. Let me tell you, Mara, you know nothing. Nothing.'

I stomped indoors to where George was lounging with splayed legs on a mattress, plucking at a guitar with fingerpickers. He wiggled them at me like talons. I thought of the horny fingertips of his other hand. From the hall, where Nana had kept porcelain figures on a small, lace-covered sideboard, one of the Weather Balloons was playing around with a microphone. Panting into it like a dog. The damp rooms, all wired to the mike, echoed with the amplified chuff-a-chuff sound, as if an unseen animal were pursuing us.

'I want to speak to you, George.'

'Come and sit by me then. Come on, pussy, pussy.' He patted the space beside him, and played a ripple of notes, mellow and exact, like a lute. Then cascaded them together, an innuendo, that reached beyond the listener's heart into the sex and vibrated against your skin, and the thing was that he knew. George looked at you and knew. *Womb fascination*, I'd heard him call it. In a session with the Wraiths, he had outlined the best technique for laying a shy girl. *Sing to her all moony and croony. Lay her on her right side so her heart doesn't thunder.*

As he took my measure, I realised again that George was not a stupid man. His bulk and easy slouch, and the affected garbage he talked, made it possible for him to camouflage his antennae. But they were always there, swinging around looking for prey. He was sensitive and manipulative, I thought, as dictators are. Or as very weak, very needy people are, and they are the most dangerous of all.

I watched his thick thumb dally on the top string of the guitar and linger before he struck the chord. Slow, building expectation. Looking at me, saying with his eyes, *This one's for you and I will have you too.* He plays on us all, I thought. He's like – what is he like? – and my eyes snagged on his beard which he seemed to be growing, or not bothering to trim. He's like a patriarch, I thought. Fucking hell. He's like the father of this family, isn't he? The high-status male in the ape troop. The one with access to all the inflamed cunts. Yes. Except mine. Me you can't have.

The panting continued, speeding up, and then the guy began to make weird moaning noises down the wire.

'Look now, Mara, this is the way it is,' George said in a quiet, serious tone. 'This is the Beloved Community. We love each other here. You ask me why? Well, man, I can't answer that. In love there are no whys and wherefores. You can hold back. Or you can come in. You're a free spirit, we know that.'

'That is such a con, George,' I said. 'Like, when the Balloons smashed all my Nana's crockery the other night – when they got into a fight – that was, aah, the *Beloved Community*, was it? That was a love-in, when Pete broke that guy's arm? What was it about Anglesey you didn't like, George?'

'You act bullish and ballsy, Mara, but I think there's just a sweet little pink marshmallow inside you. Come and show us your marshmallow.'

With a raucous, cynical laugh, Frankie let herself topple on the mattress, draping herself over George. She had a bottle of Cointreau to her lips. His hand crawled under her top and snaked round her breast. My face burned as he flexed his knuckles and joints within the sheath of green material. In came Aaron and did not blench. 'I'll put the kettle on,' he said tonelessly. 'You want a cup of tea, Mara?'

'Coffee, please, if it's no trouble,' I answered in a formal voice. The Weather Balloonman with the mike had lost control of it or drifted away, leaving it to emit a high-pitched squeal. Our distressed politeness suddenly staggered me. Aaron could enter this lubricious hell and suggest putting the kettle on, while those two are . . . probably, I thought, without turning . . . copulating on the filthy mattress on Nana's floor? Aaron stood at the kitchen window, hands gripping the draining board, tears washing down his face. I came round to his side, silently, laid my forehead on the top of his arm. He stiffened as I touched him, hating to be seen to weep. I turned him round to face me and took him in my arms. A cousinly hug. I took his face between my hands. Kissed the salt wet beneath his eyes. Nothing was said.

From the other room came the thunder of drums and bass. The Wraiths were tuning up. The fact that they were stoned aggravated the problem of their uncertain pitch and their tuning sessions could go on for an hour or more – either equably or with increasing tension that would end in a fight, depending on what they'd taken. I shut the door. In the kitchen there was a qualified stillness.

Which didn't last.

'Man, I'm shagged out,' George complained in the doorway, tucking in his shirt. 'Let's all go to bed. You come with us, Mara. Come on, Pete says he wants your holier-than-thou fucking lips to kiss the dick of his soul. I believe those were his exact words. Only quoting mind. And melon titties, he says. He reckons you are superfuckingsexual, Mara, once a guy can work your tight-ass girdle off. Only passing on what I've been told.'

'Get stuffed.'

'George, leave her be. She doesn't want that shit.'

'Oh aye, of course, you and Aaron have some kind of incest thing going. You could do with loosening up, you know that, Mara?'

'I've got to pick up Zack soon from my mother's,' said Aaron, as if this were a mundane day in a normal household. 'Then he's got his riding class.'

Aaron and I walked behind Zack on his grey pony, a round-bellied Shetland with a long mane, neatly combed. The little boy sat bolt upright with elated pride in his eyes but a pride that was speckled with fear, just enough to add spice to the outing. He was up so high. We followed like the retinue of a tiny prince, as a girl from the riding school led the pony down the lane, her young sister at Zack's heel on the other side.

'What are you going to do, Aaron?'

'I'm stuck.'

'Can't you make him go? Get Danny over and Rhodri and the boys and just throw them all out if necessary? And if that doesn't work, call the police. They have their uses.'

'What rights do I have?' he asked, gently.

'Well, surely, some.'

There was a spell in the closeness, as we accompanied the child, subdued by joy in his pony to an uncharacteristic docility. The dream rose of having Aaron and Zack to live with me, of taking Francesca's place. When he'd been a baby, I'd bonded, hadn't I, as if he were my own? And Frankie hadn't. The fact that the boy was rude and ungovernable, disliked me from some visceral awareness that I was not to be trusted with his father, was easily bored and itching to slap him in his tantrums, did not hinder that dream.

'OK then, you can't stay there. So leave the tribe to stew in its own primeval marinade, Aaron. You're welcome to come and stay with me as long as you like. You really are. Bring Zack.' I phrased it as a favour I was ready to do him and his son. 'I think you have to, don't you? I mean, you have to get Zack out of that zoo? What's he going to turn into?'

Aaron linked arms. We walked in rhythm with one another and with Zack's little riding hat as it bobbed up and down on the pony. Did Frankie actually want him anyway? Once he was with me, perhaps Zack and I would learn to like each other? We were approaching the common now, the bracken going an autumn ochre colour, blackberries already out on the briars. I had the heady hallucination that we were a family, a complete human unit, something cobbled together but perfect. As perfect as it gets.

'Hey, Dada, can you see me? Are you watching?'

'We're watching, love. You're doing great. We're watching, aren't we, Mars?'

'We're watching, Zack,' I echoed. 'Fantastic. Yeah.'

'I'll just say this,' I murmured to Aaron, so that he had to bend his head to mine. 'No, let me just say one thing, then I'll shut up. OK, so Breuddwyd isn't yours. So Zack likes George. But you're wretched, Aaron. Wretched. The needles. The squalour. The filthy fucking noise. What if one of those Wraiths ODs? And the stuff they shoplift. What if they're busted? Come on, Aaron, *think*. In the long run, Zack will suffer. If you don't want to bring him to me, take him to your mam. She adores him, doesn't she? Take him to any one of the family and get some space. It'll be better for all of you. Just say you'll come back when things are sorted.'

The rider was turning for home. His cheeks were flushed, his eyes bright and wide. The pony snorted softly as it passed us by and the smell of leather and creature reassured with a simplicity we could momentarily borrow.

'I aren't tired,' Zack protested.

'What do you fancy for tea?'

'Chips. Ride on,' he added grandly, and clicked his tongue.

'Yes, Mars, but you keep forgetting. He isn't mine.'

'But Aaron, he is, he is yours. You've been his dad since he was born, you've done all the caring, more than any father I know. Doesn't that count for anything?'

'No. Because if we wrangle over him, Zack's life will be ruined. More than it is already.'

Frankie was in the kitchen, looking at a spatula in a daze as if it and she were meeting for the first time. She seemed to be inwardly debating its function and origin. Zack hurtled in: 'Mam! Mam!' Throwing himself into Frankie's arms, he gave her an ecstatic account of the pony and how the pony knew him now, it was his friend, why didn't she come and see? why? why didn't Porge come too? where were his chips? Would Porge make his chips? He nestled up to her, tired, and sucked his thumb.

George could be seen zombified in the back room. Pete was playing a spaced-out, tuneless dirge. I closed the intervening doors to shut them into their trip and out of the child's view.

'Porge is having a nice nap,' Aaron said. He rolled up his sleeves and began to peel potatoes.

'I can't cook,' mused Frankie, still entranced with the spatula.

'It's just a fucking spatula, Frankie, get a grip,' I said.

'Is it? I can't cook though, can I, lamb, darling, doughnut, poppet, poppy seed, pumpkin?'

'You can, Mam, you can. You can do fish fingers and you can do toast. And tomato sauce, lovely.' Loyally, Zack clambered on to Frankie's lap and rested his head on her throat, giving her his fingertips to lick clean of honey. She sucked each finger and exclaimed over how good he tasted. How special and sweet. She looked into his eyes in wonderment. 'My mam can cook anyhow,' Zack beetled his brows at me, as though I had personally come in and denounced Frankie, accusing her of lacking essential maternal arts.

He sucked the remnant of a cot sheet as he scowled at me. 'You – Auntie – fuck off now.'

'Hey, you little horror, don't be rude to Mara,' said Aaron. 'Say sorry.'

Zack swerved his head away from me and knelt up on Frankie's lap, crooking his arm round her head.

'We're going to a festival, aren't we, aren't we? In Porge's lovely, lovely van.' Frankie rocked Zack to and fro, receiving and returning his wet kisses. 'But before that,' she said and smiled over the child's blond head, 'there's going to be a nice little *Blitzkrieg.* 'Cos our generation's been betrayed, do you know that, Marsie, by bloodsuckers and thieves, know what I mean, Marsie, like Annie, like, say, the whole bloody lot of blood kin, hey this is a whole new meaning for blood lines, Mars Bar . . .' and on and on she went, parroting George's philosophy. The child slept with a flushed face, his honeyed mouth open and sticky against her breast.

12

The shutters of Breuddwyd were drawn and the curtains closed. From the lane you could see how our grandmother's net curtains, in which she had taken a vigorous pride, were yellowing behind windows festooned with cobwebs. The gate had disappeared and the lawn grew wild and high. Once the grass was reddened by a swathe of blood, and one of the Beloved Community had to be ambulanced to hospital. Pete, high on speed, had scythed down all of Nana's towering pampas grass; after the last thick stalk had fallen, he had reeled round with the scythe and caught his own foot with the blade.

Something ought to be done, it must be done, said local people. They will murder each other or us. We are not safe in our beds, they said. Another time there was a deafening explosion and the police were called out, only to be told that one of the Wraiths had hurled an amplifier across the room at the climax of a song. Somehow the needles and dope were spirited away into the bracken behind the houses. But the cannabis crop was found, which had been growing there, to the amazement of the Community, completely unbeknownst. That is cannabis? Wow! Really? Hey, Frankie, apparently this is cannabis. Did your nan smoke weed then? We've never seen it before. Well, not knowingly. The Beloved Community is against all chemicals. Even cough mixture.

Francesca screwed up her eyes against the daylight. The Community stayed indoors most of the time and watched TV, huddled into its dreamy womb. But the womb was disquiet. It rang with fratricidal and infantile strife. Bottles thrown. Fighting over women. Women fighting over the men who were fighting over them.

Frankie phoned asking for sweets. *Sweeties*, Frankie lisped, like a child, but with a raw craving. Make a list, she said. Dolly mixtures she wanted, jelly beans, sherbet like we used to have, lollies, the green and red ones, can you get those nowadays? And lots and lots of Mars Bars. When can you bring them? I need them now, she insisted. *Please Marsie*. I said I couldn't possibly bring them now. Surely one of them could . . . ? No, they couldn't. They were all fucking out of it. But, Frankie, I've a job to do. I can't just bugger off to buy you sweeties. She began to weep.

I arrived at lunch with the sweets. No one was answering the bell at Breuddwyd, so I left the Lipton's bag by the door.

'Did you get the sweets?'

'What sweets?'

'The sweets you asked for. I left them at the door.'

'I didn't ask for sweets. Oh, hang on, yes I did. No, it was too late.'

'How do you mean, too late?'

'Oh, never mind. Thanks Marsie. Anyway. Auntie Hen is bringing me sweeties now so you needn't bother. And homemade cookies with hundreds and thousands and butterfly cakes. She leaves them at the bottom of the path. So she needn't see the Wraiths. She's scared of the Wraiths.'

'Can't blame her.'

'No, well, it needn't concern you, need it, Marsie, your work is so important.'

'Come round,' said Aaron. 'She needs you.'

'God, I have work to do. I have a life.'

'Marsie, please.'

'Look, I don't like George. He is weird. I don't like what's going on. It stinks there, Aaron. I hate it.'

'But please.'

Frankie was staggering round with her guitar, singing off-key, then looking astounded that her voice was coming out so untrue.

Why was she doing that, she needed to know. Why was she playing out of time? Or perhaps she wasn't out of time, she said hopefully. Perhaps this was time. Is this time, Marsie? We were in Texas at the wrong time, she said, that's the thing, we should've gone earlier when Janis was there.

Our grandmother's hearth was dead. The pouffe was smeared with brown, which might have been mud or might have been shit. Some black tarry muck stained the rug and there was a distinct smell of piss.

'Where is Zack?'

'I can't play,' she moaned. 'I'm no good. Why can't I play?' she asked me with puzzled eyes. 'Marsie, I need to know. Why can't I play?'

'Cos you're fucking wasted. Where is Zack?'

'Zack?'

'Bloody Zack.'

'Round at his fucking father's.'

'What?'

'Marsie, do you still love me? Do you? Why don't you come and see me any more? Don't you like dark places?'

She strained her eyes at me in the gloom. Asked me what I did in the world out there. Wasn't I afraid of the light? Did I know there was nuclear dust in the light? It was a fucking conspiracy. If she played certain tunes, she confided, the radiation would get worse: it would seriously damage the health of a whole generation of innocent children. She wouldn't play those notes. Ever again. Francesca's gaze strayed to the gap between the shutters, and eventually she sidled up and put her eye to it. It was as if she peered at her own compromised life out there. *We were so close,* she said. *I wish we could be children again, Marsie, just you and me.*

I thought, putting my arm lightly round her shoulders, how slight her body had become beneath the thin muslin.

'We need to grow up now,' I said. 'We can still be close.'

'No. They won't let us. You are one of Them now.'

'Look,' I said, 'you need to clean up in here.'

'Aaron won't clean any more.'

'Well, why should he?'

She bit her lip. Said there was no point anyway. Her hair needed washing: it was greasy and she kept sucking and biting the ends.

'You should sort things out. For the child's sake. Where *is* Zack? Is he playing somewhere?'

'I told you.'

'You said: at his father's.'

She had lost interest in me. Wanted to know if I had sweets for her. She was desperate for sweets, she said. She didn't want interrogating.

'Only, it doesn't make sense, does it, saying he's at his father's. His father lives here, doesn't he?'

'Nah.'

'You mean your stepfather's?'

'I mean his father's.'

'Jack?'

'Him.'

'But Frankie, are you saying that *Jack* is Zack's father?'

'Oh fuck off, Marsie, believe what you like. You always did. So fucking much you never wanted to see. Why should anything be different now?'

She splayed her fingers on my collarbone and thrust me hard away.

I said, 'Oh Frankie. Oh love.'

Frankie was fighting Pete for saying she had pitted skin. Weeping violently. *Look at your own skin, you fucking warthog. Mine are just freckles.* Then she went and hid in the coal hole, where Aaron went and sat with her, and then George went and sat with them. Sobbing that she was ugly, she wanted to get married, but no one would marry her. I'll marry you, lovely girl, said Aaron. She's already given, man, to me, said George. We don't need no fucking certificate. And if you're ugly, then give me ugly, the earth is ugly, the stars are ugly and all that has life and breath and a cock and sweet tender honey-breasts is ugly. Then Frankie began to wail that she had no breasts. She was breastless. She was not a woman, said Frankie. And if he loved her so much, why did he fuck around with Jade and Moonshine and Mari and all those girls? Why did he wound her, why did Aaron wound her? Her tears ran down her cheeks like a child's, and Zack called down the steps into the coal hole. Mam was coming, she called back, go and play. She felt so bad, she needed to shoot up, she said. Because George wanted other women. And she had to have other men because George wanted the others and because, if Aaron married her, she'd be trapped, worse than down this coal hole, far, far worse; he'd make her into nothing but a fucking mop.

'Mam. Why you crying down this hole?'

'Mam's not crying, she's laughing. Go and play on the swing. I don't want to be a mop, I want to be a guitar. I mean, play a guitar. Look at me, I can't play any more and if I can't play, I don't want to go on living.'

The child's face was a pale moon at the top of the dark, coal-smelling cave.

'Get rid of Pete,' she snivelled. 'He says I've got a pitted face.'

'Yeah, but he is family.'

'Shit, he's not *my* family.'

'Hey, baby, if you want me for yourself, I will come to you and be with you and you alone. But can you take that?' asked George, because, as he told her, he was one charismatic man, and he would lie on her heavy and he would want her to be his woman and his alone, and if he said I want you now, she must come now, and he would crush her ribs, so hard would he weigh her down, was she ready for that?

'Piss off, George, that is bullshit,' said Frankie. 'Pete is to go. Unless you tell him to go, I'm not leaving my Nana's coal hole. I'm not going to be told I'm not a woman. I am a woman. I'm a woman just as much as Marsie's a woman. Aren't I, Aaron? Am I or aren't I?'

Aaron said: 'I'm not standing for this. You're going to have to grow up. You are the mother of a child. Frankie, you are twenty-four years old. Come up when you're ready.' He started to scramble out of the hole, towards the face of Zack who was still hanging there in that artificial night like a frail paper lantern. 'It's all right, Zack. Let's go and play.' He saw me sitting in a quiet grey dress that I wore for work with the child on my lap, holding him round the waist to stop him going down.

'Oh it's all right for you!' Frankie's voice screamed from the coal hole. 'Mr Nice Guy! Mr Clean. Mr Short Fingernails. Yeah Aaron, I'm going to slash my wrists down here. And I'm going to do it good. And that is not acne, you bastards, that is chickenpox, is that, it's scars. From when I was a child. Mara gave me that.'

George said, in a gentle voice: 'Francesca, I can't make it without you.'

'Shit.'

'No. You're wrong. You gave me birth.' The coals chinked as he manoeuvred himself towards her. 'I am not messing you around, Francesca. Will you come?'

There was a long pause. They seemed to be snogging down there in the underworld. In the filth and dust. They'd couple anywhere, I thought. But wasn't there a limit to where you could copulate? The coal in your back, the muck in your orifices? You could hear them coughing. But perhaps if you were that far gone, it wouldn't make any difference. Perhaps she liked it to hurt her. She liked indignity, liked humiliation. Then a voice from the pit. George was singing: *she breaks just like a little girl.*

He shot up surprisingly, levering himself on his powerful arms, all black like a miner, and hauled her after him. The sleeve had fallen back on her arm, and the inside of her wrist was a mass of puncture marks and sores.

'Jesus,' I whispered. George seemed riled at the sight of me. He reached out both black palms, grasped my breasts and screwed them round, so that I cried out with the shock and pain. And Frankie laughed. She cackled. Because when he let go, there were two sooty palm prints over my dress.

'This is a fucking madhouse!' Aaron yelled. 'I'm taking Zack and I'm going.'

'Nah,' said George. 'You won't do that. And that was but the sign and token, Mara, of your belonging. You may need more convincing. If so, come back and I'll give you something to remember me by.'

'You're dirty, Porge,' said Zack.

'You better watch out then, son of mine.' George chased the child round the lawn, roaring while the child screamed. I stared at Frankie. Coal and tears made her cheeks look as if infinite quantities of mascara had bled there. She looked spaced. Was not well. Haggard. She examined George's prints on my clothes. He had that power, I thought, to make you feel naked. To reach across and in with his eyes. To make your heart judder and expect. Expect what? Something black and terrible. Trying to make you think you wanted it.

Pete left. He went off on his motorbike. The next time I was there, he was gone. The atmosphere was subdued and no one mentioned him at all.

There were long periods of stupor, just sitting. Their hair growing, their nails growing on fingers and toes, and the mind dwelling on that a bit perhaps, and wondering why? And birdsong outside piercing in through the slats of the closed shutters, as if someone were trying to get to them. When they got up, their seats held the shape of their arse and the place they'd rested their heads was dark with hair grease.

Sometimes they spat a bit, to while away the time. They made a trip to the toilet, having pondered it for several minutes. They craved sweets.

When they returned, the shuttered room was exactly as they'd left it, with the same people sitting in the same postions, their eyes vaguely on the television, while some endless jam by the Grateful Dead painted the walls with lashings of sound. A sound that made you feel something vital had got lost early on, and would certainly not be found on this soul-destroying voyage to the other side. The other side? Of what? What were they all doing there? It was as if the Wraiths and the Weather Balloons were waiting for an order from somewhere.

197

Frankie said: 'Come on, Mars Bar, this time you've to be with us.'

'What?'

'Come on, we're shooting up. It's fun. I'm telling you, it's fun.'

'No thanks.'

'It's oh so warm, Marsie, it's like, I'm telling you, beautiful, no pain, no fear, just this fantastic blanket all round us. Hugging us. You come too. Remember, like under the boat that day when we did the acid, you loved it didn't you, you adored it, that was a good day. Trust me.'

Frankie came across with that little-girl tentativeness on her face and said I would never know how lonely she was, and if I would just come with her, just this once, because we used to be . . . so close. And Aaron, he must come with us. The three of us. Just the once. Test the water, she said, with your little toe. It is beautiful, it is home. It is the ocean.

She got out a small bundle, wrapped in a cot sheet, and fetched out the needles and a balloon of smack. With care and reverence, as if these were sacred objects. She said, 'Trust me. If you trust me this once, I will trust you from now on, Mars.'

Jesus God, she loved it, Francesca loved it, shooting people, she said.

Stabbing you tenderly. That was a hit in itself, that was a rush like you didn't get with orgasm, she said.

'Come on, I'll always love you, Marsie.'

Just give me your arm, she said, and rolled up my sleeve. She stroked my skin slowly with her fingertips up and down, up and down, and the fingers on her left hand were horny from the guitar. I shivered and shrank away.

'Trust me, don't shrink,' she said, and I watched in horrified curiosity as she tied my arm and inserted the needle into the vein, intent, and then pushed the plunger.

Hard.

Stabbed me.

Frankie's face was next to mine, filled with curiosity, eating the experience of giving me that rush. 'Your first time,' she crooned.

'You got it from me, your first time, like Aaron, he did it with me, I've had both of you now.'

'The Prince of Darkness,' said George. 'He lives in this house. He reigns and he is risen. Almost risen.'

George and the other men started shooting each other up, in the name of Jacob Owens and the forefathers. 'It is written!' bawled George. 'It is written! Receive the Sign and Seal!' And he stabbed the needle into one of the Wraiths. You shouldn't do that, I knew you shouldn't do that. You shouldn't trust, ever. You should cut your own, keep control. You should know where the stuff came from and taste it before you inject.

'Trust me,' she said, and I passed out.

When I came to, there was a terrible cold all over me. Freezing wet and people's voices, saying *Keep awake now Mara, don't go back to sleep.* And, *Jesus, she'd never used before, you fucking idiot.* George had dumped me in the bath and was sponging my head with cold water. Cold water all around me, with vomit floating on top, a fog swallowing me from inside and the voices outside saying, *Keep awake.* I said, *Aaron.* But Aaron was not there. He was in full fuck, said George, he was pushing his poor little dick in and out of Francesca, he was a pathetic tadpole, never mind Aaron, you don't need Aaron, he has no balls. I have balls. You have balls, Mara. *You are a woman,* he said, *I could really dig. You are a fighter. I could take you on.* He splashed water all over my breasts and pulled me back when I slumped forward, slapping my cheeks. I stared at him blearily as he sluiced me with water, and then passed out again.

Clean sheets. Ironed, crisp, white. Nausea in the pit of my stomach and somehow also in my brain. I fingered the sheets. Reached with shaking hands for the plastic beaker on the hospital cabinet. Sipped water. Aaron was by the bed, distraught: bruising under his right eye. 'Oh Marsie, are you all right? You are, aren't you? Thank God, oh thank God. They've done it,' he said wildly. 'They've gone. Zack's gone, Marsie.'

'Done what?'

My mother was sitting on the other side of the bed. She said nothing but I could see that her eyes were puffy with weeping and there was a look of hectic fear and rebuke, as if my death would have been more of a public shame than an intimate loss. As if she would have liked to run away now and leave me here, wishing she had had some other child.

'Well, Mam, you should've had more than one child, if that's how you feel.' I muttered.

'What? What's she saying? What did you say, love?' Her face was near to mine and my own weak tears were falling.

'I'm sorry, Mam. Sorry. So sorry.' With a wrenching sigh, she gathered me into her arms and said I must never, never do that again. What had possessed me?

She did, I thought with terror. *She did.*

And behind her was George who possessed Frankie. And behind George, Jack, a vast silhouetted terror. And who stood behind Jack, possessing him?

My lip trembled like a child's and I allowed the tears to overflow, for it was easier that way. 'It was the first time,' I said. 'Honestly, Mam.'

'It was,' Aaron said.

'Yes, Aaron, but you would say that, wouldn't you?'

'No, really. That's why she OD-ed. Her body couldn't take it.'

'So – other people – there – gave it to her?' They spoke over me and I could feel my mother's relief at having found a way out. Her daughter was not a junky. Someone else's was. We knew who. And why. It was just a case of keeping me clear of the lost soul. For loss contaminates. I hoisted myself up in the bed, pulled up the nightgown and showed her both arms. Only one hole, flecked with blood. Likewise my legs. No holes, no blood. She burst into tears of relief.

'They should be locked up,' she said. 'That poor child, getting into that company. Never stood a chance, from the beginning. What's Annie going to do, Aaron?'

'Mummy's in a terrible state, and Pops says it's all down to me, he won't let me in. Oh Mara, you don't know. They've all gone off their heads and broken into my parents' house and turned everything over. All of them. And they've been in and beaten Jack up, and they've done over her parents' place and scrawled stuff over the walls with Susan's lipsticks and . . . It all went too far, it got out of hand, didn't it. Jesus, lovely. You could have died.'

'What happened to you?'

'Nothing much. Bit of a scrimmage. No, Auntie Leah, really, nothing to worry about. Marsie and I will never touch another drug, please believe that.'

In the pupil of his eye I saw the child, very tiny, as if he were running down a dark tunnel, on and on.

Later he and I sat in my flat together. Fragile, free. Something in me was celebrating; Aaron's vulnerability handed me back to myself. He could not do enough for me. Sprinkled my hot chocolate with cinnamon, handed it to me with tenderness. I laid a pad of witch hazel under his eye, to cool it.

'You're such a gentle, gentle thing, Mara. You're the softest person I know.'

'You calling me a fatso?' I said to make him laugh. It seemed strange that he called me soft and tender, given the violence into which Breuddwyd had degenerated. Both of us had been part of that. We stared at each other. Texas came flooding back to me: the graffiti on Auntie Midge's wall. Frankie, poor Frankie, looking for Janis. I thought of blood even while I knew it was only lipstick. The loot Frankie had snatched. And now she had robbed Annie. Apparently Annie had prevailed on Jack not to call the police; but Jack was oddly reluctant to do so anyway.

'What did she write on Jack's walls?' I asked.

'I don't know. That's the weird thing. Jack must have – he scrubbed them down and painted over them as soon as he found it. Two coats before 7 a.m. And he won't hear of calling the police.' Aaron sat with his elbows on his knees and his face in his hands, asking what did I make of that? What would become of Zack? Where was Zack now and how would he manage without Zack? Was there any legal way of getting Zack back? Every time he spoke the boy's name, it chimed in my mind, unpleasantly, like a note off-key. *Zack back*, I thought. *Zack back*. The drug must still be in my system for my mind seemed to be hovering above my own head and looking down dizzily on us both.

I knew whose son Zack was. Not George's, not yours, I thought. I allowed my heart fleetingly to grasp the huge extent of Francesca's hurt. Her stepfather's cruelty. They should have beaten him senseless while they were at it. What was the point of writing on his wall?

'I know what she wrote,' I said.

'What?'

I was silent. How could I tell Aaron where the child he loved so much had come from? How could I not tell him?

Aaron parked in front of Breuddwyd. No sound came from the house. We sat without speaking. I was determined not to interfere so that, if Aaron came to me, it must be of his own volition and not because I pulled him. Part of me meant just what I said, that I wanted Aaron's happiness. The wish flashed into my mind that Frankie and Zack should be there in the house, minus George, so that I could do the loving thing and fade into the background of their lives; the longing to love them with that gentle integrity I sometimes glimpsed as possible. But the moment I opened myself to this, I closed up again. Opened and closed, with pain and rue, several times over in as many seconds.

There was no child in the Breuddwyd garden. As I rolled down the window, I could hear wind swishing in the shattered remnant of the pampas, a small rain coming on, and a sense that everyone had gone away long ago. Everything had reverted, so that I imagined Nana might come slowly down the path, straight-backed and elegant.

Zack's toys had been cleared up and put away. A pang went through me as Aaron turned his key in the lock: I seemed to catch a rush of his anguish as he entered that empty space. The garden seat rocked and creaked slightly in the wind and the door of the shed hung off its top hinge. There was a pile of cans and bottles against the shed, like a stack of coal. I thought that violence had happened here. Horror. I thought of George sloshing cold water over my head and telling me he would take me on. But what remained was pointless disarray. As if all that had been said, shouted, aimed, had been emptied into the ears of the deaf or the dead. Rain rolled down the car windows. Aaron said nothing as he got back into the car. Out of the corner of my eye, I saw a meccano truck in his hand, a book and several tapes. Raising his hips, he slipped the toy into his jeans pocket.

He stopped at the edge of Fairwood Common. We got out and walked through the brambles, thick with blackberries, on to the heath. No one but us was out in the mist of fine rain. Aaron talked. *I wanted to kill her*, he said. *Just kill her. You know. I know you know.* He did not define what he knew, but he was right. Through my memory flitted the knowledge of how it felt on that beach near Galveston with the steering wheel under my hands, slewing it round in an arc before I took aim. I didn't shake, I wasn't drunk, it was pure hate, ice-cold. I reached now for his hand. Of course I knew. The being so drastically off-balance that one pondered the unthinkable thing. The final thing. Why was there, as we walked across the wet common, a sense that Aaron and I were just puppets? That we had surrendered to the compulsions of another person, *because we wanted to?* Why would we want to? I wondered what was there in the two of us that answered her need to repeat the old pattern of abuse?

'About Zack,' I said. 'What'll you do?'

Since I had no fridge, the wine had to cool in the bath. At some stage we were both lying in that bath, pleasantly tipsy, up to our throats in bubblebath. We lay at either end, our legs open and entwined, the water slick and oily over our skin. Zack and his mother, Francesca and her son, had dissolved away, while we began to fill in for years of hankering and not having.

'I've ached for this, Marsie. All that time. It was always you. Always. If it hadn't been for Zack, I'd never have gone back, it was bound to fall apart. But I felt, if one has a child . . .'

'I know how much you love Zack,' I said. 'And also,

sweetheart, how much you love Frankie too. So I do. I know how torn you must feel.'

He slid his hands up and down the inside of my legs as he talked, till they felt liquefied.

'I don't feel torn,' I heard him say and the steamy bathroom echoed. 'I'm here now. I'm here. With Mara. That I love. Did you know that I love you Mara?'

Under the quilt, with the curtains closed, Aaron and I huddle together in poignant intimacy. Familiars and strangers. Holding his once-precious, once-beautiful hands in mine. Tremors of shyness quiver through us both. He opens my palms and kisses them, as he used to do, which I'd forgotten, and for a moment my eyes brim. I brush his lips with my forefinger, braille-reading their shape.

There is a patience and a peace in our loving, as if voices that had raged now murmur, I'm lying curled in towards Aaron with my face against his breastbone in the crook of his arm, while his hand winnows my hair, lifting and letting it fall, rhythmically.

In the middle of the night my eyelids snap open with a spasm of apprehension. There's something in the room, surely, some moth or it could be a fly? There is no lamp for the creature to home to, no understanding that the plate of glass it butts against seals it into a world without nourishment. Of course their lives are short. They cannot know pain for as long as we can. They just exist, for a fleeting moment, an atom of sex, an atom of hunger, and finally an atom of pain.

The middle-aged man with his head on the blue pillow scarcely stirs except to frown slightly as I turn on the light and listen. Up on one elbow, I watch him. The eyeballs twitch beneath closed lids. I can hear Aaron's breathing, a faint snore, and am struck by an odd sense of violated time, as if we were posthumous. Yes, we've got up from our deaths to one another, like twin ghosts who need one final haunting.

But the love we made before we slept was not tainted, not

transgressive. No, it was kind. A form of reverencing, remembrance. Giving time to greet and let go. Aaron wakens and puts out a hand to draw my face down to his.

We drift. And later, when I wake, Aaron's face hangs over mine. 'Dear Marsie,' he whispers. 'Dear, dear Marsie.'

Small moth-kisses on and beside one another's mouths, on one another's eyelids, while we hold one another's hands and behind me morning begins. The bird chorus in the woods, the loud light reddening the sky.

Getting up, we negotiate the awkward business of dressing, breakfasting. Aaron will have to dash, he says, so much to do, got to get to Hereford by this afternoon and then off to Japan again on Saturday: no peace for the wicked, he says, and the plummy heartiness returns to his voice but still I am hearing, long after his car has scorched off down the road, the tender, private tone of *dear, dear Marsie.*

I asked him for the Etruscans back: he said he would hate to lose them, so I said to keep them in that case. But just before he left, and despite jittering on the threshold of his private and public selves, he turned and said that, if I thought it would ease anything to talk to Jack or Susan, or to speak to John, let him know. Please. Don't hold back any more, Marsie. Rely on me to be there for you and not to go chucking stuff out of windows without your say-so. I do care about you and, you might not credit it, but I have kept you in my heart over the years, though not in words: I was never all that great with words.

13

Upstairs Drs Pendennis and Khan ministered to a stream of patients, whose soles we heard creak in and out of the waiting room above our lounge, trooping to the consulting room above the kitchen. Did they hear us screwing the life out of one another in our basement flat? Our gales of laughter, the wild sonatas I played on my second-hand piano, without regard for musical decorum? Did they catch the echo of our outrageous fits of weeping?

For we wept in one another's arms from time to time, sobbed from pure love. Everyone in the upper world seemed subdued by the anxiety of illness, knowledge of mortality. Down there in the nether world there was a manic joy that danced on graves, and needed to dance, needed to insist *I'm alive now*. Nearly a year we had together. Aaron, who had become jealous and moody, seemed to feel that the best way to keep other men from wanting me was to have me and have me again, until we were both so fucked out that we slept for twelve hours at a stretch and woke, ravenous. Ate croissants which flaked onto the bed. Drank coffee that never smelt so good. Showered together while the old chaps shuffled in for their jabs above. Rubbing his face in my hair, enervated and gentle, sleeping, waking, eating, kissing, as if we were doing all these things for the first time.

I stood at the window barefoot, while he slept. Fingering the acorn of the blind I'd just raised, I looked out at the auburn red brick, amazed at the tranquillity of objects. A marmalade cat sleeked through the shadow of the dustbin, its whiskers needles of light. Ordinary things looked so good that I gazed long at the colours as if to sate a thirst.

One could live with this intensity without drugs, without music, without any aid. I stood on tiptoe, taking in the calm of the day, enjoying the balance. Then I thought: *What balance?* Wasn't I drugged now? Intoxicated with sex, alight with the thought that I had escaped and was free to enjoy . . . a man. What women had always been told they wanted, I had attained. A man. This man. What freedom was that, precisely? My reflection met me in the pane and returned her riddling half-smile. She'd been left on the other side, the free side of the glass. I turned from her, and went back to the bed.

We seldom spoke of Francesca or Zack, or the explosion of the Beloved Community, or the shell of Breuddwyd standing hollow and waiting for dereliction to set in. It was as if we'd somehow taken part in someone else's unintelligible and lurid play. Now we'd come home, for the play was over. Its freaky spotlights and bizarre script were abandoned in favour of new obsessions. Aaron wanted to give me his surname, so he said, and have children. How many children did I want? At least four?

'But I've got a surname, lamb.'

'Yes, but we'd have the same one. That would tell everyone that we belong together.'

'Excuse me but why would I want to be a Thomas when I can be an Evans?'

'Well, so that we could have the four babies.'

'Let you into a secret: you can have babies without being spliced.'

A shadow crossed his face. He was thinking about how it was easier to keep your child if the law gave you a certificate.

My four would outweigh her one, the idiot thought went through me. I was lit by the tender excitement on his face; lit but not convinced.

'Trouble is, I'm not all that maternal,' I told him.

'How can you say that? I've seen you.'

'I don't think so.'

'You can't know until you have your own.' He made no explicit reference to the perpetually absent Zack but I distinctly saw the child peer out through Aaron's greenish-blue eyes. Our children would have eyes of a similar colour, I thought. My child would be Frankie's child's second cousin twice over. Jesus, we were incestuous. But I wanted all these phantom children out of the room. To think forward would be to relinquish what we had now. The intense passion we had found peaked like a climax you wanted to delay and delay. Consummation would consign us to time. But he wanted my babies. Made of him, made of me.

It was these phantom babies that aroused the first disquiet. I had work to do, serious work. I had been born to generate change in an old corrupt order, not to sit at home and iron and bake and breed. I reminded Aaron, in a committee voice, that I was not a chattel. I had my postgraduate work in Social Policy, it was my vocation. Women must be free, I insisted, as if Aaron were a hostile audience. Of course, he agreed, anyway, who does the cooking and cleaning in our flat?

Still dissatisfied, I tried the word *vocation* on Aaron. He assured me that he would never have anything against my going back to work after the babies. 'No, of course not, Marsie: I would never want to limit you.' He knew my work was sacred to me. But he spoke less of using his economist's skills for the poor of the earth and more of gaining a foothold in a big transnational firm.

I sat in Rhodri's bar, half of a couple. A sensation of loneliness ballooned in me at this thought and I puzzled at how the sense of being at last accompanied could make me feel at once diminished and completed. Surely I wanted what I wanted? My sunburnt arms suddenly seemed alien, as if I were looking at another's. My mother's arms. I saw that my hands were folded over one another in my lap. Ladylike. Not the way I sat at all.

Rhodri said huskily, 'Not seen you in here, boy, for a long time. The usual is it?' In the Cross Keys all was stagnant. The same beery fug with its loyal row of regulars perched on bar stools. A kind of anti-chapel, Danny said, whose liturgy consisted in the fine Welsh ritual of slandering (in the nicest possible way) your absent neighbour.

'You two a couple now, by all accounts?' Danny and Aled brought their pints to our table.

'Just grooving,' I said.

'Groo–ving. Well, whatever that is, you look good on it. Especially Mara. You are blooming, never mind grooving.' He aimed a look at my braless bosom. 'Mind, you two always had something going for each other, didn't you? Thick as thieves. But I used to think, Mara, you were, do you mind my saying, the other way inclined.' Tattle was Danny's most libidinal activity; tattle and provocation.

'Did you hear about poor old Rhodri's fibrillations?' asked Aled. 'Been told to quit the booze. No fags. Ticker gone, see. Listen to him breathe, when you go up to the bar. Pitiful it is. Course he says he's fine. Quack told him his brain was already pickled, wouldn't need formaldehyde. Just quit, he said, and you're still in with half a chance. They won't operate unless you get your weight down and give up your indulgences. Rhodri says it's bollocks, his dad lived to eighty-three, smoked forty a day. You listen out for him, Mara, if you're buying the next round. Mine's a pint.'

I made my way forward to the bar. Rhodri was more purple than usual. He puffed and blew as he chatted and pulled the beer. Had his own pint beside him on the counter and sucked off the foam in a long slurp; then lumbered over to take my order. The short, panting wheezes came closer.

'So what can I get you, lovely lady?' he croaked.

I'd heard it before, the effortful shortness of breath. *Pods which pop.* Rhodri registered my stare and repeated his question. His skin was doughy, except where the telltale red capillaries in nose and cheeks betrayed the chronic drinker. But then he'd always been like that. The degeneration of the heart and arteries, the filling of the lungs goes on covertly, ignored for decades. Then the corruption shows, massively, all at once, so that even the most head-in-the-sand, alcohol-saturated character cannot continue in innocence.

I stated my order; asked how he was.

'Good, aye, quite good,' he rasped. 'Can't complain. Wonky ticker, of course,' he tapped his chest with fingers puffy with retained fluid. 'But I mean, who hasn't? Gotto – gettit – seento, but the waiting lists – see – something – chronic.'

Rhodri, the great talker, the marathon bar-stool-sitter, with his epic laugh, ran out of puff. I said, 'I'm so sorry, Rhodri, do take care of yourself.'

He hefted the pint and sipped some down; smacked his lips. 'Great medicine. Doctor's orders, girl.' As I turned with the drinks, I caught again the gargling breath in his chest. It seemed to pursue me through the press of people.

'What's up, Marsie?' asked Aaron. 'You've gone all pale.'

I stared at him, my lip trembling.

'Hey, what is it?'

I seemed still to hear it, the frothing of corrupted lungs, Rhodri, poor soul, helplessly feigning immortality. Behind him wound the endless file of ordinary catastrophes, our menfolk coughing up sputum till blood dyed the phlegm, emphysema, asbestosis, silicosis. Caswell came back, the khaki beach flecked with tar and seaweed, an ashen sea and sky. My face half-buried in Uncle David's jacket, secretly listening, breathing in the mothbally, tocacco-sweet smell. How Frankie reared up in my mind's eye in all her paroxysmic jealousy, popping the sacs of bladderwrack, olive-green and slimy, in his face. Terrifying me in the totality of her resistance to total loss. Looking at me with bale, her eyes saying, *Thief.*

'It's Rhodri,' I mumbled. 'So chokingly sad.'

'It is. It's awful. He's such a sweet guy. So much life in him.' We all agreed what a great boy Rhodri was. Raised our glasses and passed round cheese and onion crisps. The laughter gained in confidence and crashed in waves, till, lifted by a communal afflatus, we could no longer see his condition as terminal.

But I began delicately to detach from Aaron, taking myself stealthily back into my own keeping.

David's child came home. For two decades I have buried the remembrance of her homing. Cycling past Breuddwyd, I could see that the upstairs windows had been opened and the side door was ajar. I went round the house and found Francesca kneeling on the lawn, in a pale but dingy muslin smock, her back turned. Her head was down, revealing, where the hair divided, the vulnerable nape of her neck. There was something in her lap, over which she was bending. A dark shape. A kitten?

She was scarily thin. Dark circles round her eyes. Her skin was flaky and flushed with eczema, the pale cheeks covered with spots. She'd been scratching the eczema on the inside of her elbows till it bled. But it was Frankie's little-girl quality that frightened me more than the lack of flesh on her bones. I knelt beside her and recoiled with a yelp from the creature in her lap: the carcass of a blackbird. It had been dead for some time, I saw, since small flies crawled over its dulled plumage and the remains of its eyes. She said in a slow drawl, 'Don't be alarmed. She's not really dead.'

'Frankie. It is dead. Been dead for ages. Needs to be buried. It's putrid. Can't you smell it?'

'Oh Marsie, don't be silly. There *is* no death. Only love. Just love. You don't realise, of course you don't. How could you. Poor Marsie. You weren't there. Soon this bird will be flying again, can you see that? The voice is released, you see. The blackbird's voice and my voice, they're kind of released back into the wild . . . all around us.'

She looked up and gestured around with her grubby hand at the bright, overgrown garden. The tatty muslin dress was saturated. I tried to get her to relinquish the carrion to the earth, by improvising some spiel about how it must return to the breast of the earth which fed all its young. 'That's what George says,' she told me wonderingly. 'Well, something like that. Have you seen

George, Marsie? He wants you to come in. There's been a very great change.'

I looked back at the house in a panic, in case George were actually inside waiting to jab a needle into my vein, to initiate me into this very great change. But she shook her head and laughed, with mild eyes. I wondered what she was on. She said I took things too literally. George was all around us, see? George was broadcasting himself as love. You know, like radio, but you can't see the waves, can you? And everyone we'd lost was also out there, she said, all gathered into one. Not dead, just swarming, like a hive of bees. There weren't any boundaries, Francesca insisted, none.

Something was badly wrong with everything she said and the way she looked. Inauthentic. They had found out a great deal and learned some secrets, which I too might learn, if perhaps I was less hard-boiled now. Less hard.

'Oh Frankie, I don't want to be hard. I would so love us to be friends. In a right way. If you could forgive – any harm I've done you.'

'Good, that's good. If you want to be a kind person, it's good.'

But she continued with her theme. Of secret knowledge. For instance George had found out how to breathe life into dead creatures. He was repeating the miracles of his ancestor, Jacob Owens, who had passed to him the secret of how to resuscitate the dead. One day they'd stopped and George was reading, and Tessie-Bell had come across this dead owl tangled in briar and barbed wire, with a vole in its claws, and Tessie told George, who came to look, and George – she saw it herself – disentangled the owl, hugged it to his breast and breathed on it, and it, well, it just soared away.

That was the freakiest thing she had ever seen, she went on, and that was love. It was all part of the cycle of love. And on and on about George and the Family she went, for they were Familists now, it seemed, direct descendants of the Family of Love who were wandering around in the sixteenth century, or the seventeenth, it didn't really matter when exactly since there is only Now, no past at all.

I got her into the house and forced her hands under the kitchen tap. A cake of soap had been there in Nana's dish throughout the year of their absence. It was grey and ribbed and hard. I scrubbed at Frankie's hands to purge the stain. She was oddly passive and smiled with rueful pity. I dried her hands on an old cloth.

'You are so full of fear, Marsie, fear's filled you up with shit. George will show you the way out.'

I wanted to slap her face. Waken her from her daze. Unnerved I looked round at what had been Nana's kitchen. A great soup tureen in which Aaron and the girls had made soup for twenty or thirty people, now covered with grease and dust, contained what must have been the remains of the last supper the Beloved Community had eaten together: a congealed mould on the bottom. How could a woman as intelligent and shrewd as our grandmother have willed away the family home to a poor dab like Francesca? Pouring our treasure into a gaping mouth of need. Feeding the need rather than lessening it. Nana had not been senile: but it had been as if, like us, she had turned away from the proprieties of family. She had joined the great experiment. Still, in the long term, Nana might be proved right, if Frankie was going to come home and I could get her to start again.

'How lonely you are though, Marsie, how terrifyingly lonely,' she went on, in the dreary monotone which was all that remained of Frankie's voice. 'Without love, without certainties.'

'I do have love. I am standing here loving our Nana. But questioning her actions. You shouldn't have had Breuddwyd – it didn't help, did it? We weren't ripe.'

I told her how I had changed direction now and set myself to work for the greater good of the World. Work, I told her, is love in action. You can change things. The Vietnam War, I said, was not necessary: it was only happening because we were letting it happen. So we have to be out on the streets where we used to be, not in some kind of . . . hen coop with a great cock strutting round telling us stuff about love. You might as well roost in chapel and listen to sermons by bald old coots with too much tongue and not enough brain, I told her, as moon around loving the Creation without doing anything to help it. I told her about my work on the Social Policy unit and how you could change things from the inside too.

She looked bored. 'You can't change things. You can only *be* changed. The idea that you can do anything at all is pride.'

Outrageously, the voice of the chapel seemed to sound in her. I laughed and mentioned how Uncle Tony would approve but she didn't see the irony. 'You live in pride and illusion, you people of the straight, so-called normal world. George will explain to you, Marsie, better than I ever could. George will make you free too. He will.'

'Jesus, I hope not.' I gave an exaggerated shiver and grinned; but Frankie was without humour. George's codswallop had never given me severe qualms since it had never been taken all that seriously. It was just something he did, as infants dribble. Yeah yeah, everyone said, right on, and continued with whatever we were doing. But now he seemed to have taken on some sort of Messianic status.

'Don't sneer at truth, Marsie. If you snigger at truth, it's really dangerous, you know. You should be careful what you laugh at. It's all a boomerang, everything you send out comes winging back.'

'Frankie, wake up! This is me, Mara! Hallo!'

She turned away and went into the living room. The shutters had been opened and one could see a line of dark grease along the back of Nana's sofa, where members of the Beloved Community used to sit. I looked carefully at Francesca's haggard face. She looked older than her years.

She'd come ahead, she said, by herself, and Zack was coming too, and beautiful George and Jade and, oh, lots of people, whose names would be revealed. They'd all become illuminated, they'd died to the world now, they were spiritual beings, so it was important to tune in to that. Her eyes shining from that undernourished face were like Bambi's. Bambi was always a powerful figure: we'd known that as we wept at the cinema, dug our fingers into the popcorn bag, while predatory Bambi hooked our hearts. No end to the helplessness that cannot be appeased. Where were his mother and his milk? See his rickety legs. Ravenous, ravening Bambi.

Her hair had grown in the year since I had seen her and tiny plaits hung down amongst the sandy softness, reminding me of corn dollies. She had attached a string of shells to one of the plaits, along with a grey feather, but there was a tarnish about her, the lacklustre tinge of ill health.

When I told her that I had left Aaron, she shrugged. I wondered when she last ate. Whether she was ill.

Yes, she had been ill, she said, at Glastonbury, and so had Zack, it must have been something they ate or the mud or something. She lost a lot of weight at Sarum and Avebury, and then at Glastonbury she'd been really ill, but, funny thing, it was still beautiful. It was tender. Like being on fire and fire purifies, doesn't it, so all the toxins burn away. And so many, many gentle people: all of them together like flowers in a field. It taught you a lot, being part of such a shimmering mass of people, because those people were the salt of the earth, she said.

'Do you want to go home and I'll cook you something, lovely girl. Like I used to.'

Frankie didn't need to eat much, she said: you get to the point where you live on the spirit, though sometimes this craving came over her to eat sherbet or licorice or aniseed. In any case much of what people ate was poisoned. But for the Familists there was no such thing as sin, there was no such thing as bad, there was no such thing as wrong or crime or illness even. And when she did seem to be ill, said Frankie, while I sat reeling as she droned on and on, even when she got ill and was puking her guts up, there was love. There was love coming to her from them all, even from the snails.

'From every atom, and even when Zack was ill too, man he was sick and I thought we ought to call a doctor or get out of the

215

shitty field, George wouldn't let me. He took Zack out at midnight one night and let the moon's vibes play on his little tummy.

'Dilly was there, she said it was a load of rubbish, the man is mind-fucked. To be honest I never thought it would work. Lunar vibes, my arse, I said. When it didn't, I got really screwed up, and I came to blows with George – I wanted you, I called out your name, Marsie, and you weren't there. He was so angry, and I had a lousy trip, and George said he was going to leave me to go through the bad trip, and I did try to throw myself off a bridge. But he was following me, I ran for two miles apparently because I thought he was Satan. He overpowered me. In an absolute way. And he talked me back into the world of love. Even a bad trip – is – well, good, because it was just the load of shit I was carrying in my head, and once I had got it out of me, all this love came flowing in, flowing and glowing, and Zack was better and we just went on from there.'

As she monotonously talked, she was black under the eyes and I thought, *Frankie, you are wasting away.* But before the flowing and glowing had set in, I'd caught an inkling of the real Frankie. My Frankie. Objecting to the lunar rays. Standing up for herself. Calling my name.

'The thing is, you can't have a rape,' she said, 'where there is love. And in fact it was good, it broke through to me. It was good. We were one person after that.'

'A rape?'

'No, Marsie. It isn't rape. It's the Power.'

'Oh Frankie, oh love. No. Are you on something?'

'It's a new thing now we've got. I don't think I can tell you, Marsie, you're so far into the old thing, it's like trying to look through a wall. This is a more generous way to live. Really. I want you to come in. *I always want you to have what I have. And you always want what I have.*'

She didn't sing any more, she said. That had been purged from her. I sat down at the bottom of the staircase with the shock of that realisation.

Where was Frankie's guitar? Throughout our growing years it had accompanied her, like part of Frankie's body. I thought of how she'd sit on the stairwell to harness the echoes and sing with that dark, tearing voice; how, by forcing the emotion through her throat, she could sing two notes at once. All her adolescence there had been that guitar, slung across her black leather back or lying over her lap, cinnamon-freckled hands caressing its curves. So that you could not think of Frankie without seeing it in your mind's eye.

When she had talked herself out, Frankie dozed. I poked around among her things and the sole musical instrument seemed to be an old dulcimer. Later she agreed to play it: tremolo, fluttering notes without melodic line. Going nowhere. Her voice a subdued echo of itself. Then she took out a primitive wooden flute and began to blow a two-note phrase, *woo-hoo, woo-hoo*.

I said, 'Frankie, where's your voice? Belt something out for me, lovely girl. For old times' sake, if nothing else. Never mind *woo-hoo*.'

She looked up, still blowing across the mouth of the wooden pipe, as once she had blown across milk bottles, making a breathy tone to which she listened intently. Her eyes were not right and it was as if Frankie had died, but no one had noticed. Died while padding barefoot down some muddy, potholed lane and just carried on walking, all her expressions simulated by her sweet death mask of a face.

George towered, strumming a guitar, his sandalled feet up on the settee at Breuddwyd. He hardly looked like the miracle worker who could bring back decomposing owls from the dead. A pool of girls floated round him. The more I considered the new set-up, the more I pondered. Gone were the brute brother bands with their uproar. All seemed placid, orderly. The place was clean and scrubbed and there were mealtimes. On Thursday everyone went to collect their dole and shopped for the week. Each family-member had his or her own mug and there seemed to be some sort of unwritten rota according to which the women did the chores. Now we were drinking camomile tea and an air of repose and approximate normality prevailed. I sipped and listened.

The womenfolk were sitting round at George's feet in a half-circle, just dwelling on his face as if it shone. I looked from one girl to another. Tessie had an eight-month-old child, which she rocked in time to the music. The baby slept. Zack was out with Aaron: George had mentioned to Aaron that he might like to subscribe to the expenses of the Familists, mentioning that he was welcome to play with Zack any time.

'What is it with you lot?' I broke in. 'Are you all fucking deaf mutes? You give me the habdabs, you really do.'

The Familists all looked to George, who smiled and shrugged amiably. He had a glass of orange juice next to him and took a sip.

'Yeah. What?'

Nothing. Just the staring. The weird, spooky staring from girls' eyes that had learned not to blink. I held them. I wasn't going to be scared by a load of sad cases giving me the evil eye. I bent to Frankie and snapped my fingers in front of her. She didn't blink either. She was a cast of her old self. Was it their own fear they were sending out to me, or was it a warning?'

'What can I sing for you, Mara?' asked George.

'Give Frankie her voice back, that is all you can do for me, George, you fucking fake.'

He'd learned his guitar techniques from her, it dawned on me, stripping her of them. How could a person do that? Gut a girl, like a herring? I looked at his glib mouth as it grinned and sang; he'd swallowed her.

'You're worried about your cousin,' he said calmly, over their heads. 'I know that. Francesca is fine. She is in a safe place. She's resting. Don't be grieving, we all need to rest. Mara, I would never, never hurt her. She is precious to me.'

Was that mind-reading? Or was it lucky chance? He was talking about her as if she were elsewhere, on some other continent. How had he done this to Frankie, sucked out the juice from her marrow?

'I will show you,' he said. 'How it's done.'

'I'd like to fucking show you something, George. And that something is the door of my Nana's house.'

George nuzzled the waist of the guitar with his beard; his eyes smiled but not his lips.

Aaron came in with Zack, just as I was telling George to go screw himself.

'I do think ... we could try to get on with George, Mara, couldn't we?' Aaron privately suggested. 'He's mellowed. The really bad apples have all gone. Just a few poor waifs he's trying in his own rather weird way to nurture.'

'He doesn't respect people who try to get on with him, hadn't you noticed?'

I tried to explain that George was threatening us, that something bad was going to happen. He said that was a fantasy. That the whole cult-of-love thing was drifting apart and we were all growing up. For instance, he said, you have grown up Mara, you live a respectable life now, well, I don't mean respectable as in Respectable, but your work ...

'Please don't tell me about my own life, Aaron. You know nothing about my life. I don't like to be condescended to.'

He was sorry, he said, that he had been insensitive. It was bound to be difficult between us until we found our way back to being just cousins, as we would. But all we had to do was wait for this thing at Breuddwyd to disintegrate. Zack was his priority. George would let go, because after all he often said that he wanted to go to India, make a spiritual pilgrimage, and when he went, Aaron would be waiting. He said, don't be afraid. What he would try to do was to bring them into our family.

Which family?

Well, ours. The Evanses, Thomases, Menelauses. In that way, little by little, there would be a calming. A leavening. Obviously.

Zack rebuked us all by his profound and patient absorption in the world as it was. He was a great child for pointing out objects of interest, waving his arm, pointing his finger without strain, as if the arm were made of putty not yet set hard. He was an intelligent, rather grave boy. He had been to Findhorn and had learned to garden, sacred gardening in which you saw the angel of the plant. Zack told us about the angel of the pampas, a lady with white hair; the seaweed deva all green and frondy. We spent his birthday at Llangennith, where he was carried round on people's shoulders, thrown from George to Aaron and back again, squealing with excitement.

George had a four-pack of extra-strength beer beside him on the sand. I wondered if he was asleep. Getting up, I sauntered over and swooped down on the cans, extracted two and dropped the remainder back. Jade shot me a furtive look of amused shock, like a naughty schoolgirl. I beat a retreat into the dunes. Glancing round, I spotted him raising his head dopily and stretching out an arm to where the cans used to be.

Wants his baby's bottle, I thought. *Ah diddums*. I climbed the steepest drift of sand. It reminded me of myself and Frankie and Aaron running away to where the destroyer had made its fantastic appearance. The rusted hull, the exciting smell of its innards, a ship to pirate and possess. In the shadowed lee of a dune, where the sand was cold, I sat down among the reeds and opened a can. Liquid happiness dulled the image of Aaron pottering on the shore with Zack. Just there the wreck had been, I thought, exactly there by the dried-up stream; and, lying back, I watched the sky, waiting for the rare sun to break through the clouds. I rose on one elbow to finish the first can and immediately cracked open the second.

George's face loomed above me.

'Enjoying your privacy?'

'I was until you came. Won't your harem be wondering where you are?'

He laughed. 'It's you I want.' I began to scramble up but he grasped my wrist and jerked me back. I landed with a thump on my hip.

'I prefer it,' he said, 'if people ask before they take what's mine.'

'Thought you didn't believe in private property. Thought you were into "to each according to his need". As long as you get more than your share and all the bloody girls as well. I mean, how old are those kids you fuck around with? Anyway, have your fucking beer,' I said, and poured it straight over his head. 'Why don't you just clear off, back where you came from. Down some bloody sewer like the rat you are.'

'Now wait a minute,' he said amenably and just let the beer sluice through his hair and trickle over his head. He sucked some off his moustache and chortled, letting go of my arm. 'I've something for you, remember.'

'What?'

'Do you want it now?'

'No. I don't want anything from you. Ever. Look, George, leave Frankie alone. Will you? She's so gifted and so bruised. You've got plenty of disciples: why do you need her? Sorry about the beer. Just let her go.'

A worm of fear coiled inside me. But the thing was, not to show it. Like a dog, he could scent fear. George, I thought, was a troubled and turbulent man, out of control, needy and endangering. If I did not fear him, he had no power over me. The trouble was, I did fear him. But what was there to be afraid of? On a public beach. He couldn't harm me. Not out here. Then I thought: this is his fear, he's projecting it on to me.

'There's nothing I'd like better than to talk, Mara. You are intelligent. You don't take shit. You think I've interfered with Frankie? You and I both know that she was fucked up years ago. You and Aaron, you have hardly made it better, have you? But I have given her . . . a sort of peace.'

'Otherwise known as death.'

How did he tick, I asked myself. I tried to imagine his father the pastor, his mother the pastor's wife, the scent of piety mingling with the Sunday joint. I could see a tablecloth, white and starched, a brood of children sitting round the table eating

221

up their greens, sending donations from their pocket money to missions in Patagonia or China. Or was the father a ranting orator, who'd chasten the children of Babylon over their boiled eggs?

'How did you get on with your father, George?'

'Fine. A man of kindly rectitude, charity and forbearance,' he intoned, as if this had been forced down his throat from a young age. 'Devastated he was, when I gave up my studies at Lampeter. Or rather, when Lampeter booted me out. I'm not knocking my father. But my way lies in another direction, another country. I feel this charisma in me, or at least I am led to see that other people sense it, do you dig that, Mara?'

'You don't see your way, then, to going back home to Anglesey?' I looked curiously at his mouth; he was gnawing his whiskers, meditatively exploring them with the tip of his tongue. His saintly father must be relieved to know that his hairy hippie son had carried himself off to the south, and would be unlikely to pop up in chapel to embarrass the minister and offend the congregation. George sat with his arms on his knees, the beer drying on his face in the sun. I felt that, if I could think of the right question, he would reveal the point of weakness. It lay somewhere about his claim to charisma. He was asking me to confirm that claim. Almost pleading with me, like a child. The troop of women was not as dependent on George as George was dependent upon them. But the more he had, the more he would need; for his own sense of self was so feeble.

'You know, Mara, you and I have a destiny.'

'We have not.'

'We do. You are my likeness. I've been doing a fair bit of research and I am led to the sense that you are to bear a manchild and he shall be called . . .'

'Oh for fuck's sake.'

'All things are pulsing together, Mara. If you just pause a moment,' and he placed his thumb on the veins of my wrist. It pressed, bulbous and strong, as if to hold down a string. His physical strength disconcerted me and I winced in pain. 'No, just be still, very still. You can hear the love. Hear it. I think it's time. I can feel your beautiful blood beating. I hear you, Mara. Now you try and listen too. Gentle down.'

'All I can fucking hear is you droning on and on. Don't you ever stop preaching? It doesn't work on me, George. All that cosmic shit. All that narcissist-infantile come-fuck-your-father, have-a-new-name, now-you-are-my-creature Rasputin stuff.'

His grin then was surpringly shrewd. It told me that this was why he was after me, because I held out. Because I disproved his so-called cosmic gifts. Because I knew that a dead seagull was a fucking dead seagull and that it was always going to be dead. I had made a monumental error in taunting him; I could have given him the slip.

You don't want love? He had me under him, his hand shoving my top up over my chest. *You are crying for love, sweetheart. I hear your cries. Let them out.* His beery mouth covered mine. He kneaded my breast with one hand; grasped my wrist with the other.

Get off – you – fucking – disgusting – perverted – animal. I wrestled, wrenching my head sideways. George laughed. I did not believe he would hurt me. The silky words contradicted the violent actions.

'You're not insulting me – Mara – calling me an animal. Animals are honest . . . now lay your head back. Look I don't want to hurt you – you hurt yourself. I want you – to be free. Animals are full of love, open your legs. Every hair of your head . . . every blade of . . . grass . . . every . . .

Panic burst up into my brain. The shock of my helplessness. The cringe as he rammed his chest against mine, knee between my thighs.

No. Someone's coming, they're coming, look over there, don't, please no please.

Mara, I know . . . it's a fight for you. To get pure. To feel the love. Don't give up now, little sparrow . . . you're like a . . . fledgling . . . in my hand.

Off me. Mouth full of sand. Hand round my throat. Eyes bulging. *No.*

And if that fledgling . . . twists around . . . the hand might . . . crush . . . crush its . . . bones . . .

No. Hands tightens. Throat. Can't call out. Pain grasping me down there, scalding me. *Hurting me.*

It's only what you like. Bit at my neck. Hurting as he hammered in. *And . . . want. Open up . . . fall loose. You want to, Mara, say you want to . . . all you have to do is say . . .*

On and on, the sick voice. I opened my eyes as he pumped in and out. The quivering dunes glinted with hints of buried cans, buried glass. I called with a tiny voice for him to get off me, get out. Was I bleeding? I could smell blood. Would he kill me? My knees bent up and I tried to roll him off.

Yeah yeah. I know, I know, baby, here it comes.

Tears squeezed from my eyes as he slammed into me. Gulls called, lewd, terrible calls just by my ears, the breeze whipping through the reeds at my head. His mouth gnawed and fingers travelled: a language of touch that said there is no love, there is no love at all, there is no love or pity in the world, only vileness and night, and this was what Frankie had known from way back, but I had been shielded, and it was as if he had come as her messenger. So I would know forever. Imprinted with that knowledge. I was a flinching, cowering mass of fear and shock, a cut of meat on the sand exposed. One, two more pushes and he'd done. He toppled on to me, a dead weight.

Now that was love. I am love, you are love, we are one, ah sweet fucking Jesus.

I wrenched to one side, to shift him. To get out of my ear his sick mantra. His chest on my front was wiry, sticky with sweat and beer. With odd matter-of-factness, I remembered Frankie's voice, saying, confidentially, that he was hairy all down his chest to the groin, and he was.

Please will you let me go? Supine, I put the petition with sudden quietness, looking straight up into his eyes.

Yeah, sure. He was up and wriggling into his jeans. Limber, powerful maleness. Unwashed. Sand in every orifice. I had his semen in me; as I scrambled into my shorts, my knees were jelly.

He was on the point of turning to go. As he turned, I launched myself at him from where I was kneeling. Used to play rugby with the lads and knew how to tackle. And George was clumsy, lumbering off-balance in the drifting sand. I sank my teeth into his calf and he yelped. I jerked his foot out from under him and he splayed face-forward down the steep dune. Yes. As he slithered, I rushed down after him and threw my whole weight on him as he staggered to his feet. I punched, poked at his eyes and slammed his head back. He grovelled before he could right himself, I spat, than waded fast and panting up to the top, to a crest visible from the beach, where suddenly they all appeared in blessed ordinariness, the semicircle of the tribe, children playing quoits and building castles, the tide far out. They would hear me if I called. They were a guarantee of safety. As I whirled round, I watched him get up, and I jeered, weeping.

George coughed, rubbed sand out of his eyes. Departed, tucking his T-shirt into his frayed jeans.

I crumpled. I hadn't won anything. Was soiled, every inch of my skin, the inside of my body. I knelt and retched amongst the reeds in the sea breeze, corruption in every pore, sand in my hair, eyes, anus, everywhere, slime between my legs. I limped back to the beach with my arms clutched in over my chest. The bay opened out, immense; an innocent scene. George was lying with his hat over his face, arms beneath his head, bare feet sticking out at angles. Dead to the world. Fucked out. He must have sauntered back, smug, satiated, and fallen fast asleep.

'Hi! come and eat!'

I shook my head. It was as if a door in my mind had been thrust open and there would be no way to draw it safely closed.

Across the large perspective of the bay, Frankie and Zack were playing frisbees just before the gleaming sheet of water left by the outgoing tide. I was caught by the graceful motion of her in her transparent Indian skirt. She was playing serenely; Zack intensely, attention focused on the game. The yellow frisbee spun high and she plucked it from the air with languid ease. I focused on Francesca's remote face with an extraordinary clarity: beauty bereft of its old expressiveness. Mockery and malice, delight and exuberance were quenched, leaving the face blank. She missed the frisbee and the boy laughed. He dashed here and there, with all his young appetite for movement and play. She stood still and looked in my direction. Now I knew what she knew. There was nothing to be done except to walk shuddering and subdued with your leaden legs slightly apart because of the damage to the intimate tissue.

No. That was what he wanted me to think. He had gone complacently to sleep. Had assumed he'd gutted me as he'd gutted them. Not so, not so.

I turned away and began to walk, fast. I would not mirror her, be broken like her. I would never be George's creature. I began to run and the pain rang in my belly and blood streamed down my legs, and I'd got a nosebleed.

Reaching the first copse of the bracken forest, I stopped dead beside someone's caravan, where, outside on the pale sandy path a little girl was hunkering, letting the sand drift through her fingers dreamily. The child looked up. I could not go on, for the memory of Frankie's childish face beset me; the moment when my father nearly offered her sanctuary and me a sister, clumsily pulling her blonde head against his midriff with his great hand, with a compassion that died almost at birth.

Now that I bore my cousin's scarlet pain between my own legs, in my own scourged heart, I could not leave her to George's intrusions. I turned back the way I'd come and climbed to the crest of the dune in an agony of effort.

George still slept where I'd left him. His women and the children had gone down to the shell-line, where they were picking about like long-legged birds among the jetsam. Zack and Aaron were diminishing figures scampering across the ribbed sand to the sea.

Frankie was standing where I'd left her, arms dangling at her sides. I waded to her against the current of my throbbing hurt. I

226

was snorting blood now, blowing bubbles of it through one nostril. Francesca winced; her expression, or rather lack of it, did not change but she reached both arms round me and took me in to her, drawing me close, delicately so as not to hurt my wounds.

'I'm not leaving without you,' I said. 'If I have to drag you.'

She would come with me, she whispered, but where to? Together Francesca and I began to hobble our way off the beach and up the dunes. To the telephone. I dialled and got through to Uncle Tony. Mother. The straight world. The authorities.

14

Elin with her hair up in a sassy topknot, Pritchard the Prick, Miles Caradoc the new man at gynae and I have unfortunately coincided at coffee.

'Yes, we're proud of our Pain Unit', Pritchard is bragging to Caradoc. 'Did you have anything like this at Gloucester? State-of-the-art but low-tech, low-cost, there's the beauty of it. We had Ralph Singh over, the guy who developed mirror theory, last month, you know the man? You should read his book, it's a classic. He was impressed with the creative work we're doing.'

'We? Who is *we*?' I whisper to Elin behind my hand as Pritchard gasbags on.

It appears that Pritchard not only mooted the idea of the unit in the first place but has encouraged and supported us at every point and may himself be writing a short paper on telescoping. Pain shrinkage to you, he informs Caradoc. One of many fascinating phenomena: the phantom shrinks until the lost foot, say, is perceived as being attached directly to the stump. Now, we take this for a good sign...

'So,' I say to Elin as she and I retreat, leaving Pritchard to impregnate Caradoc with his newly thieved beliefs, 'Who the fuck are *we*? Since when did he do anything but sneer at our work and leer at your bottom?'

Elin, smiling, takes my arm for a moment. 'Never mind, we'll be philosophical because we need guys like that with the big fat egos, don't we. What do you think of my hair? Do you think it's daft? Hey, I read about the American Indian use of juniper berries for amputees, did you know they call them ghost berries?

There's one hell of a lot of knowledge out there which is just being ignored and, oh Mara, by the way, I'm pregnant, I hope you're pleased, I'm not jacking in my work, don't worry, no way. Hey, put me down!'

Ghost berries, I think, back at the flat, brewing up tea and checking the store of dark chocolate I keep in the fridge for comfort. Perhaps that's what I need. But no, just stare the ghost in the face, examine it in the mirror and watch it shrink. They live on our fear, as bodiless as smoke.

George has presumably served his sentence and, for all I know, could have returned to his native Anglesey a reformed man. How George enjoyed conducting his own defence, denouncing me as a bull dyke and female impersonator, a deviant Women's Lib man-hater with a castration-wish. And advertising himself as a man of sorrows acquainted with grief, a minister's son and devout ex-student of Theology, who had only wished to help society's castaways to make a respectable life for themselves, tilling a patch of soil for the greater glory of Christ. He had attempted to reestablish the Primitive Church at Breuddwyd, and if he had failed, well, didn't St Peter and St Paul fail? Failure could be holy, if you did not judge from the world's perspective.

His beard, hair and nails had been trimmed and he sported a grey suit. But his spitty rant delivered him into my hands. George's father and mother, mild and bowed, sat every day in court.

Francesca was dead: we had scattered her. The ice had begun to form around my heart, the cold iron had entered my soul. I conducted my own case. The times had thrown George up and now the times were dragging him down. I watched his cocky display falter under my interrogation; his big mouth dwindling to a little round O.

'Do you or do you not claim to be the Son of God?'

I led George through a virtual library catalogue of the books he had filched, from which he had divined his apocalyptic destiny and his role as impregnator of the Virgin Vessel with the Ancient of Days. All this he denied. But like the gasbag he was, once he got going on this juicy topic, he was unstoppable.

His women sat in the gallery and sobbed at George's sentence. Afterwards Jade told reporters that in her opinion Mara Evans had spiritually raped George. For I was not a woman but a perversion of the natural order, an opinion that George had strenuously maintained in the dock, hoping to align his kind of hippiedom with the norms of the straight community. The feminists in court had got up and cheered when George was sent down. A cluster explained to reporters the political significance of my victory in terms of women's emancipation.

I slipped away and returned to Menna. She was in the bath when I came in, and Charley was soaping her with a yellow sponge. Menna clapped her hands to see me.

'I heard,' said Charley, low-key. 'Well done, Mara.'

'Well, it's over. How's she been?'

'Fine. We've had a lovely time together, haven't we, chickabiddy?' Charley's partner Nerys came and we toasted the judge and jury in champagne. Menna lay on my lap asleep; I could not bear to let her out of my sight. I homed to Menna. She was the Pole to which my quivering compass tended; she earthed and stilled me. Menna and my work. Frankie's child was mine, as much mine as if I had not delivered but borne her.

But Zack had fallen out of our hands. He was shed like a leaf, twisting as it fell: that was how I saw him in my mind's eye. George's father and mother had custody of him, and perhaps, said Aaron, that would be best for the child he had loved as his own. Perhaps the sober, kindly Owens would manage not to rear a second George this time.

'Aaron,' I said, 'you make me sick with your spineless pusillanimous bloody reconciliation to things as they are. You should have fought for your child, as I've fought for mine.'

He said he didn't know what pusillanimous meant but would look it up in the dictionary. The cases were not the same, he said. Menna's mother had made it clear that I was to take her place but no such provision had been made for Zack. Zack was not his biological child and seemed happy enough to go to his grandfather. Aaron would be allowed to visit, he was sure.

'Well OK, Aaron, let him go. It's up to you.'

'There are circumstances,' he said, 'under which you have to let go.'

'No. There aren't. I think I've adequately proved that.'

He looked at my jutting 'don't-mess-with-me' chin and, presumably remembering my whirlwind conducting of the court case, backed off. I was always quick to judge, slow to listen. I allowed Menna to fill my entire horizon and her head to eclipse the blue-green globe I'd set whirling in inner space at Dilly's years ago, and to whose fragile safety I'd dedicated myself. Or did I interpose Menna between me and the world, a refuge sheltering me from its raids and claims?

Edging aside the screen I've erected and maintained through the years, I hesitantly allow myself to dwell on moments in those last months in which Francesca and I shared Breuddwyd together.

I hold her wrist and coat the eczema on her arm with cream. She is all warm from the shower, which has softened the abraded skin. The best time to cream her is just after a shower and there is some mild satisfaction in doing so, covering each sore patch with the emollient. Passively she lets me. Pale arms, picked scabs, needle punctures. The murmur of our voices, chiefly mine, cajoling her to eat and drink. It must be morning, judging from the blanching light on her face and shoulders. Her belly rounding out, Menna's presence announcing itself against all Frankie's denials.

I cajole her to see a doctor, sign on at the hospital; and I am sporadically out of my depth with worry, as if I'd been appointed her parent or guardian by default. She shouldn't be taking any drugs, none at all. Won't the child be born an addict? Frankie assures me that she takes next to nothing. Honestly, she is way past all that.

How can I get her to the doctor? My own mother ventures to the back door with bags of groceries and we whisper but I say nothing to Mam about drugs. I keep her up to date with the preparations for the trial; she begs me to come home and be looked after. She does not beg me to bring Francesca along for a share of the same treatment. Manages not to say, *You two have brought it on yourselves*.

Frankie lurks in the background, listening in. Does not miss much. She may be out of it most of the time but, when it counts, she is alert. As I smooth the cream into the hectic skin on the inside of her elbow, she says, 'If any quacks come here, Marsie *cariad*, you know I would not be able to stay.' Quiet, subdued recalcitrance, in sorrow never anger. The dry softness of her moth-lips brushing my cheek. 'And where would I go to?'

She is not really pregnant, Frankie says. It is a false pregnancy. It is in the eye of the beholder. She is just getting very fat from overeating.

I learn not to say that she under-eats. I tiptoe round her and the confrontational eloquence I will learn to use against George is not yet available to me. I am hunkering down licking my own wounds in the lair where we've gone to ground, she and I, and from which I venture as rarely as possible, and always with an unhinged apprehension that the louring sky will fall on me; that people jostling me in the streets mean no good. Some days I am afraid of my own shadow. I've been penetrated by doctors' instruments in the examination after the rape. I have been left to lie in a cubicle with nothing on my nether parts, while forensic voices discuss me on the other side of a curtain. A flashlight photographer has shot the view between my legs. I have been pierced by police questions, probed by a solicitor, reduced to long phases of dumbness. I am in no position to take the burden of Francesca's helplessness. But just for that reason, I am the only company she will tolerate.

I am haunted by the living wraith of Francesca, a waif who shadows me, keeping close as I make tea and toast. Carries the plate back to the settee for me and tries to oblige me by pretending to eat. Even when she is too wasted to get up and shadow me, her eyes follow me. Or I will find her quietly waiting outside the loo, where I have gone to pee and sat staring at the door with its many cracks and blemishes; a wan smile lights her face when I reappear, as if I had been away for months and left her pining. She takes my hand, gentle as a little girl who wants something from you; holds it lightly but drags heavily on my spirit. Sees that I am trying to recover and hangs her whole weight on me, determined that I shall not. For we are twinned and equal at last. So she thinks. She spooks me and she blesses me with her terrifying trust.

We have entered into a pact of mutual forgiveness and, whatever this entails, I will not willingly break it, even though I wear her as a ball and chain. That Janis song she used to screech: 'Ball and Chain'. I used to inwardly object that the blues were retrograde. We middle-class whites had no right to the blues. We created our own shackles and should crack them off for ourselves and one another. I understand better now as I drag Francesca the length and breadth of our prison, that the blues are her legitimate music too. I wish she would sing them now, sing anything.

Do we talk much? In my memory there is a silence between us, but I suppose we talk of everyday things. I am torpid, my spirit taking a deep rest. But I have little doubt that I will emerge from this chrysalis state. I'll not give up as Frankie has done. However supine I am at this moment, I know I shall crawl away, raise myself to standing, career around a bit and then walk; walk free. She turns to me to think for her; can scarcely work out how to do up her own buttons and does not trouble to wash herself, though she will if I nag her. She likes it best if I give her a shower. She hums then. Looks at me with wondering eyes as I take care of her. I think of Zack as I cream her arm, and I believe she does too. But we do not say his name.

Although she doesn't sleep, you can hardly call her awake. She's a somnambulist, a body whose soul is elsewhere. She passes out from time to time. Where does she get the stuff? She must be seeing someone. Either she is very crafty or I am farther gone than I know. We share a bed but when I am deep asleep, she slips out and goes downstairs. I hear her leave by the back door in the middle of the night and, occasionally looking out of my window, see her crouch in her shift in the back garden. She is always so careful and fastidious with her gear. Keeps it clean and neat, in the way addicts just don't. Squirrels it away somewhere I can't find it but do I look very hard? I doubt it. I imagine rather than see the flash of a needle. A numb laziness possesses me much of the time, and this must look to Frankie like a duplicate state of her own. In that false calm I neither remember nor feel George's violation. I blank him out but the cost of this is that I have to blot out everything else too.

I ask Frankie what she wants to do when the baby comes.

'Take care of him, Marsie, if any baby should come, he is for you. You are in my place. Don't let anyone else get their hands on him. I've written it down.'

'You're not going to die, softgirl. Are you honestly expecting *me* to deliver it? Here?'

'I don't really think there will be a baby. We'll have to wait and see.'

Later she becomes afraid. Says she's haunted. Whimpers that, oh Marsie, there's something dreadful inside her. Feel, she says, feel, and I place my hands on her belly and feel the knobbly elbow or knee squirm round inside her. In spite of myself, I break into a smile. Like a father feeling his child, I listen enchanted. Place my ear to her belly and listen to the soughing of a life through the cotton nightie, the thinning wall of flesh.

'That's your baby, Frankie.'

'Where do you think Zack is then?'

'Well – with his grandfather, isn't he? With Mr Owens. He's fine.'

No, she says, he's in her. It's Zack she's carrying again, and it's some kind of punishment, she can't bear it, she can bear anything but she can't bear that. Ranting on and on, pure gibberish, so that I move into maternal mode and tell her she's being silly. But terror is not silly. It is real. She shrinks from herself. I lay her head on my breast and sing to her. I sing all the old folkies she used to sing when we were teenagers. My voice seems purer, more focused. Frankie listens and is comforted by the music, if you can call it that, but she does not join in.

The maelstrom of blood when Menna erupts, nearly three months early.

Francesca's belly a violent theatre of conflict. Muscles slamming drum-tight. The waters gushing out hot over my hands, sheets awash.

The child comes bursting and sliding out so fast. There's scarcely time to think. A disembowelling. The head's going to tear free. A purple head, like an otter or a seal, scarcely human as it crowns and is thrust out into my hands.

Thick, plaited cord, oh my God, what is coming now?

The massive afterbirth in my hands, hot like an external heart. Steaming. What should I do with it? I panic. Look for a bucket or somewhere to put it.

Francesca is altogether forgotten until a keening begins. That smoky, throaty voice, some grating song, or is it a cry of distress? I don't even look at her face. It doesn't go on for long.

For the afterbirth is still attached.

What should I do with this great lump of liver?

When my father came in from his rounds and my mother was preparing the steak and kidney for tea, he would gag, because he said this was woman's work. Oh yes, and eating it's yours, is it? said my mother with businesslike bloody hands.

Jesus, the slithering baby's not crying, its elongated head is like a bloodstained pixie's, blue. Is it breathing? What do you do? With this lump of meat? It's like a butcher's shop in here, with me the crazed, incompetent butcher.

The kitchen scissors blunt on the cord. I hack but they slide. Doesn't matter. Never mind the cord. Leave it. Just get to the baby.

Baby's not breathing yet.

Let it die? She would want me to let it die. Yes. Let the baby go. So I attend to cutting the cord instead, with pinking shears, and manage it, so at least we shall have a tidy death. The afterbirth lies where I dumped it on Nana's pink quilt.

In fact, I think the baby's already dead. Gone. A girl, Francesca has got a girl, oh my God, you're a little girl, aren't you? Her eyes are open and they are so like Zack's, when he came, almond slits of sheer speedwell blue.

So instead of letting the baby die, I abortively blow my breath into her, suck it out. Mouth-to-mouth doesn't work, how could it work? Jesus, Jesus, what to do? Get a straw, that's it. Baby must live. Frankie was drinking the Coke through a straw, so we've got straws. I hurtle with the baby into the kitchen. You *aren't* going to die, never.

The blue baby is in the kitchen with me, under the smeary light of the naked electric light bulb. I insert the straw into its gullet and suck. Free its blocked air passage; either that, or Mother Nature does it for us, because music hits the air. Weak music, but clear and true nevertheless. The thin piping of a wail, pumping in and out the fragile lungs.

The baby cried! She cried! You cried!

I wrap the little bellowing body in a cotton T-shirt, all bloodstained as it is, then call the ambulance with the baby in my arms. Shaking with shock. I return to find the bed empty, a trail of blood across the floor.

I tell this to Aaron and Uncle Pierce in the Oystercatcher, not about the trail of blood but about the empty bed and how I hardly had time to register it, before I was swept off in the ambulance with the newborn child, everyone assuming I was the mother. And although I wanted to tell them, I was mute with shock. I delayed, fatally.

'The empty bed,' I say. 'She was just gone.'

About the bloodstained room, I shall not speak. I give them a white image without the gore. They are men; what do they know? And we are in a pub, scarcely a place for stomach-churning detail.

'My dear Mara,' says Pierce. 'I can see that the experience is still with you.'

When I came in Pierce rose and I knew it was the man on the bus, the one I had seen with the neat haircut and his collar of corduroy. He manoeuvred round the table to take me in fragile arms. Pierce has shrunk; was never a big man, but age (and he must be ninety) has leeched his bones and blanched his skin, depleting the blue in his pouched and lashless eyes. I feel a huge, daft burden in these slight arms. And why did I think I was coming to judgment? Pierce was always so clement. But austere in his mercy, so that you felt much was withheld.

'It's the kind of shocking experience,' Pierce goes on, 'that stays with you.'

'Oddly enough, it's only recently that it's come up. Since the TV film. Things I'd buried.'

'Poor Marsie, it must have been traumatic,' says Aaron. He and I have a closeness since we spent that last night we don't talk about together. 'I mean, birth *is* traumatic. It just is. Without all that extra horror.'

He was there for five out of the six births of his youngsters, he says. Wouldn't have missed it. Not for the world. 'But the first time, well . . .'

'Rather worse for the mother, I imagine,' says Pierce, with the wry astringency which always mediated his principled goodness and made it humanly tolerable. 'You have a very level-headed daughter there in Menna, Mara dear. That is to your credit.'

I don't think I can claim credit but I smile bleakly at him.

'Bethan says you always mothered her lovely. She remembers how you would not put Menna down and how Menna clung to you like a little monkey.'

'Does she say that?'

'Well, of course. We were all impressed by how you were with Menna. Not easy for you, Mara.'

Of course they all knew whose baby Menna was but, oddly, the family seemed to have no trouble in identifying me as her true mother. Having read that you could breastfeed a child that was not your own, I set myself to doing it. And though there was not enough to satisfy Menna, the miraculous milk came. She drew down my milk, my lovingkindness. Overriding my grief for Francesca; mastering my heart by her milky-mouthed sleeps at my breast.

Level-headed is the word for Menna, I think. I told her the truth when she was perhaps six and she shrugged. *You are my mam, Mam*, was all she said, without raising her head. I'd been bracing myself to break the truth to her for weeks: I knew you had to. All the books said so. And there she was in the sandpit with her bucket and spade, not looking up, taking in this information but sticking with her habitual allegiance. A careful child always, she patted the moist sand level in the bucket with the back of the spade, upturned the bucket in one clean and rapid motion, and removed it, leaving a perfect mould with a star on top. A small irregularity in the star she daintily reshaped with one nudging forefinger. Sat back on her heels. *You are my mam, Mam.* Don't raise the matter again, her cautionary posture seemed to say. This subject is now closed.

Had I done my duty? I told her again when she was eleven, to make sure she'd taken it in. '*Yes, I know that*,' she responded with neutrality, a faint hint of annoyance. Then when she was eighteen, I thought I would ask her again if she would like to know more about Francesca, but I refrained or bottled out. And then, when the film was shown and her mother's face seemed to thrust itself into our world, I saw her light up as if she'd been tinder-dry all these years, waiting for the flame. I waited, as I'd waited for my punishment for an imagined theft. None came. It seemed that Menna was concerned for me rather than for herself.

And that is it, I think, as Aaron is telling Pierce about his children and saying how he must come to the new Breuddwyd at Hereford, must come for a week, or a month. I'm thinking that there was no theft. None whatsoever. The baby was my free gift from Francesca. And Menna knows that. Menna is not a dreamer. She isn't susceptible to that allure. So she is careful for and with me.

Pierce says, 'Now don't you turn round, Mara, if you don't want to – but Jack is over there in the corner.'

'Oh my God.'

'You leaving good beer, young lady?'

I look into the eyes of the old soak I've been aware of for some time, out of the corner of my eye, the sort of chap that, if you meet his eyes, will seize you in a one-sided, embarrassing conversation and not let go.

'Sure. You're welcome.'

'Well there's a darling. I don't mind if I do. Shame to waste good – Hallo, Pierce my boy. And who are these? Well well, it's the girlie who bolted and ... you are Mr Aaron Thomas. Privilege to meet you.'

Jesus, you smell. You are unwelcome everywhere you go. In station waiting rooms the passengers budge up in their seats to put space between themselves and unwholesome you. You drink the dregs of women's beer. Perhaps I shouldn't loathe you, my flesh shouldn't crawl, for you have come to grief.

'What's it to be?' asks Jack. He is wearing strange Russian-looking headgear, a mangy fur cap with ear flaps, which he keeps clamped on his head even though the pub is fuggy and warm. 'Family reunion, calls for a celebration. No, I insist,' he slurs. 'Drinks on Pierce, your round I think. Don't mind whisky, my boy, if you press me. Not changed at all, you haven't, girl. So what are you doing with yourself, Margery?'

I tell him I'm working at the Institute.

'You always had such bright promise, I used to think, Mara,' says Pierce. 'And you're doing a worthwhile job, pain relief, theory of pain relief?'

'Give me some,' puts in Jack. 'Only joking ha ha. Pain relief. Pain in plenty we got by here. In my old gut for instance. Whisky, mind, is very kind to pain. I hear you're a moneybags and live in a palace, Aaron. Annie will be swelling her chest like a blooming pouter pigeon.'

I try not to breathe while I look at him. But when I do, the smell has gone. Weird. Perhaps I dreamed the smell. He looks, in point of fact, quite clean, though eccentric in that Russian-style hat and the leathers. Yet a minute ago I could have retched. His teeth are stained with nicotine, and one front tooth is missing. He'll charm no more ladies but does that make him harmless? His mind's half eaten but does that relieve him of half the guilt?

Aaron goes to fetch the drinks. His hand brushes my shoulder as he passes behind me and I lean back momentarily, taking comfort and courage from his presence. Between the two of us, at some deep level, there is peace.

'She won't have me,' he tells me, hangdog.

'Who?'

'The wife so-called. Chucked me out. Of my own house. I've not two brass farthings to my name. Tell you straight.'

In my mind the wreckage of Susan shuffles in slippers through thick dew at the end of her garden, penned behind iron bars.

'Said I was a lush. Said I to her: "what's a lush?" Innocence, see, that's innocence for you. I suppose you haven't a pound going spare for an old man, Margery, have you? Clean out of fags I am.'

'Mara.'

'Pardon?'

'My name, Uncle Jack. Is Mara.' I glance sideways at Pierce, for guidance as to whether I should produce the pound coin. But the moment I use the word *Uncle* to Jack, a trembling sets in. Pierce can offer no help. He seems unable to make a judgment, for not only is the dilemma insoluble, since the man's brain is already well and truly pickled, but mild and transient kindness is all one man so infirm and tottery can offer.

I pass Jack the pound and, having just recalled that he'll need two quid if he's to have the smokes that agree with him, so why not make it three, man, he's off to the bar and ordering a stealthy drink behind our backs. I don't have to look. I can see the characteristic way he lopes, without having to turn. But he's back.

'Hey, Marge, I'm going to need another quid. So make that a note, won't you? Call it a fiver. That'll do fine. Pay you back, cub's honour, when my Giro comes through.'

'Very sad,' says Pierce softly. 'Nothing to be done.' I reach for his hand, which accepts mine with a pleased pressure.

'No,' I agree and pause. 'I'm very glad to see you, very. So sorry I hardly ever wrote.'

'Well there you are.'

We're all of us fading, I think. Only the dead leap into the light in intense colour, astounding us with their unrestrained vitality. They never had to pass this way through the long dulling of sensibility we endure, or submit to the tedious sameness of everyday responsibilities. The short period I shared with Frankie is so near the surface, and my questions to Jack so near to bursting through, that, looking at my reflection in the window, I see that I am slanting forward, shoulders high, pent as if to take or give a blow.

'My present concern,' Pierce is saying, 'apart from our current atrocious assault on Iraq, is Madagascar. Things are not good there.' He begins to explain.

'Uncle Pierce,' I butt in, shoving aside the huge need of Madagascar for every kind of amenity, for decent trade terms, for democracy, healthcare, pain relief of every kind. In place of these I substitute one child. 'Do you ever think about what happened to Francesca, in that last day. Have you ever thought that it might not have been suicide after all, that someone – finished her off? Perhaps that was all there was to it, her despair, but . . .'

'What do you want to ask, dear?'

'About Zack . . . and if Jack . . . do you ever think? Could it possibly have been that he was the father?'

'Oh the poor lass. What's the sense of speculating? I'm an intuitive, see, same as you, Mara, I see things I'd rather not. And I felt for the dear girl, to the marrow of my bones. There was a gentleness she had, a gentleness not commonly seen before David died, bless him, and the world knocked it out of her. And there was the loss of her little boy too.'

'Aaron says you've heard from Zack.'

'John. I did do. Some years ago, every so often. There was one time he just came into the Quaker Meeting and sat down. When I looked up, suddenly there he was. But then he left before I could speak to him. I wondered for a minute if I'd gone daft in my old age and started seeing things. Around six years ago, I believe that was. Seven perhaps.'

'How did he look?'

'Good-looking young fellow. Tall, you know. Well over six foot. Towering sort of chap.'

'Still flaxen blond?'

'No. Not really.'

'What does he do?'

'Well, he was working as a gardener last time. Modest fellow though. Called himself an odd-job man. He sent me some photos and then there was a bit of a gap, whereupon he began to write to me, and when I got my computer, of course, we started to email one another. We had some thoroughly good chats.'

'Susan said to me, when I visited, that Jack had killed girls and buried them in the cellar.'

'Oh, Susan, well, her poor mind's not what it was, and she'd probably latched on to some murder story on the news. But, you know, she was never a bad woman. Flighty is the worst you could say. And a regular beauty in her time, you know. It must be hard to live with those looks and nothing to go with them. And as for Jack: there must be something, way back in his childhood, that accounts for it all. We have to meet people on the human level, don't we? However hard that may be.'

It was what we used to think back there in our balmy hippie heaven, that we could reach out to everyone. Ultimately. All understood. All forgiven. I consider that Pierce and his ilk were radicals before we were born. However did they live with the constant disappointments? Better than us no doubt, because they didn't pretend they could live without egos of their own.

'So Margarine,' says a booming voice, lost somewhere between aggressive and jolly, 'have you beaten up any defenceless blokes lately? Joined Gay Lib ha ha.'

So Jack remembers everything. I stare at him. He knows my name perfectly well. Offers me a crisp and thrusts a couple into his mouth. Removes the bag before I can take one, which he relishes as a great joke. Aaron puts down the drinks on the table, a pint of beer for Jack and no whisky. Jack looks round and asks where the chaser is, has it been left behind? Aaron says there are no chasers. Jack, sucking the froth from his pint, makes do, remarking that it's your skinflint that ends up with the fat wallet. Then he laughs.

'What are you laughing at?' I ask him.

'Me? Laughing! Oh a sin. I've committed a sin, Reverend. Oh I'm a rotter, I am, a singular sinful rotter.'

'I said, what are you laughing at?'

He stares, uncertain. My look queries whether he has any right to live, and he reads it clearly. Seems to grope for his account of how things were: the account he has agreed on with himself at some earlier date, and told himself over and over until he believes it.

'No good looking at me like that. Like a criminal. Nothing to do with me. Done it herself. A good spanking I gave her once or twice, oh aye. Had *that* coming to her. For sure. Spoilt, she was. Bad friends. Bad cousins, I could say, but I won't point the finger at you two. Can see you're all over each other, always were, always will be. Now if that isn't incest, I don't know what is. But back then, man, I could tell you a thing or two. Nothing I could do. Drugs, you know. And she'd say, barefaced mind, beer's a drug, coffee's a drug – but I explained no, I said no, you got it wrong girl, beverages are those. And what did she say? My arse, she'd say, beverages my arse. Way to talk! Heroin, cocaine, she done the lot. Dropping bastards here and there, lost count I did. Hippies, hundreds of ruddy hippies by there, dropouts, bloody short back and sides they needed. In the end she comes running back to me, see. My little girl. Comes back to me.'

I think he's finished. He seems to have dried up. There's an addled expression in his eyes. What has he said? he seems to be wondering. Has he said anything that might be used in evidence against himself? He murmurs, 'Don't mean no harm now.' Adds, 'Shattered man.' Then it comes over him that he hasn't finished.

Hasn't finished by half. There in the fug of the bar room, he digs both arms down between his legs, in the gesture of a little boy rubbing against his private parts and thinking that he is not detected, so that it seems obscene, he says with a coy leer, 'She was my beauty girl.'

A silence seethes between us. I will have the truth out of him if I have to wring it out. But how do you extract truth from the mouth of a man whose brain is addled? Can such a man be made to pay?

Words dribble from his lax mouth.

'But why would she do that? String herself up in the ruddy garage, creeping in behind my back, for her mam or me to find? Obscene is that. I'll tell you why she done it, want to know? The honest-to-god truth? She did it to get back at me. Because I disciplined her. I wouldn't stand for the little tyke's nonsense. Oh no. She comes back and she hangs herself by the neck from the beam! No business to act like that she hadn't. Loved her, see . . . but bad blood was that one, delinquent. Wanted to shame me but was I going to be shamed? No fear. Fill up my glass, someone. Well, don't all sit there staring, it's not a ruddy court martial. Loved her like my own. Often had her on my lap, put Smarties in her little mouth one by one. And what do the two of you do to pay me back? One of you near breaks my skull open, the other sets me up! Pins her own death on me! So what's that you got there then, Margery? Oh no, that bloody locket. Where's the hair? There was a scrap of hair in there. Funny thing she did, Susan. Came running out when I got the girlie down. She'd been doing her nails, and I'm speechless, I'm holding the girlie and her face is purple, and there's her mam with an emery board in one hand and ruddy nail scissors in the other, always prinking she was before she let herself go, so what does she do, she gives this wail and cuts the girlie's curl off! Before she's even got nextdoor to call the police. And even Susan's bloody saying I killed her now. Well, you three Holy Joes, I was exonerated, exonerated good and proper, and the coroner said so and the police say so and everyone knows so. Long time ago it was, mind. Cruel, wicked thing to do. And you two thick as thieves wouldn't even let me scatter her darling ashes! No! You were going to do it, not having *soiled hands* like mine do it, you don't remember that? Funny how people only remember what they want to, isn't it? You snatched her away from us. And Susan said, *Let them, Jack, don't make a scene.*'

'It wasn't like that.'

'Have it how you like, Margy-Bargy. You always did. Well, I pulled down that garage with my own hands. And you needn't look at me like that, miss, those are her eyes in your head. Her eyes in your head, and nasty with it, vindictive and cold. You don't think I've suffered?'

I pause, breathing deep and calm. Yes I do, I do think that in his own way Jack has suffered, and that it is true Francesca took her own life. She went home to finish things, perhaps to be closer to Uncle David, to follow him. In the end, Jack was an irrelevance, a casual trespasser.

'You have suffered and you will go on suffering, but you will never atone for what you did to her.'

He weeps, this shambolic human, the maudlin tears coursing down his cheeks.

'Who are you to judge?' he sniffs.

'No one. In much the same boat as you.'

'My beauty girl, she was.'

15

Versions are all you have. Having talked it through, Aaron and I agree our version. The air of truth in Jack's account came of his being off-guard, unable to censor what came out of his mouth. We have to let go, let her go, Aaron and I agree, sitting in my flat under the lamp, while the open curtains frame a rectangle of rainy darkness. We link hands gently. We shall always have her in us, Aaron says. You and I will always be close, even though we are so different. We never knew at the time, how different we would turn out to be. We were like embryos uncurling, preliminary forms of life.

Aaron and I scan the picture Uncle Pierce has given me into my computer.

'Well, why don't I invite him, say you'd like to be in touch? Menna has met him.'

'Really. Has she?' Why does Aaron know things about my Menna that I don't know? I've drunk a lot of red wine since we got back from the Oystercatcher, on top of the beer in the pub; and red wine doesn't agree with me. I'm a mass of nervous suppositions. If Menna fell in love with Zack? with Aaron? She has no boyfriend, as far as I know. I think she's a bit in love with Aaron: how could anyone help but love him, he's remained in some indefinable way so . . . porous. He's a sponge. But, no, he's no threat to anyone's boundaries. He hears the edge in my voice as I react to not knowing that Menna has seen Zack, and the indignity of having to ask him rather than herself, 'Does she know, Aaron, he's her half-brother?'

'Yes. But it's all right, Marsie. Really it is. They seem . . . a bit more grown up than we were at their age. She's tremendously concerned for you, Mara. You've been her rock and she needs you to be OK. You're such a strong person, you gave her that. Look, here comes the picture. Yes, it's a good likeness, the expression especially.'

We hold the image between us, at the window. It is hard to see in John the fat-cheeked child with that flaxen hair and the giddy, uncoordinated movements. All over the place, Zack was. In this snap, for one cannot call it a photograph, the young man looks older than his years, wears an olive green pullover and has a subdued air. He has been reading and the book is still open on his lap. There is a paper clip in the corner of his mouth, which adds to the impression that he has been caught unawares. My guess is that he dislikes having his picture taken, for he does not smile at the camera. A shelf of books behind him, with titles I can't make out. No, said Pierce, he does not seem to have taken after his mother particularly. He seemed rather a grave young man, contained. Reserved. I respected him. He had spent some years at the Findhorn Community, and their ethos, you know, had made a considerable impression.

'I'll invite him. Like I said. It will be good.'

'What will he make of all your grandeur? And the decanter collection?'

'Take it solemnly in his stride.'

Everyone is there: Auntie Hen in pride of place, Seth and Joe and their wives, Annie resplendent in grey silk with pearls, Pops, and a host of others. Pops, who is all thin shanks and age-spotted knuckly hands, is saying, 'Well, well, even if I do say it myself, the boy has acquitted himself well in life. He is a credit to us. Oh yah. Done us proud, haven't you, Aaron?'

Aaron is saying, 'Oh, I'm just your average bloke, Dad.'

'Now, darling,' Annie interrupts her husband, 'you know he doesn't like boasting. Shush now.'

'Well and that's to his credit too,' says Pops. For here it can be demonstrated once and for all that the Thomases climbed to the very top of the hill from Port Talbot. They climbed so high as to rocket out of Wales altogether.

Of the survivors from that generation, apart from Pierce, who's on his way, only Susan and Jack and my mother are not present. Over a cup of tea, Hen is expressing her amazement that her nephew lives in this perfect castle.

'I know, Auntie. It's fantastic, isn't it?'

'Amazing, it is. I hope you're not coming down with a cold, dear. There's a lot of virulent bugs about.'

'I've had a bit of a cold but it's on its way out now. I'm sure I'm not contagious.'

Aaron explains that he's not long off the plane from Japan, excuse the rumpled outfit. A tempest of compliments from the tribe, streaked with diguised envy: hadn't he done well in life? But didn't the foreign food make him ill?

'Aaron has a natural bent for business,' purrs Annie.

'Bent is the word,' I murmur to Aaron, who gives one of his dreadful social laughs. 'It surprised me really, the knack I did have for business. Never had all that much ambition, did I, Mummy?'

'No, darling, we had the ambition for you.' She pats his knee. 'And you amply fulfilled it.'

Looking away from him in a complex of emotions, I meet Aaron's eyes in the mirror. He said, *Marsie, dear dear Marsie*, that night.

'Seth is no slouch, is he? By no manner of means. And look at Menna. She's done brilliantly.'

'Seth,' says Annie, preening, and I do not begrudge her the pleasure, 'and Joe, and all our grandchildren, and, of course our nieces too . . . they have all done well in their chosen spheres. I'm sure your mother, Mara, is as proud of you as we are of our boys. How is dear Leah these days? Tell her we ask after her, won't you? Whenever she and her husband would like to come down and talk about old times, you know there's always a bed for her.'

'She doesn't get about much.'

'No, you said. So sad.'

My mother could not have been more delighted to get away from 'the tribe', as she called them. Second marriage suits her, and the knowledge that she will never again have to wash a man's socks or kowtow to his prejudices, not that she is knocking Dad, but Alan, as a childless widower and, the icing on the cake, an only child, is a tonic after the Evanses, the Thomases and the Menelauses. *Rhy dynn a dyrr*, she says: *Too tight breaks*. I'm shifted back to the months after Francesca's passing, when Mam was there for me.

'What do you and Menna need?' She opened her bag as if she could produce several grand from its depths at a moment's notice. 'Now, no objections please. I don't know what happened between the three of you, Mara, I don't know and I don't want to know, I've always felt you were all a bit unhealthily close, but, well, there you are. But Francesca, you know, it was coming from the word go. She was so unstable, the poor pet. Do you remember her with Dad? She put out her hand and asked to be punished, God love her. And then when she took up with those dropouts. But you will be fine. You are not alone, not by any manner of means. Not while I'm around.'

I remember that I put out a hand across the kitchen table at Breuddwyd and she clasped it for a moment. We'd never been deeply close, like other mothers and daughters I knew, always in and out of each other's houses, each other's lives. No one had ever said, *You two are more like sisters than mother and daughter*. And that was a relief. You could be too close. The space was there to be reached across.

Menna, I remember, was sleeping in her cot, wearing a suit of rainbow colours, with her arms and legs in a kind of star-shape, abandoned. Safe.

The doorbell goes and, because Menna is nearest, she answers it. Uncle Pierce and John. When she runs out, I see that she and he are in one another's arms. As John looks over my daughter's shoulder, Francesca's wraith leaps upon me, like a nemesis that is so long feared that, when it comes, one is almost relieved. I see a mirroring expression to my own on the faces of Annie and Pops, of Tony and Henrietta and the others of that generation. It sweeps across the landscape of their faces like weather. And then it passes away. Because this excessively tall man does not recapitulate anyone in an obvious way. He is grave, cordial and little inclined to smile. You could conceive a resemblance to Jack, to George or to Aaron, if you chose to read one there.

'Oh now, this is champion. Just champion,' says Tony. 'Pleased to see you, my boy.' He gives a little cough and makes the introductions. I become recessive and I try to fade into the background. God, I hope Menna and John are not too close. No, surely not. Their gentle ease with one another is surely the natural feeling of kin for kin. Family love that has not yet had a chance to dim into comfortable banality.

Great to see him again, everyone says. Well a well. After all these years. There you are. Constraint and embarrassment. A child who was not supposed to exist; whose nativity was a shame to the combined Thomases, Evanses and Menelauses. Faced with a grown-up human being, so tall that he stoops slightly, with broad hands that gesture to cover his shyness, the family gathers him anxiously into itself. After all times have changed: so many things that used to be hushed up are out in the open, they remind themselves. But what a lot he will have to tell us. So many stories.

'Here's my mother, your Auntie Mara,' says Menna.

I emerge from shadow, stretch out my hand to shake his and he takes it with polite reserve. There is no immediate sense of recognition. John's accent is a strange amalgam of North Welsh and Scots, a voice without humour or volatility.

At table, sitting between the Etruscans, next to Aaron, John tells us that he has left Findhorn. He feels his work is done there and that the time had come to leave. He and his partner, Madeleine, have in fact completed a cycle. Of course there is a tiny little wrench to leave a place where he has learnt so much, but there's no sense of leaving roots. You take your roots with you, after all, says John, if you like gardening analogies as he happens to do.

Many questions are not being asked, as the folk around the table gaze at the self-possessed young Scot with the long, thoughtful face. The only sign that Aaron is moved is that he is drinking nonstop. He glances at John occasionally, and without particular expression, falling back on his business persona.

You need to try this, says John seriously: take off your shoes and go barefoot on the soil. You will realise you are connected to the mother planet. Living earth. With a sort of heartbeat. It may sound silly at first but that's just because we're used to walking on pavements. I often walk round now without any shoes, and people no doubt think I'm cuckoo, but once you've experienced the roots, the humus beneath the earth, it's just a natural thing to do. In contact with where you came from, in the deepest possible way, the most sensuous way. And of course you will go back there.

'I used to go barefoot,' I say. 'My parents were not thrilled.'

'And quite right too,' says Uncle Tony. 'I remember all too well how you threw your shoes into the Tawe. Your poor father was quite beside himself.'

Menna giggles. It seems that I did all the adolescent things for her and that she has rebelled by proxy. Her half-brother gives a rather theoretical smile.

'And anyway, Mara dear, whatever the rights and wrongs which I don't think we need to debate, because you've got your shoes firmly on your feet now, I trust,' says Bethan, 'John means something entirely different, a *spiritual* experience, isn't it? As I recall, you were not walking on the earth but on the pavements of Swansea?'

'I'm sure he won't do it in Swansea.' Annie touches the corners of her mouth with a napkin and flashes an alarm signal to Pops.

'No, it is better on the bare earth,' says John. 'And you know, if you get down to ground level, you see so much more. Like the seeds breaking through the asphalt.'

'Oh you should have seen my drive last year,' says Hen, tuning in to the conversation. 'Moss, see, it's the moss that does it, it's stronger than a gang of men with pickaxes. Breaks up the asphalt something chronic.'

'Moss is powerful,' says John, nodding. He is eating salad with a fork, having refused the meat and cheese dishes. A vegan no doubt, as well as a Buddhist and an ecologist. He talks as if he were giving sermons, perhaps in the style of his foster father the minister of Anglesey. How dour he is, how humourless. Pierce says that Findhorn is a fine place, with an ethos we can all relate to and John tells the whole table about sustainability and its relation to spirituality. The discipline and duty – indeed, the absolute imperative on us – to preserve the planet. He has planted trees in Scotland, where deforestation had laid the land completely to waste. For the birds, he says, are our neighbours. It may seem a strange thought. Not strange at all, says Aaron, no, I feel it myself. Oh, I love birds, but not pigeons mind, says Hen. And not gulls, they are a menace, the vermin of the skies, adds Bethan.

Our neighbours the birds, repeats John solemnly.

'I hope you are not a pagan, young man, or some kind of animist or pantheist,' Tony objects. 'I imagine you are just speaking poetically.'

'Well,' says the grave young man, 'it's complex, isn't it? I am not sure that we want to label beliefs as this or that.'

'Oh yes, I think we do,' Tony says.

'Well, perhaps I'm a sort of Buddhist. But I've seen so many good people from all kinds of spiritual background,' says John who is not Zack and I can see so clearly how he is not Zack even though the man who walks barefoot in moist, dark soil is surely one with the child who raced round the garden and who picked up sea urchins at Llangennith with passionate curiosity.

'Each person,' says John, 'has within her or him the capacity to be a wise teacher. This is my belief. I do a lot of meditation to discover mine.'

'Don't look at me, I'm not a wise teacher,' I say. I too have drunk far too much. 'I'm an ignorant struggler. Or straggler.'

'If I can be, so can you.'

'I don't think so. No. It would have been made manifest by now.'

'Not if you hadn't sought within.' He looks me straight in the eyes and I engage for the first time with his distinct resemblance, around the eyes, to both Menna and their mother.

'Zack,' I say. 'I mean, sorry, John . . .'

He blinks, lowers his eyes so that he's looking at a point just below mine.

'Do you remember me at all, John?'

'I've seen your face in photos, Mara.'

'Of course.' I prefer to recede into the background. But I can see that he is remembering something. John is the kind of man who would keep his own counsel, hazarding little of his inner self and travelling lightly over the earth, observing the terrain, his pale eyes taking in the larger scene.

But then he blurts, 'Funnily enough, I do remember pampas feathers. Waving in the air. And a pony's mane and his hooves clip-clopping. Those are not Anglesey memories. I remember my mother, Mara. At least I think I do. And Aaron of course used to visit us regularly, with his pockets full of lollipops and Crunchy bars. Papa would confiscate them, you know, Aaron, as soon as you'd gone. That was why I bolted them. You have to understand that Papa was rather a, what shall I say, rigid character, and he had his prejudices. South Wales being one. He'd had his trials, of course, but a heart of gold. I do ride still. Actually, it is one of my chief pleasures.'

'Oh, very well spoken,' says Hen in the kitchen, taking the glasses as I wipe them and carefully lining them up. She has refused to bung them in the dishwasher. 'Though I couldn't say I could make out much of what he was saying. Very nice and quiet though. Quiet-spoken men I do like.'

I wonder if he can sing. The child of the universe.

Reflection

Every time I remember Rhossili differently. Aaron and I stagger about on the cliff top at Worm's Head indecisive about where to throw the ashes. Out there, the calmest of days is betrayed by shivers of wind. It comes in from the grey sea, whose waves far out from shore bend back on themselves. Patches of yellow gorse cringe low to the turf.

Aaron and I have ceased quarrelling, not because we have reached consensus on which of us has the right to the ashes, or whose prerogative it is to throw them, but because we've wrangled our shocked and depleted selves empty. I clutch the urn to my ballooning jacket and he lets me. He's dressed absurdly in a thin cotton top with a hood and stumbles forward ahead of me. My hands around the urn are so cold, I imagine losing hold, sending the vessel tumbling down over the rocks.

We stand, looking out over the wilderness of water. Wondering how you do this kind of thing. We haven't planned what to say, what to do. We've been too busy hating and fighting one another.

Now we open the urn between us, and the wind has dropped. *Shall I just . . . shake?*

No, Mara, we'll scatter her with our hands, yes? More loving.

We scoop and fling. Little of her reaches the sea. She lies littered around the rocks, the soft sift of her there, and I see a gull glide down and perch where she is. Each time I remember it differently, with Aaron licking the dust of Francesca into himself or me receiving a little powder into my mouth or eyes by the grace of the breeze.

I set the marble jar down on the rock beside me.

What now, Aaron? I ask.

I don't know. It's a close moment, I'd forgotten. Francesca swirls around on the rocks, her fragments are lifted up, brushed away. Soon all her particles will be scattered. Aaron takes my hand; we stand there confounded.

I do not know how it has come to me but I find the answer. Something not entirely false, not flat and dreary. Not a plain goodbye. I am singing, in a croaking rasp the wind tears from my throat. *Not fade away.* I cry it into the void. *Love that's love will not fade away* ... As we turn our backs, our hands uncouple, and a sense of her exposure overcomes me. Exposed on the rocks for birds to peck at, to blow back up and lodge here where families picnic and lovers kiss.